BABYSITTER OF THE APOCALYPSE

WE DON'T SACRIFICE KIDS TO ZOMBIES

BOOK 1

COURTNEY KONSTANTIN

BABYSITTER OF THE APOCALYPSE

AUTHOR'S NOTE AND DEDICATION

This book was completed just before the passing of writer friend Javan Bonds. It feels only proper to dedicate this book to him. Javan was a force to be reckoned with, one I loved to torture and plot against. We had a fun friendship and I appreciated his passion for not only writing, but the genre we shared. I wanted to share the forward Javan asked me to write for his last book. I was flattered that he asked me, after he'd had some much bigger authors writing them for him. If you are so inclined, please continue to support his work. https://www.javanbonds.com/

Anyone that knows me, would know if I went on and on about how amazing Javan is...I had my body snatched and these weren't my words. So I won't do that. What I will do is talk about Javan, as the insane writer that he is.

As writers, we have the ability to create characters in any likeness we choose. We create characters that our readers can laugh and cry with. And then, once we've pulled the readers in, we throw the characters into the worst situations we can conjure, with no promise that everyone will come out unscathed.

In the time I've known Javan, the one thing I find that stands out about him as a person, is the character he is in real life. I will admit, when he's not eating marmite or making a fool of himself with hot sauce, you sometimes want to reach through a computer and strangle him. Which would be wrong...because beating up blind people in wheelchairs isn't a nice thing to do. But I digress...

The thing about Javan and his writing is that he creates a powerful picture that draws readers in and demands their attention. From messages from a "Screenwriter" to a man playing pirate (I mean even I want to do that), to birds getting the zombie virus, Still Alive 10: Zombie Deliverance, continues a story of resilience. The series isn't the typical zombie apocalypse story, with Javan putting his own demented spin on the world the survivors are living in.

The Still Alive series gives you heroes that are created out of normal people, that could be anyone in the world. And even when those heroes aren't exactly normal (cause Javan's mind ain't normal) you can still laugh with them as they stumble through the zombie apocalypse.

I NEEDED A DRINK. Any stiff, straight, not watered down alcohol would do the job. Even gin, the one thing I detested only slightly less than not having any booze at all, would have been welcome. The desire for booze hit me like a freight train, knocking some of the sense out of my brain. The alcohol wanted to be a priority. However, the apocalypse didn't offer that many choices in what was a priority.

A sharp pain in my chest caused me to gasp and open my eyes. Looking down, I was greeted with a gap tooth smile. I quirked an eyebrow at the almost two-year-old and waited to see what she wanted.

"Vick...," the little girl said, her version of my first name, which is Vicki.

"Tina," I replied, as if we were having the most normal of conversations.

There was nothing normal about where we were. We bumped and bounced on the school bus bench, causing Tina to head butt me in the chest. Again, I had to take a deep breath to catch the air she kept knocking from me. I wrapped my arms tighter around her little body, hoping to keep her from braining herself on my sternum, or bruising the crap out of me.

The little girl couldn't sit still, and wiggled until she'd climbed up me to stand, balancing on my thighs.

"Jesus Christ, kid. This isn't a freaking circus act," I mumbled.

The moment the words left my mouth, my gaze slid sideways, catching sight of the black and white habit that sat two rows ahead of us. Looking around the school bus, I could admit it was the strangest group of rag tag survivors I could have fallen in with. A priest was behind the bus wheel and a nun sat with another young woman, praying as we drove through the night.

My life was like a grim joke now. I'd heard them all; a priest, a nun, and a bartender with two kids who aren't her own, all walked into a bar. But that's what life was now, a big fat joke. When an illness swept the world, causing the dead to not be officially dead anymore, I could have made all the zombie jokes I knew.

Now, I was still struggling with coming to terms with the new reality I trudged through. Almost two months before all this, I'd locked myself away in my small dingy apartment. I was prepared to wait this all out, when my next-door neighbor pounded on my door with her two kids. I almost didn't answer. If I was being honest with myself, I sometimes wish I hadn't. She'd shoved the two kids into my apartment, and begged me to watch them so she could save her sister. Before I could tell her I'd never even kept a house plant alive, I was alone in my home with a five-year-old, Gabby, and an almost two-year-old, Tina.

For a week, I told myself that their mother would be back. By the second week, I had run out of food that Tina could successfully eat. I raided their apartment then and came back with a treasure trove of kids' supplies. I felt successful, as if I had taken the first big step to actually making sure the little goblins didn't die. Until I turned and found a very disappointed Gabby, staring at me from the bedroom I'd left her in.

Gabby informed me I shouldn't leave them alone and then she listed all the things that could happen. Her horror stories ranged from running with scissors, Tina climbing into the oven and it miraculously turning on and her or Tina falling from the second-floor windows. I stared at her in disbelief, wondering who taught the small child the things that happened in scary movies, but she just stared back at me as if I was a complete idiot. She wasn't too far off.

The safe zone over the border in Canada seemed like the only option I had, because no matter what I really wanted, I couldn't just leave the girls behind. It wasn't a simple trip and if it hadn't been for the group with the priest and nun, we would have starved to death. When we got to the safe zone, I had hoped we'd found a place to be safe for a while. I was wrong. Nothing was safe anymore.

Within the first night, the safe zone fell and our temporary bliss had erupted into screams, gunfire and blood. The nun, who I just finally learned was called Sister Ann, came to find us and led us back to the school bus, the same one that brought us to the zone. With zombies pounding on the side panels, the priest guided the big vehicle out of the neighborhood and back onto an open highway. Both the nun and the priest said continuous prayers for the fallen they couldn't save.

That had been two days before. Father Allen, who also finally introduced himself, switched off driving with another man. I didn't bother learning about him because I didn't really care. I had two people, small people, that I had to take care of. That was the extent of my world now. And as we drove through the night, without stopping, looking for a new safe place to be, I shared a bus bench with the two of them.

Next to me, curled up in a small ball with her head on a

pillow, was Gabby. I was pretty sure the child could sleep through a tornado, should one strike us suddenly. Her face was soft in sleep. The only time she was quiet was when she was asleep. It made me wonder why women had children, if they would do nothing but listen to little opinions and arguments for the rest of their lives.

Tina, who had been sleeping against my chest, was now a full ball of energy in the middle of the night. Luckily, the adults didn't sleep any better than I did, and Tina's squeals didn't seem to bother anyone. I locked my arms around her legs, so she could see over the seat and through the windows. Sister Ann had turned to see us and she appeared with a sippy cup filled with milk, made from powder we had in the back of the bus.

"She probably would go back to sleep with some milk," Sister Ann said with a kind smile.

I didn't have the energy to return her smile, but Tina reached up with grabby hands and took the cup. Throwing herself back against my chest again, she started sucking down the milk at warp speed. I again, was trying to catch my breath from her forcing it out of my lungs. Sister Ann laughed lightly.

"They really are the inspiration to keep going."

I thought about it for a moment before replying, "I guess."

I had no inspiration for surviving except keeping myself from being eaten by the dead. In the beginning of the sickness, I did what I always did. I avoided people. My life had consisted of my tiny one-bedroom apartment and the bar I tended. When people started dying left and right from an unknown illness, I wasn't overwhelmed with grief or the need to save anyone else. My goal was completely self preservation.

Tina's white blonde head finally rested, as the sippy cup fell from her pouting lips. Her mouth continued to make a drinking motion, but her eyes had fluttered shut and Sister Ann quickly caught the falling cup. The little body felt heavy against mine and I finally could take a deep breath of relief. Sister Ann draped a light blanket over us both and ran her hand over Tina's head.

I could understand why the adults looked at the kids the way they did. Something about children represented what was pure about the world. Something zombies and the plague hadn't been able to reach. At least not yet. They were also the new start that humans were going to need if we were going to survive as a species in this world. When I looked at them, I saw innocence, but I also saw weakness and liability.

When it was just me to keep alive, I was able to take all the extra steps to keep myself healthy. Before we understood the real threat of the illness, people still went about their business somewhat normally. I worked for a few days, with a completely empty bar, until the owner ended up sick and shutdown. Assuring me it was only until he was feeling better. I never heard from him again.

Shutting myself away in my apartment for days, I lived off ramen, frozen burritos, and whiskey. It was enough to keep me sane. Finally, when the ramen ran out, I strapped on a pair of snorkel goggles, I had only used once, a medical grade mask under a handkerchief and latex gloves. The looks I got from people didn't bother me, especially the ones that were coughing or looked pale and sweaty. I was going to keep myself healthy.

One trip to the grocery store was all I could make before the dead started to attack the living. The surrounding apartments quickly became empty as neighbors panicked and evacuated. Another plus to having no one to worry about, I had nowhere else to go. So I stayed alone and quiet. Until the girls showed up. Then I realized I hadn't stocked up on enough whiskey to make it through.

I gently pried my shoulder-length, plain brown hair from Tina's chubby fist. She had a habit of wrapping her fingers in the strands and holding on for as long as my scalp could handle it. Even though I was pretty sure it was an early sign of a serial killer, I let her use my hair for whatever comfort she needed. I would do whatever I had to keep her from crying the high-pitched screech she could build to. Sometimes I wondered if being deaf during the apocalypse would really be all that bad.

Gabby shifted next to me, her foot digging into my hip, and I scooted further toward the end of the bench. I would have moved, but when she started to fall asleep, she would feel scared and made me promise to stay next to her. I wasn't sure what she thought I would do, but I stayed put. Shuddering, I didn't want to think about the lecture the little girl could give if she woke up and I was gone.

My gaze drifted to the window of the bus. There was nothing to see. Everything was pitch black outside. But in my mind, I could imagine the dead wandering the sides of the road. My imagination was probably going way further than what was actually outside. The girls and I had been in a few close scrapes, and I wasn't sure how I would protect them if we got into any more. I had failed at a lot of things in my life, but this was one thing I actually wanted to do right.

Closing my eyes, I tried to let my exhausted body recharge itself. But too many thoughts plagued my mind. It was true that I had no one in the world now, but I had come from somewhere. That was something I didn't know about either. Growing up in the foster care system, When I was 18, I aged out after never being adopted. When.the state is no longer responsible for you, they really don't care what happens to you from there.

I barely scraped through life working at a fast-food restaurant for a few years until the manager tried to sexually assault me after closing one night. I broke his nose with a box of frozen chicken nuggets. It wasn't the first time that I found when it was a young girl's word against a grown man, the girl rarely won.

Charged with assault, I was fired from my job as the man quietly dropped the charges. My guess was he didn't want the video footage from the office where the attack happened to see the light of day.

Getting the job as a bartender at a local watering hole seemed like the best option. The owner was an old angry man who wanted nothing to do with me, except for me to do my job and to pay me. I lost myself in the bottle more often than not since I knew alcohol could dull the pain. Working where I had easy access to booze was a positive I needed in my life. I had always kept my drinking under control, no drunk driving or public intoxication. At least not where I was caught.

Hiding away as a bartender, doing nothing with my life, had not prepared me for what was going on in the world. I knew nothing about how to provide for two small children. Even before there were zombies, I barely kept myself alive some days. These thoughts plagued my mind as I was trying to sleep and I could feel myself start to sweat under Tina's weight on my chest.

Taking a deep breath, the baby's sweet smell filled my nostrils. I had once heard a joke about babies smelling good, to prevent parents from eating them. Sounded like evolutionary brilliance to me. Even without getting regular baths, the baby still smelled good. I didn't hesitate to lower my face just slightly, to focus on my breathing and Tina's smell. Eventually, my mind settled, and I could get a few hours of sleep on the bumpy bus.

I was awakened from a dark dream by something poking me in the face. Startling awake, I looked around and squinted against the harsh sunlight that was filling the bus. When I turned to the side, I found Gabby's face almost level with my own. She was sitting up on her knees and holding onto the back of the seat to keep herself upright. Her finger was still pointed at my cheek, and I glared at her.

"We gotta figure out a better way for you to wake me up, kid," I groaned.

"You're drooling on Tina's head."

Bringing my hand to my face, I found Gabby wasn't wrong. A stream of wetness was on the side of my chin. I used my shoulder to wipe my face and ran my hand over Tina's blonde hair. She was slightly damp, but had slept through the impromptu saliva shower. I was feeling stiff and badly needed to pee. Looking around the bus, I found many people were still sleeping, but Sister Ann was awake, slipping around the supplies in the back. I wasn't sure the nun ever actually slept.

When she walked back up the aisle, she handed a juice pouch and a bag of fruit snacks to Gabby. She also handed me a container of puff treats for Tina when she woke up. I noticed we must have stopped while I slept, as the priest was no longer driving.

"Sister, are we stopping anytime soon?" I asked.

Suddenly, Gabby started bouncing next to me on the seat, nodding her head emphatically.

"Need to relieve yourself, little one?" Sister Ann asked.

I raised an eyebrow, but didn't mention that it was me that had asked about stopping and yes, I needed to pee.

"Yes, ma'am," Gabby replied.

I had to stifle a laugh. For some reason, the habit wearing nun earned the utmost respect from the five-year-old. Where I was lucky if she gave me full sentences that weren't dripping with sarcasm and attitude. I hadn't thought their mother was religious, but really, what had I known about them before they were dropped off at my house? I had heard Tina crying through the wall more than once, but it was easy for me to put on headphones and drown out the noise with music and whiskey.

Sister Ann moved toward the front of the bus, where she shared some quiet words with the driver. The man nodded, but his gaze was sharp on the road as he moved around vehicles that cluttered the highway. I sat up straighter, able to focus more on our surroundings. We seemed to be passing through a small town with remnants of chaos all around.

Burned-out vehicles still smoldered near a convenience store, the front of the store only a charred remain from where it had also caught on fire. We slowly rolled by a residential area and I stared. Though this type of destruction was normal now, it was still hard to stomach. I had avoided scenes like this for the first month of the apocalypse. Now I see them each and every day.

The street was littered with the remains of the lives that had once happily resided in the homes. Grass had overgrown and flowers wilted and died. A suitcase lay open with clothing still inside. Dark stains spotted the sidewalk and there was no mistaking what had caused them. Far off in the distance, the jilted movement of a body became visible. The zombie had clearly not had anything to catch its attention for a long time as it shambled toward the moving bus.

"God save and protect those that lived in this town," Sister Ann murmured.

"I don't know that God was on this street, sister," I replied.

The nun was well aware of my feelings about religion. Especially the talk of God. I found it unreasonable to believe in a higher power that would allow so much death to happen on the planet at one time. But then again, why was I surprised? If I remembered biblical stories well enough, he also created a planet wide flood because he got a little pissy. The big guy must have really been feeling put out to create walking monsters that wanted nothing more than to feast on your flesh.

"We won't stop until we're out of this town," Sister Ann said, completely ignoring my negative God talk.

I just nodded and kept looking out the window. Gabby

turned to look, but I moved her to sit on the outside of the bench, so she could move across the aisle and color in a book. I couldn't protect her from everything. She had already seen some of the worst. But I didn't think it helped her little brain to constantly see what had happened to the only world she knew.

Tina began to sniffle and rub her face against my chest, the sure sign she was finally ready to face the day. Her arms, which had been tucked between us, came shooting up in a stretch. One tiny fist smacked me on the lip and I threw my head back against the bus seat. I wasn't sure, but sometimes I thought Tina did things like this on purpose, likely to pay me back for snapping her in the face with a seatbelt. It was only one time, but I knew the kid hadn't forgotten.

Sister Ann, who was still standing in the aisle ahead of us, turned to reach down for Tina. The little girl smiled at the nun and held her arms up.

"I'll get her changed. Why don't you stretch your legs?"

I nodded, grateful to have my body to myself for a moment. If it wasn't Tina laying on me or being strapped to my body in some contraption, it was Gabby wanting to always hold my hand, to be glued to my side. I stretched my own arms up and turned my neck from side to side. Sleeping sitting up in the bus seat hadn't done my abused body any good.

That reminded me, I was only a few days from almost dying from starvation and dehydration. After leaving my apartment building with the girls, we tried to get to Canada on our own. Things were going ok, until a horde of zombies trapped us, forcing us to climb a water tower without enough food and water to last even a few days. If the bus hadn't come by and Gabby hadn't still had the strength to stand and wave, all three of us wouldn't have made it off that ledge.

The picture of Tina's tiny body, not moving, as they pumped IV fluids into her on the bus, was something that haunted my nightmares. Though I knew I couldn't control the zombies, the predicament felt like it was entirely my fault. I stood from my bus seat, listening to my knees and hips crackle and pop. Pulling my hair into a ponytail, I stretched my arms and walked up and down the aisle to get my hips moving.

With a clean baby on her hip, Sister Ann returned to her seat and gave Tina a cup full of milk to start her morning. The baby slurped and leaned against the nun, completely trusting of the woman she had only known a few days. At what age did kids learn about stranger danger? The thought floated across my mind, as well as wondering if stranger danger even mattered in the apocalypse. Everyone was in danger, living and dead, until they could prove they weren't.

The bus slowed, and it pulled off onto a large shoulder next to the highway. The guy behind the wheel stood up and faced the bus. Including me and the girls, there were only eight people that had made it onto the bus. Since fleeing the safe zone, everyone had found their own spaces within the aisles and had kept to themselves. Even though the priest and nun moved between people to pray and ask if they could help them.

"We're going to take a bathroom break here. Everyone, keep your eyes open. I see nothing moving out there, but you never know," the guy announced.

I fought my urge to roll my eyes. If anyone didn't actually know they needed to be careful at this point, they didn't deserve to keep surviving. Gabby's head popped out from her seat and her eyes searched until she found me. Without a word, she made her way to me and grabbed onto my hand tightly. We followed the group as everyone filed out of the bus into the bright morning light.

It hadn't taken me long to realize Gabby couldn't squat on her own. After being peed on twice, we finally found a process where she hooked her arms around mine and I hung her between my legs. She would pull her legs up and would pee between my feet. Sometimes a bit splashed on me. But since the only bodily fluid I couldn't handle was vomit, and as long as my socks weren't soaked, I considered the bathroom break a win.

Overgrown weeds lined the side of the road and you could see the pollen that was dusting everything in the early spring days. I led Gabby by the hand to the back of the bus, with everyone else going off in their own directions. Privacy was scarce when we were all just using the road as a bathroom, but something in me wanted to protect Gabby as best I could.

Once we were out of sight of everyone else, I stood and looked around us. I used my hand to shield the rising sun from my eyes. Gabby danced next to me, her little face screwed up in concentration. There was nothing around us that seemed like a threat, so I turned to the little girl.

Fumbling with the waistband of her leggings, Gabby pulled them down to her ankles with her underwear. I put out my arms, like we had done several times before. She tried to hook her arms around mine, but slipped off one arm and dangled. The urgency to pee struck her and while she was hanging over one of my legs, she let loose and I stared at the side of the bus as hot liquid slid down my leg.

"I need a damn drink."

CHAPTER 2

"I'M NOT EATING IT," Gabby said for the tenth time.

My patience was already running thin, and we hadn't even gotten back on the road yet. When we ran from the safe zone, after it became the unsafe zone, we had very little in the way of supplies. A lot of what the group had gathered had been unloaded, and we couldn't grab everything on our way out.

Which brought me to my predicament with Gabby. The girl had to eat something, and we were serving everyone portions of oatmeal, made with powdered milk, warmed over a tiny propane camping stove. Tina chomped away happily and played with two cars I had grabbed and shoved in my bag before bugging out. On the other hand, Gabby gagged with the first bite and refused to try it again.

"Come on, eat some of this and you can have another juice pouch," I said, repeating my desperate attempt at bribery.

I was positive that bribing her was the wrong way to go about taking charge as a responsible adult. But this felt even more difficult than handling the regulars at the bar. With them, all I did was threaten to call a wife, the cops or take their keys and suddenly they were on their best behavior. No matter what I promised Gabby, she just glared at me over the bus seat.

"Listen, neither of us is having a great day so far. You peed on me, remember? I'm wearing the last pair of clean leggings I have, with no washing machine or Walmart in sight. The least you could do is eat what we have for breakfast and remember, we aren't in the position to be picky."

I hadn't raised my voice, not wanting to bring too much attention to us, but Gabby's lip trembled, anyway. A string of curse words flew through my mind, but I bit my tongue before I let them fly like arrows at a five-year-old. Instead, I slumped into the seat next to her, laying my head back to stare at the ceiling.

Suddenly, Sister Ann appeared next to us, her face a mask of kindness and compassion. I wasn't sure if there was ever a time she wasn't in that mode. Her hands disappeared into her habit and when they reappeared, she had a small snack sized bag of candy coated chocolates. Gabby's eyes went wide as she looked at her hand and then up into Sister Ann's face.

"How does chocolate oatmeal sound, Gabby?" Sister Ann asked.

Gabby nodded her head enthusiastically, and the nun sprinkled a few candies on the top of her food. The little girl was slow to scoop up one candy with oatmeal. Her gaze cut over to Sister Ann, and I knew the little manipulator was thinking about eating the candies off the oatmeal. But apparently, she wouldn't do that with the watchful eyes of God on her.

"Good girl," the nun said.

I saw Gabby push down her gag reflex, but she chewed slowly and finally swallowed with a big gulp of water. I wasn't so mean that I enjoyed watching her struggle. But I also knew the chances of food were slim and we had to take what was available whenever it was. And sometimes that included oatmeal that tasted like sludge.

Father Allen made his way to us and he stood smiling down at the girls and then at me. I just flashed a small smile before picking up a car that Tina had dropped.

"I hope you ladies are comfortable. We're going to get going soon. We are low on fuel and need to find diesel vehicles to scavenge from."

I nodded my head, knowing diesel was going to be harder to come by than regular gas. But the bus was large and felt way safer than the initial van I had found for the girls and I. That vehicle had also been stolen right from under my nose, so having more people to keep an eye out also made me feel more secure.

"I can help siphon from other cars if we find any. I did that a little before, when we first bugged out," I offered. My voice gave away the insecurity I felt in the task, but I had to pull my weight somehow.

"That would be very helpful, Vicki. Thank you," Father Allen said with a small bow before returning to the front of the bus.

A few moments later, the rumble of the bus engine started. A thump next to my window made me jump, and I leaned over to find a zombie scratching at the side panel of the bus. The sound of the people inside and wandering outside to cook and stretch must have attracted it from wherever it had been. It was a young woman, and it threw its head back, groaning into the air, trying to find its prey. Its dead eyes locked onto my window, the groan rose, and its hands scrabbled harder against the metal, as if it could climb up and reach me. Its pale pink dress was torn to shreds around her legs, showing peeling flesh where others must have feasted on her living body.

The bus hitched slightly as it was put into gear. As we pulled away, I watched the zombie get spun in the place. I lost sight of it as it fell, but I knew it would just climb up and continue until it found a meal. I felt a slight shiver go through me. To stay alive, it felt like we had to just keep moving until the end of time. That thought suddenly made me feel extremely exhausted and even though we hadn't been awake long, I leaned my head back and closed my eyes.

"Vicki, do I really have to finish?" Gabby's voice cut into my mental nap.

"Yes. Even the bites that don't have chocolates." I didn't bother opening my eyes.

My hand was on Tina's leg, making sure the girl didn't slip while the bus moved. Gabby was on her knees on the other side of me, the bowl of oatmeal on the seat. I heard a loud, annoyed sigh that made me wanna say something snarky, but I just let myself be exhausted. The mental aerobics of keeping up with Gabby was taxing on my sober mind. Another few gagging sounds and she announced the oatmeal was done.

Opening my eyes, I took the bowl and put it on the ground to be disposed of later. We didn't have any real plates or bowls, so we were using paper or plastic and also empty cans to be reused for warming food. It was the best we could do with the slim supplies we had. Gabby clambered up onto the seat and leaned against me for a long moment.

"Oatmeal sucks," she said.

"Sorry kid, things just suck right now. Hopefully, we have the chance to find more food soon."

The morning breakfast had been all the oatmeal packets we had. The water was running low and that meant powdered milk couldn't be mixed, even though the girls desperately needed those calories. We had uncooked pasta and dried beans, which also faced the problem of not having enough water. A box of fruit snacks and a box of juice pouches. The adults easily agreed those were set aside for the kids. Then we had a mix of small bags of potato chips and a couple of packages of jerky that had been missed when the bus was off loaded.

It wasn't enough, and we all knew it. Somehow, Sister Ann and Father Allen continued with their belief that we would find some sort of salvation. I didn't voice the opinion I had about that being absolute rubbish. Salvation wasn't out there, I was sure of it. We had to make it ourselves, figure out how to survive, and just keep moving.

An hour later, the bus slowed again, and I lifted my head from where it rested. Looking out the windows, I saw we had entered another one of the small towns that seemed to dot this highway. They all looked almost the same. Small gas stations, small strip malls with the same five types of businesses, maybe one large box store and several clustered neighborhoods.

The bus drove toward the small gas station and I knew it was time to get serious. The bus couldn't continue to run on fumes. When the engine cut off, everyone sat quietly for a long moment. I was not a leader, but we were wasting time and daylight if we just kept sitting. Grabbing a hunting knife that I'd found in the safe zone, I slipped the sheath into a small back-pack. I didn't have pockets or a belt to hook it to, so I had to hope I could get it out before it was too late.

Hoisting Tina into my arms, I made my way up the aisle, where Sister Ann and Father Allen sat, whispering with the driver. When the three looked up at me, I shifted uncomfort-ably. I wasn't trying to be a hero or someone to follow. But I had two children I didn't want to see starve to death. So, if that meant I had to get off the bus and handle business, I would be the one to do it.

"Sister, can you watch the girls?" I asked.

The nun solemnly nodded and held out her hands for Tina. Gabby ran up the aisle and grabbed my hand before I could head down the bus steps. Turning, I looked down at the little girl, waiting for some sort of quippish rules she wanted to impose on me.

"Vicki, you'll come back, right?" She asked.

"Yeah, kid. I'm not leaving for long."

Her face started to screw up, and I grimaced. She was winding up for something, and I wasn't sure what it was. Suddenly, she was wrapped around my waist, hugging herself to me and almost making us both tumble down the bus steps. At the last moment, I grabbed the front bench seat to keep myself standing. Gabby's little shoulders shook as she cried, and I just stared at her dumbly.

Realizing everyone was watching me like a hawk, I huffed out a breath. I found her locked hands behind my legs and pried them apart carefully. Once I was out of her little vise, I crouched in front of her, so I could look her in the eyes.

"Hey. Have I left you behind yet?"

Gabby shook her head.

"And that's still the plan. Remember how I used to have to leave the apartment once in a while because we needed food? Well, this is the same thing. I gotta make sure you and your sister stay alive."

"Mommy didn't come back." Gabby's voice was quiet, and I almost missed the words.

Yikes, I thought to myself. Gabby was a smart kid for her age, even so, she was traumatized. How could she not be? Her mother dumped her with a complete stranger that barely knew how to care for a houseplant. I knew their mother had every intention of returning; she loved the girls. But the apocalypse had different plans for us all.

"I know, your Mommy wasn't able to come back. But look, kid, I'm not going far. Just out there to see if I can find supplies. You can watch from the window if you want," I said, hoping to give her some sort of consolation.

She nodded slightly and climbed onto the seat behind Sister Ann, moving as close to the window as possible. I took a deep breath and met the nun's gaze for a moment. Her look was heavy and said so many things without her opening her mouth. I didn't think I wanted to know what she was thinking at the moment.

One guy on the bus volunteered to go searching with me, and he quietly followed me down the steps. The air was cool and felt cleaner than what was becoming stale on the bus. With my eyes peeled for any sort of threat, I slowly made my way to the gas station glass windows. Though there was a lot of destruction surrounding the building, the windows and door seemed to be intact.

On the ground I found a metal pipe, the end of it covered in dried blood and I stooped to pick it up. Swinging the pipe, I continued toward the building until I could tap on the glass of the door. Almost immediately, a dead body slammed against the door. The zombie was wearing a gas attendant uniform, the logo still clear on the chest. But that was about the only thing that wasn't covered in blood or ripped to shreds.

The zombie was once a young man. Now he was slamming unnaturally into the door, trying to get to a meal. The flesh of his arms had been bitten and peeled, revealing white bone stained with blood in places. My mind worked, trying to figure out how he got locked in the station and also that ruined. Just as I was going to give up, another figure appeared, moving slower, joining the zombie at the door.

"It's just two," I murmured, hoping the guy with me could hear.

When I glanced over, the guy was hopping from foot to foot nervously. I rolled my eyes, figuring he was likely going to get himself, or someone else, killed. And it would not be me.

"I'm going to swing this door open and let them out. You lead them away from the entrance and I'll hit the last one in the head. You take the first one. Can you do that?" I asked.

The man's gaze flashed over to me, and I could see the fear painting his face. Internally, I was screaming at the guy to get the hell over it and join the program. We were living with zombies, there was no getting around it. And we needed what was inside the station. As I stared at him, his wide eyes dominated by white, I waited for a response. He finally jerked his head in a nod and I turned toward the door.

Grasping the bar that ran across the door, I nodded to scared guy and he hesitantly nodded back. I took a deep breath and pulled. The door didn't budge. I tried once more, and even so, it didn't move an inch. Cursing in my head, I moved back to look closer and realized the door was locked from the inside. I almost smacked myself in the forehead as I realized, of course, if the door was open, the zombies would have pushed their way out to get us at this point.

"Need a new plan," I said.

I slowly walked down the wall of windows, peering inside the store. Most of the products were still inside, though there was blood and entrails splashed against the walls or smeared along the windows. When I got to the end, the zombies moved my way. Suddenly, deciding the fastest way in was through, I motioned to the guy.

"Keep them at the door," I said.

"How do I do that?" He asked.

"Dude, they want to eat you. How do you think you keep them there?"

If it was possible for him to go more pale, he did at that moment. But he visibly gulped and walked toward the door, tapping on the glass, causing the zombies to look back at him. They seemed to rationalize that the man was closer, so they wandered back to the door and started slamming against it again. The man jumped and a small yelp came out of his mouth, and I held back the cackle that bubbled up.

Stepping back from the window, I swung the metal pipe I had like a bat, slamming it in the window. It didn't shatter like I'd hoped, and the impact sent waves of pain through my arms. But a small crack formed and fissured slowly. Not waiting for the zombies to decide the louder human would be tastier, I slammed the pipe into the cracked area. The glass broke, flying into the store.

Immediately, the thick, grotesque smell of the dead wafted out and I couldn't stop the automatic gag I had. The zombies had completely abandoned the man at the door, knowing I was within reach. I watched as they made their way down the windows until they reached the one that was broken. Remembering we were out in the open, I risked a quick glance around. Breaking the window was like ringing a dinner bell.

When the zombies got to the broken space, they leaned into it, like they expected glass to still be there. The young man was the first to tumble through and fall to the ground. I didn't wait for him to figure it out. Quickly, I swung the metal pipe down, slamming into the back of the zombie's head. The crack of the skull was loud, but it didn't stop him. His body continued to work to stand, so I swung again, grunting as the impact embedded the pipe into the brain matter and the body collapsed at my feet.

Just as I was celebrating my first win, the second zombie tumbled and hit my leg, causing me to sprawl on the ground. Dimly in the back of my mind, I heard muffled screaming, but I couldn't focus on anything but the dead fingers that were reaching out for my booted foot. I crab walked backward on my hands and feet until I had enough distance to stand. The zombie took the same time to get itself upright. My eyes fell to the metal pipe that I had dropped as the zombie's shuffling step kicked it out of reach.

I found the scared man, inching away from the fight, and I

wished I had the pipe just so I could throw it at him. Swinging my pack from my back, I shoved my hand in and gripped the hunting knife. I threw off the sheath and dropped everything as the zombie came toward me. I waited, trying to figure out the best place to stab it, knowing I couldn't put too much thought into what was happening.

Just as the zombie was about to fall on me, I shoved the blade up into its face, through its eye socket. The feeling of the blade piercing the dead eye and sliding along bone made me break out in goosebumps. As soon as the body fell, finally lifeless, I turned and puked up my oatmeal breakfast. My stomach continued to revolt for a moment as I tried to calm myself. I had just shoved a knife into an eye and brain, and I did not know how I found the strength to do it.

I realized as the pounding in my ears faded, I could hear screaming and banging again. Glancing up, I found Gabby's tear-streaked face at the window, watching everything that had just happened to me. Crap, I thought to myself. I hadn't wanted her to see this kind of violence or see the monsters that were around every corner. Sister Ann sat next to her, trying to pat her on the back to calm her.

"I'm fine," I called, hoping she could hear me.

Knowing I couldn't make her feel better until I could get back on the bus, I turned to retrieve my backpack. At the dead zombie, I grimaced, but leaned down and gripped my knife handle to yank it from its face. I stared at the blade for longer than necessary. This world wasn't something I was ready for. Not that blood bothered me. I used to love watching all sorts of slasher films. And there were plenty of times some drunk in my bar would fall and crack their head open. But having to kill things, even if its defending myself, was beyond the scope of the life I had expected.

"Are you ok?"

My gaze snapped up and my eyes narrowed as I stared at the man that had all but abandoned me.

"No, thanks to you. You shouldn't even be out there," I snarled.

The man had enough brains to look contrite, and his pale face colored with red. When he opened his mouth again, I held up a hand to stop him. Leaning down, I used the clothes on the zombie to clean my blade. I then went to pick up the metal pipe I had found and walked toward the storefront. The man's steps behind me indicated he was following me, even if he was completely useless.

I carefully stepped through the broken window, ensuring I didn't get caught on any of the jagged pieces that were still stuck in the frame. The smell inside was almost impossible to breathe through. I pulled my shirt up to cover my nose, hoping it would help somewhat. Some of the fridge doors were open, showing rotting pre-made lunches, fruits, vegetables and milk products. Those things only added to the dead stench that had been building for days.

Near the front of the store, I found a stack of reusable shopping bags. Grabbing two of them, I shoved them at the man that was just ghosting behind me with no idea of what he should be doing.

"Anything edible goes into the bags. There's not much. But it'll hopefully get us through a few days."

He nodded and with a straightforward task, he moved away and started shoving chips, pretzels, trail mixes and cheese-flavored snacks into a bag. Next to the front counter, there was a rack of maps. All of them seemed to be for places in North Dakota, giving me an idea of the state we had to be in. I grabbed one of each and then found the address of the station under a plastic mat on the counter. With a pen that was on the register, I scribbled the address, not really sure it was useful, but thinking it would be a starting point for the maps.

Behind me, the man had filled two bags, and he just stood watching me. I rolled my eyes, wanting to growl at him. I wasn't his leader or his chief or whatever. He could make decisions and figure out what he needed to do on his own. But whether it was fear or lack of intelligence, the man needed someone to tell him what to do.

"Take the full bags to the bus. Come back for more," I said, waving him away with a hand.

I grabbed two more bags and went toward the small area that sold medications and other toiletries. Reading nothing, I grabbed handfuls off the racks and shoved them into the bags. I grabbed all the feminine hygiene products, knowing that was going to be an issue sooner rather than later. The last period I had was right before I bugged out with the girls. Though I had lost track of days, I was pretty sure I had a couple weeks still.

My bags were stuffed by the time the man appeared again, sweat appearing on his temples. As I made my way to the window, I stopped and unlocked the door instead so we wouldn't get sliced up. I propped it open with a rock from outside and headed toward the bus. The doors swung open just as I got there and one woman from inside took the bags from my hands.

The man and I each made two more trips of full bags of any products we found at the station. I went back once more and waved the man off, looking for something very specific for me. Searching behind the counter, I didn't find the liquid gold I was searching for. Frustrated, I tore out the area under the register and the sound of metal stopped me.

On the ground at my feet was a flask, and I just stared at it for a long moment before picking it up and unscrewing the cap. The smell of whiskey wafted from inside and when I carefully shook it, it felt about half full. I praised God, though I knew he wanted me to quit. I had promised, after all. But I guess he shouldn't have sent a plague that made dead people walk and try to eat me. I couldn't survive this stress without something to take the edge off. Weighing my options, I shook the flask in my hand, listening to the liquid slosh around. I could leave the flask on the ground and walk away, pretending I didn't need the liquor to make it through the apocalypse. Or I could slip it into my pack and no one would know anything about it.

My hesitation didn't last long, and the flask found its way into my backpack. To cover up how long I was taking, I grabbed two more bags and made another sweep of the shop. I found a stand with sunglasses and grabbed a handful of them. There was a turnstile with kids' books and I shoved as many as I could into the bag as well. On a back shelf, I found batteries, jumper cables, work gloves and more items that could come in handy as we were on the road.

I made my way back to the bus just as a collective groan rose from behind the vehicle. I peered back onto the road and saw a group of about ten zombies tripping down the road. As soon as I was back on the bus, the man behind the wheel fired up the engine and we were back on the highway within moments, leaving the small group behind. Taking my two bags down the aisle, I first stashed my backpack in the row the girls and I slept in. I was careful to hide it, to keep anyone else from poking around in my findings.

Then I took the two shopping bags to the back of the bus, where we were keeping all the supplies. A woman was sorting what had come from the bags. She smiled brightly at me as I approached.

"That was really brave of you," she said.

I shrugged. "Someone was going to have to do it. We were running low."

She took the bags from my hands and smiled at the books before handing that one back to me.

"Only two people on this bus will use those."

I nodded and flashed her a small smile. She continued her sorting, and I went back to find the girls. Gabby was on her knees in her seat, watching me, and when I got closer, she clambered down into the aisle, wrapping her arms around my waist.

"Hey, what have we said about walking around when the bus is moving, shorty?" I asked.

Gabby mumbled something against my stomach, but then she released me and climbed back into her seat, a determined look on her face. Sister Ann was in the seat behind her, and she motioned for me to come sit with her. I handed the bag of books to Gabby first and joined the nun. Tina sat on the Nun's lap and was climbing around, trying to get to her sister. I reached around and picked a random book and brought it to the baby, who plopped down on the nun's lap and started pulling at pages.

"She was terrified," Sister Ann said.

"I wasn't feeling all the great either."

Sister Ann nodded and continued. "I know you're not their mother and definitely weren't looking to be one. But you're the only constant in their lives now. I hope you realize how important that is to them both."

The weight of her gaze made me look away and long for the flask that was hidden rows behind us. I didn't want the responsibility of kids. My brain knew that. However, when we had initially gotten to the safe zone in Canada, I wasn't ready to just hand them over to adults that were ready to raise children. And that proved to be the smartest decision I could have made. When the zone fell to the dead, the girls were with me, and I could easily save them again. There was no knowing what could have happened to them if I had let someone else take charge of them.

Father Allen came to sit across from us, saving me from having to respond to the nun's examination of my role and responsibility with the girls. He had one of the maps I'd grabbed unfolded in front of him.

"Very smart to grab these, Vicki. I think I've pinpointed where we are. You were right that we're in North Dakota and we've just been heading west, since we came back into the states," he said.

I nodded and waited for him to continue.

"We don't really have any ideas of where to go. Large cities seem dangerous. Maybe find a small town with a neighborhood that is behind gates?"

"Gates didn't help the safe zone," I replied.

Father Allen contemplated the map.

"I think there were too many people there. They weren't quiet. A lot of lights and vehicles." He said the words as if he was talking to himself, so I didn't respond.

We sat in silence for a long period before the bus slowed again. Father Allen glanced up and stood. Sending me a small smile, he turned and made his way to the driver. I watched as the peered through the windshield and the two men exchanged a few words. Then Father Allen turned and found my eyes again. His gaze told me what was coming, and I threw my head back against the bus seat. Nothing was going to be easy.

CHAPTER 3

A DIESEL POWERED city bus sat abandoned on the side of the highway. Bloody handprints and splatter painted the windows. But the door was wide open and nothing seemed to move inside.

"We have a few gas cans under the bus, so we could fill those," Father Allen was saying to me.

I stared at the bus and the other cars that were crashed or abandoned haphazardly along the road. The bus engine quieted and everyone sat on the edges of their seats, waiting to see what I would do. When I looked behind me, every gaze was locked on me, as if I was going to save them. The idea turned my stomach, and I found Gabby's eyes watching me. I tried to pretend she and Tina were the only ones on the bus. The only ones I had to help, protect, and save. Even that was more pressure than I wanted, but it was more manageable than the additional adults watching me.

"I need someone to watch my back while I work," I said.

"I'll do it," Father Allen said.

In a few minutes, I had gathered the supplies I would need, glad I immediately found a use for the work gloves I found at the gas station store. Father Allen opened the storage area under the bus and pulled out two five-gallon gas cans, a length of hose and a funnel. I'd only siphoned gas a few times and only twice where I didn't end up with a mouth full of gas. I wasn't looking forward to the process, but we needed the fuel to keep going to wherever our destination ended up being.

At the city bus, I checked the windows first, ensuring there weren't any zombies hiding and waiting for a meal to walk by. The inside was worse than I had imagined, pools of dark, dried blood, pieces of flesh and what I was pretty sure were long pieces of intestines littered the bus floor. But there were no bodies, so whoever or whatever did the damage made it off the bus at some point. We moved until we found the cap for the gas. I cursed quietly when I saw a keyhole.

"Makes sense. They wouldn't want people stealing the gas," Father Allen whispered.

I just nodded my head, because I had already come to that conclusion. His voice also reminded me to keep my language under control. Religion didn't rule my life, but I still felt awkward sounding like a sailor in their presence. I stared at the fuel door that hid the prize I needed. Slowly, a thought came to me and I looked toward the open door of the vehicle. The priest followed my gaze and then looked back at me.

"We need the keys. My bet is, the driver could open this door," I whispered.

Together, we moved along the bus, until we got to the open door. I knew there were no zombies inside, but I didn't really want to step foot on what felt like a coffin on wheels. I caught Father Allen doing the cross, and I had to grit my teeth to not make a smart ass remark on how he wasn't protecting us with that. Taking a deep breath, I focused on the steering column where the keys should be and didn't look anywhere else.

Stepping onto the bus, my foot made a squelching sound that I knew I wouldn't want to think too hard about. At the steering wheel, I looked quickly and found keys hanging from the ignition. Carefully, I pulled them out and almost jumped back out of the bus.

"What is it?" The priest asked me.

I shook my head and walked back to the fuel door. Was I supposed to tell him that the bus felt haunted, like too many people had died inside and their souls were trapped? How could I explain that the air felt too heavy to breathe? Instead of trying to voice the sickness roiling through me, I focused on the keys and the fuel door lock. After the third try, I bit back the cheer I almost let loose, with a key slipped in and easily turned. Father Allen patted me on the shoulder and for a moment, I felt good about the recognition from him.

I set up the supplies and started the siphon process. When the diesel almost passed my lips again, I spilled some on the ground instead, before leading the hose into the tank. The fuel flowed freely and I wiped the small amount that had hit my chin. I knew I was going to stink like gas and I looked up at the sky to throw my anger, when realizing I was wearing my last pair of clean leggings. If it wasn't bodily fluids from a child, it was gas or blood. I couldn't stay clean to save my life.

The process of getting the gas from bus to bus was long and annoying. The city bus was only about half full, but with the five-gallon gas cans, it was slow going. I lost track of the number of times we moved gas to our bus. Sister Ann came from the school bus to give us each a bottle of water that we luckily found at the gas station store. Though it was early spring, the sun beating down on us was warm and I was slowly beginning to sweat. Just another reason to know I was going to want a shower and clean clothes really soon.

I wasn't built for the apocalypse for many reasons. My desire to be clean was one of the big ones. I didn't take pride in much in my life, but cleanliness was important. I hadn't had an actual shower since we left my apartment, and the little baths we could give ourselves with baby wipes did very little. My top focus was keeping the girls as clean as I could, especially Tina, with her diaper butt that could easily get red and irritated.

My mind was wandering as the final diesel was flowing into the five-gallon cans. We had just enough extra gas to fill one of the cans and we added that to store for emergencies as we traveled. Father Allen and I stunk like fuel, but none of the adults complained. Gabby, on the other hand, had no problems voicing her displeasure the moment I sat down on a seat near her, Sister Ann, and Tina.

"You stink, Vicki." She held her nose dramatically.

"You're no flower these days," I replied.

"I smell better than you," Gabby protested.

I opened my mouth to shoot back some kind of your momma joke and quickly realized that was the wrong road to go down. Instead, I did the only mature thing possible. I stuck my tongue out at her. She responded by crossing her eyes at me. Relenting, because what was the point in arguing with a five-year-old, I laid my head back on the seat. The bus rumbled to life again, and we were once more moving down the highway, with no plan or destination.

Darkness fell before we found any sort of shelter. We decided that since we didn't have a specific destination in mind, it would be safer to just park and sleep, instead of driving through the night. The adults would work shifts to ensure there was always a lookout. Since we weren't moving, it was easier for people to create beds throughout the bus. I made a small cocoon of blankets and clothing for the girls to sleep side by side on the floor, in front of the seat I would lie on.

I tried to be comfortable on the small seat, but it was close to impossible. Even with almost everyone sleeping, the bus was loud with soft snoring, movement and murmurs. I tried to block it out, desperate for a few hours' sleep before it was my turn on watch. When I fell under the power of unconsciousness, it was dark and dreamless, just the way I wanted it. It felt like minutes had gone by when I was gently shaken awake by the woman that had watch prior to me. Her face was kind, but it was clear she was exhausted.

Wiping the sleep from my eyes, I nodded and slowly sat up. I checked on Gabby and Tina, who were both still curled up together, sleeping peacefully. They were relatively safe within the bus and I didn't feel uncomfortable moving toward the front of the bus for my time at watch. I wandered quietly down the middle aisle, being careful not to step on the heads or feet that were sticking out all over the place.

The front seat of the bus was big and uncomfortable, but it bounced and I had to control my intruding thoughts so I didn't wake up the entire vehicle. We had parked at a small truck weigh station that had no other vehicles around. Now, all I could see was the inky blackness surrounding us. The moonlight did little to illuminate the small building we drove beyond, or the trees that lined the station. I double checked that the doors were locked at least three times, before I felt comfortable sitting, so exposed in the big windows.

I listened to the night noises of the bus, but some of the outside noises also filtered through the cracks of the windows and door. An owl hooted, constantly calling to whoever would listen in a nearby tree. The buzz of a fly that was stuck inside caught my attention and I watched it as it continued to try to find that one open spot to get out.

Strangely, I related to the fly, and I felt as if I was also stuck in a box of glass. On each side of the box was another threat or worry. One side held the girls. I had decided during the short stop in the safe zone that they were going to be my responsibility. I didn't really know what that meant or why I felt like I had to keep them with me. However, I wasn't going to just leave them with another set of strangers after they had to come to me in such a horrible fashion.

On another side of the box were the zombies themselves, of course. The apocalypse wasn't something I had expected ever seeing, despite all the movies, shows, and books about it. They all felt too science fiction for my mind to consider. Yet, here I sat keeping watch, in a dark school bus. Counting me, as far as I knew, there were only ten people left alive on the planet. The rational part of my brain told me that was ridiculous, but that was how small my world was for now.

I could even see the alcohol outside of my box. That thought made me consider the flask I had found, but only for a split second. I didn't want to be irresponsible with my shift on watch. Not only were the girls on the bus, but the others as well. I couldn't risk being drunk or even a little tipsy while watching for threats. But at that moment I thought about it. I could almost feel the burn of the liquor as it slid down my throat.

A hand on my shoulder caused me to jump and cover my mouth before a squeaky scream escaped. Sister Ann looked down at me, her habit in place perfectly, her face wide awake with no signs of exhaustion. Maybe God was real, and he had blessed the woman with youth and the ability to handle anything without her habit being even a little dirty.

"I didn't mean to scare you. You were deep in thought," she said.

"Yeah. I was never much of a heavy thinker before all this." I rubbed my hands over my face.

Sister Ann suddenly sat on the ground next to the driver's seat and arranged herself before looking up at me expectantly. I just stared down at her for a long minute, but she didn't say a word, just smiled kindly up at me.

"I'm not much of a talker," I said.

"But I'm an amazing listener."

"Part of the job, I guess." I gestured to her clothes.

Sister Ann's smile widened, and she smoothed her hands over the material on her legs.

"I think I was good at that, before the job called to me. But now, I do the listening from a different place."

"What place is that?"

"From my father's love. He's bestowed that upon me and I give that to others," she said.

The talk about God had me fidgeting, and I pulled on a thread that was coming loose at the bottom of my t-shirt.

"I know you're not a believer, Vicki. That's ok. It doesn't mean he's left you."

My gaze snapped up to hers then, and I could see the moment she registered anger in my eyes. Her smile softened again, to look more consoling.

"I think if he even exists, Sister, he's left us all."

When I expected her to defend her position and her God, she didn't. She just nodded her head, as if she agreed with me. She didn't speak, and I knew she was waiting for me to continue. And I found I couldn't stop the words from tumbling out.

"If there's a God, how could he possibly allow zombies to exist? How could he allow such an illness to sweep the world and torture the survivors? Some of which, wear his uniform, like you and Father Allen. Not to mention the number of religious people that have died as well. How is that some sort of grand plan he has? He left two little girls orphaned with a person who has no idea how to keep them alive. And now we have no idea of where to go. How can you still believe after all of that?"

Sister Ann didn't say a word until she was sure I was finished. She then looked into the dark bus, studying something I couldn't see. I was beginning to wonder if the nun was a little confused in the head and believed she was speaking to God at that very moment. She turned back to me; her face open and thoughtful, the raging I had against her boss not phasing her in the least.

"I can understand where you're coming from, Vicki. But do you know what I see when I see those two girls?"

I said nothing, just shrugged my shoulders and waited.

"God put them in your hands, because he knew that even if you weren't exactly equipped for the job, your heart was. He has confidence in your ability to care for the survival of those sweet babies. And they represent survival for me. Because when we are finally on the other side of this, it's the babies that will save humanity," she said.

I didn't respond, because I definitely didn't agree and was sure arguing with a nun was a sin. If God had some plan for the girls to survive, he would have brought some sort of survivalist into their lives. Not someone who would have them stranded on a water tower, without food and water, to where they almost starved to death. But as I thought that, I realized exactly how we were saved. And it was by a nun and a priest. The idea made the hair on my arms stand up, but I still didn't tell Sister Ann what was in my mind.

"Now, your shift is over. It's my turn. How about you try to get a few more hours of sleep? The sun should be up soon and then we make plans for survival," Sister Ann said as she stood from her position on the floor.

I moved to stand and when I was right in front of her, the nun put her hands on my shoulders.

"They need you, Vicki. Not some other stranger. You. Don't forget that."

Feeling slightly creeped out, as if the nun could read my mind, I moved away from the front of the bus and carefully found my seat turned bed. I checked on the girls, confirming they were both fast asleep, which made me wish I was their age and could sleep anywhere. I wasn't sure how I would fall asleep again, so I quietly fished the flask out of the bottom of my pack. After the heavy thoughts from the conversation with the nun, I needed something to put me to sleep.

The first burning gulp felt like coming home and alarm bells rang in the back of my mind. It was dangerous how good it tasted. The second gulp felt more normal and warmed my body from the inside. Using all of my strength, I closed the flask and pushed it back into my pack. I hoped the two shots would help my racing mind slow just enough that I could block out all of my intrusive thoughts.

Laying my head on the pillow I had created out of plastic bags and a blanket over it, I was careful to get comfortable without making too much noise. Eventually, I had my face hanging partially over the side of the seat, so I could easily see the girls. For some reason I felt calmed by their presence, their safety, their sweet deep breathing sounds. As I fell asleep, I chastised myself for getting too attached to them. They weren't my kids, and there was no way of knowing how long any of us would survive.

A thin string of slobber landing on my forehead announced that morning had come. In my dream, it was a zombie about to bite my face, and it was blood and gore dripping onto my face. But when I was startled awake, I realized it was only Tina, who was standing by my head. She looked down at me with a toothy grin.

"Vick! Morning!" She cried.

The bus was still fairly quiet, so I sat up quickly and picked up the baby, shushing her before she woke up the entire group. When I looked forward, I saw Sister Ann was still sitting in the driver's seat on watch. The light of dawn was illuminating the inside of the bus and she turned when she heard us moving around. She waved her fingers at us, though I knew it was really for Tina who was heavy with a wet diaper.

In the back, I set up the diaper changing supplies I needed, before laying a wriggling Tina on a seat. She tried to roll off, but I grabbed her leg, flipping her onto her back. She let out a giggle, as if we were playing a game. I hadn't gotten enough sleep, ever in my life, to be entertained by a baby trying to escape a diaper change. I shoved a box of cheese crackers into her hands, so she had something to play with, while I did my best to change her diaper.

Gabby met us, rubbing her eyes sleepily. She leaned against my hip, watching my process.

"It's backwards," she mumbled.

"Huh?" I tilted my head to look at the diaper.

There was a design on the front when I folded it up that looked right. And it seemed to fit. But Gabby reached over and showed me how the little tabs to close the diaper would go from front to back instead of back to front, making it very hard to fasten. I also could tell the diaper would be low in the back and I didn't want to deal with that mistake later. I nodded to Gabby and lifted Tina's behind with her ankles, flipping the diaper around.

With the near disaster avoided, I yanked Tina's sweats back up her legs and noted that she wasn't nearly as chubby as she had been when her mother first dropped her off. I wondered if that was normal growing or she really wasn't getting enough food still. Back in the real world, I would have pulled out my cellphone and searched the web for the answers to all the questions I had. The only thing I could do was feed her whatever I had when she was hungry. Wasn't that the same as feeding a pet?

Snorting a quiet laugh, as I translated Tina and Gabby into clingy cats, I carried the baby back to our area. The adults on the bus were slowly moving around, and Father Allen took over the driver's seat from Sister Ann. Shortly after, the sound of the bus door opening had everyone migrating toward the front of the bus. Sister Ann took Tina off my hands with a smile and the little girl giggled as she threw her arms around the nun's neck.

Outside, I led Gabby to the back of the bus again, taking in our surroundings and finding a private place. This time, I had my feet and legs well out of her stream and she could relieve herself without trouble. I sent her back to the bus and did my business. When I boarded, the bus rumbled to life and Father Allen swung the door shut.

"Where are we going?" I balanced against the front seat so I could easily speak with the priest.

"I pray for God to show us the way," he replied with a smile.

"Doesn't God expect his flock to make their own decisions sometimes?" It took everything to hide the annoyance in my voice.

"Of course. He made his children very resilient. We just have a lot of road ahead and we could use a little guidance."

I stood quietly for a moment, realizing he wasn't completely wrong. No one on the bus had any ideas about other safe zones. No one had suggestions of places to try. Most of them had either lost their family in the beginning, or didn't have any to search for. We were a group of people wandering without an anchor to keep us in one place.

"Maybe moving is the best idea. Just keep going?" I suggested.

Father Allen smiled kindly over at me, before focusing on the road and pulling us away from the weigh station.

"If that's our path, then we must walk it. Or drive it, as it seems. But to continue moving, we will need to find more fuel." He tapped the gauge in front of him.

When I peered around his shoulder, I could see we were

just over half a tank. I knew that could keep us moving for a while, but we had to have plans to add more to it. We also had the need for many additional supplies. Proper food, fruits and vegetables, even canned, were going to be necessary for the health of everyone. And clean clothes. The girls and I were on our last set and with them, there was no knowing how long they would last. Tina had blown out more than one diaper and, without the ability to wash anything, I threw her pants from a bus window.

"We're going to need to stop for gas and supplies. Probably going to need to risk a larger town," I said.

Father Allen said nothing, but he did nod, so I knew he had heard me. Assuming the conversation was over, I moved back into the depths of the bus and decided to sort through some supplies to find a suitable breakfast. I grabbed two juice pouches, noting there were only two left, the box of crackers I had let Tina play with and a package of jerky. Tina probably wouldn't be able to completely chew the jerky, but I figured if I ripped it small enough, she wouldn't choke on what went down.

I found the girls with Sister Ann. Gabby was coloring on the bus seat and Tina was standing on the nun's knees, trying to play with the woman sitting ahead of her. The woman wanted nothing to do with the baby. I had noticed she had really kept to herself on the bus, but especially with the kids, she completely hid from them. It made me wonder about her behavior, but really, I had enough to handle and didn't need to be the woman's support animal.

Scooping up Tina, I motioned for Gabby to follow and we sat together across from the nun. I held the juice pouch as Tina drank, because she tended to squeeze them and shoot juice everywhere. I batted away her hands as they tried to grab on. Luckily, she knew how to use a straw and she sucked away happily. Gabby's nose turned up at the jerky, but when she saw my "I'm not doing this today" face, she popped a small piece in her mouth and chewed.

When both girls were fed, the adults started handing around whatever food we had for breakfast. The gas station store provided little beyond road trip snacks. But it was better than a completely empty stomach. There wasn't much to do except sit and wait. The girls played with the books and little toys we had brought. I studied the map, where Father Allen had marked our location. There was a town coming up, if we were right about where we fell on the map. I pointed it out to Father Allen, and he nodded his agreement.

Soon, the buildings of civilization rose in the distance, and everyone held their collective breath. At times, I wondered if the zombies had hit everywhere, or if it was only the large metropolitan areas. But as we entered the town, burned out skeletons of cars greeted us. There was smoke in the distance, billowing from a neighborhood area. Father Allen carefully drove around obstacles in the road, some of which were bodies decaying in the midmorning sun. I kept my eyes straight, not wanting to study every dead body; to tell the story of how they died and fell onto what would be their grave.

A mid-sized store came into view, and when Father Allen looked at me, I nodded. That was what we needed, though I wasn't looking to guide anyone. I just knew what I needed to find for the girls and I. If I could do that with more people to watch my back, the better chance for me to not die. There were a few zombies in the parking lot and they immediately turned as the large bus caught their attention. The metal pipe I had found at the gas station was sitting on the dash of the bus, because it was covered in drying gore and I didn't want it near the girls. I grabbed it now, prepared to handle the few zombies I could see.

Sister Ann came to the front of the bus as the priest parked. She brought my bag and had Tina on her hip.

"You need to be careful. Remember, you have more than yourself to live for now," she said quietly.

I looked back, and I could see Gabby's fearful but determined expression over a seat. She then turned and took up her position at the window to watch me. Two of the other women on the bus stepped forward to go with me. When the same guy from the gas station stepped up, I pinned him with a hard stare.

"We aren't going to have the same issues here, are we? Because if so, stay on this bus," I said, my voice low and threatening.

The man swallowed hard, and his face went white.

"We're good. I want to help." His voice shook, and I knew I would have to watch him closely still.

We grouped at the closed bus door, watching for the zombies that were headed toward us. I could hear Father Allen blessing the people behind me and I was sure it was meant for me too, but I didn't believe in his invisible protections. With my backpack on and pipe in hand, I nodded to the priest to open the door.

I took a deep breath before rushing out, not wanting to be a slow meal for the zombies. One shuffled toward me, wearing a Metallica logo t-shirt and a knife handle protruding from its chest. I didn't hesitate. As it raised its hands toward me, I brought my pipe up and swung with all my strength into the side of the head. The zombie collapsed, its skull completely caved in. I stepped forward and studied the knife handle before reaching down and yanking it out. A long serrated blade was exposed, and I whistled low at my new fun weapon.

Behind me, one woman squealed, and I turned as the other swung a bat at the second zombie in the parking lot. She hit it in the shoulder first, sending it stumbling to the side, before swinging overhand and coming down on the top of the skull. When it didn't fall immediately, she actually growled and lifted the bat again, slamming it down with all her might. The zombie crumpled into a truly dead mass and the woman's shoulders heaved as she stared at it.

"Nice," I whispered.

The woman turned and looked at me, her eyes bright with the adrenaline that was pumping through her. The second woman didn't seem to have a weapon, and I wasn't sure what to say about that. While the man was standing off to the side with his knife in his hand, that he was unlikely to use. I noted he hadn't stepped up to help with the other zombies, and my eyes narrowed. I marked him as a liability in my book and there wasn't much he could do to show he could be helpful.

I led the way to the store doors, which stood open, broken off of whatever track they had been on before. The store held several stenches. Some were from the zombies and other smelled like rotting food that had probably been in refrigerators that were no longer running. The darkness inside the building made me nervous, but I steeled myself, thinking about the supplies we desperately needed.

Yanking a flashlight from my bag, I clicked it on and illuminated the first area, where shopping carts still stood to one side. Dried blood smeared along the ground told an all too familiar story. Slowly, we filed in, the women and man following me and my light. As we entered the actual store, grimy skylights filtered a dull light in places, making the large warehouse not completely black.

I moved toward the register area first, needing bags or boxes to gather whatever supplies we could find. My feet crunched over broken glass and someone behind me kicked a can that spun and hit the wall. The noise reverberated through the store and I froze, waiting to see if there would be any response. When everything seemed to stay still, I continued moving until I found a register that still had a small stack of plastic grocery bags.

Separating them into four piles, I handed them out to the others in my group.

"We shouldn't split up, but it would be faster if we did," I whispered.

All three of their faces looked scared, though the woman with the bat had a bit more determination in her gaze. I didn't want to be stuck with any of them, and I really didn't want to feel responsible for someone else.

"How about you three stick together? I have the flashlight and I can handle an area on my own."

When none of them argued, I knew it was my best bet. And I hoped that with three sets of eyes, someone would make sure they didn't all die. We split into two directions and I made my way down aisles, pointing my light up to read the signs above each. When I found the baby aisle, I almost cheered out loud. The diaper displays were destroyed, but I took my time finding two packages that would fit Tina.

I grabbed whatever jars of baby food that was left. I had tried a fruit one when it was the last food we had. And honestly, it didn't taste half bad. And it was easy calories for Tina. I also threw in baby shampoo, lotion, powder and the last tube of diaper cream I found. I had two full bags now, heavy in my hands, and I had only grabbed baby stuff so far. Shaking my head, I made my way back to the store entrance, keeping my eyes peeled for any threat.

Outside, the sun was a sudden brightness that made me squint, but I could easily see there were no more zombies in the parking lot. When I approached the bus, the door swung open immediately. I handed the bags over to the man at the door.

"Most of it is baby stuff, if you can put it by my area," I said, feeling awkward, but determined to make sure Tina had what she needed.

The man said nothing, just nodded and disappeared. Father Allen still sat in the driver's seat, controlling the door.

"The store has been trashed, and it smells like a dump on fire, but I think if we take our time, we'll find plenty to keep us going," I said.

"Be careful. Where are the others?" Father Allen asked.

"I let them go as a group to check another part of the store. I was thinking —" An ear-piercing scream echoing out of the store cut me off.

My thinking hadn't gotten very far.

CHAPTER 4

WITHOUT THINKING, I turned and sprinted from the bus. I
heard the door swoosh shut behind me, and I was grateful the
priest did what was necessary to protect those on the bus. If I
had to worry about the girls, I wouldn't be able to focus on what
was right in front of me. The vehicle wasn't impenetrable, but it
was large and could move if anything too big came its way.

As I entered the store again, a figure came running at me
and I raised my metal pipe. My mind barely registered the
fearful face of the man, as I pivoted to make sure we didn't
collide and I didn't brain him. He didn't even stop when he saw
me, just continued running for the bus. I instantly realized the
women weren't with him and I didn't wait to ask him questions.

Inside the store, I turned the way I had originally seen the
group go. Using my flashlight, I shined a clear view up each aisle
until I got to the very end. There I found more than just the two
women I was expecting to find and my brain couldn't seem to
connect the dots of what was happening. A scream tore from
the mouth of the woman that held the bat. She was holding it
out in both hands, shoving a zombie back. A quick count told
me there were five of them.

I didn't immediately notice the second woman, but when I looked down, I could feel the bile trying to rise my throat. Two zombies had fallen onto her body, their hands digging into her stomach, pulling out her insides and shoving the flesh into their mouths. Her sightless eyes were pointed my way, her face frozen in a mask of desperate pain and death. Fury rose in me and red seemed to tinge my vision.

Stepping forward, I swung my pipe down on the first zombie that was eating the young woman on the ground. Its head caved in with a satisfying crunch and it fell over the dead body, knocking the other zombie back. The dead couldn't handle confusion. They just continued to move, to grab and eat. I didn't give the zombie on the ground the chance to touch the woman's body again. Using the end of the pipe, I slammed into its face over and over, until gray matter flew.

Suddenly, a person appeared at my side, a baseball cap on their head, turned backward and their face hidden by a bandana. I startled, almost whirling to hit them, but stopped just as they slammed a knife into a zombie that had turned toward me. Running to the woman with the bat, I grabbed the shirt of one zombie. It was an employee of the store who had won the employee of the month at some point, the large logo on the back of the ruined shirt boasted. With all my strength, I flung the zombie away from the woman and myself, making it land with a thud against a nearby display.

Stalking to it, I lifted my pipe before getting to it and swung like a baseball player determined to hit a home run. The neck of the zombie snapped, and the head fell to the side at an unnatural angle before the whole body collided with the ground. When I turned back, the mystery person had already stabbed another zombie. The woman with the bat was wailing on the third with her bat, her screams of fear having changed to frustration and vengeance. I stood back and looked around, ensuring there were no more monsters coming and let the woman have her revenge.

When the noise stopped, I heard the bat clatter to the linoleum. I turned and found the woman staring at her arm and her body began to hitch in sobs. I picked up my flashlight from where I had dropped it and shining the beam on her arm. There, against pale white skin, was a perfect bite missing from her arm. Blood oozed and flowed down her arm and puddled on the ground. Curses flew from my mouth. I rushed to her, throwing down my pack to remove my shirt, but the mystery person ripped the bandana from their face and tightly wrapped it around the bite.

I looked at the person and realized it was a man, probably a few years older than me and surprisingly handsome, even covered in zombie gore. His bright blue eyes flashed to me and I just stared, not really sure what to say. He had dark hair on the longer side and the beginnings of a beard, looking rough after a few months of the apocalypse.

"Did you get bit?" He asked.

I shook my head. I hadn't even given the zombies the chance to notice me before I started my attack. Shaking myself out of my confused stupor, my eyes narrowed. Before I could think, he turned back to Krista and shoved his knife blade into her head, preventing her from turning and attacking the people that knew her.

"Who are you?"

"Just happened by and heard the screams. You with the bus out there?"

It wasn't lost on me, he hadn't exactly answered my question.

"Thank you," the bitten woman mumbled.

The man turned to look at her, sympathy on his face.

"Of course. I'm sorry I couldn't do more."

"How did this happen?" I asked the woman, realizing it all seemed to have happened in a split second.

"We were searching over here and that guy with us, Trevor or whatever, opened that door over there." She pointed toward an employee only door that was now shut. "Before we knew it, these zombies came streaming out. But instead of helping us, he ran and in the surprise, they got Krista. I tried to stop them, but then they were on me, and I couldn't do much but push them back. Her screaming, god it was horrible before she died."

I knew they were bad, because it was what I had heard before I ran back into the store. I let the story settle in my head, and something beyond disgust and anger flooded my veins. It was clear the woman could see, because her face drained of any remaining blood it had. The new guy stepped up to take her arm, when it seemed like she might collapse. Turning back toward the grocery store door, I stalked through the aisles, with my metal pipe at the ready.

When we broke back into the sunlight, Father Allen and the other man from the bus were off the vehicle, trying to console the weasel, weakling Trevor. He was blubbering about almost dying, but I moved right into his space, dropping my pipe to grab him by his collar. My approach shocked him so much, it wasn't hard to slam him into the side of the bus. I pressed a forearm against his throat, holding him against the yellow panel while staring at him.

"Vicki!" Father Allen's voice seemed miles away. The roaring in my ears was drowning out all the protests.

"You left them," I growled.

A squeaky noise came from his mouth and his face was getting redder by the moment. A hand suddenly fell on my shoulder, not to stop me, but to get my attention.

"He can't answer you if he can't breathe." The voice of the stranger was close to my ear.

I moved my forearm, just a millimeter, allowing Trevor to gasp in oxygen. And as soon as he did, he began bawling again. I was a moment away from crushing his windpipe to give him something to cry about, but the stranger's hand on my shoulder tightened just a fraction. He then leaned so close to my ear, I could feel his breath move through my hair.

"A little girl is watching you through a window, and I'm not sure you want her seeing you murder someone," he murmured.

His words seemed to shock something inside me and I took a measured step back, allowing Trevor to collapse into a ball on the ground. Everything in me wanted to kick him and keep kicking him until I could get the vision of Krista's body out of my mind. However, I knew nothing would wipe the scene from my memory and it would likely haunt my nightmares for a long time.

I shrugged off the hand of the strange man that had appeared out of thin air. Turning, I faced the shocked faces of the people from the bus, as well as the sick face of Connie, as she leaned heavily on Father Allen. I pointed furiously at Trevor on the ground and spoke quietly.

"He opened a door, letting zombies into the store. Then ran like a coward, leaving Connie and Krista alone. Krista is dead! Because of this piece of trash. Now, Connie has been bitten...," my voice trailed off as the meaning of that settled with all of us.

Father Allen embraced Connie, holding her tightly to his side. She was pale and visibly sweating as she tried to stay standing. Blood had begun to drip from her arm, the splattering sound loud to my ears. Sister Ann came out of the bus holding a first aid kit. She set to unwrapping the bandana and applying a clean bandage to the bite on Connie's arm. They slowly moved her next to the bus and sat her on the asphalt, where Sister Ann continued her ministrations.

I turned toward the stranger again. The man stood back from the group, studying each of us.

"Who are you?" I asked again, hoping he'd give an answer this time.

His eyes shifted from me to Father Allen and then to Sister Ann. Something settled heavy in my stomach and I tightened my grip on my pipe. He didn't pull out a gun to shoot the zombies, only used a knife. So, if he threatened anyone in my group, I knew I would have a fighting chance.

"What church are you with?" His question caught me off guard and it seemed to surprise Father Allen too, as his eyebrows rose.

"I doubt anywhere you would know, son. Originally, we were from Oklahoma, an Eastern Orthodox Church there. We've been traveling by bus since shortly after supplies ran out."

The tension in the stranger's shoulders seemed to loosen, and he finally sheathed his knife.

"My name is Theo. I'm sorry, I've just had some trouble with a group that would believe they are a religion." His hand drifted to his forearm, which was wrapped in a bandage.

"What's that?" I asked, pointing at his arm.

He dropped his hands, as if he hadn't meant to give away so much, and just shook his head.

"It's not a bite."

I looked over at Connie, who was already looking gray with illness. Theo was tan and healthy, even if he was probably a little skinny from the lack of supplies. I didn't need him to unwrap his arm to prove that he hadn't been bitten. He'd be showing illness signs he couldn't hide. I looked around, realizing I did not know where he had come from or if he had people.

"Are you alone?"

Theo nodded. "I've been running on my own...since my run-in."

When he didn't elaborate further, I stepped to whisper to Father Allen. I asked if he wanted to bury Krista's remains, though we would need to wrap her in something so everyone didn't see how badly the zombies had shredded her body. He nodded with a solemn look on his face and then inclined his head toward Connie. I knew he was saying we would need to dig two graves.

"I'm going back in there. We need supplies. He's not going with me," I said, pointing at Trevor, whose sniveling had turned into hiccuping that made me think of Gabby.

The reminder of the girl made me look up, and I saw her white face pressed against the window. Behind her, the third woman on the bus sat with Tina, who was enthralled with a book in front of her face. I waved at Gabby, who immediately waved back frantically.

"I'm ok," I called out, loud enough for her to hear me through the glass.

She nodded and pressed her lips together, keeping herself together. The other man who drove the bus moved to my side and volunteered to help gather supplies. I knew it was impossible to have two men as bad as Trevor in one small group, so I nodded. Then Theo stepped forward and waved his hand in a small wave.

"I could help. It seems you are a smaller group and might have space on the bus for one more? I could help with supplies here and down the road as needed. Also, I know how to hunt, if we can find a bow or a gun with ammo, so fresh meat. The bus is like the box trucks I used to drive, so I could help with driving, too."

"You sure seem to be trying hard to convince us, Theo. What are you running from?" I asked.

During my time in the bar, I watched more than one person try to drink away their worries with alcohol. Sometimes those drunks were talkative, and it was always as if they were trying to convince anyone listening that they weren't bad, that they weren't hiding, and that they could stop drinking at any time. Hell, I even told myself that all the time, but I was determined to get back inside the grocery store to find more liquor.

Theo was shifting from foot to foot, and his eyes moved around the parking lot as if he was just waiting for something. He didn't seem like someone that felt safe and I wasn't sure if that would put the girls in danger. I looked over to Father Allen, who I figured had to decide. It was his bus. And I had no doubts that he wouldn't turn away a person in need.

"Son, you are welcome to join our band of travelers. I only ask that once we are on the road, you give us a clear picture of what has happened to you," Father Allen said.

I rolled my eyes, thinking he could hijack us before his story was finished. But I didn't speak up. I wasn't a leader and would not try to act like one. Gathering the empty bags from the bus, I turned and headed toward the store. I didn't wait for Theo to follow, though I heard his footfalls behind me.

Though I was pretty sure the grocery store was clear now, I was still cautious as we entered, afraid all the noise we made had brought something else out of hiding. Nothing moved, but I didn't breathe normally as I went away from the aisle that had Krista's dead body. I was careful to not trip on any of the products that were spilled across the floor, but I checked to see if anything was still useable.

One of my bags filled up with crackers, canned tuna, chip bags, and dried fruits. We turned into an aisle that used to have canned vegetables and beans. The shelves were practically empty, but I felt desperate. Using my flashlight, I shined along each shelf, finding two cans of kidney beans, three cans of green beans that were all different cuts and one can of corn. Theo took the cans and didn't say a word. Further down the aisle, I was ecstatic to find two packs of fruit cocktail cups. I knew the girls would love them and it would get them some vitamins.

When we finished with the aisle, I stood, feeling lost at the end. Theo stepped up next to me and motioned for me to follow him deeper into the store. I hesitated for a moment, wondering if this was the moment he tried to murder me. I studied his back as he disappeared into darkness and debated going back to the bus and driving away. Then I remembered he had the fruit cocktail cups, and I wasn't leaving without them. They were worth risking my life.

I followed him, but as I was looking at aisle names, I saw beer and wine. It wasn't my normal drink, but I headed there first. It did not surprise me to find it completely wiped. People that drank didn't screw around when it came to stocking up on their booze. One unbroken bottle of pink-colored wine lay in the middle of a sea of broken glass. There was no hesitation in my steps as I trudged across the glass and picked up the bottle. I had no idea what kind of wine it was, but it had an alcohol percentage on the label and a twist-off cap for convenience.

Slipping the bottle into my pack, I knew it was wrong to hide supplies. But I needed this wine to handle each day that I had to face. I promised myself not to get loopy when I needed to be there for the girls. The rest of the time was fair game. When I made it to the end of the aisle, I was swinging my bag back on and Theo had come back to find me. He looked at me questioningly for a moment, but he still didn't speak, just jerked his head to the side for me to follow.

When he found what he was looking for, he stopped and picked up a big white pail. He held it up for my flashlight and I realized it was freeze-dried meals, made for backpacking. I read the label, and it listed Mac and cheese, beef chili and spaghetti with red sauce as the main meals. I nodded enthusiastically.

"That's great. We should grab as many of these sets as they have," I said, pitching my voice low to not draw unwanted attention.

Theo nodded and pointed. There were three additional pails, and I suddenly felt rich. I had a bottle of wine in my pack and we had enough meals for at least a few days for everyone on the bus. I wondered why the pails were left on the shelf. As if reading my mind, Theo finally spoke.

"People usually go for all the regular stuff, canned foods, rice, pasta. They forget about outdoor gear. This is always where the outdoor meals are."

Weighed down with two pails and the bags we had filled, we quickly made our way back to the bus. The group of people was still milling around outside, with Connie sitting on the ground, looking gray and unmoving. Trevor sat off to the side, and I was glad no one was trying to console him for his idiotic behavior. They saw Theo and me coming out, and eyes widened when they saw everything we carried.

Sister Ann met me, and I held up one of my pails. Her face lit with a bright smile.

"He always provides," she said.

"Well, Theo and I did, but sure," I replied.

Sister Ann didn't take offense, just patted me on the shoulder as I moved toward the bus door. We left the items at the top of the steps so someone could store them in the back of the bus with the rest of the supplies. I emptied the plastic bags we had filled and turned to Theo.

"You good with another run inside?"

"I got your back," he said with a nod.

Squinting at him, I found myself confused. He didn't know

me or anyone in my group. And he was almost tripping over himself to be helpful and agreeable. In my world, no one was this nice. I had to make an exception for Sister Ann and Father Allen, but their excuse was religion, not just natural kindness. I was sure Theo was hiding something, and that something was probably dark and psychotic. For now, I would let him help me carry stuff, so we could get back on the road.

We made two more trips from the store, before more zombies took notice of us. I made sure to retrieve clean clothes for myself and the girls. I also grabbed extra shirts, shorts, leggings and undergarments that the other survivors could use. No one had given me specifics, so I did a lot of guesswork. I also loaded another two plastic bags with baby supplies I found, because I just felt that would be the hardest stuff to find. Then also found additional cans of powdered milk, which was also a huge score for the girls.

The last thing was cases of bottled water. The grocery store had a huge water display in the front that was clearly before the pandemic. Though it was crushed and empty in places, there were five cases we could salvage. All five went onto the bus last. By that point, my energy was lagging, and I was starving. I could feel myself getting cranky and I was just done taking care of everyone for a bit.

Theo moved away from the group to dispatch the three zombies that had wandered into the lot randomly. I couldn't even muster the energy to follow and help, but the man didn't seem to need any help. It was clear he had been on his own, surviving, with little support. He killed the zombies as if he had been born to do it and got very little blood on himself. I found myself feeling jealous of the way he could move.

The sound of Father Allen praying made me turn and look at Connie. It was clear she had passed, as the priest slowly lowered her body to the ground. He did a crossing motion over her and then he produced a knife that I had no idea he had, and slid it smoothly into the side of Connie's head. I closed my eyes, letting my head fall back. The day was more than halfway over and I was exhausted.

"I saw sheet sets inside. Maybe we can wrap the bodies in those?" Theo asked.

I opened my eyes and looked to where Trevor was still sitting. I badly wanted to walk up to him and just kick him as hard as I could and keep kicking him until we had three bodies to bury. When a better idea came to my mind, I walked slowly to him.

"Get up." My words were more of a demand than a request, causing his eyes to snap up to me.

"Wha...what?"

"I said get up, you sack of useless meat. If we're going to bury these women, you're helping. Because this is your fault."

Trevor stared up at me with his pale face, shock in his expression.

"I...I can't. I don't want to go back in there," he said, pointing a shaking finger at the store.

"Why is that, Trevor? Because you let a woman get ripped to pieces inside. And then let another be bit and die out here? Is that why, Trevor?" As I spoke, I crouched in front of him, bringing my face close to his.

"You will either help with the deaths you caused, or I will make sure you never step foot on this bus again. I will make sure you are left here to live out your few remaining days. Alone. And I will not wish for your death to be quick."

The entire group had gone silent as I spoke, my words dripping with violence. I didn't even care that Father Allen and Sister Ann could hear me. If Trevor didn't get to his feet, I would absolutely follow through with my threat, even if I had to throw him from the bus while it moved and hope he broke his neck. Trevor's eyes went to the people standing behind me, and I knew immediately he wasn't getting the reaction he had hoped. The begging in his eyes shuttered, and he stared at me with stark fear.

I wasn't moved.

CHAPTER 5

AS WE ENTERED the store again, the oppressive feeling of the darkness and silence weighed on me. Theo gestured for us to follow him. Though he didn't know any of us, he agreed to come into the store with Trevor and me. I could admit, I was partially glad he offered, because I didn't trust myself alone with Trevor. If we ran into zombies, I would likely throw him at them and run.

In the home goods section, we found dark colored sheet sets. I also grabbed several duvets and fleece blankets. I wanted to stock up on anything we could use to make living on the bus more comfortable. Outside, I loaded the blankets for the bus onto the steps of the vehicle. After I pulled the sheet from the plastic, I clutched the dark fabric in my hands. Theo and I laid it down next to Connie before moving to her body.

"No, Trevor, you get her shoulders. You aren't just going to stand by and watch," I said.

Theo looked from me to Trevor and back, as if he was going to argue. Whatever was on my face clearly told him it wasn't for him to speak up. Trevor was visibly shaking as he moved to position.

"If you drop her, I will punch you in the face," I growled.

Burying two practical strangers that shouldn't have died wasn't how I wanted to spend my day. But here we were. And it was Trevor's fault. I could see Sister Ann's concerned face out of the corner of my eye, but I would not acknowledge it. She clearly could see how close to the edge I was teetering, and I didn't need the push.

Trevor hooked his hands under Connie's arms, and I grabbed her legs above her ankles. Moving together, we carefully laid her in the middle of the sheet. Trevor handled her with care, so I didn't get to throw the punch I was holding in. Sister Ann stepped up and put a small cross on Connie's chest and we wrapped the sheet around her body, tucking it under.

Ripping open the second sheet, I stood, looking at the store. Theo moved to stand next to me, his presence feeling too heavy.

"What?" I asked, when I couldn't bear it any longer.

"You sure you want to do this? She was pretty messed up," he said.

I desperately didn't want to go anywhere near her body. There were a lot of things I could handle, but a body that had been torn apart like that, wasn't something I wanted to face. It was something that happened in this world, and there was no denying it.

"It doesn't feel right to leave her in there, just decomposing," I replied.

"Did you know her well?"

I couldn't contain my snort laugh at that.

"I don't really know any of these people well. Even the kids that are my responsibility, I barely know them."

I could feel Theo's eyes on me, but I didn't turn. The questions I was sure he had, were ones I didn't feel like dwelling on.

"Ok, then." Was all he said.

"Let's go, Trevor. That was the easy part," I called over my shoulder.

Trevor's shoulders slumped, but he didn't beg or plead his case. No one seemed to be stopping me either, which was surprising. I wondered if Eastern Orthodox churches believed in corporal punishment. Or if the priest and nun wanted Trevor to serve his penance for what he had done by opening a door and abandoning the women to the dead.

As we got close to the place Krista's body was left, I averted my eyes, looking at shelves and the ceiling. I waited as long as I could before I looked down at the woman's destroyed body. Her facial expression hadn't changed, forever frozen in fear and pain. Her limbs splayed to the sides, as if she was going to make a blood angel among the entrails and ripped flesh.

A gagging noise caught my attention, and I whirled to where Trevor was covering his mouth. Torn, bloody bodies were hard enough to stomach. I couldn't handle vomit. Which I knew seemed weak for a bartender in a dive bar. But it was well known, with patrons, co-workers and the bar owner, that I didn't do puke. I had almost beat a man with the bat we had behind the bar when he talked about wanting to puke, but he refused to go to the bathroom. My threats and the swing that nearly missed his head made him think twice, and he rushed toward the back of the bar, where the hallway with the bathrooms was. No regulars dared puke in the bar when I was there from then on.

"If you even think about puking right now, you better go back outside. Evacuate your stomach and get back in here. You will help. It doesn't matter how long we have to wait. Krista isn't going anywhere," I snapped.

I didn't miss the smirk on Theo's face. The man had been around for less than four hours and already he felt like a conundrum to me. Trevor stared at the both of us, my flashlight pointed at his chest, waiting for his decision. He visibly swallowed and nodded that he was ready. Theo produced a handful of latex gloves, and I gratefully accepted a pair. I hadn't thought about the gruesome mess we would put our hands on.

It was no small task to lift Krista's remains onto the sheet. Trevor continued to gag audibly, and I had to keep my stomach controlled as well. When we laid her on the sheet, I reached over and closed her eyelids. I couldn't handle seeing her desperate fear any longer. Something inside me didn't want her buried with that look on her face. Together, the three of us wrapped her body tightly, the material almost immediately soaking through with the blood that remained on her body.

When we got to the entrance of the store, Father Allen met us.

"We found a grassy area in the back of the store. Even if they are just shallow graves, it would be as good of place as any. We'll need shovels though," he said.

"There's a gardening section toward the back of the store. I saw the sign," Theo replied.

The priest nodded and turned on his own flashlight to head into the store. I felt awkward allowing him to go in alone, but he had survived this long somehow. I didn't need to protect everyone. That wasn't my job. Even if it felt like people were looking to me to help, to provide. They didn't know me well enough to know they shouldn't hedge their bets on me.

We changed direction and headed toward the back of the store. It was easy to find the spot Father Allen was speaking of. It was a small pretty meadow full of bright green overgrown grass. Carefully, we laid Krista's wrapped body off to the side. We then retrieved Connie's body and also moved it. By the time we came back to the bus, Father Allen had leaned three shovels against the bus. Theo immediately grabbed one, as did the other man from the bus. Trevor collapsed on the ground, leaning against the bus. Clearly not any additional help. Father Allen took the last shovel, smiling at me.

"You've done enough, Vicki. I think Gabby would benefit from seeing that you are well."

I opened my mouth to make a smart comment, but when I saw Theo studying me, I just nodded and trudged to the bus. When I climbed on, I heard Tina's high-pitched laugh as the woman holding her lifted her high above her head and brought her down quickly. Gabby was sitting quietly in the same seat I had left her in. She had a fruit cup in her hand and she was eating slowly.

"Hey, kid."

Her gaze flew up and locked onto my face. I had no idea how ragged I looked, but her eyes narrowed and she studied me from head to toe.

"I'm fine. Just tired. And dirty. You girls want to go outside and get some fresh air?" I was sure being constantly shut up on the bus wasn't good for either of them.

Gabby nodded and drank down the sugary liquid from the fruit cup as I nodded an approval. That was really the best part of a fruit cup. I reached over and plucked Tina from the woman's hands when she held her high, causing the baby to squeal in my ear. I grimaced, but put her on my hip and led the way for Gabby out of the bus.

Both girls squinted in the sun, but I had them stand right in the middle of it. They needed the sun, the warmth, the vitamin D. I did a quick check of the area and noted that there weren't any zombies coming our way, but I didn't want to be reckless. I picked up my pipe with my free hand and walked the girls in a big circle around the parking lot. Tina wiggled to get down, and I put her on her feet, holding her hand as we slowed the walk so she could get some exercise too. Gabby found a bush that was suitable to pee behind and we both relieved ourselves.

When we came back to the bus, Sister Ann had brought a blanket and some of the girls' toys out. She laid out the blanket, and we all sat, so they could play in the fresh air and waited for the graves to be dug. I wondered how long it would take to dig two shallow graves with three men working on them. As the sun dipped low, I wondered if the burial would happen before dark.

Sister Ann busied herself with going through some of the fresh supplies and picking things to make for dinner. Boiling water over the camp stove took a long time, but once it was done, she could pour it into the freeze-dried food pouches and everyone could eat a filling dinner. I helped Tina get more macaroni in her mouth than on the ground. Just as Sister Ann was about to make food for the three men digging, they appeared from the side of the store, looking sweat drenched and filthy.

As the men set down the tools, Sister Ann brought water and wet wipes for them to clean up somewhat. They then sat on the ground and inhaled the food that the nun had made for them. Even Theo, who ate without speaking or making eye contact with anyone.

"Is it done?" I asked.

Father Allen's weary eyes met mine, and he nodded. I didn't know what to say then. I didn't really know either of the women and didn't think they knew anyone else on the bus. It was just more loss of life, a meaningless loss that should have been avoided. The idea of the pain Krista went through made the anger come back, but I pushed it down into a box so I didn't freak out the girls.

A familiar groan broke the silence, and I shot to my feet. A small group of zombies were making their way toward us. All the adults stood, seeing the same thing. Gabby grabbed my leg, hiding partially behind me, while Tina babbled to herself and ate more crackers that she had dropped on the blanket. For a moment, I thought since she was eating them from the blanket and not the asphalt, that made it ok.

"We should pack up," Father Allen suggested.

No one argued. I picked up Tina and handed her to the woman climbing onto the bus. Gabby quickly followed, but turned to look back at me.

"Go on, I'll be on in a second. Just need to pack up supplies."

I popped open the storage area under the bus and fit the shovels in around the gas cans. There was no knowing where we were going or what we would face. I didn't want to leave anything behind. All the adults, except Trevor, of course, grabbed things to put back on the bus. I was the last to climb on, just as the zombies were reaching the vehicle. Father Allen was behind the wheel, the bus roared to life, and the door shut soundly behind me. A zombie banged into it a moment later, but I just stared at its decaying face as we pulled forward and it was spun away from the bus.

Everyone gathered near the front, with Theo in the middle. It was time for the mystery man to spill his story. I still wasn't sure if I would need to get him off the bus to protect my girls, but I wouldn't allow anything to hurt them. Theo was a wild card, a blank spot on the board. He had been helpful, which earned him some points in my book. But I still wanted to know what was going on with him.

When he realized all eyes were on him, he sighed and looked at his hands. I could see dirt was still caked under his nails and there were callouses on his palms. He unwrapped the bandage from his arm, making me think he was bit after all, and now he was going to admit it. But instead, I gasped when I saw the wound he had been hiding. A patch of skin was raised, pink and extremely angry. At first, I couldn't tell what I was seeing, but when he held it out in front of him, I realized it was a brand of a skull.

"I mentioned a religion I had a run in with. They call themselves The Children of Z. But they don't worship God or Allah, or Jesus. Nothing you would guess about a religion. Not even the devil. They're so much worse."

"There are agnostic religious groups that just believe in general that God is unknowable, so they are still spiritual, but in their own way," Father Allen called back.

Theo had begun to shake his head as soon as Father Allen spoke, but the priest couldn't see him from where he sat.

"It's nothing innocent like that. These people...they're evil," Theo said. His voice came out so quietly that Father Allen asked him to repeat his words.

"He says they're evil," I called out.

"That's not an exaggeration, and I'm not using the word to be dramatic. They did this to me, because you either join them, or they feed you to their deity." Theo thrust out his branded arm for everyone to see. Father Allen's eyes flashed to the big mirror above his head, and his frown deepened.

A moment later, the bus was being pulled off the road, behind a strip mall that looked clear. Father Allen locked the door and shut off the engine. He stood and came to Theo, lifting his arm so he could see the mark better.

"A skull? Who is their deity?"

"The zombies. They don't kill them. They live with them, tied up around their camp. And they see feeding people to them as the sacrifices needed, so they are blessed with eternal life," Theo said, his voice monotone and distant.

"Blasphemy," Sister Ann murmured and crossed herself.

"You could say that. I escaped two days ago and have been on the road trying to put distance between us since. The car I had ran out of gas this morning, before I found you all at the store. Seemed like fate to stumble upon a group," Theo said.

"How many people are in this group?" Father Allen asked.

Theo shrugged his shoulders. "I had no way of knowing. It was also a thin line between the believers and the ones that were just doing what they had to for survival. Not everyone was bad. But I guess they just aren't strong enough to escape on their own or fight back."

Everyone was quiet for a long time. Gabby's hand slipped into mine, and I realized I should have probably put her in the back of the bus so she didn't hear the conversation. There were still so many questions to ask, but it was dark outside and everyone was exhausted after the long, sad day. Sister Ann appeared with the first aid kit. I watched as she ripped open a small tube of burn cream and carefully applied it to Theo's brand. He grimaced, but didn't make a sound as she applied clean gauze and secured it with medical tape.

I could feel the weariness in my bones. Picking up Tina, I took both of the girls back to the seat we used for our sleeping area. Opening one of the new duvets, I fluffed it up on the floor and laid Tina in it with a sippy cup of rehydrated milk. Her eyes were fluttering before she even popped the milk into her mouth, but she drank with ease. I realized the feeling I always felt was relief. Every time I saw the girls eat or drink, a bit of relief settled in my chest.

Gabby crawled in next to her sister and curled around her. I covered them with a fleece blanket and Gabby smiled up at me.

"It all smells new, not dirty like everything else."

"I know, kid. I hope we can find somewhere to take a shower, eventually. Maybe even do laundry. Who would have thought I would actually want to do laundry?" Wrinkling my nose at her, she smiled again.

I sat with my legs tucked under me, watching the girls as

they fell into a deep sleep. I set Tina's cup aside, now completely empty of milk. The baby would sleep well with a full belly. Ahead of me, Sister Ann was handing Theo bedding and showing him to a seat that wasn't taken by anyone else. I was pretty sure it was where Connie was sleeping before, but Theo didn't need to know that. She was gone, and that meant someone took her place.

Once I knew the girls would not be waking up and asking for something, I quietly opened my pack and slid out the bottle of wine. My mind tried to tell me it was a bad thing that all I had done all day was think about when I could get to this bottle. But after the day we'd had, I would take anything that could take the edge off. I had no doubt that when I closed my eyes, I would see Krista's staring face, horrified as zombies consumed her.

I shivered as I thought about the woman and resolutely twisted the cap off of the wine. The sound of the metal breaking open felt loud on the quiet bus, but no one paid me any mind. Not even bothering to sniff the wine, I put it to my mouth and tilted back until I got a full swig. I swallowed quickly, the wine too sweet to savor or keep on my tongue for too long. It didn't warm me like straight alcohol did, and I would probably need to drink half the bottle to take the edge off.

An hour later and three-fourths of the wine gone, I started to feel warm and fuzzy. It took all the control in my body to screw the cap back on the bottle and slip it back into the bag. If anyone knew what I was doing, they didn't say a word to me. Which was the best decision they could make. I didn't have a good excuse for my drinking, but I would fight anyone that tried to take away my coping mechanism.

With another of the new fleece blankets, I curled up on my bus seat, checking the girls once more. I burrowed into the blanket, realizing Gabby was right. The blanket didn't smell stale or like a dirty body. It helped me forget that I probably had blood somewhere on my clothing. It helped me not think about the shower I could desperately use. It helped me fall into a dream-less sleep, at least for a little while.

The darkness of sleep wasn't guaranteed, though. I blinked against harsh light, but I knew it wasn't the sun. Instead, it was grocery store lights that were brighter than anything I had ever seen. I was in the middle of a spotlight, toppled shelves on either side of me. Ahead of me, a figure emerged from the darkness, entering the spotlight. It horrified me to see Krista's frozen face staring at me, the same horrific gaze and expression still there. But instead of her being dead on the ground, she was slowing moving toward me.

Her body had been so destroyed, I couldn't understand how she was standing. When my eyes took in the impossible, I felt vomit rising in my throat. I was pretty sure her intestines were trailing on the ground behind her, still attached to something in her stomach cavity. Each footprint she left was a perfect bloody print of the New Balance sneakers she wore. I couldn't rip my eyes away from the bright red blood on the perfectly white grocery store floor.

Something smoothed my face, and I could hear screams. But I realized the screams were mine and the hands on my face were small and warm, not Krista's trying to eat me. My eyes shot open and Gabby stood next to me, her hands patting my cheeks. Her hair was sleep messed, and it was still partially dark on the bus, dawn just barely appearing.

"What?" I croaked.

"You were screaming, Vicki," Gabby said, her voice tinged with a little fear.

Just as she said that, Tina let out a wail from the floor. Gabby moved, so I could get to the baby, hoping to hush her before we woke up anyone else. When I got Tina into my arms and sat up, Theo was suddenly at our side. He didn't look like he had slept a wink, but his eyes were bright and awake. I patted Tina's back as she pressed her little face into my neck. Her little body trembled, and I knew my screams had woken her and scared her.

"I'm...I'm sorry," I whispered to Tina, but also looked up to Theo to convey the same sentiment.

"It's ok. Makes sense you'd have nightmares after yesterday. Well, after a lot of what's happened in the last few months." His eyes were so blue, I had a hard time pulling my gaze away.

Other people rustled on the bus, and soon Sister Ann appeared. Her hand fell to my shoulder, patting me. She also produced a sippy cup for Tina, which always seemed like magic. The baby grabbed it and shoved it into her mouth as she sniffled and hiccuped. Gabby climbed up next to us and leaned against me. I put my arm out so she could cuddle in. I wouldn't admit it to anyone, but I needed their comfort as much as they needed mine.

Theo sat on a seat across from us, and I could feel his eyes. I let my head flop to the side so I could meet his gaze.

"What?" I snapped.

"Not a morning person, are you?"

"Oh, Vicki isn't a day person," Gabby replied.

"Whose side are you on?" I muttered to her.

"Quite the gray sprinkle on a rainbow cupcake, huh?"

My mouth dropped open, shocked at his insult. That somehow didn't feel like an insult, as he delivered the words with a crooked smile. Gabby's body shook against mine as she giggled and nodded. Theo leaned so he could see the little girl's face, and he crossed his eyes at her, causing her giggles to intensify. My head began to throb, the beginning signs of a hangover creeping up on me.

"It's too early to be ganged up on."

CHAPTER 6

THE NEXT DAY was slow and calm. We decided to stop driving far distances until we really had a set destination in mind. Everyone was still feeling the effects of the long day before and losing two in the group. We were a small group as it was. And though I didn't really know the women well, it was painful to be front row to their deaths.

We had driven into a smaller town, and Father Allen found a church that had a small playground behind it. A fence closed in the playground and there were no zombies to be seen. Gabby bounced up and down on the bus seat when she saw the play structure with two slides and a few swings.

Before everyone got off the bus, Theo and I checked the church for survivors or zombies. Father Allen had hoped that a group of survivors may have taken refuge in the lord's house. I didn't have any such illusions. The stained glass windows were broken in places. The pathways to both entrances were over grown, not showing any signs of living or dead walking through often.

At the back door, I tapped on the wood, waiting for a sign of something inside. When a body thumped into the doors, I sighed and stepped back. Theo and I shared a look, and we both shrugged. If the priest wanted into the building, we would have to deal with whatever was behind door number one. I took a moment to evaluate my body, making sure my breakfast was settled with the cup of coffee I could drink. I had no desire to puke up any of my beloved caffeine. The food and drink had helped ward off a full-blown hangover. I knew that pink wine wasn't my friend. That wouldn't stop me from finishing it the first chance I got.

Theo gestured for me to go to the door. He counted down on his fingers and when he held a fist, I just stared at him.

"That means open the door, Vicki," he said.

"Maybe just say that?"

Without warning, I flung open the door, stepping back to hide behind it until the zombies came out. First was a largish man, wearing a similar outfit to Father Allen. Except his was filthy, and he was missing one full sleeve. The zombie's eyes latched onto Theo and it stumbled down the few steps that brought him to level with him. Theo didn't hesitate. He had already pulled his knife, and he dodged one way, drawing the zombie with him, before quickly dodging back the other way and slamming the knife into its temple.

Just as I was going to step out, the door was pushed back into me, and I stumbled. Theo's eyes came up and widened, telling me there was more than just one coming out of the church. Turning, I did a quick hop and jumped over the railing of the entrance. I ran to stand next to Theo and took in the four additional shuffling bodies that were making their way to us. Their groans rose and echoed inside the empty church.

Without a plan or understanding between us, Theo and I broke apart, causing the zombies to choose a meal choice. The first that came for me was an elderly woman, wearing a bright pink mumu dress. She stumbled, because one of her sandals had slipped off her foot and was tied around her ankle. The shoes reminded me of one of the old drunks that used to come to my bar. The woman had been a grandmother and would show up with shirts that said something about grandma's garden with a bunch of names on it. She had the same utilitarian type of shoes.

The memory made me momentarily sad. The grandma from my bar had actually been a sweet woman. She definitely had a drinking problem. But she was never angry or cruel to anyone. And she always called me by little nicknames, that no one in my life had ever thought to use. The zombie was within striking distance, but I was so lost in my thoughts, I wasn't focused.

"Vicki!"

Theo's voice shook me from my distraction, just in time for me to push the zombie's outstretched hands to the side, spinning her like a top on her unstable feet. Pushing the kind grandma from my mind, I swung my metal pipe with enough force to dent the side of the zombie's head. It fell into a heap, tripping the second one coming, making my job that much easier. Swinging down on the moving head as it tried to snap at my legs, I heard the moment the skull cracked. The body went limp over the old woman zombie.

Turning to check on Theo, he was cleaning his blade on the shirt of one zombie he had ended. I walked over to him, feeling awkward.

"Thanks for that," I mumbled.

"Where did you go?"

I looked over my shoulder and could see the sandals that had thrown me into my memories.

"She reminded me of someone."

"Family?" Theo asked.

I stiffened. Talking about myself and my past wasn't something I was comfortable with, even with people that knew me well. I wasn't about to spill my foster kid sob story to a stranger.

Spinning on my heel, I went to the open door of the church and studied the inside. The broken windows allowed bright light to spill in. I couldn't tell how long the zombies had been inside, but it had been long enough for them to smear gore along every wall and door.

"I don't think Father Allen will find what he's looking for in here," I said when Theo joined me on the steps.

"Might as well let him look, since we cleared it out."

When Father Allen entered the church, I could see tears in his eyes. He and Sister Ann slowly walked down the middle aisle, crossing themselves and murmuring quietly. I knew that was my sign to find something else to do. I made my way back to the bus, where everyone was climbing down the stairs into the fresh air.

Gabby ran from the woman holding her hand and came to me. She stood in front of me, bouncing on the balls of her feet.

"Can we go play now? Can we? Come on Vicki! Please?"

"Slow down half pint. Yeah, as long as we're careful, you can play for a bit." I ruffled her hair affectionately before I even thought of it. Her eyes widened, and I stepped back. I was not getting attached to these kids.

Clearing my throat, I took Tina's hand and led both girls to the play structure. Luckily, the zombie bodies weren't visible from the fenced play area. As we went through the gate, Theo jogged to catch up with us. He secured the gate behind us and we both set our weapons within reach, but keeping our hands free.

"Race you to the top of the slide!" He yelled.

Gabby's laugh rang loud, and I winced, looking around for any zombies that might hear her. Theo got to the ladder first, but he pretended to trip and stumble, just to let Gabby ahead of him. I watched as he protected her from slipping and falling until they reached the top platform. Gabby looked down at me with Tina and waved wildly at me. I lifted my hand in a small wave, not quite as caught up in the craziness.

The baby pulled away from me and I looked at all the items, judging none of them safe for a baby. Tina fussed, and I swung her up in my arms to keep her from running. But she fought, trying to get back on the ground. I knew she wanted to be a part of the fun, but I didn't know how to do that without her breaking her skull.

Suddenly, Theo was at our side. He held out his hands, and Tina threw her body toward him, seeing him as her salvation.

"I don't think...," I said.

"It's ok. I'll put her on my lap. You'll see," Theo replied in the silence.

What did I think? What did I even know about taking care of a baby? I knew she needed fresh air. All living things needed that: food, water, sun. I rubbed my forehead, realizing I was listing off what I needed to keep a houseplant alive. I knew baby proofing was some sort of colossal task. And I couldn't baby proof the entire world.

Tina's giggle pulled my attention, and I found Theo and her at the top of the slide. My stomach flip-flopped as she wriggled and tried to escape Theo's grasp. But somehow, he smoothly sat down, with Tina on his thighs. They slid down together and landed on Theo's feet. Tina's face was flush with happiness as she giggled and begged for more. Theo let out a deep laugh, that caught me off guard, before heading back to the ladder.

I realized Gabby wasn't on the slide anymore and my gaze flew around, trying to find her. My heart thudded when I found her on the swings, trying to kick her feet up and back. She was barely moving, and I could tell she was concentrating hard with her tongue sticking out between her teeth.

"Vicki, can you push me? Just to get me started? I was

learning how to swing by myself...before...at school," she said, stumbling a little at her explanation.

Her mother had been teaching her. I had seen them on the small rusted swing set by our apartment before school. My heart ached for the little girl and all she had lost in such a short time. She and Tina had gotten such a limited time with a mother I was sure loved them. And now they were stuck with me.

I walked to stand behind her and grabbed the chains of the swing, pulling it back slightly. When I let her go, she kicked her feet out hard, leaning back, before she swung backward and she bent her feet under her. I stepped back to watch as she continued to pump her legs, getting herself higher than I had, all on her own.

"I'm doing it! I'm doing it, Momma!" Gabby cried.

Her words caused me to freeze and I could feel myself stop breathing. Gabby immediately stopped kicking her legs, and she slowly came to a stop. Theo and Tina had just come off the slide and were standing off to the side. I knew Tina didn't understand, as she tried to tug Theo back to the ladder, but his eyes were glued on Gabby and me. Panic flared, and I was at a complete loss for what to say. I stood there, next to the swings, my mouth opening and closing like a fish.

Theo came to crouch in front of Gabby. The little girl's head was down and her shoulder shook with what I was sure were tears. Theo grabbed the sides of the swing to keep her still.

"Hey, little one. Can you look at me?"

Gabby just shook her head, not making eye contact.

"You miss your momma, huh?"

Gabby nodded her head.

"I bet she loved you and Tina a lot. She even gave you to someone who would keep you safe when she couldn't be with you anymore." His tone was quiet and soothing. I knew I should have been taking notes.

"Vicki didn't really want us." Gabby's voice was so quiet I almost missed what she said.

Her words were like a crushing vice around my heart. I had never told her I didn't want them. But I guess there were times I let my annoyance and frustrations get the best of me. She wasn't a baby like Tina. She was old enough to read the room. Wanting them had never really factored into anything. Even when we got to the safe zone in Canada, I could have given them to a mother that had other children. However, I couldn't get over the fact that their mother had trusted me.

"I don't think that's true, little one," Theo said, hedging while he looked at me to say something.

I knew I had to say something, though I was sure whatever came out of my mouth wouldn't be nearly as good as what Theo was saying.

"Vicki isn't a mommy. She didn't have kids. I know it's hard to be a mommy." Gabby swiped a hand under her nose and finally looked up at Theo. He reached up and wiped the tears from her pink cheeks.

"No, I'm sure it's not easy. But ya know what? Just in the two days I've been with you, I've seen how Vicki takes care of you. Makes sure you're fed. Made sure to get you fresh blankets and clothes. Pushed you on the swings. Maybe she's trying?" He whispered the last words, as if they were sharing a secret.

Gabby snuck a look at me and I tried to smile, but felt like I was grimacing.

"Maybe. She got us blankets that didn't smell dirty. And she found us fruit cups."

"Right. And she sleeps right next to you, watching over you. I saw her last night," Theo said.

Gabby nodded and looked into Theo's eyes.

"It's ok to miss your Mommy, little one. Vicki knows that

too. You can talk to her all you want, in your head or out loud, if that makes you feel better."

"Really? Do you think she can hear me?" Gabby asked, hope threaded through her words.

"I think that if she can watch over you, she is. I wouldn't doubt it for a moment."

Suddenly, Gabby pitched herself forward and fell into Theo, wrapping her arms around his neck. He easily put his own around the little girl, hugging her tight. When she pulled back, she wasn't crying anymore. Tina had found her way over and was reaching up to hug her sister.

"Gabs, swing!" Tina said.

Theo swooped Tina up into his arms and sat on the swing next to Gabby's. He kicked off with his feet and pumped, while holding one arm around Tina in his lap. The baby giggled and tried to kick her feet as well. Gabby would not be left behind. She got back into her swing and tried to kick off, but her feet didn't quite reach. Unfreezing my feet from their place, I moved behind her and pulled her back like I had before.

"Thank you, Vicki," Gabby said, just before I let her go.

I wasn't sure what she was thanking me for, but it didn't matter. Taking care of her wasn't a favor or something I needed gratitude for. Being responsible for the girls gave me a purpose I wouldn't have had if their mother hadn't dropped them at my door. Maybe I didn't understand how she could leave her girls to go look for her sister in the city. What I knew, was she wouldn't have gone if she had known she wouldn't make it back. I wasn't a mom, and Gabby knew that. But I could understand emotions and their mother had loved them completely.

Later, I had a sleeping Tina on my shoulder and Gabby was holding onto Theo's back as he carried her. Father Allen and Sister Ann had finally appeared from the church, each of them holding books, but nothing else. They revealed that there were no supplies in the church. It was likely the group of people that had turned into zombies had never planned on staying there for any length of time.

On the bus, I sat with Tina in my lap, not wanting her sleeping on the ground when we drove. I didn't have any car seats and honestly wasn't sure about the protocol for a school bus. But in my mind I pictured her tiny body flying forward under the seats if someone had to hit the brakes too hard. I would not be responsible for that kind of accident.

Gabby sat with Sister Ann, a box of animal crackers in her lap as the nun read to her from a book. I hoped it wasn't the Bible, because I couldn't answer questions that could come from that. Outside, Theo and Father Allen were adding the remaining fuel to the bus, and I could hear their conversation about finding more. Theo didn't sound concerned, and he reassured the priest. Somehow, the guy always had the answers and was always upbeat. I knew he was too good to be true.

Looking for more fuel was just part of life now. We were always looking for something. More fuel. More food. More water. More protection. More, more, more. When I put it all together in my mind, it made me completely stressed, so I tried to push it all into a box and slam the lid down on it. When I did that, more things popped up, and I had to keep shoving.

What happened when we ran out of diapers? Or the dehydrated milk that was holding Tina over at night? What about baby wipes? We used them for so much more than Tina's butt. I knew they wouldn't last forever. Would I be able to figure out how to make things from whatever I found? I knew before disposable diapers, mother's used cloth and reusable materials. Looking down at Tina, I thought about some of the diapers I had changed. I held back the gag that wanted to rise with the idea of having to rinse out a cloth to reuse after one of those messes.

With everyone back on the bus, we decided to move on from the small town. But there was no actual destination in mind. Everyone watched out the windows for any vehicles we could scavenge fuel from. With what the bus had, we could likely go a few hundred miles, but then what? Father Allen had switched driving duties with the other man that knew how to drive the bus. The priest was sitting in the front seat, poring over the books he had brought. I imagined being religious in the apocalypse had to be confusing, and he probably desperately needed answers from the books he had studied for so long.

Theo found his way to the back of the bus, where I sat with Tina. As he passed Gabby, she held up her hand and they high-fived. I stared at the interaction and a weird emotion swirled around my mind. It took a second, but I finally realized it was annoyance. Theo had somehow won over my charge within 48 hours. It had taken days for the girl to talk to me, except to ask where her mother was. And even now, she didn't smile and have some secret handshake with me.

The offending man plopped down in the bus seat across from me. I kept my eyes straight. My cheek was resting on the top of Tina's head, and her smooth hair slid across my skin.

"So, I know they're not yours. But, what's the story?" Theo asked.

"You ask a lot of questions, don't you?" I shot him a side eyed glance in time to see him shrug his shoulders.

"I haven't had an actual conversation with a human in... well, quiet awhile," he replied.

That made me turn to look at him. I studied his face. If I were to judge his age, he was likely a few years older than me. Small laugh lines had found their way around his eyes, but not deep enough to make him seem over middle-aged. His hair was a wild mane that somehow looked fashionable, even though I was sure he hadn't had a haircut since the beginning of every-thing. I had to fight the urge to pat my shoulder length hair that hung dully around my face. His eyes were the most arresting feature of him, though, a blue gray that was bright and beautiful.

The last thought made my cheeks heat slightly. My inner voice chided me, insisting that I keep my mind on more impor-tant things.

"So how long were you held by The Children of Z?"

A pained look crossed his face, and he took so long to speak, I didn't think he'd answer.

"Two weeks."

"Did you agree to join them? Is that how you got the brand?"

"No, absolutely not." His eyes were angry as he met my gaze.

"How did it happen then?"

"They brand those that they want to force into their congre-gation. There was a woman, one of the higher members of the group. She wanted to keep me. She thought I'd be the perfect pet." His last words were so soft I almost didn't hear him.

"Pet? I'm not really sure I want to ask," I said.

"It's probably whatever you could imagine. I caught her attention and even when I fought and killed one of their people, she still refused to allow them to feed me to the zombies they kept around. It was just pure stupidity on their part that I was able to escape one night. I was either going to escape or kill myself before she could do whatever she wanted to do." He let out a long breath and turned so he was facing the front of the bus.

The way he laid his head back told me the two weeks The Children of Z held him captive were worse than he could tell. And just talking about it seemed to exhaust him.

"Do you think they're looking for you?" I asked.

"I hope not."

I stared at his profile for a long moment, knowing I hoped they didn't look for him either. Desperate to change the subject, I turned toward him, my arms wrapped around Tina's form so she didn't flop around.

"Obviously they're not mine. They were my neighbors and lived with their mother. We lived in a three-story apartment building in a small suburb. There were fewer zombies in the beginning. A few weeks after the initial illness started, when communications fell, their mother knocked on my door and asked me to take them. She needed to go into the city to save her sister. I guess the sister was a nurse and had stayed in the city to help. But when communications failed, she couldn't reach her anymore. So, she wanted to go after her, but didn't want to put the girls in danger. She never came back."

Theo had turned to watch me as I told the story. I left out all the mishaps I'd had with the girls since they were dropped off. My inability to take care of children was clear to anyone around me.

"And you never left them. That's admirable."

My mouth dropped open. A lot could be said about me. Now and back with the world was real. Admirable wasn't one of the words I had ever heard. I didn't even know how to respond to that. Theo smiled when he realized he had rendered me speechless.

"So, how did you three end up on this bus? I get the feeling you weren't hanging out at the church with the priest and the nun," he said.

"Well, that story would be on my list of failures. We got run up a water tower by a horde of zombies. We were there for days. Tina and I, well, we almost died. But this bus showed up, and they got the three of us down. There used to be a doctor with us. We lost him in Canada. He nursed the three of us back to relative health before we got to the safe zone."

"The Canada safe zone? I heard of that one. There was a lot of talk about it among the Children too."

"What did they say about it?" I asked.

"They wanted to raid it for supplies. Their group just kept growing. Desperate people looking for someone to protect them from death. They had so many people with children begging to take them in, because they had no idea how to find safety on their own. The Children of Z would make them swear their allegiance and put them to work. They kept their word mostly. They didn't allow the kids to die. The parents weren't always kept alive, though," Theo explained.

"The same night we arrived at the safe zone, it fell to what I think was a horde of zombies. But they had strong walls. Do you think The Children of Z had something to do with it?" I asked.

My mind whirled with the implications. Since we had run from Canada, I had wondered how the stronghold had fallen so easily. The night had been quiet until the first screams, which told me something strange had happened. But before hearing Theo's description of The Children of Z, I hadn't thought there was some enormous threat out there besides zombies. The look on Theo's face told me he didn't think it was impossible, either.

"I wouldn't be sure. They had people coming and going all the time. I have no idea how big they really were," he finally replied.

We fell silent, each in our own thoughts. Suddenly, the bus screeched to a halt and my shoulder slammed into the bus seat in front of me. I heard Gabby cry out as she lost her animal crackers and Sister Ann soothing her. Theo shot to his feet and moved toward the front of the bus until he was near the front and could crouch and look through the windshield.

"What is it?" Father Allen asked the driver.

"People blocking the road," the driver called back.

"Back up," Theo said, his voice icy.

"I'm not sure I can," the driver replied.

Father Allen stood so he could see around Theo.

"Maybe we can help them. It's only right to extend our hand to support survivors."

"No, Father. Those aren't people you want to help. See what's painted on that van?" Theo pointed to one side of the windshield.

I couldn't see around the men, but apparently, Father Allen saw whatever had Theo scared.

"These are The Children of Z, I guarantee it. I'm not sure if it's the same group I ran from. But they had groups going all around to scavenge supplies to feed the main camp. This might be a scavenging party—"

A volley of bullets cut Theo's words off. I ducked behind the seat, cradling Tina against my chest. The noise woke the baby, and she immediately began to wail. I put my lips near her mouth and shushed, hoping to calm her. Her arms slid around my neck and I held tightly. Sister Ann rushed by me and Gabby followed until she got to me.

"Sister Ann says to follow her," Gabby said.

"Theo!" Sister Ann called down the aisle as I heard more gunshots.

This time, the bus seemed to tilt slowly one way, and the driver yelled from the front, "They're shooting at the bus!"

Not knowing Sister Ann's plan, I stood, pushing Gabby toward the back of the bus to the nun. She had the carrier for Tina in her hands and she pushed my shoulder so I could spin, and she started shoving straps around my arms. We smashed Gabby between our legs, but she didn't complain. Theo made his way back to us and his face had gone white.

"I'm afraid they're looking for me," he said.

"You were brought to us for a purpose. You saved Vicki and helped us when we needed you. Now, we need to ask something more from you," Sister Ann said as she tugged me around again, fastening the pack across my chest and stomach.

"I'll do whatever I can," he replied.

Yells from outside could be heard, but no one from our bus was opening the door.

"They're threatening to shoot in the windshield! Everyone take cover!" Father Allen cried.

Sister Ann, Theo and I dropped together in the aisle. Gabby was in front of me and Tina now, and her face was stricken with fear. I gathered her closer to my body, throwing up prayers that any bullets that came in hit me and not the girls. Warmth behind me told me Theo was trying to block my back as well as protect the girls. When the gunshots came, the windshield didn't shatter, but cracked and then broke into big safety glass pieces. The driver was on the ground, and Father Allen lay in the middle of the aisle.

When the shots stopped, Father Allen just lifted his head to look around.

"Is anyone hit?" He called.

No one said anything in response. All I could feel were two small, trembling bodies in my arms and a body pressed against my back.

"We only want the supplies. Did we hear a baby crying? We could provide a good life for any kids!" A man bellowed.

I turned my head to meet Theo's eyes with my own frightened gaze, and he shook his head.

"We have to go. They can't get their hands on the girls," he whispered.

"That's exactly what you're going to do," Sister Ann said from the back door.

She had a duffel in her hand, the one I had come to them with. It was packed full and barely zipped. The nun was standing at the emergency door and was looking around. She then popped the door open as quietly as possible. She motioned for us to come forward and I stood, both Tina and Gabby, in my arms. Theo moved behind us, following the exit.

Sister Ann handed the duffel to Theo and took Gabby from my arms. The little girl hugged the nun tightly.

"God protect you, little one," Sister Ann whispered into her hair.

"Sister? Won't you come with us?" I begged.

Theo pushed past me and jumped from the bus, crouching to the side to hide from any eyes. Looking up at Sister Ann, he held out his hands for Gabby and I felt extremely confused, as if they had shared a plan I wasn't aware of. With Tina clinging to my chest, I turned to Sister Ann to search her face for a clue to what was happening.

"Vicki, these girls are the survival of us all. I told you before, they are the future of humanity. That's what children are now. Protect them, make sure they grow up, and fix the world. Love them in your own way—"

More threats being screamed from the front of the bus cut her words off. Sister Ann looked toward Father Allen, and I turned to look as well. Father Allen nodded and waved goodbye to me. It was then I knew they had always planned on protecting the girls, no matter what came at us. Yet no one had told me they would sacrifice everything, just to make sure we kept living. I felt tears of fear and sadness rush to my eyes as I stared up at Sister Ann.

"You can do this, Vicki. There's so much more in you than you have found. Now go! Take care of those angels!"

With her parting words, Theo was suddenly there, his hand up to help me down with Tina. I climbed down and turned just as Sister Ann was pulling the door shut. I was about to cry out, tell her to come with us, but shots on the bus shocked me into silence. Theo tugged me to a run, until we were sliding into the drainage ditch on the side of the road, screams and evil laughter echoing behind us.

CHAPTER 7

MY FEET SLID out from under me and I landed on my butt, sliding down to the bottom of the steep ditch. Theo yanked me up by my hand and prodded me to run into the tree line and further away from the bus. He carried Gabby in his other arm, though the little girl had all of her limbs wrapped around him as if she wouldn't be letting go anytime soon. Tina was still in my arm, one of my hands being pulled by Theo as we ran.

I didn't know how far we had gone, but I couldn't breathe and Tina had head-butted my nose more than once, making it hard for me to see through the tears in my eyes. Pulling back on Theo, I forced him to look back at me. I must have looked as bad as I felt, because he slid to a stop and helped me sit down. He looked behind us, checking to see if anyone was following. He disappeared behind some trees, leaving me and the girls sitting in the overgrown grass.

Gabby crawled to me from where she had been sitting and pressed against my side until I slid an arm around her. I concentrated on breathing, trying to stop the black spots that were popping up in my vision. I closed my eyes for a moment, but when I did, all I saw was Sister Ann's face as she closed the emergency door behind us, locking herself on the bus that was likely her tomb.

"Why did those people do that?" Gabby asked in a watery voice.

"I don't know." My voice was a broken croak, and I needed water badly.

I was sweaty, but also my chest was soaked with tears from Tina's quiet cries. Even the baby realized how dangerous the situation was. Though she couldn't stop herself from crying, she did it almost silently as we ran. I leaned to the side and slid the duffel bag to my side. Tina sat in my lap, her legs around my hips, her head buried between my breasts. Gabby was on the other side, so I struggled with the zipper with one hand.

Heartbreak threatened as I saw what was in the bag. All the supplies I needed for the girls were there. Tina's diapers and wipes. The last of the dehydrated milk. Tina's sippy cups. Books were shoved in too. I found bottles of water at the bottom of the bag and I pulled one out. Holding it to Tina's little lips first, I carefully helped her drink a little down before handing it to Gabby. The little girl drank deeply.

"Slow down, little one," Theo said as he reappeared. "Don't wanna upset your stomach."

Gabby nodded and handed the bottle back to me. I had no need to listen to Theo as I chugged the water down my parched throat. The moment it hit my empty stomach, I could feel it turn, but I refused to show it. I held the bottle out to Theo, who finished the last half and slipped the empty bottle back into the duffel.

"We aren't being followed. Not yet, at least," he said.

"Why would they follow?" I asked.

"It's only a guess, but I think they would want the kids.

Unless the people left on the bus could convince them there weren't actually any kids."

"What do you think they did to them?" I whispered, not saying the exact words with little ears that could hear.

"Probably what you're thinking," he said.

What I was thinking was that everyone on the bus, people who had saved my life twice, were now dead. And that the last thing Sister Ann did was save us for the third time with her quick thinking and sacrifice. I leaned my head back against the tree and fought the urge to just bawl my eyes out. I didn't want to scare the girls, and I knew we couldn't stay still for too long.

Theo sorted through the duffel some more and pulled out a folded packet of paper. It was the map of where we were. I didn't know how Sister Ann had gotten it into the duffel so quickly, but the woman was a genius in my book. I shot a prayer to the God I wasn't sure I believed in, just to say that if Sister Ann was up there, she deserved all the benefits.

After studying the map, Theo turned and looked across the field on the opposite side of the road.

"There's some sort of smaller back road that winds through some towns that way. I think we need to stay off the highway for as long as we can. Maybe we can find a working vehicle that way and get further away."

I nodded. I didn't have any ideas. We had nowhere to go, no idea of what was safe. His idea was the best we had at the moment. After a few more minutes of rest, Theo helped slide Tina back into the carrier. He found one of her pacifiers in the duffel and he gave it to her, which she started sucking relentlessly.

"She's probably almost too old for that," Theo mentioned.

"It's what keeps her quiet. She can have the damn thing for the rest of her life," I replied.

Theo gave me a sad smile, but nodded his agreement. I didn't know what the rules were for babies Tina's age. And I honestly didn't care. I was going to let her have whatever she needed for comfort. I shifted and adjusted until the backpack was mostly comfortable. Gabby climbed to her feet and stood next to me, waiting. I held out my hand, and she grabbed it with a grateful squeeze.

We slowly left the shade of the trees, looking both ways as we entered the ditch next to the highway. Theo held up his hand to stop us and he climbed up the hill, staying low until he reached the top. He stayed there, still for a long moment, and I crouched next to Gabby, prepared to grab her and run straight back into the trees at his signal. Both of the girls stayed silent, Tina's sucking on her pacifier the loudest noise I could hear.

Finally, Theo turned and motioned for us to join him. I pushed Gabby ahead of me to help her. Theo slid down and offered his hand to the little girl. He pulled her up the rest of the way before turning and offering his hand to me. With little trouble, he helped pull me and Tina up the hill. At the side of the highway, Theo stood, indicating it was safe to show ourselves. I brushed off my leggings, cursing in my head about the lack of clean clothes again.

He had put the duffel on his back, everything we had for survival in one bag. Once we stopped for rest, I was going to have to search the bag and see what else was in there. The one thing I knew we didn't have was my backpack that had the remaining pink wine. That loss struck me hard, but when I pictured it sitting on the bus that was likely full of dead bodies now, I didn't want to think about it any longer.

We quickly crossed the two-lane highway, reaching the other shoulder in seconds. Theo slowly slid down the hill, holding Gabby's hand to make sure she didn't tumble head over feet. I followed more slowly, knowing if I fell, I could crush Tina under me. At the bottom, we immediately set out across the dirt field.

"When we get to the road and find a car, where are we going to go?" I asked quietly, walking next to Theo with Gabby between us.

"Where were you going to go? Do you have people to find?" He asked.

"No people. No safe haven to speak of." My words were clipped, but Theo didn't get the sign that I didn't want to talk about it.

"No one? You had no family before this fall, that you might want to go find?"

"I told you before that you ask a lot of questions, right? I just wanted to make sure you heard that."

Theo just flashed a small smile before waiting for my answer.

"I never had family. Grew up in the system. I don't remember my mother or father. That's fine, since they didn't want me, anyway. Aged out at 18 and have been on my own ever since," I said.

I immediately saw Theo's eyes fill with the exact emotion I wanted to avoid. Pity or sadness, both things I didn't feel for myself. Never knowing what it was like to have a genuine family, probably saved my life when the illness first started, so I was ok with it. And I also didn't have to feel the pain of losing that family to zombies. I lifted my chin and just glared at Theo long enough for his eyes to clear. He moved his gaze back to in front of us.

We were totally exposed in the dirt field until we got to a row of trees in the distance. I hadn't felt nervous at first, but the hair on the back of my neck seemed to stand up as we got further into the field. I looked around us, but saw nothing moving or any visible people watching us.

"Denver," Theo suddenly said.

"As in Colorado? Yup, that's a city and stuff."

"It's where I was headed. I didn't have time to tell everyone this, but I'm actually from the East Coast. I was living in New York, thinking I was going to hit it big time with some big financial company. Sitting behind a desk as a low level mail room intern, if you can believe it, as zombies appeared in the office and started eating people. Anyway, I immediately knew I needed to get home."

"And home is Denver, Colorado?" I asked.

"Yeah. My parents and one sister live...or well lived there," he said.

I looked over at him, realizing again I did not know what it must be like to lose a loved one. The likelihood that his family was still alive was definitely slim. But I wasn't going to say that to him.

"Denver sounds like as good of a place as any. We aren't going to be walking there though," I replied.

"We definitely need wheels. Something will come along, I believe it."

Theo's well of positivity didn't seem to have a bottom, and I wasn't sure how long I could stomach it. After what had just happened not even two hours before, I couldn't think of anything but drowning myself in an enormous glass of whiskey. Something that would not happen anytime soon, since we barely had enough supplies to keep us alive for a few days. There were much more pressing matters than my coping mechanism. Even if I couldn't keep my thoughts completely off of it.

When we reached the trees on the opposite side of the field, I felt like I could breathe a sigh of relief. The shade of the branches hid us as we continued. Further beyond another empty field stood a big farmhouse. We stared at it for a long moment. It would be perfect for a night's rest if there were no one in it. The only weapon we had was Theo's hunting knife. My metal pipe and knife were left behind on the bus. Facing a group of zombies wasn't something we could really handle at the moment.

We continued in the tree line until we came to the end of the property and found a dirt road that led to the gate of the home. Climbing over the fence was easy work with Theo helping Gabby over and then making sure I didn't tip over with Tina on my chest. As we walked, Theo consulted the map again. He traced his finger over lines and he nodded to himself. I hoped that meant his annoying positivity was getting us somewhere.

Darkness appeared before we reached the asphalt. Gabby had asked to be carried when her feet began to ache. So, we put her on Theo's back, with her sitting on the duffel and holding onto his neck so she didn't fall backward. His hands were still mostly free, and he said he was fine when I asked to take her from him. Gabby laid her head on his shoulder, and I could see her eyes wilting. Both girls had complained about being hungry and Tina was fussy with a diaper that badly needed changing.

"We need to figure out sleeping arrangements. The girls need to eat, too," I said.

Theo pointed to a copse of trees off the dirt road.

"I was thinking those. Thick enough that we should be well hidden."

I nodded and followed his lead. The copse was thick with trees and brush, making it difficult to walk through without tripping. Eventually, we found a tree with a clearing under its low branches. I helped Gabby climb down, and Theo took Tina out of the carrier. Both girls moved around the clearing, walking a circle around Theo and me. I reminded them to stay close and not to leave the small clearing and Gabby agreed, taking Tina's hand.

I kneeled next to the duffel and unzipped it. Diaper duty was the first thing I needed to worry about, so I pulled out those supplies. At the bottom of the bag was a crumpled tarp, something I had pushed into the bag when we left the apartment. I pulled it out, and Theo grinned.

"That's perfect for cover. I'll work on a tent."

Somehow, he produced paracord that I had seen nowhere, and in a few minutes, he had a tent structure over our heads. The girls ran in, giggling that there was no door. Theo chased them for a moment, before I grabbed Tina on one of her run bys.

"Diaper for you, kid," I said, as her legs kicked.

I set into changing her, feeling horrible that she was so wet. But there hadn't been a chance to stop before. I gave the wet diaper to Theo to dispose of far from us and strapped on the clean one. I did it the right way on my first try this time, and I felt somewhat accomplished. With her dressed again, I turned her loose with Gabby and dug into the duffel. I realized Sister Ann must have used the duffel for foods that were for the girls because there was so much that I had gotten specifically for them.

We didn't have any way to heat water, so the freeze-dried meals were out. But we had crackers, fruit cups and a bag of jerky. It felt similar to when the girls and I had first fled my apartment. We struggled to find food and almost died. I shook my head, pushing those thoughts out, as I handed a cracker to Tina and a few to Gabby. They both ate hungrily, and I turned to hand a sleeve of crackers to Theo. He shook his head and pointed to the girls.

"Take it from me. We do them no good if we starve ourselves," I said, pushing a handful of crackers into his hand.

Both girls ate a fruit cup as well and a few pieces of jerky before they got sleepy. We had one small baby blanket in the duffel that I had brought for Tina originally. It was just big enough for the girls to lie on, so we got them settled. I mixed a cup of milk for each of them, wanting the extra calories in their stomachs before sleep. They fell asleep so fast, I didn't even have a chance to worry that they wouldn't sleep out in the open.

"I'll take the first shift. You sleep with them," Theo whispered.

I nodded and curled up next to Tina, with my back to the tent wall. I put my arm around the baby to make sure she couldn't get up and wander without me waking. But as I tried to find the sweet baby scent she used to have, sleep felt elusive. The tarp and trees blocked any moon or starlight, so I couldn't even see the wisps of eyelashes on her face. But I could feel her body rise and fall as she breathed deeply in sleep. I counted each breath. As I got to fifty, my breathing evened out and slumber finally came.

When Theo shook me softly, I felt as if I hadn't slept at all. But when I checked the time, I realized I had been out for five hours. I sat up quickly, rubbing my eyes. Theo had a small flashlight lit, but his hand was keeping the light from the girls' faces.

"You let me sleep too long," I whispered.

He shook his head. "I wouldn't have woken you at all if I hadn't started to nod off. You seemed peaceful."

"Sleep is the only peace we seem to get anymore, isn't it? Try to get some yourself, before morning."

Theo laid on his back next to Tina, not cuddling her like me, but blocking her from rolling from the tent. I moved to the foot of the tent that pointed out into the trees. The moon's beams filtered through the branches, which only worked to make the shadows look as if they were dancing. I yawned and squinted into the darkness, trying to ensure none of the shadows were more than that.

When the sun warmed the dawn, the shadows were exposed, finally settling my nerves. We were alone in our small copse. No living or zombie had stumbled upon us in the night. I crawled from the tent to stretch my stiff back and joints. I walked a circle around our clearing before going behind a nearby tree to relieve myself. The area was really pretty as the sun slowly appeared and warmed the darkness to morning.

I continued my watch from outside the tent until I heard whispered voices inside. When I peered in, I saw Tina poking Theo in the cheek. I was just about to grab her and pull her away when I saw a small smile appear on his face. Gabby was already sitting up, a book on her lap. I motioned for her to come to me.

"I'm going to let Gabby pee. Can you keep Tina for a minute?" I asked.

Theo nodded without opening his eyes, making Tina giggle. Gabby climbed to me and we got her business done with no hazards this time. On the way back to the tent, she picked up a stick and dragged it around the dirt, drawing circles. It made me think about her education and the lack of learning she had with no society. That was a problem for another day, though. We had enough to face out in the wide open, with no vehicle and no safety.

When we got back to the tent, Tina was running circles around Theo, who was untying the tarp from the trees. I took the time to mix milk for both girls and let them eat the last fruit cups for breakfast. Theo and I ate the beef jerky. The two of us crouched, looking into the duffel as he repacked the tarp.

"We're going to need to find supplies soon," he said.

I didn't really have anything to add to that. It was definitely the first worry of the day. We had freeze-dried meals we could attempt to eat without hot water. If it came down to it, we would have to choke them down. I just wanted to find the faith needed to keep going down this road. To keep surviving. To know that everything would work out and we would find what we needed. I didn't have that faith now.

Once everything was packed and Tina was strapped onto my chest again, we set out from the grouping of trees, back to the dirt road. It wasn't long before we discovered the asphalt back road that Theo had found on the map. He traced his finger along it until it connected with several other roads in a tiny town.

"Here. We'll find something here. It can't be over three miles."

For once, fate was in our corner, and the walk wasn't quite three miles. It still took almost two hours with a five-year-old that had stubby legs. Theo offered to carry her a few times, but Gabby wanted to be independent until she didn't. By the last half mile, she was really lagging, and I wasn't giving her options anymore. She was on Theo's back again when we saw the outskirts of what looked like a rest area, more than a town.

The first buildings we came to were a gas station and a small store with the windows smashed to pieces. There was a mechanic across the street, which looked untouched. Theo headed that direction first. Sitting in the parking lot was what I would label a mom van. It was a minivan with sliding side doors and a back hatch that swung up. It was clear Theo wanted that car, as it was the first one he went to.

After settling Gabby and Tina near us on the asphalt, Theo went into the mechanic shop. He was hoping they left the van because work had just been done on it, and its owners hadn't picked it up yet. I wasn't sure we could be that lucky, but when the van suddenly beeped next to me, I jumped two feet in the air and whirled, looking for a threat. I almost smacked Theo when he walked out with a big grin, clearly laughing at my reaction.

The van doors slid open smoothly, and we looked inside.

The inside was fairly bare, but it had plenty of seats and some-where to store supplies. We decided to put the girls in the captain's seats in the second row and keep the third row folded down.

"I think these two seats fold under the floor too. Making the area flat. We could camp out in it on the road. I think this vehicle is perfect," Theo said, as we were putting the duffel in the back, between the girls' seats.

"Yeah, if you're a mom, driving six kids to soccer," I muttered.

"Don't be ridiculous. A mom could only fit five kids in this. Little kids can't sit in the front seat because of the airbag," he replied.

I stared at him. I didn't know the information about the front seat airbag. Filing that away, I just shrugged and moved to climb into the front passenger seat.

"We still need car seats," Gabby complained from the back.

"We know, little one. As soon as we can find any that will work, we'll get them," Theo replied in a soothing voice.

I kept my mouth clamped shut, because my response would not be so kind. The kid was obsessed with the rules. And at some point, she needed to learn that the rules didn't really apply anymore. I glanced back, and she was fiddling with her seatbelt, as it either came across her neck or hit her in the face. Grum-bling, she flung it behind her arm, so she was still strapped in, but not hindered by the belt.

I hid the smirk on my face as Theo climbed into the driver's seat. We held our breath as he turned the key and when the engine started, he smiled over at me. I leaned over and tapped the gas gauge.

"It's almost on E."

Theo's grin faltered, but the happiness didn't fall from his eyes. He turned the van back off and held up a hand as he climbed out. He disappeared inside the mechanic's shop again. When he reappeared, he had three gas cans in his hands. He also had a crowbar under his arm and several bungee cords. When he came to my side of the van, he motioned for me to open the door.

"Just need to find hose and a funnel, and we'll be good to go."

"We can just cut a water bottle in half for the funnel. And I'm sure one of these businesses has a water hose attached to it," I said.

Theo looked over at the convenience store. I saw the wheels moving behind his eyes and I knew before he opened his mouth that he was going to suggest going inside.

"We need better weapons before we go in there," I said.

He held up the crowbar and handed it over to me.

"Smaller than the pipe you had before, but it'll do just as much damage, if not more."

I took the metal bar from him and hefted it in my hand. It wasn't any lighter than the pipe I was using, but it was longer. And it also had a sharp end on the curved side, just in case I needed to try to impale someone. I shook my head at my internal thoughts, wondering how I had become the person thinking about what would break through a human skull.

"Let's move the van over there. We can lock the girls inside and go in together. Better to watch each other's backs," I said.

Theo agreed, and jumped back into the driver's seat. There were also two smaller cars in the parking lot of the gas station, and if there were no zombies around, we could start scavenging for gas there. Theo parked the van near the front of the store. I turned to look at Gabby, preparing the speech about how she needed to be aware of her surroundings.

It wasn't the first time I had left her alone in a vehicle. That time, someone who turned out to be a threat had appeared and

Gabby took the initiative to hide her and Tina inside. I needed her to be smart like that again. But she seemed to already know where I was going to go and before I could speak, she opened her mouth.

"We'll hide if anyone comes."

"Good girl." I couldn't help being a bit impressed with how well Gabby was handling things.

Leaving Gabby with a bottled water, so they could have a drink while we were inside, Theo used the remote to the lock the van. It made an annoying honking noise when it locked, and we froze, looking around for anything or anyone to come investigate. When nothing appeared, we both let out a gush of air, and Theo grinned at me. I couldn't pull it together enough to smile back. There was just nothing to smile about.

The windows of the store were demolished, someone clearly wanting in that didn't have access. We stepped into the building, boots crunching on the broken glass. The sound was loud in my ears when in reality it wasn't the alarm it felt like. The shelves in the store were pushed over and products had fallen into the glass. Careful not to cut ourselves, we each took a small section and sorted through what was left. Eventually, we had a pile of road trip snack foods and the big surprise of a case of water behind the counter.

Working together, we took our haul to the van. We learned the hard way that opening the hatch of the van also set off a beeping noise we couldn't seem to stop. Theo looked at me with a cringy smile as we waited for the sound to quiet. We quickly loaded up what we had found, just as I noticed a figure in the middle of the road making its way toward us. At a distance, I couldn't be sure if it was zombie or human. The walking wasn't clear. But it was definitely coming straight to us.

Theo ran around the store quickly until he found a length of garden hose on one side. Using his large knife, he cut it from the spigot and ran back to the van. He paused only long enough to see that it was indeed a zombie coming down the road. Throwing the length of hose at me, he climbed into the driver's seat and turned on the engine. I wanted to cheer out loud as it turned over so easily. Theo quickly threw it into drive and got onto the road. We drove away from the zombie threat, and I continued to watch until it disappeared in the side mirror.

CHAPTER 8

A FEW MILES down the road, we came to a blockage in the road and Theo slowed the van. We both searched the area around the cars, the incident with the bus too new for us both. After trekking across the two fields and going through the back roads, I hoped The Children of Z didn't know how to find us. I still held onto the belief that Sister Ann never would have admitted that the girls were even on the bus. However, that didn't mean someone sniveling and begging for their life, like Trevor, wouldn't have spilled all the information.

"What do you think?" Theo murmured.

"I don't see anything," I replied, my voice just as quiet.

"We need the fuel. These cars would probably fill those tanks."

I nodded at the obvious statement. While we had driven, I had cut the length of hose and had used one of the empty water bottles to create a funnel. Neither would be perfect, but it was the best we could do for the moment. I wasn't sure how the plastic bottle would do with the gas, but we'd find out once we tried to use it. Picking up the crowbar, I nodded to Theo that I was ready.

"Ok, little one. Same rules, okay?" Theo called back to Gabby.

I turned my head in time to catch her nod, as she undid her seatbelt to see between the front seats. Her eyes widened slightly, but she moved over to her sister's seat and sat with her, just in case. When we got out, instead of using the remote and making the honking noise, Theo locked the doors with the mechanism and closed his door quietly. We met at the front of the van, still looking around for anyone that could jump out at us.

"This feels creepy." I rubbed the back of my neck, goose-bumps rising over my body.

"Let's hurry," Theo said, nodding his agreement.

The first car had almost a full tank of gas. It was the biggest jackpot either of us had found so far. Using the five-gallon gas can, Theo went back and forth until the van was full. Then we worked to fill the gas cans completely as backup. I realized what the bungee cords were for then, as Theo strapped the cans on the top of the van. It was much better than exposing the girls to the fumes that couldn't be contained.

While Theo situated the fuel, I stared, peering into cars we hadn't checked. I came to a vehicle with the driver's window rolled down and a dead body sitting in the seat. Moving closer, I gripped my crowbar tightly, studying the man that had been the driver of the compact sedan. He had been wearing a business suit, but he had thrown the jacket into the back. It looked like he drove away from work and just kept going when things started to fall apart. Suddenly, his head jerked toward me, and I let out a shriek.

Jumping back, I realized I was perfectly safe, as the zombie was still trapped in his seatbelt. Looking around, I realized that somehow zombies had gotten to the vehicles and had eaten part of this guy's face through the open window. But once he died, they left him to turn. His body was slowly decaying. I stared, wondering if the decay happened faster without fresh food, or if it happened at the same rate, no matter what.

"Are you ok?" Theo's voice came from behind me, causing me to scream again and spin.

He held up his hands in a surrender motion and I lowered the crowbar that I had been prepared to brain him with.

"Not the best time to sneak up on people, just a note," I growled.

"Got it." He peered around me and saw what had scared me before. "Yikes. Guy was a sitting duck with his window down like that, I guess."

I nodded and looked back at the guy. Somewhere deep down, I felt bad for the zombie, so I took the sharp end of the bar and shoved it with all my might into the side of its skull. When I pulled it out, blood covered the metal, and the zombie slumped, its head smacking the door.

"Could have just left it," Theo commented.

Shrugging, I moved to the next vehicle to peer in. This one had open doors and no bodies inside. There was a suitcase in the backseat, so I pulled it out to the road. Unzipping it, I found women's clothes, about three sizes too big for me. I was not in the position to be picky, so I grabbed the flannels, sweatpants, and jeans. Theo came to me with a ripped grocery bag he had found in another car that had batteries and a few flashlights in it.

"No food anywhere," he said.

"I didn't find anything either."

When we felt like we had done all that was necessary, we made our way back to the van, to find the girls both curled up and sleeping in the folded third row. With Theo's help, we moved them back to their chairs, which leaned back enough to allow them to continue to sleep, but to have at least a lap belt across them. Then we continued in a general West direction.

The car was eerily silent, except for the sound of the engine and the rhythmic thump of the tires over cracks in the asphalt. I hated uncomfortable quiet times, and it made me feel like I needed to fill the void. But I had nothing to say and instead just stared out my window. I missed my smartphone with the music streaming app. Though there was no cell service, I thought about how I just left it behind on my coffee table. The music was downloaded onto the device and I probably could have still listened to it. I wanted to kick myself for not thinking of that before.

"So, you aged out of foster care, huh?" Theo asked.

"Quite the conversation starter, aren't you?" I shot back.

"You really should come with a warning label. Might be spicy or bite," Theo replied with a large grin.

"I bite hard, so maybe think about that before asking questions."

Theo looked away from the road to study me for a long moment. I pointed at the road and he just grinned again. I didn't understand this guy. And I wasn't looking to get to know him. But for some reason he wanted to push and pull at all my nooks and crannies and figure out who I was. As if he knew exactly what I was thinking, he continued.

"Do you plan on going your separate way with the girls once we get somewhere that looks good for you?"

"I...what? What does that mean?" My voice came out a little cracked, because when the idea of being alone came to my mind, panic pushed everything away.

"You are very determined to not get to know me. You don't want me to ask about you. So, I thought maybe you didn't plan on sticking together for long?"

I pulled my knees up, planting my heels on the edge of my

seat. Wrapping my arms around my legs, I rested my chin on my knees and stared out the windshield.

"What's the point? We all die," I said, my voice barely above a whisper.

I saw Theo's eyes flash up to the rearview mirror, and I knew he was checking to see if Gabby was still asleep. Knowing Gabby couldn't keep to herself for a long period, I knew the silence from the backseat meant they were still sleeping. I also knew they would be hungry when they woke up and that would be the first words out of the little girl's mouth.

"It doesn't have to be that way," Theo whispered back.

"What control do we have? Look at Sister Ann and Father Allen. The nicest people I've met, well, in probably my entire life. And they sacrificed themselves so we could get away. How do I know you'll last, or I will, for that matter?"

Theo chewed on that for a long moment. He wasn't one to just spit out the first words that came to mind. That was how I communicated. I rarely thought for too long about the things running through my head, before they sprinted off of my tongue for others to hear. That type of behavior seemed to always earn me labels of smart ass or confrontational. Well-earned titles I was typically proud of.

"I guess I don't. But, neither do you. There's no knowing that I won't last longer than anyone else you meet. Also, what if something happens to you? What happens to those girls?"

I couldn't contain the grimace on my face. Of course, that was always a possibility. I wasn't living in some bubble separate from the rest of the apocalypse. A sick feeling settled in my stomach when I thought of the girls being left completely alone because I was stupid enough to die. It almost happened once, though they probably would have starved to death with me. And I couldn't even handle thinking about that near failure.

"I hadn't really thought about it, because it's not like there are babysitters on every corner these days. When we left my apartment, I only had one idea of a plan. Canada. And well, that failed. So now I'm just doing what I can to keep us alive, day to day."

"I would take care of them if something happened to you." Theo's answer was immediate, and his voice held no hesitation.

"Why? They're practical strangers to you, just like me."

"Does there need to be a reason? Beyond the fact that they are innocent, defenseless children? Protecting them and providing for them is only the natural and responsible thing to do. Isn't that why you're doing it?"

I huffed out a breath at that question. I didn't have an obvious reason I was doing it. But I just knew I couldn't leave them behind and I couldn't just hope some random woman that knew how to mother would come along and rescue them from me. When I thought about the deeper reasons I might have for it, I pushed them aside. I wasn't looking to get super emotional about any connection I was building with the two sleeping ankle biters.

"Maybe your childhood has something to do with it?"

Theo caught my side eye glare, and his smirk widened. I could see how he was going round the subjects, to keep coming back to me.

"Listen Freud, I'm not lying on your therapist's couch right now for you to tell me I have attachment issues."

"Don't need to be a therapist to see that from a mile away," Theo said.

My fist itched to punch his face. I knew my issues and had lived with them for my entire life. Who could really blame me for not wanting to be attached to anyone or anything? No one in my world had ever wanted to keep me, protect me, or provide for me. That wasn't going to suddenly change in the apocalypse.

I didn't respond to Theo, just kept staring out the windshield, watching the vehicles we passed and the wide open spaces around us.

"Sorry, Vicki. I'm not trying to be annoying. I'm also not saying I want you to leave or take off with the girls as soon as we get to Denver. I hope we can stay a group as long as fate allows it."

I tried to stare at him without him noticing. He talked like a philosopher, not like some guy trying to get out of a mail room to work in finance. Theo was too good to be true, and I wasn't sure how far I could trust what was coming out of his mouth. As long as it was safe for the girls and me, we would stay with the weirdo until a better offer came along. Even I realized how unlikely that offer would be, but I wasn't placing all my eggs in one basket.

"Why did you want to work in finance?" Getting the subject back on him felt the safest way to move forward.

"Why does anyone want to work in finance? Money. Financial stability in my adult life. To have enough money to buy a house, have a family, all those bells and whistles."

His answer was brutally honest, and I had to admire that. When I asked questions, he answered. He wasn't trying to hide behind anything, or pretend. If he was lying, he was extremely good at it, because he didn't hesitate.

"That was always your plan? Money, wife, house, kids? White picket fence and all that?"

Theo shrugged, but didn't take his eyes off the road.

"I didn't see the need for anything else at the time. Now I wish I had spent all my time hoarding supplies and having an unground bunker built. Hindsight, ya know."

I snorted at that. More than once I had wondered about real hoarders, who had been screaming about the end of the world for years. They probably wanted to tell every living person they told them so, but that would mean coming out of their shelters and interacting with people. Most of them didn't want to do that.

We fell silent then, because Theo wasn't going to attempt to ask me more questions about myself that I wasn't ready to answer. And I didn't really know what else to ask him, to get to know him. It didn't take long for a whining voice to come from the back of the van and, as predicted, the girls were awake and hungry for a late lunch. So we could stay on the road, I clumsily climbed over the middle console to get back to the supplies and get food for the girls.

"Vicki, when will we have real food again?" Gabby asked quietly.

"I thought kids loved junk food," I replied, as I handed her a bag of mix that had pretzels, cheese crackers and nuts.

Gabby rolled her little eyes at me, making me grind my teeth. I had more than one foster parent get mad at me for my sarcasm and the rolling of my eyes. And though most of them weren't very fond of me and they made sure I knew it, I could understand the infuriation that came with someone less than half your size, with an attitude larger than life.

"Not all the time. It doesn't fill us up for long."

Sometimes the five-year-old sounded like an adult. Of course, I knew the nutritional value difference between junk food, crackers, jerky and fruits and vegetables. I had hope we would find something canned along the way, so I could get something more substantial into them, but we had what we had.

"We'll find something," I said.

I gave Gabby a water bottle and filled Tina's cup with water as well. Hydration wouldn't be something I'd forget this time. Both girls gulped down the liquid, so I knew they needed it. I threw a bag of chips up to Theo and put water bottles in the front cup holders for us both. Then I brought a bag of jerky to share and climbed over the console again, this time not falling on my face.

"We could stop and build a fire for dinner. Heat water and eat some of the camping meals," Theo suggested.

I nodded. That would make Gabby happy. And hot food would help them fall asleep better when they turned in for the night. I turned to see the girls happily munching and looking out the windows. Imagining a mother using the vehicle for her brood, I could understand the appeal. Reaching the kids was easy. It was open and airy inside, so a long drive didn't feel stuffy. The back, with the third row folded down, made ample storage space. Not that we had a lot to store at the moment, but I pictured stacks of cases of water and canned foods. My stomach growled then, and I shoved a piece of jerky into my mouth.

True to his word, Theo scouted for a safe place to stop as the sun started to dip. We discussed we didn't want to build a fire when it was completely dark. It would be a beacon to anyone or anything looking for living people. I had no doubt that people out in the open like this would be likely to steal from anyone they found, because survival was only for the fittest.

Eventually, we came to a dirt access road and Theo pulled down it slowly. He only went so far that hid the van from the road, but not so far that we could get stuck with no way out. When he turned off the vehicle, the silence was thick. Both of us stared out the windows, our heads on a swivel, checking for anything moving toward us. The surrounding trees hid the vehicle, but it could also hide threats we didn't know of yet.

We waited about five minutes, letting the girls unstrap themselves and climb all over the car, until they ended up in our laps. Theo held Tina, and I was impressed with the way he redirected her hands over and over as she tried to hit the car horn. In my mind, I was feeling tempted to tie her up, just to keep her still. But Theo just handled her as if it was second nature.

Once we were sure the coast was clear, the four of us climbed out of the car. I put Gabby on the ground next to me and she reached her hands up to the sky, then looked at me and started doing her pee dance. I sighed and nodded, calling through the open doors to Theo that I was taking her to pee behind a tree. He nodded and was lifting Tina above his head while she pretended to fly.

With the business at hand done, we trekked back to the van, where Theo was opening the hatch and pulling out diaper supplies. I raised an eyebrow at him.

"I used to babysit. My sister is twelve years younger than me. So, my parents had a built-in babysitter when she came along. She was a surprise baby."

He told the story as he deftly removed Tina's wet diaper and put on a new one. He didn't even have to study the diaper for a long period to determine the front like I did. Tina also seemed to lie perfectly still for him and even raising her legs when he needed her to. He was annoying. I had to fight the urge to snatch her up as if she were my possession and he was trying to steal her away. The feeling was so foreign to me; I put it away to evaluate when it was quiet and I could think for myself.

"Why don't we take a little bit of a walk into these trees? Get some energy out? Then build a fire before dark and heat water for the food?" Theo suggested.

Inwardly, I mocked him for having a good idea, one I should have thought of. I wasn't above pettiness, but I didn't want to show it to Theo. Instead, I just nodded and took Gabby's outstretched hand. Theo hitched Tina on his hip, and we started slowly walking through the trees. I couldn't keep myself from breathing deeply and enjoying the freshness in my lungs.

I wouldn't roll the van windows all the way down after seeing the zombie in the car with the wide open access to it. Wasn't about to make that mistake. So, the van got stuffy and then stinky when Tina had a dirty diaper while we were still driving. I did not know how something so small could make a smell so damn toxic. But yet she did. I threw that diaper from the van window while allowing just a little fresh air to circulate in to save our noses.

Before the apocalypse, I wasn't an outside type of person. I didn't appreciate nature the way many people did. The concrete jungle was my home, and I was ok with it. Now, the lush green of trees and the shrubs that grew at their feet felt freeing and inviting. In my mind, the cities felt like barren wastelands, full of the dead, just trying to multiply their own numbers by attacking anything that attempted to live there. I didn't want to be there any longer.

Theo suddenly whooped and rushed over to one side of a tree. Turning, he thrust Tina into my arms and I stared at him as he freaked out over something he was digging up. They were some sort of honeycomb looking fungus and I wrinkled my nose.

"What in the world are you doing?" I asked.

"These are morel mushrooms. They grow wild out here. They're edible." He turned to grin at me with a handful of the nasty-looking things and I just glowered at him.

"If you hadn't noticed, we have two kids with us. How are we going to feed them those?" I asked, even though I was the one thinking I wasn't eating wild mushrooms.

"I'll eat it. If Theo cooks it," Gabby said.

I looked down at her, and she was smiling at Theo as if he was her hero.

"Traitor," I muttered, but no one acted like they heard me.

"If we chop them up small enough, we could mix them into whatever camping meal we make. That way, we're getting something fresh too," he said. He then looked up and really studied my face.

"Vicki, this is the way it will be, eventually. We'll run out of canned vegetables and fruits. The girls especially need fresh foods, to be healthy, to continue to grow."

He wasn't telling me anything I hadn't already thought about, stressed about, had nightmares about. My worries centered on the girls and their nutrition on the regular. Even if I had been used to living on ramen noodles, frozen burritos and chicken nuggets most of my life, I knew it wasn't healthy. Just thinking about that made my mouth water for a burrito, but I pushed the thought aside.

"How do you know so much about this, anyway?" I asked, wanting to change the subject and forget about the delicious frozen burritos.

Theo shrugged, looking back down at his dirty hands. "We camped a lot when I was growing up. My dad taught my sister and I all about edible plants. He was a doctor, but was always really interested in herbs and the powers of natural healing when it could be done. He also believed in science, so he was a weird hybrid between the two."

I wondered what it was like to have knowledge taught to you by people who loved you. I once had a teacher in the seventh grade, that took a special interest in me. She was kind. When I would come to school with nothing but a snack, she would sit with me in her room and share a sandwich. She would joke about how I was too skinny and that she definitely wasn't, so I was helping her out. In class, she would subtly point things out for me to study more, or to pay attention to, because she knew where I struggled. She was the closest thing I had ever had to an adult that took the time to teach me.

"So, you're sure those aren't going to send us on some trip that will have us seeing colors that don't even exist?" I asked.

Theo barked out a laugh. "You can be funny when you're not crabby."

"That didn't answer the question."

"You really need to learn to trust. You think I'd get two young kids high on wild mushrooms?"

I shrugged and studied my scuffed boot. Theo stood, moving around the trees, bending and digging up additional mushrooms, until the bottom of his shirt that he was using as a basket was full. I was sure Theo had what people called an infectious personality. I couldn't help but look at him as someone that was just an infection. For some reason, the girls loved him and I just followed along, because being alone would have been much worse.

Back near the van, I started collecting branches and dried brush that was on the ground. Theo set up a small circle of rocks and dug down just slightly for a pile of kindling. Theo dug out a package of lighters he'd found at the store. Carefully, he opened the packaging, taking just one lighter out. He stored the rest back in the duffel bag. They were precious tools until we found anything else to use.

The fire started small, but eventually it was big enough to boil water in an empty can. After washing them, Theo cut the mushrooms into small pieces. Once the water boiled, he added them to the can and waited for them to cook through. Then he added the water to the camp meal packet of spaghetti and meatballs. He folded down the packet to allow it to cook with the water. Then he started the process again.

We had agreed to eat only two meals between the four of us for dinner. Both girls had full cups of milk, though I was feeling nervous about the powdered milk dwindling. I was thankful for the calories they were getting now, even if Theo and I cut way back for ourselves. The girls' needs came first.

The second packet Theo mixed was a chili that he and I would split, since Gabby immediately hesitated when we suggested it. But noodles and sauce were perfect for little kids' taste buds. Using a small camp fork, I put noodles into Tina's needy mouth. She chewed with gusto and then drank her milk. Gabby used the same fork and took a meatball, which she took bites off of, until it was gone.

The chili wasn't horrible, which Theo and I took turns with. While I fed Tina, Theo held out the spoon with chili for me. I didn't think twice about taking the offering, because my stomach had been growling for hours. If the mushrooms tasted like anything, it didn't hurt the bland taste of the meal. And the girls didn't seem to notice the extra little bits in their bites. I tried to think if mushrooms had any real vitamins, but I couldn't be sure. I decided since they grew from the ground naturally, they were doing some good for both girls.

The stars were appearing as we finished eating and the girls started to feel drowsy. Gabby laid her head on my leg and Tina climbed until I was cradling her against my chest. Theo kicked dirt over our embers and stood to arrange the van. I heard the middle seats go down and then Theo appeared, lifting Gabby into his arms and carrying her to the vehicle. I stood to follow with Tina.

Theo had made the entire van flat in the back. He laid the one small blanket out for the girls to curl up on. I placed Tina next to Gabby, and they used jackets to lay their heads on. Theo and I each took a side and then we pulled all the doors shut and hit the lock mechanism. We were essentially safe, and neither of us stayed up for watch.

"Vicki?" Theo whispered over the girls, who had started to breathe deeply almost immediately.

"Hmmm?"

"What do you think we'll find in Denver?"

I didn't answer. Because nothing I could imagine was good.

CHAPTER 9

IT'S easy to say the worst alarm clock in the world is a screaming child. Also, being elbowed in the cheekbone, along with that scream, would ruin anyone's morning. I heard Theo curse, which made me think he also got something to the face as we both bolted upright in the back of the van. Gabby was scrambling from our sleeping positions and her mouth was wide open on a continuous scream.

"Gabby! Stop!" I cried, reaching to put my hand over her mouth.

I noticed her eyes were on me and I turned to see what was causing her extreme freak out. Against the window was a zombie, its mouth pressed against the window. Broken, jagged teeth gnashed, as if it thought it could eat its way through the window to the humans inside. I had a sudden thought of a tuna can and shook my head to think more rationally.

"Ok, ok. It's alright, little one. We'll just drive away, ok?" Theo said, in a low, soothing voice.

There was a bit of pleasure when I noticed a red mark appearing on his forehead. Gabby had gotten him good in her fight to get away from the window. I looked over at the zombie again. It was an old man who looked like he was decaying even before he became a zombie. The old jean overalls he wore were ripped and faded. His gray hair was shooting out in all directions, with a piece of his scalp flapping where it had been torn away.

I grabbed Gabby and pulled her into my lap, pressing her face to my shoulder, so she didn't have to stare at the dead man any longer. She clung to me like a monkey and I used my arms to pull Tina in with us, as Theo slowly backed the van off the dirt road. The zombie tried to follow, but tripped and fell without the van to hold it up. I could see it struggling to its feet through the windshield, but it had no chance of catching up to us.

On the asphalt, Theo carefully turned the van and drove, while I held onto the girls in the back. Once we were a decent distance away, he pulled over to the side, and we quickly fixed the seats so the girls could strap in. Tina's diaper was changed, and we all did our business outside. I made each of the girls their morning milk and gave Gabby a fruit cup. While Theo drove, I sat on the floorboard, feeding Tina the fruit from another cup. She wanted to do it herself so badly, but food was scarce and we couldn't afford to let a baby lose what there was.

Theo consulted the North Dakota maps again and began to build a path south, so we would eventually cross over into Colorado. He didn't pressure us to hurry or be patient with no stops. But I knew at times, when his gaze was faraway, he was wondering if we'd make it in time to find his family. We switched off driving, so I drove into the night and Theo took care of the girls. We decided not to stop this time and just ate snacks and gas station foods we had. Theo slept in the front seat while I drove.

We crossed into South Dakota before we switched drivers and filled the tank with the gas we had on top of the van. I fell asleep easily in the passenger seat while Theo drove. When I woke, the sun was high in the sky and the girls were playing in their seats. I stretched and looked over at Theo, noticing the tightness around his tired eyes.

"How did I sleep through their morning routine?" I asked with a yawn.

"You were dead to the world. The girls and I played the quiet game, to make sure we didn't wake you," he said as he smiled up into the rearview mirror.

"Who won?" Gabby called from her seat.

"I think we all did, little one! Vicki woke up on her own. You girls did a good job," Theo replied.

Gabby let out a little whoop and Tina tried to mimic her until the two of them dissolved into giggles. I looked around and realized we were on the outskirts of a town.

"Are we looking to stop?" I asked.

"The van is getting low on fuel and we used the last we had to fill up last night. Plus, anytime we can find more food, that's a good idea. We're running pretty low on a lot of things."

I nodded, knowing this was just the way of things now. Theo slowed the van to a crawl as we studied the first set of houses we drove by. It was a ghost town, with nothing moving to give us any sign if there were people or not. As we drove by one house, I swore I saw the curtains shift and I tapped Theo's arm to point it out. We slowed further and could see a person moving behind the fabric. They didn't seem to want to contact us, so we continued driving.

We found a parking lot with quite a few abandoned cars outside an elementary school. There were also military vehicles parked there, but we could see no one. Theo pulled into the lot, and we each grabbed our weapons. The crowbar I carried wouldn't do much against a human that might want to shoot me. I just hoped they tried to talk before pulling the trigger.

"We should make sure there aren't people inside the school before we take gas. We don't want to steal from survivors," I said.

Theo nodded his agreement. Neither of us wanted to create hardship for others, or face a fight we weren't prepared to handle. I turned and got the girls settled, Gabby knowing the routine now. When we left the van, we used the inside locking mechanism, so there was no honking noise. Gabby's head peered through a back window for just a moment, but when she saw me looking, she waved quickly and ducked down.

I shook my head as we walked. That girl would be the death of me in one way or another, I was sure of it. I tried to get my mind in the moment and followed Theo to the nearest wall of the school. The gate around the buildings were wide open, providing no protection from anything. The windows were grimy and dust covered. I ran my finger along one of them, watching as a path of clear glass followed.

"No one has been out here in a long time," I whispered.

"Or they haven't cared about the windows," Theo replied.

We moved toward a door that was partially propped open with a brick on the ground. The interior of the school was pitch black, and I saw no reason to continue inside.

"Theo, if anyone was in there, it wouldn't be so dark and quiet."

Just as I spoke, something metal clanged inside, the noise echoing toward us. Theo raised an eyebrow at me, and I just stared at the opening. Something felt terrible about the school and I didn't think I wanted to go anywhere near it. Theo stepped toward it, and I reached out and grabbed his arm. When he looked back at me, I just shook my head.

"Can't you feel that? It feels like death. There's nothing living in there, Theo. I just know it. Let's just get our gas and go."

As if my words brought something to fruition, a ghastly hand reached out from the darkness and wrapped around the door. On impulse, I rushed forward and kicked the brick as hard as I could with my booted foot. It skidded inside and I slammed my body against the door. Theo joined me, even if his face was covered in confusion. The starving groan that rose from inside was enough for us both to panic and throw all of our weight into securing the door.

The hand of the zombie that was reaching for us through the gap was preventing us from closing the exit. It didn't feel any pain, as we continually crushed its wrist between the door and the frame. On our third slam, we looked at each other and timed our push, so all of our strength was behind it. The sound of crushing bone was barely audible over the moans that were joining the first. The hand fell limp and finally disappeared inside, and we could slam the door shut.

Slowly, we backed away from the door, waiting to see if we had done the job fully. A chorus of noises was now echoing inside and I realized I was right. The school was nothing but a tomb for the dead. As we put distance between us and the building, I noticed things I hadn't seen before. I pointed down the wall, where I could see broken out windows.

"Are those bullet holes?"

Theo followed my gaze and nodded affirmation.

"So, someone was shooting into the building. I wonder if that was before or after the people inside became zombies," I mused.

Suddenly, the doors in front of us burst open, and a scream was ripped from my throat. Theo quickly took in the scene before grabbing my hand and sprinting for the open gate entrance. Once there, we slid to a stop and Theo worked to close the gate entrance.

My eyes were frozen on the horror coming our way. Over

twenty zombies appeared as they staggered and tripped to get out of the school. The door behind them swung, but stayed open as more bodies pushed through. I could barely see that the inside was a push bar and it must have popped open when all the bodies pushed against it just right.

There were women and men. Some adults were in military uniforms that must have belonged to the vehicles in the parking lot. But the thing that was going to give me nightmares was the children of all ages. I couldn't help but wonder if there were family units among the zombies. Did they know they were family? Or had family members turned on each other and feasted until they spread the disease?

"Vicki! Help me!" Theo called, breaking into my thoughts.

I grabbed one side of the gate that was stuck behind overgrown weeds and dirt. As I started yanking, the gate only made slight movements.

"I think it's stuck!" Panic seeped into my voice.

Theo got the other side closed, but it did no good without the other to latch onto. He came to me and we pulled together. I looked up at the zombies again. They were gaining ground faster than we were moving the gate.

"It's not going to work. We need to just run," I said.

"The fuel...," Theo's voice trailed off as he calculated the time and distance just as I had.

"We'll find something else." I grabbed his shirt and tugged him back until we were both running for the van. Theo suddenly changed direction and ran straight for the military vehicles. I ran to keep up, confused about what he was doing. At the first vehicle, he went straight to the back and yanked on the doors. Surprisingly, they sprang open. He looked around and cursed under his breath before moving toward the other one. There, he also pulled open the back doors and immediately found what he was looking for: a handgun.

Without another word, Theo grabbed my hand and started running back toward the van. The zombies had already come out of the gate and we were their primary target as they moved toward us. Theo unlocked the van just as we got to the doors. He slammed the fob into the ignition and the tires screeched as we turned for the parking lot exit. Gabby and Tina slid around the back until I climbed over the center console and gathered them into my lap.

"What's happening, Vicki?" Gabby asked.

"There were too many monsters there, kid. We just gotta find somewhere else to get gas."

After a few turns, Theo finally breathed a sigh of relief as he slowed the van to a stop. I peered over the seat, so I could see out a window and saw we were in a residential area. There were no zombies to be seen, nothing moved down the street. Theo laid his forehead against the steering wheel, and I wasn't sure what to say. The fear of this world was growing each day, and we only had each other for support in surviving.

"Are you ok?" I knew the question was dumb, but I wasn't good with communicating, so it was the only thing I could think to say.

"Yeah. Glad you stopped me from going into that building." His voice was slightly muffled, but he didn't sound upset.

"It was probably supposed to be a safe place for those people. Something the military was going to barricade, maybe? Obviously, that went wrong."

Theo just nodded against the steering wheel. I put the girls in their seats and looked around the neighborhood a bit more. The driveway we were in front of led to an open garage with two cars. There were broken windows on the house and the front door stood open. A large brown stain marred the white door, telling a larger story of the house. I tapped Theo and pointed.

"No one is living in that house. We should take any gas they have in those cars. Pull the van into the driveway."

When he lifted his face, I could see his blue eyes were haunted. I could almost see the reflection of the zombie children, because it was all I could see in my mind as well. I tried to smile, knowing it looked more like a grimace. There was no way to console each other over what we had seen, what the entire world likely looked like. For me, having a plan helped keep me focused on moving ahead. One foot in front of the other, as if I was trying to pass a DUI checkpoint. As long as no one tried to get me to say my alphabet backward. I could barely do that forward when sober.

The girls climbed into the back of the van again, Tina thinking this whole thing was a great game. She kept climbing and making herself fall in dramatic fashion. And then she would erupt into a fit of giggles. I wondered what went on in her head. Gabby was older and was well aware of how dangerous and scary things were. She could also realize they had lost their mother. I wasn't sure how much of that Tina realized. And that thought made me even more sad. Would she remember how much her mother loved her?

Theo moved the van, and we both climbed out cautiously. Again, I was sure I saw people moving within windows, but no one called out or opened a door.

"You're much better at this than I am. I'll watch your back while you get the gas," Theo suggested.

I nodded, though I didn't think I was good at it at all. At least I wasn't getting mouthfuls of gas anymore, though I still ended up smelling to high heaven somehow. One car had a full tank, likely filled just as the breakdown of things was happening. The people in the house probably had an escape plan in their minds, or at least wanted to be prepared for a long drive.

Instead, somehow, they had all died, if the blood splashed on the door and porch were any sign.

The van had a full tank, and we had an extra ten gallons by the time we were done. We stood facing the house. The gun Theo had found was in his hand, pointed at the ground. All I held was my trusty crowbar.

"Do you know how to use that?" I asked.

He lifted it up, checked the chamber and then ejected the clip, looking to see how many rounds were left. He slammed it back home and pointed it back at the ground.

"Yeah. I don't have perfect aim or anything. And without more ammo, it won't help for long. But for now, it's a good weapon."

I just nodded and stared at the house and the door from the garage that led inside.

"Should we do this?" I didn't mean for my voice to sound frightened, but there was a quiver in it.

"If we're stopped here, we need to look for supplies. Even a pan or pot we could use over a campfire would make cooking some actual food easier."

He was, of course, correct. I sucked in a breath, giving myself an internal pep talk and to get myself together. Theo led the way, and I followed closely, checking each corner of the garage for threats. It was doubtful there was anything in the house with the front door wide open. But if there was nothing to grab a zombie's attention, they just seemed to wander aimlessly. There was no knowing what would be inside. Theo's hand was on the garage door and he reached back to confirm I was close.

When he opened the door, the smell was the first thing to hit me. It was a mixture of rotten food and death. I pinched my nose shut to make sure I didn't gag as we stepped inside. The garage door was near the front door and we could now see the full story of the blood on the front porch. On the ground in the living room, there was a dead body. Flies swarmed around it, buzzing happily on the perfect specimen for them. I didn't move closer, but the wound to the face was clear, and I was fairly sure it was a zombie that someone inside the house had killed.

There was nothing but silence and buzzing insects inside. We stood still, just listening and waiting for anything to surprise us. When nothing did, Theo led the way further into the house, where we expected a kitchen to be. The tile floor was littered with broken glass and ceramic that I guessed were plates and bowls. There was a full shelf that had been pulled down, and the fridge stood open. That was the source of the horrible stench. Theo used his foot to push it closed.

I went to a pantry door and was just about to swing it open when something slammed into it from inside. I jumped back and almost slid on the glass. Theo was at my side immediately, staring at the door. A grunting moan came from inside and we knew it was a zombie.

"Probably only one," Theo mumbled.

I held up the crowbar, and he nodded. He went to the door and looked at me for confirmation. Yanking the door open, he stepped back so the zombie didn't see him. Dead eyes locked on me immediately and hands that were shredded to pieces lifted toward me. It had been a woman, and looked as if it had been in the closet for some time. The inside of the door was marred with scratches and then lines of blood and gore as the zombie had tried to fight its way out.

When it was within striking distance, I didn't wait. I brought the crowbar up across my body and, with an arching back arm swing; the metal slammed into the temple of the zombie. The dead eyes didn't change, but the body buckled in on itself and fell onto the shattered glass. For good measure, I brought the bar down on the back of its head as well, until I heard the crunch of bone.

"Ok, ok. I think it's done," Theo said, holding up his hands to get my attention.

I was out of breath. I just looked down at the mess I had made. Brain matter and blood covered the crowbar. I felt sick and couldn't handle the sight. Quickly, I wiped the bar off on the zombie's clothing, knowing its time as a beauty contestant was long over. Theo went into the pantry and made a tsking noise as he looked around. When I joined him, I saw what he was seeing. So much of the products that had been in the pantry had either spoiled or were ruined by the zombie battling itself and the need for fresh food.

We could recover a bag full of canned goods. Vegetables, beans, tuna and olives all went into a paper bag. There were two plastic bags of pasta that had expired but weren't gross, so we risked it. I was excited to find two boxes of generic cheese cracker snacks in the back, away from the nastiness of the zombie. After searching some cabinets, we found the pots and pans and took a couple of small ones, as well as a strainer, for the noodles. On a last minute thought, I grabbed the boxes of plastic snack bags. I didn't know what I'd use them for, but I knew with two kids they would come in handy.

Outside, we took our time loading the supplies and organizing the back of the vehicle. The girls played near their seats. Theo and I would pause and look around, making sure nothing was sneaking up on us. In the distance, a sound echoed into the neighborhood, and my hand froze over a box of crackers. Theo similarly stopped moving, and we both listened, waiting. Turning from the van, we watched the road and the surrounding houses.

At the end of the street, a black vehicle appeared. It hesitated, but I knew the moment they had spotted us. As it drew closer, I realized it was a more dark green, and it was clearly a military vehicle. I had no trust for other survivors and had had no reason to trust the government that had failed to protect its citizens. I turned abruptly and waved to get Gabby's attention. When she met my eye, I signaled for them to hide and be silent. Her eyes widened with fear, but she didn't disobey. She pulled a blanket over them and popped Tina's pacifier into her mouth.

"Should we close the trunk?" I whispered.

"If we do it now, it's like we're hiding something," Theo replied.

"We are hiding something!"

Theo glanced back and turned more fully toward the approaching vehicle, using his body to shield the van. I busied myself with the supplies again, because I knew my face hid nothing. I stacked up the two cases of water we still had, so they partially blocked where the girls were sitting as well. When I heard the vehicle pull to a stop behind us, I slowly turned, concentrating on keeping my face blank.

A man in the passenger seat rolled down the window and peered at us. Theo immediately went into his charming personality. He smiled widely and raised a hand, while stepping forward slowly.

"Wow, it's been so long since we've seen anyone else! How are you guys? Where are you from? Near here?" He fired off questions, as if he was overwhelmed, but I could see his eyes were slightly guarded.

"You two alone?" The soldier asked, not cracking a smile or answering any of Theo's questions.

"Yes, it's just the two of us. We're making our way to Colorado," Theo responded.

My eyes ping ponged back and forth between the men. I didn't trust myself to say a word. I picked up on how Theo wasn't giving them all the information. Not telling them about the girls and not telling them exactly where we were going. I just nodded my agreement about Colorado and turned to close the trunk of the van.

"Why there? Have you heard of the Rapid City installation?" the soldier asked.

"Know people out there. And no, we haven't heard of any installation."

The soldier looked inside and exchanged quiet words with the driver and someone that was sitting in the back. The windows were tinted, so all I could see was the outline of someone's head. There was no way to tell if they were male or female. When the soldier turned back toward us, he was also popping open the door and stepping out of the vehicle. I pressed myself against the back of the van, refusing to move and allow them to see the girls.

"We're the last active military regiment in the country. We are gathering survivors in Rapid City. You'd be safe there. You should follow us back. It's not far from here," the soldier said.

I studied him carefully. He was armed with a handgun on his belt. I could see other weapons inside the vehicle, between his seat and the driver. With the door open, I could see the driver better and realized he was a basic copy of the passenger. They were both clean cut, their uniforms perfectly pressed and spotless. Even the boots the man stood in were shined and clean. Everything about it felt off.

Theo casually put his thumbs in his front pockets and shifted. He subtly moved to block me and it was then I realized that while I was studying him, the soldier had been staring at me the entire time. His eyes were hot and if the van hadn't been blocking my way, I would have stepped back. I knew what lecherous looked like, and the man's face was painted with it. My stomach turned as I imagined what he was probably thinking while he gaped at me.

"We appreciate the offer. But we'll continue on our way.

Once we find our people, we'll be sure to spread the word," Theo said.

The soldier side stepped, so he could see me again. The smile he sent me had promises that I wanted nothing to do with.

"What about you, sweetheart? You'd be well taken care of if you came with us." His head indicated the vehicle and a quick glance confirmed the driver was staring as well.

I swallowed and just shook my head, not sure how to reply. The soldier made to step forward, but Theo stepped back into his path, not allowing him to get closer to me.

"My wife is fine staying with me. I've kept us safe for this long. Like I said, we appreciate the offer. And we'll mark it on the map." Theo's voice had gone arctic, and I could see the set of his shoulders tensing.

His handgun was in the back of his pants, hidden from the soldiers. I wondered how fast he could pull it, if the men really tried to fight. The soldier looked from Theo and then me, his eyebrows pulled together, as if he was trying to determine if Theo was lying. It wasn't lost on me that Theo was painting a lie, and I needed to play into it. Cautiously, I stepped forward until I could slide an arm around Theo from behind and rest my head on his back. His body was rigid and on high alert. I just waited for the signal that things were going to go down a road we couldn't come back from.

The silence stretched out and I could no longer see the soldier or the vehicle. Hiding myself behind Theo, I actually felt safer and less on display for eyes that I didn't want studying me. I felt dense, not thinking about the threats from the old world that would easily carry over into the apocalypse. I had to be walked to my car almost nightly after work, due to whatever drunk thought they were going to take me home that night. Rarely did it get physical, because I knew how to deflect intoxicated intentions. But now, with no law, judges or juries, people who wanted to take what they wanted had nothing to stop them.

"Alright. Remember, we in Rapid City are here for you. For any of your needs. You remember that too, ya hear, sweetheart?"

My mouth felt like ash as I realized exactly what the man was insinuating. I just nodded my head against Theo's back. I didn't attempt to make eye contact. That would only encourage the conversation further, and that was definitely not what we were looking for. Theo nodded, and then his arm shifted until there was a sound of palms slapping together. Holding tightly to him, I let him know I had his back should things go downhill. But, after the handshake was done, I heard the door of the military vehicle close and the engine revved until it was moving away from us.

"You're shaking," Theo murmured.

Quickly, I released him and stepped back. He wasn't wrong. It was like my system had been flooded with adrenaline suddenly and I didn't have any way to spend the energy. I felt sick to my stomach, and I took some deep breaths to make sure I didn't make myself puke. Theo turned to watch me but said nothing. I held up a hand as I closed my eyes and focused on calming my heart. A tap inside the van had me whirling and Gabby's face was peering from the edge.

Theo opened the back hatch, and the girls were right there. Tina almost pitched forward, so I picked her up and put her on my hip.

"Are they going to help us?" Gabby asked, looking down the road.

"They weren't looking to help all of us," Theo said cryptically.

We quickly got the girls settled in their seats, giving them each a baggie of crackers to munch on. Theo didn't look at the map, but immediately went in the opposite direction of the military vehicle. He wound around the small town, checking the mirrors constantly.

"You don't think they'll follow us, do you?" I whispered.

I glanced over my shoulder, making sure the girls were busy with their snacks and toys. Gabby had her tongue between her teeth, trying to focus on a coloring book, despite the moving vehicle.

"I really don't know. But they didn't exactly give me a trusting vibe."

"Me either. Do you think this Rapid City place is real?"

Theo took a moment to consider my question, as he took another turn, which brought us to the back of a grocery store. He stopped and looked at me.

"Something must be real, because I have seen no one that clean and polished since this all started. They must have power wherever they're from. And running water."

I nodded, because those were all thoughts I'd had when I saw them.

"What I do know is, any man that looks at you that way isn't one to just follow without caution," he continued.

I couldn't disagree. The memory of the soldier's eyes on me made the hair on the back of my neck stand up, and I immediately had to look around to make sure I wasn't being watched. I didn't want to need Theo, but I couldn't help but think about what could have gone differently if I had been alone with the girls and the soldiers had stumbled upon us.

CHAPTER 10

WE SPENT the rest of the day hiding behind the grocery store and arranging the fresh supplies. I glanced at the building more than once, badly wanting to go in and see if I could find any sort of powdered or boxed milk that hadn't expired. We were almost out of the supply we had started with, and I didn't want the girls to go without.

I stared at the can in my hand for a long moment, realizing I didn't know what was healthy for the kids. What did they really need? I was assuming they needed milk, vegetable and fruits. I picked up a can of vegetables and read the nutritional facts, noting all the vitamins that were listed. All of that was really important for growing kids, I had no doubt.

Theo started a small fire on the asphalt with dead wood he had found in the green space behind the store. We added two cans of peas to one pot we had taken from the house and waited for the liquid to steam. He added crushed up mushrooms, without the girls seeing. Once the peas were hot, I spooned some into one can and smashed it into a puree for Tina. When I came toward her with the food, her little mouth was working in anticipation. At the first bite, she frowned, but then swallowed and opened for more.

Gabby sat with Theo on the back of the van and ate quietly, without complaint, though I could read the displeasure on her face. Both of the girls finished their peas and mushrooms completely and each had a cup of milk to wash it down. I gave them each a fruit snack pouch as well, to fill them up so they would sleep well.

I stood facing the store, my mind whirling. Theo joined me and just waited quietly.

"I'm going to go inside," I said.

"I'll come with you."

Shaking my head, I motioned behind us. "Stay with the girls. I'm tired of leaving them alone. But I also don't want anyone else taking risks I could take myself."

Theo frowned, but he didn't disagree. I expected him to try to stop me. However, the truth was, one of us had to stay alive to take care of the girls. The stronger of the two of us, the more prepared, the smarter, was definitely Theo. I wasn't trying to just sacrifice myself, but I wasn't blind to who would take care of the girls better.

I grabbed my crowbar and an empty backpack. Gabby watched me without a word.

"I'll be back, kid. Just seeing what this store has to offer. Maybe I can find some juice or something else for you girls to drink." I plastered on a bright smile, that didn't phase Gabby in the least.

As I walked away from the van, I refused to look back, as if I was saying goodbye and needed one last look. I needed to show I could provide for them. I knew nothing about forging wild plants, fishing, or hunting. So far, I had realized I could kill a zombie or two out of sheer anger and fear.

The front of the store didn't look any better than any of the others we had encountered since the beginning. The doors were completely gone, ripped off their hinges and taken somewhere. Trash created a path from the entrance, across the parking lot. It was difficult to not feel immediately deflated. I couldn't imagine there was much left inside the building. I took just a moment to feel bad before gathering just enough hope that made me still walk into the dark inside.

Flicking on my flashlight, I shined the beam in front of me. The inside looked much like I had expected. Displays had been destroyed. Someone had pushed shelves over, toppling multiple aisles together. I reminded myself that we weren't too proud to dig through the trash as needed. Using the beam of the flashlight, I searched under the shelves. When I found what looked like an intact plastic bottle, I reached in and pulled out a pack of Gatorade drinks.

The small win gave me more energy to continue to look through the mess. My light illuminated a wet circle of dark material and I debated within myself. Slowly, I walked toward what I knew would be a gruesome discovery. In the back of the aisle I had been searching, I found a man's body propped in a sitting position against a dark freezer. His hand still held the handgun that he had used to end his life. I could see the bite on his leg that never had the chance to fester and infect him, as he took things into his own hands.

As carefully as possible, I reached over and removed the gun. I knew nothing about it, but I couldn't be sure Theo wouldn't find it useful. I slipped it into my pack and prayed it didn't somehow go off and shoot me in the back. That would be my luck in life. Shoot myself and die from an accidental wound, instead of something like a zombie attack.

Moving back toward the aisles, I found two partially crushed boxes of cereal and one box of oatmeal packets. I wanted to cheer out loud, knowing the girls would love both finds. Stacking my finds by the door, I continued to search each aisle. I didn't find any sort of milk substitute, but I had known that was unlikely. I was excited when I found two cans of apple juice, though I had never seen canned juice before.

When I brought the first armful over to the van, Theo whistled low and made space in the back of the van. It took three trips, but I was able to get everything packed away. I even found one fleece blanket that hadn't been soaked in blood or other unknown substances. We rearranged the back of the van again, knowing we would need to constantly move things to sleep inside the vehicle. It was still our safest option.

We laid the fleece down, so we all had something softer to lie on than just the carpeted backs of the van seats. The girls were fairly exhausted and curled up without complaint. I begged Gabby to not wake us up with screaming even if she saw a zombie. I had to reassure her over and over that the doors were locked and she was safe inside. Once the girls were asleep, I pulled out the gun I had found inside the store.

"I wasn't sure if it was like the one you have or if you could use it," I said, handing the weapon to Theo.

He turned it over and pulled out the clip to check the bullets.

"It's not the same caliber as the other one, but it's better than nothing. Having two can't hurt anything."

I shrugged. "I wouldn't know. I've never shot one."

"Maybe I could teach you."

I thought about the idea for a long moment. But I knew I didn't like the idea of being responsible for a weapon like that, especially not with the girls around. I shook my head and picked up my crowbar.

"I'm doing fine with this. I wouldn't feel safe around the girls with that."

Theo didn't push. He packed the guns away in his bag and

put it in the driver's seat out of reach. I lay next to Tina. As I tried to get comfortable, the baby rolled toward me and dug her hand into my hair, holding me hostage. I sighed and adjusted until my head was comfortable on a small pile of clothes. Wrapping my arm around her little body, I pulled Tina into me until we were cuddling. It had become her normal routine, and I didn't see any reason to keep fighting it.

The next morning, when we got back on the road, we headed straight for Denver. We had enough food to make the trip, and we were topped up on gas. Theo was eager to look for his family, and I wanted to get as far away from the Rapid City military installation as possible. I hadn't been able to shake the unease sitting in my stomach after meeting the soldiers. All night I had woken, believing someone was looking in the van windows. But every time I looked around, all I saw was empty moon lit glass.

With the girls full from breakfast, the first half of the day was easy. We didn't hit any blocked freeways that slowed us down. There were also no other moving vehicles in the area. I didn't speak my inner thoughts, because everything was dark and negative. Theo's family could still be alive. The possibility wasn't zero. However, what made them so special that they survived when clearly almost no one else did?

We had to stop three times at cars along the road, to fill up the van and then refill the gas cans. But Theo was determined to reach Denver before nightfall. I wasn't sure if it was all that likely, but I would not be the negative Nancy in his world. We had enough of that on our own.

The van had a CD player but only came with country music CDs, definitely not my favorite. However, once the silence was just too much, I popped one in so we could have music on our road trip. The music seemed to make the girls happy as they danced along in the back seats. Every once in a while, Tina would slide from her seatbelt and I would have to climb back to secure her again. I kept trying to look for a car seat that would work for her, but I got distracted way too easily.

It was after dinner time when Denver's skyline came into view. Theo started to speed through, cutting off the freeway once it was too clogged to even drive along the shoulders. It was clear to me that people had tried hard to evacuate. As far as the eye could see along the freeway, it was bumper to bumper vehicles. Some were crashed. Some were twisted black remains from fires. And roaming zombies bumped along in the spaces, also not able to move far from what would be their tombs.

When we got into a neighborhood that was familiar to Theo, his fingers drummed against the steering wheel. His impatience was palpable, and the van was thick with it. I watched the buildings we passed, seeing how the condition of the neighborhoods got worse the deeper we went. But I didn't say a word as Theo took corners too fast.

Suddenly, he hit the brakes, causing the van's tires to screech and the vehicle to skid to a stop. Theo threw the gearshift into park and jumped out without turning off the engine. I stared in horror as Theo ran for a burned out foundation and remnants of a house.

"Vicki?" Gabby's small voice broke the silence of the van.

"It's going to be ok, kid." My response was automatic. I didn't truly know if anything would be ok again.

Reaching over, I turned off the engine and pulled the keys out. I popped open my door and stepped out onto the sidewalk. A mailbox had been knocked to the side and was laying at my feet. It had been painted canary yellow with flowers that were faded from time in the sun and snow. I locked the van doors behind me, wanting to protect the girls.

Theo was on his knees, pulling at half burned wood, tossing pieces haphazardly to the sides. A vehicle could be seen under the roof of the attached garage. I walked toward it and peered through the windows, confirming there was no one inside. I didn't try to move any of the rubble, afraid of creating a tidal wave of destruction that could bury Theo and me.

There was nothing that indicated his family had tried to leave the house and got caught when it fell down around them. But that didn't mean it did not bury them under the piles of ash, wood, brick and other materials. But Theo continued to dig with his bare hands. I waited on the sidewalk, as the sun disappeared behind the buildings left standing and soon the moon was all that lit the neighborhood.

Tina began to cry in the van, and I knew I couldn't wait much longer. I could hear Gabby trying to shush her, but the baby was getting uncontrollable. Her exhaustion was at a breaking limit.

"Theo?" I called, keeping my voice low, so not to draw attention. So far, we had pulled no zombies our way, and I didn't want to risk it.

Theo's shoulders slumped, and he bent low over the pile he had been digging in. Looking back at the van, I made sure there was no one around the get to the girls and then turned my flash-light on to make my way to him. His body shook in a way that told me he was crying and I was afraid to see what he had found. I knelt and studied the side of his face. His eyes were squeezed shut and his hands were fisted on his thighs.

Carefully, I put my hand on his shoulder and squeezed softly.

"What is it?" I asked.

Tina's wails were echoing, and I was stuck between getting the girls settled and getting Theo back into the van. When Theo didn't acknowledge me, I moved my flashlight beam to the hole he had created in front of him. Leaning over, I saw that once he removed the first layer of debris, he could see into a large space below. Everything was burned almost beyond recognition. I could just make out melted frames that were probably hung on walls. The frame and springs of a couch were covered in pieces of the house that had fallen.

I moved my flashlight beam around until it settled on what looked like a skeletal leg with a melted shoe at the end. I stared for a long minute, my brain not comprehending what I was looking at. So many other things came to mind, but it was just me grasping at straws, trying to make it not reality.

I leaned back and covered my mouth. Theo took a deep, shuddering breath next to me.

"They didn't make it out," he said in a broken voice.

"How do you know it's not someone else? Maybe they evacuated and someone else was using the house." I tried to pull any rational explanations from my thoughts, anything to console Theo.

Tina let loose a loud scream that made my head spin to look behind us. The sound also seemed to shake something loose in Theo, as he climbed to his feet next to me. Down the street, I could see movement, but it was too dark to be sure of what was coming our way. There was no way it was a welcome wagon, bringing us a basket of freshly baked cookies and a house-warming gift.

"We have to go." His voice was solid ice, none of the Theo warmth shining through.

I couldn't disagree. The figures in the shadows were multiplying, and soon our exit could be blocked. My heart ached for Theo's loss, even if my mind knew this was what he would find and he should have expected it. Having people meant you had something to lose. As if to remind me that I wasn't a lone ranger any longer, Tina screamed at the top of her lungs. And then Gabby's pitiful cries joined, and I knew we were up the creek.

Theo hurried away from the hole he had found, away from

whoever was burned below. He hurried toward the little girls that were relying on us, that needed us to keep them alive and fed. As he got to the driver's door, I unlocked the van. I climbed directly into the back with the girls and held the keys out for Theo. He didn't make eye contact as he took them and fired up the engine.

As I slid the van door shut, something slammed into the other side of the vehicle. Gabby screamed and scrambled toward me. I grabbed her and shoved her into her seat.

"Stop moving. And for the love of everything, stop screaming! You're going to make my ears bleed!"

Theo pulled from the curb slowly, hitting another zombie that had stepped into our path. It bounced off the front of the van and landed in a heap. Tina was still on the ground, trying to climb to her feet, but wasn't able to with the van's movements. Her crying continued until I plucked her off the ground and held her in my lap in her seat. I secured the seatbelt around us both while she buried her wet face in my neck.

"Where are we going?" I asked as Theo turned off of his family's street.

"Somewhere quiet for the night. Then we can think about it." His answer was clipped and short, but I didn't take it personally.

Theo drove as if he knew the area, taking decisive turns toward an unknown destination. I watched the black buildings pass until we came to a large sign for a hotel. Theo entered the parking lot and rounded the back of the building. When he turned off the engine, everything fell silent. Theo rubbed his face hard before turning in his seat to look back at us. Tina had fallen asleep as soon as I was holding her. Gabby had wide, scared eyes, but she had stopped crying.

"I used to work here. We'll still sleep in the van, since it's the safest thing. But we should be safe from anyone stumbling on us," Theo said.

I just nodded, without a clue of what to say. My parents were gone long before I knew who they were. I had lost no one that actually meant anything to me, so I wasn't sure how to empathize with him. Instead, I slowly got to my feet with Tina in my arms. I had to hunch over inside the van, but I could move enough for Theo to put down the captain's seats to create our sleeping area. We didn't bother with organizing, just pushed all our supplies to the sides and found places for our feet to lay.

I laid Tina down carefully, but her grip on me was steel, so I awkwardly laid down with her at the same time. Normally, Gabby would lie in the middle, but she hesitated and moved to lay on the other side of me, moving until she could put her little arm around my waist. Immediately, I felt too hot and uncomfortable. We were all sweaty and filthy, making me feel sticky and disgusting. I kept my body completely still, although I was feeling claustrophobic, with two little bodies attached to me.

Breathing through my nose and out my mouth, I worked to slow my heart and the panic that was rising in me. They were less than half my size. I could throw them off immediately if there was an emergency. I reminded myself that they were completely reliant upon me to live, to survive. And while I wasn't always excited with the responsibility, it wasn't their fault and definitely wasn't their choice to be stuck with me.

Movement on the other side of Tina caught my attention, and I looked up to find Theo sitting with his back against the driver's seat. I could only see the side of his face as he gazed out the window. As I stared, a tear rolled down his cheek, and he dashed it away roughly with his palm. The panic in my chest rose again, the serious emotions happening, making me feel completely uncomfortable and out of place. I couldn't decide what the right thing to do was. Reach out to him? Let him mourn in private? I finally decided to close my eyes and put my face into Tina's hair. My fumbling attempt to console Theo would not help him in any way.

I didn't think I would fall asleep, but before I knew it, I was in a dreamscape that felt all too familiar. I found myself in my apartment, alone, drinking a glass of whiskey. A loud banging on my door made me jump, and I ran to answer, afraid of what could be happening. It wasn't so much a dream, but a memory. When I swung the door open, the girls were there, but this time, it wasn't their living mother bringing them. They were screaming, with a being behind them, that had been their mother.

In my dream, I hesitated, watching as the zombie made it toward the girls. Her hands were up, her face was already covered in blood. The scene felt confusing, as it was no longer my memory but a nightmare conjured by so many days of horrors. The blood on her face made me look down at the girls again, and the nightmare took on a different color.

Tina now laid lifeless at my feet. If I hadn't seen her alive just moments before, I wouldn't have known it was the same baby I had been taking care of. Her face was completely gone, bloody bone showing through in places. I stumbled back into my apartment, tripping over my coffee table and falling back. At the door, a second growl rose and my breath felt like it was ripped from my chest. Gabby, with her throat completely ripped out, was stumbling toward me. Her stare was the dead, vacant hunger that mirrored her mother's behind her.

In my dream I screamed, while in the waking world, my name was being called and my shoulder was being shaken. My eyes popped open, only to squint against the sun that was coming through the van windows. Tina was sitting on Theo's lap, her face fearful. But it was Gabby that had her hand on my shoulder. I scrambled back from her for a moment, before I realized she was alive and not a zombie child trying to eat me. Her eyes were wide with questioning and the edge of worry.

"I'm sorry," I said, holding up a hand for them to give me a moment.

Looking around, I tried to grab hold of reality and make the nightmare fade. I crawled to the small side window that popped out and opened it to get fresh air on my face. I sat there for a long time and no one spoke, except Tina's random noises. The van moved, as Theo bounced her on his knee, giving me the time and space I needed.

Eventually, the fear from the dream faded, and I could push the remnants back. I moved toward the supplies and pulled out a can of juice. Using a manual can opener, I opened one side and poked a hole in the other for ventilation. It was a muscle memory, as I used to have canned pineapple juice at the bar. I poured a cup for each of the girls and carefully walked over to them on my knees.

They trained their gazes on me with trepidation and wariness. I thrust the cups out. Tina took hers with gusto and shoved the sippy nub into her mouth. She hesitated for a moment when she realized it wasn't milk, but then drank with gusto. Gabby was slower, taking her cup and bringing it to her mouth. All the while never looking away from me.

"You were yelling my name," she finally said.

"In my sleep?" I turned and moved back to the food, not wanting to admit that she was a zombie in my nightmare.

"Yeah. Were you having a bad dream, Vicki?" Gabby asked.

I shrugged. "I don't remember. But if I was yelling, it must have been a bad one. It's gone now."

Dried cereal went into snack bags and I handed one to each girl. They began shoving the food into their mouths immediately. Looking around the van, Theo and I could confirm there weren't any immediate threats. Climbing from the van, I stretched my back and hips. My body was screaming at me, which told me I probably laid on my side between the girls the entire night.

I watched Theo out of the corner of my eye. His movements were sure, and he didn't seem exhausted. But that didn't confirm that he had slept a wink all night. The silence between the two of us was continuing into a new day, and I wasn't sure I could handle the nerves it was causing in me.

"Did you sleep?" I finally asked.

"Some," he replied.

I cursed in my mind. His short answer didn't leave me anything to build on. I knew I was going to have to start a conversation I didn't really want to have.

"Theo, you don't know it was them in there. And you don't know if there was more than one person," I said, keeping my voice calm and quiet.

"They weren't going to leave until I got here. If I hadn't gotten taken by The Children, I would have been here way sooner."

"That's not your fault," I insisted.

"I trusted the wrong people. It's totally my fault. And now, somehow, my family home burned down with my family in it." His voice was rising, and I grimaced, looking around us. He took a deep breath and turned to look at me.

"I'm sorry," he said.

"I'm still not convinced," I replied.

He scrubbed his hands through his already messy hair. I would be irritated with him later, with how it still fell into fashionable waves when he finished.

"And if they weren't in there? If they aren't dead? What do I even do?" He asked.

I had actually thought about our next steps before I fell asleep. My mind wouldn't stop working. While I wasn't sure what our next steps would be, I had thought about what Theo could try with what he had left. I didn't know what it was like to have people you'd want to find as the world fell apart. But I wanted to help Theo survive what was to come.

"What about leaving them a message? I saw the mailbox. What if we put it back up and leave a letter in there? A note to tell them where to find you? I don't know where that is yet, but when we have a destination, we could put it in the mailbox."

Theo looked over at me, hope sneaking back into his eyes. It was the look I was used to with Theo, and it made me feel more comfortable in our situation. Then he smiled, and I was suspicious of what was going on in his mind.

"I have an idea about that," he said.

CHAPTER 11

"YOU AREN'T SERIOUS," I said.

The small smile that Theo had shown me earlier in the morning was now full blown across his handsome face. I stared, deadpanned, at the chain-link fence and beyond in front of the van. Gabby climbed from her seat and stood between our front seats, so she could see what we were looking at.

"Are we flying somewhere?" she asked innocently.

"Neither of us can fly those things," I grumbled. Then I turned wide eyes on Theo and said, "Can we?

Theo just laughed and shook his head. After he'd told me he had an idea, we had packed up the van, strapped the girls into their seats and started driving. I had been nowhere in my life, so I was at a complete loss as Theo made his way through the neighborhoods until he could find an open freeway on-ramp. I had asked questions, but Theo just kept telling me to wait.

Now, we sat outside a chain-link fence, staring at the Denver International Airport. We weren't by the terminals, though. Theo had wound around until he found an access road that took us right to a chain-link fence that was locked with a padlock. On the runway, several planes sat, abandoned mid apocalypse. There were the remnants of yellow inflatable slides hanging off the sides of some of them. More ominous were the planes that still had sealed doors.

"What are we doing, Theo?" I asked.

"We need somewhere to live, right? We can't keep driving to nowhere. I thought about the airport, because it's in the middle of nowhere. And a plane, well, it's up high, away from zombies if they did somehow get beyond the fences. We can bring whatever we need out here. Stay for a while," Theo explained.

I tried to picture it, and it didn't really make sense in my mind. But Theo seemed so worked up about the idea. I wasn't about to deny him. He was right about the fact that we had nowhere to go. We didn't have any safe places in mind. I wasn't someone that trusted just anyone, so I would be fine if we found a way to survive just the four of us.

"Uh. Ok," I replied.

"What about you, little one? Wanna live on a plane for a while?" Theo asked, turning just a little so he could look at Gabby.

Her little face screwed up in concentration and I was sure she was having some of the same reservations as I was. But then she smiled at Theo, her complete trust in the man, and nodded enthusiastically.

"I'd like to not sleep in the van anymore," she said.

"When I was a kid, I used to make my mom bring me here, so I could watch the planes. I once told her I'd live on one. She laughed. But now I have the chance," Theo said.

I had only dreamed of living in one house, with a family that wanted me. Childhood fantasies were something I had spent little time on. When I looked at Theo's face, I could see this was his way of pushing away the grief and trying to move forward with something. I decided the best I could do, was support his plan, even if I couldn't see how it would work. I could give Theo this, after all he had done for the girls and me.

"It's better than going back to Rapid City and finding out what those men had to offer," I murmured.

"If that was even an actual place," Theo replied.

I nodded. Sighing, I motioned toward the runway.

"How do you intend on getting us out there?" I asked.

Theo whooped, and Gabby mimicked him. From the back seat, a squeal joined, and even Tina was feeling the excitement. All I felt was a headache coming on. However, I realized that if the planes were intact from their last service, I might find the one thing I needed most. Alcohol. Even mini bottles would be better than nothing. That thought gave me the boost I needed to focus more on Theo's dream coming to life.

We drove around on the access road until we found a security entrance that was likely used for deliveries. A rail and concrete columns that had been brought up from the ground blocked it. Clearly, someone had tried to break in before security was gone. Theo tapped the steering wheel for a moment, before putting the van into park and climbing out.

I watched as he went around the front of the car and slowly approached the security stand. The door of the small building was closed, and Theo jumped back as something slammed inside. He leaned over and peered into the windows, looking for an open spot. When he saw whatever he needed, he nodded and pulled his hunting knife. Opening the door, Theo took a step back. I held my breath, waiting for the appearance of what I knew had to be a zombie.

The figure stumbled out, arms outstretched, trying to reach the only living thing it had probably seen in months. The uniform gave away the story. It was the security officer that was probably trying to protect the airport as the plague rampaged. It continued toward what he thought would be his meal, and Theo danced to one side before slamming his knife into the zombie's temple. The security guard, turned monster, collapsed and Theo pulled it away, hiding it behind the security office.

When Theo appeared at the office door again, he held his nose. I could only imagine what type of smell was stuck in the small space, with a zombie decaying day after day. He disappeared, and I waited patiently with the girls climbing all over the van. When the concrete barriers dropped into the ground and the rail lifted, my mouth dropped open.

Theo came out with a huge smile on his face, running back to the van. Within moments, we were driving on the runway, looking at the planes parked at gates and planes that were lined up along the runways. I couldn't help but wonder what was happening inside the airport buildings. During the beginning of the plague, people had panicked and tried to travel all over the world to get away from populated areas, or to get to family. I was sure the building was full of zombies, just waiting for someone to stumble upon them and release them to feed.

"There!" Theo cried, and he turned the van toward a white and green plane that was last in the line of the planes.

I realized immediately why he was shooting for that one. While many of the planes either had sealed doors, telling us there was nothing good to find, and others had the remnants of slides, the plane Theo pointed at had a set of stairs parked at its front entrance. It would give us a way to get into the plane, without having to find a ladder or some other mechanism. Immediately, it felt too good to be true and butterflies were swimming in my stomach.

We pulled up next to the stairs, and Theo looked at me.

"Should we check it out first?"

I nodded, not prepared to take the girls into a situation we would have to fight our way out of. Gabby knew what we were saying and immediately had taken Tina to sit on the floor by their seats. I climbed back to get water for them and gave them snacks before leaving them. When I left the van, I had my crowbar at the ready.

Turning a big circle, I felt uncomfortable and couldn't put my finger on why. But then I realized it was the most open space I had been in since the apocalypse started. I would have thought being able to clearly see around me would be a comfort. But for some reason, it was making my skin crawl and would take time getting used to.

Theo was already on the steps, waiting for me to catch up. He pointed down at the front wheels of the plane.

"Someone already put the blocks in, so this plane isn't rolling anywhere," he said.

I nodded. It was just something else I wouldn't have thought to worry about. Theo was noting things as we went. We both studied what open windows we could see. No movement showed, and we carefully entered the fuselage. At the entrance of the row, there were discarded suitcases, purses, laptops, and phones. But as we looked up and down the aisle, there were no living or dead people inside. We carefully checked the bathrooms, the cockpit, and even the small closets that were used by the flight crew.

"There's really no one in here," Theo mused.

"Did you expect something else?"

"I wasn't sure. This just feels like a good place to hold up, ya know? No one is just going to stumble on you. Zombies can't get up here," he said, as he lifted a suitcase out of his way.

"Maybe no one sees this as a comfortable living situation? I know as a kid it seemed fun. But looking at it now, where are we going to sleep?"

I had so many other concerns, but my first was, the only open spots were in the front and back areas where the small flight attendant areas were. There were the aisles, but we would have to lie out our beds every day and that seemed like a lot of work. Not to mention not a good way to control the movement of Tina if she couldn't fit next to me or Theo.

With my words, Theo crouched and looked at the ground, before kneeling down and crawling slowly.

"What in the world are you doing?" I asked incredulously.

His head popped up over a seat again and looked at me. "I'm seeing what tools I need."

Standing up, he met me at the front of the plane.

"See what I see, Vicki. Just for a minute. I know you think I'm as sharp as a bowling ball. But I have a vision." He flashed me a grin that was almost his normal signature, but there was still that tightness that was pulling at him.

"Please, go ahead, lord bowling ball." I gestured, opening my arms wide.

That made Theo bark out a laugh before he started talking, gesturing around as he described his picture.

"We'll use the back flight attendant area for supplies. Maybe we can even find a generator to run outside and run a power cable up to the backdoor. I'll remove at least three of the back rows, toss the chairs out. We'll create a play area for the girls, find them more toys, kids need toys. And we'll create a sleeping area. Until I can find the tools, we'll make the aisles work for sleep, but I promise Vicki, we'll make it comfortable."

I really tried to see what he was describing. Theo's excitement was probably something people found infectious. For me, it was overwhelming and felt disingenuous. In my world, getting excited over something was usually the sign that things were going to fall through the cracks and disappointment was on the horizon. That life experience made it really hard to just jump on board and believe in the dream.

What I knew was we couldn't keep driving with the girls in

tow. They needed a break, needed a home for even a little while. Having some sort of home base where we could collect supplies, make actual meals and sleep full nights was a priority. And though the plane idea felt insane to me, I didn't have a better option.

Theo was watching me the entire time, waiting for my reaction. His bright smile slowly dimmed as he realized I wasn't just jumping for joy with the idea. Feeling guilty for bringing him down, when I knew he was wrestling with a lot more at the moment, I tried to paste on a smile. I nodded, though maybe not enthusiastically.

"Ok. If you see all that, I think we can try it out. I'm sure rent is cheap," I cracked.

Theo smiled and patted my shoulder.

"It's a steal."

He headed toward the door, but I went back into the flight attendant area. I had seen a drink cart during our initial search, and I had to know what was on it. Pulling out the first drawer, I found canned sodas and juices. I filed away the fact that those would be useful and pulled out the next drawer. I could have cried when I saw the perfect rows of mini bottles.

Checking over my shoulder, I confirmed that Theo had gone back to the van. I grabbed the first bottle my hand could touch. Vodka. Without a thought, I opened the small lid and downed the entire contents on an empty stomach. The alcohol burned down my throat in a familiar way, though my stomach roiled slightly. I found a bag for trash and put the small bottle in it, as well as some other trash I found on the ground.

That was how Theo and the girls found me, cleaning up trash, to hide the evidence of my fall from grace. Gabby immediately began to run up and down the aisles and Tina tried to follow as fast as she could. By the time they made it down the aisle twice, I had filled the bag with napkins, newspapers, magazines and a few rotting food products. Theo took a moment to study the back door and figured out how to open it, motioning for me to toss the trash out.

The long fall to the asphalt below made my head go fuzzy, though I was figuring the vodka was probably flowing through my blood stream too.

"We need to figure out a way to keep the girls from falling out," I said.

"We'll keep it closed most of the time. The air will flow better when it's open, but we'll only do it once or twice a day."

I nodded and turned back to the girls. They had bright smiles on their faces as they climbed into seats and played with the seatbelts. Even if I wasn't sure about the plan of living in an abandoned plane, the girls were clearly happy. It was new for me to judge life based on the reaction of two children, but that was where things were now.

Theo and I took turns going to the van, bringing the supplies up. I brought the girls their toys and books so they could play and keep themselves somewhat busy until we finished. I also gave them cheese and crackers, since it was getting close to lunch and I didn't want them getting too hungry. The anger that came with that was just too much at the moment.

I snuck one more bottle from the cart as I was grabbing a can of juice for the girls. This one felt more typical, and my stomach didn't feel as upset. I also found airline pretzels, and I chowed down on a bag, just to make sure I didn't puke up pure alcohol. Theo found me at the cart and he grabbed a soda for himself, but didn't even bother checking the rest of the drawers. I handed him a bag of pretzels and smiled, which I knew looked suspicious by the look he gave me in response.

With the girls settled with juice, crackers and pretzels, Theo and I started going through the carry-on bags that were left behind. We stacked all the electronics in one aisle. Every bag had either a tablet, laptop, phone or some sort of headphones. If we could get a generator up and running, there could be a use for something. I had high hopes for some sort of downloaded movies or entertainment. I missed music and sounds other than people's voices around me.

Going through people's belongings felt morbid, especially when I reminded myself that most of these people were likely dead. When we found purses with wallets, I couldn't stop myself from peeking at passports or driver's licenses. After a while, all the faces were the same, and I stopped looking. However, purses proved to be a treasure trove for medications. We had a nice supply of over-the-counter pain, allergy and cold medications. There were also laxatives and other stomach medications that could come in handy. We packed all of those together in one bag and put it with the plane's first aid kit.

Suitcases were full of clothes, shoes, toiletries and more. We only got through the first few overhead bins before the girls got restless and the sun started to get low in the sky. I found one small suitcase with a popular kids cartoon character on it. The clothes inside were a bit big for Gabby, but they would be useful once we could figure out a showering situation. I mentioned that to Theo while I was sorting through it.

"Camp shower. I've been thinking about a few things. We need a place for a bathroom, that's somewhat sanitary. Also, need a way to shower. I wonder if the water is still running somewhere, to make it easier for us," he said.

So that was our next project. We packed the girls back into the van, something they weren't super excited about, and drove toward the airport building. As we got closer, it was clear there had been complete chaos at the end, with vehicles crashed or abandoned haphazardly. A trolley that must have been carrying luggage had been tipped over and the suitcases were strewn across the ground.

With night approaching quickly, we didn't find the water source we were hoping for. However, we found a catering truck. The smell coming from inside was putrid, but we were both pretty sure there were items that were sealed and still edible. Holding my nose, I sorted through airline snacks, finding nuts, crackers, pretzels, cookies and candies. We loaded the van up of everything we found edible, including cases of water that were left.

At the plane, I realized I was again in a second-floor apartment, lugging groceries up the stairs. But now, I had two kids in tow that I had to somehow keep from following me every time I went back down to get another load. On my last load, I passed Theo on the stairs, only to catch Tina with one arm as she tried to topple off the top step and follow him. I carried her under my arm like a football as she struggled and argued to follow Theo.

"Kid, if you make me drop you and then cry like I did it on purpose, we're not going to have a good night," I growled.

Gabby's head popped up in a row and she slowly sunk back down, recognizing quickly that my mood had soured. I didn't know if it was because two shots of booze wasn't enough, was wearing off, or that I wanted more, but my mood had twisted. Knowing the little bottles were within reach made me itch to drop Tina in the nearest seat and drown myself. But I didn't. I took the baby to the row Gabby was in and sat her down carefully. In my head, I was dropping her, and she was bouncing off the seat, just so I could teach her a lesson.

"Watch her so we can pull together food for dinner, ok?" I asked Gabby.

The five-year-old, who was barely old enough to learn to tie her shoes, nodded solemnly, as if watching a baby was totally in her wheelhouse. I sighed and walked back to the open door to wait for Theo. The last load was one more case of water, which he dropped near the cockpit. We had no need for all the components in there, so we were using it for storage of clothing and other items we may need later.

Theo closed the front door, not completely, but enough that neither girl would escape in the night. The plane pitched into almost complete darkness and I switched on my flashlight.

"Lights, we'll need to think about that too," Theo murmured, adding to a mental list I could actually see him making.

Dinner consisted of packages of beef jerky that weren't even big enough for the girls, nuts, fruit snacks and a can of corn. The girls were happily full by the time the food was done, though my stomach barely felt like I had anything in it.

"Tomorrow, we'll figure out a cooking set up. Maybe near the backdoor, so we can cook inside with the door open for fumes. Or maybe under the plane belly," Theo said.

His uncanny ability to read my mind irked me. I could read drunks on a barstool. I often could guess drinks, or knew it was too much long before the drunks fell off their seat. Theo smiled too much. I was pretty sure there was no way he was as happy as he acted, so I guessed he hid his true feelings under the blinding smiles and optimism.

We had collected all the travel blankets, airline blankets, and neck pillows. With the two blankets we had in the van, we created a nest for ourselves on the hard ground in the back of the plane. There was barely enough room for the four of us to lie together in a row. Theo and I laid on our sides, so we could enclose the girls and ensure no one went wandering off in the middle of the night.

Gabby slid her hand into mine and I jumped, still not used to being touched all the time. But when she squeezed my palm, I wrapped my fingers around her little ones.

"Will we get beds?" She whispered.

"That's the goal."

"Sleeping on the ground sucks," she said.

I choked on a laugh, wondering if sucks was an okay word for a five-year-old. But then decided it was better than some things she'd heard me say.

"Yeah, it does suck, kid."

She moved closer until she could tuck her head under my chin. In my head, I reminded myself that kids craved physical touch. If I allowed myself to think about the memories of my childhood, I would remember the number of times I needed a hug so badly, but there wasn't one adult that cared enough to even try. I didn't want Gabby to have those types of memories, along with losing her mother and living through an apocalypse. With that thought, I put an arm around her back, and she melted into me.

I could feel Theo's eyes on us, but I didn't dare look up. Tina was already asleep on her back, next to him. I knew I could trust him to be aware of the girls, to not let them get hurt, or leave the bed during the night. He was strangely positive, and that gave me pause. However, that didn't mean he wouldn't do the best for the girls.

After my nightmare the night before, I wasn't sure I would get a full night's sleep. The warmth of Gabby flowing into my skin helped me fall asleep much faster than I expected. Thankfully, I wasn't cursed with any additional nightmares. The only thing that woke me was the girls' restless movements. I had learned early that they didn't stay still ever when sleeping.

When sunlight was peaking around the edges of the window shades we had pulled down, I stretched and found Gabby still asleep next to me. Theo and Tina were wandering somewhere on the plane, but they were so quiet, it hadn't woken me. Carefully, I climbed out of our nest, making sure I still covered Gabby with a blanket. I found Theo and Tina standing near the open door, fresh air flowing into the fuselage.

"Good morning," Theo whispered as I approached.

Tina giggled a little as he held his finger to her lips, reminding her to be quiet.

"I don't know how you keep her quiet. I couldn't for a month living in my apartment." I frowned, feeling quite disgruntled.

"It's all a game, really," he said.

I looked beyond him, out onto the runway and at the airport beyond.

"Any movement? Threats?" I asked.

Theo shook his head.

"Earlier, the sun was just perfect, and I could see movement in the windows. I'm pretty sure it's all zombies."

"That's freaky to think about. It was probably thousands of people trying to get away, and just a few sick people could have started a mini apocalypse inside." I couldn't stop the shiver that went down my spine.

Theo just nodded and looked toward the windows that we couldn't see into any longer. I suddenly wondered if his family could be inside. Maybe they were attempting to get out of the city and got caught like thousands of others. The shadows in Theo's eyes told me he likely had some similar thoughts.

"Vicki?" Gabby's sleepy voice came from behind us.

I turned, and I knew what she always needed the moment she woke up. I also needed it, the bathroom. We had decided until we had some sort of setup, we would walk to the strip of grass in the middle of the runway to do our business. I led Gabby down the stairs and across the runway. The wide open area again made me feel nervous, but I constantly moved my eyes around to make sure nothing snuck up on us.

By the time we got back to the plane, Theo and Tina were

downstairs. Tina was in her last clean outfit and Theo had changed into clothes he had found in one suitcase. She had a cup full of water and was chugging away on it.

"It's time we go shopping," Theo said.

"Shopping?" I just raised an eyebrow at him.

"Well, it sounds better than looting, stealing, robbing? Doesn't it?"

I snorted. "How about scavenging? Surviving? Trying not to starve to death?"

"Nope. Shopping sounds much better. We're going shopping." Theo's bright smile was back and both of the girls were falling into it.

Gabby flashed me a big smile, and I just grumbled and jogged up the stairs. In a row in the back of the plane, I had thrown clothes that were somewhere around my size. Most of them were too big, but that was better than too tight. I changed into a pair of sweatpants. They were too long, so I tucked the bottom of the legs into my boots. I threw on a clean oversized t-shirt and with just those changes, I suddenly felt like I had a brighter outlook for the day.

Theo had the girls strapped into their seats when I returned, and I heard him promising Gabby that we would find car seats for them today. It hadn't been on the top of my priorities list, even if it should have been. My list started with alcohol, went to food and bedding supplies. I knew Theo's list was much longer, because he was the planner.

Climbing into the passenger seat, Theo pulled us away from the plane and I watched as the other planes and airport passed the windows.

"Do you think our stuff is safe out here?" I asked.

"As safe as it could be anywhere. Eventually, we won't leave as a group. We'll have a better set up and maybe not even have to leave often."

I tried to figure out how Theo's optimism worked. Was it a never-ending well that just fed him all day long? Maybe he had a drinking problem too, and he was drunk most of the time and I just didn't know it? That thought made me want to laugh, but I pushed it down, knowing Theo would ask what was so funny. No, I was sure Theo's cheerfulness was with no liquid help. I probably hated him.

CHAPTER 12

"THIS ONE SEEMS right for her weight," Theo said.

He was pointing to the fourth boxed car seat we had found in the store we were in. I was surprised and suspicious to see how the outskirts of the Denver suburbs were less destroyed. Theo saw it as a sign and was reassured we were doing the right thing by staying in the area. I reminded him we had little choice in the matter.

"I guess." It was the fourth time I had said it, because that was all I had to add to the conversation.

I knew nothing about car seats. I could read a box like anyone else. But I didn't know which type of harness was most effective, or if she should face forward or back. Though Gabby filled in the gap on that, insisting that their mother hadn't turned Tina around in her car seat yet. According to two of the boxes we read, she could be turned around now that she was almost two. I just wanted whichever seat was easiest.

Gabby was easy. She walked directly to a display and pointed to the seat that looked like the one her mom had in their car. It was some sort of grow with your booster and I grabbed it from the display and put it in one cart we were pushing. But

Gabby insisted she didn't want the blue one from the display and Theo searched until he found a box with a pink one of the same make and model.

The searching for baby seats felt like it took half the day. Then there was the time it took to install the devil contraptions. There were so many straps and buckles, I didn't know where to even start. So, I stood like a statue while Theo worked, reading instructions as he went.

Once that task was done, Gabby was excited to climb into her seat. She could buckle herself in and I could see immediately why she was happy. The straps didn't hit her in the throat and she could see us much easier in the front seats. Tina didn't enjoy being strapped in and she started to wail when we tried to test out the seat. I pulled her from the car, shushing her, looking around to make sure she didn't bring an entire horde out of hiding.

We went back into the store and took our time through the food aisles, taking whatever we thought we could cook. I was excited to find a section of shelf stable food for preppers. I threw three large cans of powdered milk into my cart. It would be unlikely for us to finish those before we had to move on. Or someone made us move on. The nagging thought didn't leave my brain.

Together as a group, we slowly went through the canned food areas. The jarred pasta sauce area had been cleared out and other jars were broken on the ground. The effect looked bloody, even though there were no bodies around. Theo left Gabby and Tina with me, as he carefully walked through the glass and bent to search the entire shelf. He turned with a smile when he showed he had found two intact jars.

The back of the van was half full with just food, but we also needed supplies to create beds and something to cook on. In the bedding area, I found mattress toppers and beds in a bag with comforters, sheets, and pillowcases. I loaded a cart with pillows for sleeping and throw pillows. When I rolled by the kids bedding area, I found large pillow stuffed animals and I grabbed ones I thought the girls would like.

Once the bedding was added, Theo and I stared at the lack of space.

"We have to get a camp stove. Proper food needs to be cooked," Theo murmured, more to himself. Again, I could see his mental to-do list rotating behind his eyes.

"We'll make it fit if we find one," I replied.

I was ready to get back to the plane. Since leaving my apartment, I had missed having even a slight moment to feel safe. To feel like we had a place to be. That was ours. Scavenging in the city felt like a risk every time we did it, even though I knew it was necessary for survival and comfort.

Theo drove us to a sporting goods store. We studied the front. The glass doors had been shattered from the inside, and the glass littered the sidewalk across the front. Theo parked the van across from the entrance and checked his gun, as was his habit.

"You stay here with the girls. No need for all four of us to go inside. Honk if there're any problems," he said.

I wasn't going to argue. The relative safety of the van helped calm my anxiety and I could give the girls their lunch snacks. I watched as Theo disappeared into the darkness of the store. For a short time, I could still see his flashlight beam bouncing around inside. Once he disappeared, I climbed into the back and pulled out packs of crackers and beef jerky for the girls to start on. I also had a can of orange juice to split between the two of them. Every few moments, I would glance back at the store to ensure Theo wasn't in trouble.

The sound of a cart being pushed caught my attention, and I could see Theo's flashlight beam. An echoing squeaking sound accompanied the cart, and it made me wince. I climbed from the van with my crowbar and checked the area. As the cart got closer to the door, the noise got louder and banged around the buildings in the shopping center. Theo paused inside the doors for a moment, looking at something on a rack, when I heard another sound coming from behind me.

Whirling, I immediately found what new sound had joined the mess. Two zombies had responded to Theo's call with the cart and were shambling toward the van, the girls, and me. I moved to the other side of the van, watching as they approached, unsure if I could really handle two of them. In the back of my mind, I heard the cart again, but I was too focused on keeping us safe.

One zombie began to pull away, my movements encouraging it to increase its speed. Even that speed was a slow walk. But it was enough that I could hopefully deal with one at a time. I moved quickly to meet the first zombie, just as Theo's cart pulled up next to the van. I lifted the crowbar above my head and brought it down on the top of the zombie's head.

The crack noise was loud, but the zombie didn't fall immediately. Dead hands reached out to grab at my shirt. But I pushed them to the side and brought the metal bar down on its head again. This time, the blow knocked it sideways, so I could bring my weapon down a third time in the same place. The crowbar smashed through the skull and the zombie stopped moving.

The second zombie was a small man in a mechanic coverall. He was slowed down by one pant leg someone had ripped down from his thigh and a huge strip of flesh that joined it, dragging at his feet. I could feel bile in my throat as I noticed all the details. This time, I didn't hesitate to hit the zombie in the temple, causing it to buckle to one side. I hit it again, as it tried to grab at my feet. I didn't stop until my crowbar came away with brain matter coating it.

I was breathing hard by the time Theo came running to my side. He looked around, his hunting knife in his hand.

"Are you ok?" He asked.

"I handled it."

"I can see that. I asked if you're ok."

I looked over at him, prepared to snap something rude. But his face was only filled with concern, so I bit my tongue and just nodded my head. He nodded in response and looked out toward the main street again. Way off in the distance, there was more movement and suddenly an engine sound broke the silence.

"Time to go," Theo said, grabbing my arm.

We ran back to the van, where Theo had left the cart. A large box was in the cart, with a large picture of a flat top griddle. I caught just a glimpse of a brand name with the word black in it, but didn't bother paying attention as we opened the back of the van and rushed to find space for the grill. We smashed the bedding bags around the girls and fit in the grill. The whole time we worked, I was sure the engine was getting closer.

Theo shoved propane bottles by my feet and we climbed into the van. I had my knees in my chest as he turned and headed toward the parking lot exit. Just as we were about to turn out, a vehicle appeared and skidded to a stop in front of us. Theo cursed loudly and slammed on the brakes.

"Bad word!" Gabby cried.

"Not the time!" I yelled back.

The vehicle in front of us was some sort of black upgraded jeep, with large tires meant for rock climbing, black gas cans strapped to the back and pitch black tinted windows. We just stared through the windshield for a long moment, waiting to see what would come next. Suddenly, the driver's side window rolled down and the face that appeared completely shocked me.

An older woman with wild, red, frizzy hair poked her head out of the window. She was wearing dark glasses to cover her eyes, but her grin was huge and I was pretty sure she was missing a tooth. Theo and I didn't move a muscle. But the woman waved at us like a madwoman.

"Hi! Hello! Oh, hello!" She yelled.

"She is going to bring the dead out from their damn graves if she doesn't shut up," I murmured.

Theo's hand went to his door, and I reached over and grabbed his arm.

"We know nothing about this woman. She could shoot you the moment you climb out!"

I expected him to ignore me, but his hand went to the window button instead. Rolling it down, he leaned slightly out to reply to the woman.

"We're just going!"

A frown appeared on the woman's face and she popped open her door. My jaw dropped open as she jumped from the jeep, and I realized she was less than five feet tall. She reached into the jeep, raising on to tiptoes so she could reach, and pulled out a weapon that she strapped onto her back. It looked like the handle from a shovel, but with a hatchet at the end. She then turned back to the van with a huge, inviting smile on her face.

"It's been a while since I've seen anyone else around here. Are you new to the area? Or have you always been here? You're real right? I'm not just seeing things?"

We didn't respond, just watched her from the safety of our vehicle.

"Is she a bit crazy?" I asked in a quiet voice.

"Maybe if she's been alone for a long time? What do you want to do?" Theo suggested.

The woman had her hands out in the open and was slowly walking toward us.

"I guess answer her. I don't want her getting too close to the girls." Glancing over my shoulder, I could see Gabby's eyes were wide and locked on the woman in front of us.

"We're just passing through," Theo called out.

"That's ok, that's great! My name is Bet. Short for Betty, which was short for Elizabeth. But in my old age, shorter is so much better. You're passing through. Do you have somewhere safe to go?"

Just as she yelled at her last word, she swung her weapon off her back and my hand went to my crowbar. Theo's hand hadn't left his gun the entire time. But instead of rushing us, she turned back toward the Jeep and the zombie that had approached. I hadn't even noticed it come into the parking lot. Bet swung the pole once in a large arch above her head, before grabbing it with both hands, jumping in the air and slamming the hatchet down into the head of the zombie. The entire movement felt like a dance, more than a fight.

I murmured a curse under my breath, not willing to get called out by Gabby for language at the moment. Theo repeated my sentiment as Bet yanked the hatchet free and gore flew from the zombie. Without preamble, she strapped the weapon back on and came back to face our van.

"Where were we? Do you know of a safe place to go?"

"We heard of a place called Rapid City in South Dakota," Theo replied.

Bet frowned and shook her head.

"I heard about that place. But I heard stories. I'm not going near that. Wait...so...are you real? Or am I talking in my head?" Bet asked, as she started to pace in front of the van. Her voice dropped, and she continued to talk to herself, motioning with her hands.

I cut a look at Theo, and he just shook his head at me. He didn't have any answers about the baffling woman in front of us, either. Bet continued pacing, wringing her hands, talking. And something about her tugged at my heart. There was clearly not something exactly right in her mind, and that wasn't her fault.

My hand was the one going toward the door now, and Theo caught the movement. He grabbed my arm to get my attention, and I turned to look at him.

"Have your gun ready. If she comes at me, shoot her. Anything else happens, you get out of here with the girls," I said.

"Vicki...," Theo started.

"Look at her, Theo. I don't trust anyone that's outside of this van. But that woman, she doesn't have people. She's lost. I just want to reassure her we aren't a figment of her imagination."

"I have your back," he said, releasing my arm.

The sound of the door opening caused Bet to freeze and look over at us again. I carefully climbed around the propane tanks and placed my feet on the ground. Standing up, I realized I had overestimated her height. I towered over her. But she didn't seem afraid. Instead, her smile bloomed again, and she stepped forward. I held up a hand to stop her and she froze, but didn't stop smiling.

"You aren't talking to yourself. My name is Vicki and I'm definitely a real person," I said, raising my voice just enough so she could hear me.

"Vicki, short for Victoria?"

"Just Vicki." I shook my head, thinking how I only knew my name to be Vicki and nothing fancy like Victoria.

"It's nice to meet you, just Vicki," Bet said with a huge smile.

"Have you been alone for a long time, Bet?"

The woman looked at me, tilting her head as she studied me.

"I've never known a Vicki. Not a Victoria either. So you

couldn't be in my head, right? Like if I was making you up, wouldn't you have a name of someone I already know?"

"Sure, Bet. That sounds likely. Like I said, I'm not in your head. I'm real. My car is real. And I'm positive you're real, too."

That caused Bet to bark out a laugh. Suddenly, she moved on quick feet toward me. Fear caused me to step back before I caught myself. Behind me, Theo's door opened, and I knew he was keeping a close eye on things. Bet shoved an empty hand toward me and it took me a second to understand she wanted to shake my hand.

Hesitantly, I held out my hand and slipped it into hers. Her grip tightened, and she pumped up and down longer than necessary. And once the handshake was over, she continued to grip my palm. She pulled me close and gazed up into my face with a serious look.

"Hi, Vicki. I'm glad you're not in my head."

"Me too. Seems it might be a bit confused," I replied.

That got a smile from Bet.

"Sometimes it is. Your friend is nervous. Wanna tell him I didn't hurt you?" She said.

"I'm fine," I called over my shoulder.

"So, you're passing through. Going where? Coming from where?" Bet asked.

"I hope you understand, but we're not really comfortable sharing our secrets. Have you been alone long?" I asked.

Bet nodded. "My husband died during the first wave of the plague. I avoided people after that, not wanting to get sick too. But by the time I came outside again, the dead were everywhere and people were gone."

"Just gone? All of Denver is empty?" I stared at her with wide eyes.

"From what I've seen. I lived downtown, in an old neighborhood that hadn't been torn down for those big high rises yet."

Bet waved her hand back, as if we could see the Denver cityscape.

I could feel my palm sweating against Bet's. I had loosened my hold, but she continued to grip it, as if she believed I would disappear as soon as she released it.

"But you've just stayed in the area?" I asked.

"I live in my Jeep and stay wherever is safe. No where else to go. This has been my home for forty years."

"So just a lot of zombies everywhere, no living holed up around here?" I asked.

Bet just shook her head, but added nothing. For some reason, I wasn't scared of the old woman. I felt sympathetic to her plight. But that sympathy wasn't enough for me to open my arms and life to her, not when I had the girls to protect. Thinking of them made me want to turn and check on them, but I fought the instinct. I didn't want to give Bet any reason to study the van any further.

"Well...like we said. We're just passing through, also just living from place to place. We might stay in the area for a little while, I mean if we find somewhere to stay. Maybe we'll run into you again," I said.

This time, I pulled my hand from Bet's and wiped it against my sweats. I saw how her eyes flitted from me to Theo. She was looking for something to say, somehow, to continue the conversation. I looked around and still saw nothing that gave me worry.

"Sure, sure, sure. I understand, right? We all gotta be safe somehow these days, right?" Bet said, stammering slightly.

"Right. So, uh, see ya around?"

Bet nodded sadly, but she let me move toward the van. Theo was still standing in his open door, not showing his gun, but I knew it was at his side. Bet spun and went back to her Jeep, but she stopped and looked back at me.

"Could we see each other again, Vicki?"

I looked over at Theo before I responded. He just shrugged his shoulder, leaving the decision on my shoulders.

"Sure. How about tomorrow? We'll meet you here, in this parking lot. Same time?" I replied.

Bet's smile was huge and hopeful. With little thought, I actually liked the quirky little woman. She nodded her agreement and jogged back to the Jeep. I watched in fascination as she tossed her weapon into the passenger seat and then launched herself from the ground up into her driver's seat, without the help of a step. She waved in an exaggerated manner at me before peeling away, making a loud noise that was our signal to get moving.

Back in the van, Theo let out a huge gush of air as he started the engine again.

"What was that?" He asked.

"A very crazy old lady. I like her."

"From that, you decided you liked her? I'm more worried she'll chop someone up in their sleep."

Bet just didn't strike me as a crazy serial killer. Just a woman that had been alone for too long, without a great handle on reality. But what she could do was kill a zombie with some finesse. I wasn't sure about her age, but she moved with the agility of a young person. The more I thought about our brief interaction, the more I became curious about who Bet was and where she had come from.

Theo drove around the area for a while, checking corners and watching behind us. I had no doubt that Bet wasn't following us, but I wouldn't argue with Theo's caution. Eventually, he pulled us into a hardware store parking lot. There were smaller stores bordering the lot as well. I studied the names, not seeing anything that would be really useful, except maybe the dry cleaner.

"I'm going to check for some tools. Anything that might help me remove some of the seats. Do you want to stay in here with the girls?" Theo asked.

Suddenly, I spied a shop that boasted old fashioned kids' toys. It was an antique shop, but the enormous poster told me there might be something the girls could use that wouldn't need power or batteries. I pointed to it, and Theo nodded. I climbed from the van and strapped on the baby backpack. Tina was slid into the pack by Theo and we got everything secured, while Gabby climbed from her car seat.

I had a bag in one hand and my crowbar in the other. Gabby's hand was wrapped around my wrist that held the bag and I had made her promise to not let go unless I specifically told her to. Even though she had her own little opinions, she was learning that when I gave her instructions; it was for her safety and she needed to follow them.

I turned my head for just a moment to check as Theo entered the hardware store. He was out of sight within moments, and I turned toward the antique store. The windows and door were intact on the store, which didn't surprise me. When I pulled on the door, I almost fell backward as it opened without trouble. However, a loud bell rang out throughout the shop, something that clearly ran on a battery to announce when customers entered.

Gabby started to step forward, but I pulled her back.

"We always wait," I whispered.

"To make sure the monsters aren't inside?" Her big eyes looked up at me and I nodded.

She turned her gaze into the store and I saw her eyebrows pull together as she studied the interior. After a long minute, when no sound came, I pulled out an old metal milk jug and used it as a doorstop. Once I was sure the door wouldn't swing shut and cause the bell to ring again, I led Gabby into the store.

Tina babbled behind me and I reached back to make sure I could pop her pacifier into her mouth.

The front of the shop consisted of glass cases full of odds and ends. I glanced through, not seeing anything that was particularly necessary. After a few cases, we came to one that was full of knives. It had a sliding door in the back, so I made my way there and opened it. I tested a few of the pocket knives and found a few that were still sharp. I slipped those into my bag. We could never have too many knives.

There was also a display of cast iron cooking equipment and I immediately wanted to take a pan and a huge pot with us. Pulling them from the display, I moved them to sit outside so I could load them into the van later. Gabby stayed by my side, moving her hand to hold on to Tina's backpack while I moved things. She didn't complain or make any more noise than necessary.

In the back of the store, we found what we'd originally come in for. There were shelves along the wall that held a number of older toys. Gabby pointed to a doll, and I pulled it down for her. There was also a white bunny, and I grabbed that for Tina. In addition, I packed up a Rubik's cube, a play typewriter that I knew Tina would love slamming on, a bag that held a Mr. Potato Head and a lot of his accessories, and a few retro Barbie dolls.

Back in the parking lot, we found Theo stuffing tools on the floor under the bedding that was in front of the girl's feet. I shoved the bag of toys into whatever open spot I could find before getting both of the girls back into their seats. I retrieved the cast iron and brought them to the van. Theo caught sight of them and gave me a thumbs up and a smile. It took some work, but we eventually got everything to fit, including us, though my knees were still pressed against my chest since the propane was on the floor in front of me.

Theo drove straight back to the airport, no longer worried about being followed. The nice thing about the Denver airport was it wasn't in the middle of the city. As we headed toward our little hideaway, we left the congested city behind. I watched, wondering if Bet was right, if there weren't living people surviving somewhere in what was once a large bustling city. Something in my chest released, and I started to think we might feel safe for some time.

We arrived back at the airport just as dinner time was coming. I jumped from the van and pulled up the security bar. We kept it down, even if it provided little safety. The thought was, it could possibly deter other living people from wandering onto the runway. As we drove toward our plane, the airport was still completely still, without a thing out of place.

Theo checked the plane again, just out of an abundance of caution. Once it was clear, I helped the girls into the plane and left them in the back with their new toys and strict instructions to not move while Theo and I moved things around. He took his tools upstairs, and I pulled out the cooking implements, leaving them under the belly of the plane.

Together, Theo and I built the grill and hooked up the propane. We immediately agreed on a pasta dish for dinner. Hot food was something we hadn't experienced fully in a long time. I filled up a pot with bottled water and we put it on the grill burner, waiting for it to boil. I brought a box of pasta and a one of the pasta sauces we found. Twenty minutes later, we had hot noodles covered in a red sauce that smelled better than anything I could think of at the moment.

Inside the plane, the girls inhaled the food that was put in front of them. I made sure they each got seconds and ate until they were completely full. They drank juice to wash it down while Theo and I enjoyed sodas. While Theo hadn't been watching, I had cracked open another mini bottle and downed the alcohol, giving myself an additional warmth that even the food couldn't provide.

That night, we still had to sleep in the back of the plane in the small flight attendant area. The girls fell asleep fast, and I was sure that was due to them having really full stomachs for the first time in days. Theo grabbed my hand that I had wrapped around Gabby and squeezed.

"This is going to work, Vicki."

For the first time, a small glimmer of hope poked through my darkness.

CHAPTER 13

THE NEXT DAY, our first goal was running water. After driving around the airport building for a little while, we finally found a spigot. When we turned the knob, clear water poured out, and we cheered quietly before turning it back off. I wanted to dive into it and wash away all the filth I felt on my skin. However, we did not know what the quality of the water was.

"We need a big pot and a good way to boil it. The propane stove won't be good for that," Theo mused.

"What if we built something that could hold a fire? Some sort of fireplace? Away from the plane?" I asked.

That went on Theo's mental list, and we decided it was our next big goal. We needed more water for drinking, cooking and showers. The girls were getting ripe and the four of us in the van created a hot box of stink that was almost poisonous. Together we made a list of the largest pots we could find, plastic buckets, some sort of closed container for cleaned water and a camp shower set up.

We tried the box store we had shopped in the day before. Along with our list, I had agreed to meet Bet again today. We didn't decide on a time, and I was worried if we didn't show, the old woman would start believing she was the only living person on the planet and go even more insane than she already was.

Before we could drive back, we had to fill the van with gas. We used the last of the gas in our cans and strapped them to the top of the van to refill while we were in town. The girls each had a new to them doll as they got strapped into their seats. Tina was sucking away at her sippy cup, full of milk that I had mixed for her before leaving. The milk was one accomplishment I felt I could pat myself on the back for.

Just before lunch, we pulled into the parking lot for the box store and there was the blacked out Jeep, sitting in front of the doors. Bet was sitting on the hard top roof, just watching the entrance to the parking lot. When we pulled in, she climbed to her feet and held her hands over her head, waving us down, as if she wasn't the only thing moving in the parking lot.

Theo pulled the van up to a group of cars that had been left. We had agreed I would speak with Bet alone again, because she seemed comfortable with me. While I chatted with the baffling old bat, Theo would get the van topped off and fill the gas cans. Once we handled Bet, we would get into the store and see if we could find everything on the water list.

"Vicki! You came back!" Bet called across the parking lot.

I hurried toward her, using my hand to motion to her to keep it down. When I got to the Jeep, Bet slid from the hard top to the hood before using the front tire to climb to the ground. She spun toward me and rushed forward. Again, her quick movements gave me pause, and I halted my steps. Bet seemed to understand, and she slowed. Her lips moved soundlessly, as if she was talking to herself.

"Hi Bet. We agreed to come back. I wanted to make sure you knew we were real people and not just in your head," I said.

"Right, right. You're real. I think I know that now. You and your man, driving the van."

"Not my man, but yes." I still didn't mention the girls, not being sure how Bet would react to knowing they were also in the car.

"Well, there's not many people living these days. If he's not your man, he'll be someone else's soon, I'm sure," Bet replied with a laugh.

I just shrugged. I didn't look at Theo that way and we had met no one else that looked at him that way either. Losing my partner in this wasn't something I felt like I had to worry about so far.

"So, are you still passing through? Or will you stay awhile? There's no one else here. It would be nice to have more living people around," Bet said.

Theo and I had discussed what we wanted to reveal to Bet and what we didn't. She had found the places we were scavenging and would likely look for us in the future. I had convinced Theo it would be better for her to know seeing us was a possibility, instead of surprising her each day.

"We're going to stay around for now. So, we'll probably run into you from time to time," I replied.

Bet's eyes lit up, and she bounced on her toes.

"Oh, oh, oh...that's great news. I'm thrilled to hear that!"

I liked Bet. But I wasn't trying to make friends. The woman looked way too excited about the prospect of us being nearby.

"So, yeah. We have things to look for today," I said.

The light in Bet's eyes faded, and I felt guilt rise. But Tina took over for me and released a tremendous scream that bounced around the buildings. Bet's eyes went to the van and they widened slightly, before settling back on me.

"Not your man? But your baby?" She asked, cocking her head to the side.

Unconsciously, I stepped to put my body between her and

the van. She tilted her body to look around me, but I danced in front of her, forcing her eyes on me.

"She's not your concern." The edge to my voice caused Bet to snap up straight and pay attention.

"I'm no threat to a baby or to you, Vicki," Bet said softly. I could detect just a hint of pain in her voice.

I took a deep breath, trying to calm my nerves and my immediate need to protect the girls. It was impossible to know of all the threats we would face. Theo's concerns were sitting in the back of my mind, making it impossible to trust Bet at face value.

"We don't know you yet," I said.

"Right, right. No. I understand. I wouldn't trust me either. Weird old lady, all alone out here in this wasted city." As she spoke, Bet ran her hands through her bright red hair and paced back and forth.

There was nothing for me to say to that. It was true. Bet was a stranger. A weird woman who was zooming through the broken city in a tricked out Jeep, killing zombies with a hatchet stick weapon that I couldn't even put a name to. Although I found her slightly endearing, I didn't trust anyone beyond the people in my van.

Behind me, the van engine started back up and the vehicle approached us slowly. I knew Theo wouldn't come too close, because he didn't know that Bet knew about the baby. It was my signal to excuse myself from Bet and get us back on track with our goals for the day.

"It was good to see you, Bet. Maybe we'll see each other again in a few days?"

She stopped pacing and looked over at me. A small smile appeared and her hope sparkled slightly again. It tugged at my heartstrings, but I pushed it down, remembering who came first.

"That sounds great, Vicki. Good luck finding the stuff you

need. This area is probably good to check, not as many zombies. Don't go into Denver though, not downtown. There are huge groups of the dead wandering around, just looking for something to eat."

"Thanks for that warning. I don't think we'll go much further than this."

"You have somewhere safe to sleep? To live?"

I paused for a moment, trying to evaluate what information I wanted to reveal. I decided with the vague truth.

"Yes, we're safe. As safe as anyone can be these days."

Bet nodded an agreement and turned to make her way back to the Jeep. She vaulted up into the driver's seat and rolled down the window to look back at me.

"See ya soon, Vicki with her not her man and baby."

Her joke seemed to be hilarious in her mind. Her laughter flowed out the open window as she drove out of the parking lot. Anxiety drained from my body as the engine sound of her Jeep faded into the distance. Theo pulled the van between me and the store.

"How did that go?" He asked as he climbed from the vehicle.

"She knows there's a baby. She heard Tina scream."

Theo looked in the direction of Bet's exit. "Do you think that's a problem?"

I recounted the conversation to Theo, so he could come up with his own conclusions. He nodded as I spoke, while opening the van doors and getting the girls ready to go inside. We brought a backpack for Gabby to wear as well, so she could pick things she wanted to take back to the plane. As Theo strapped Tina onto my back, I finished my story and turned to look at him.

"What do you think?" I asked.

"Not quite sure. So far, it all seems fairly normal for a woman that's been alone for months."

There was nothing to do about Bet, so we focused on our needs. The four of us made our way slowly into the store. Now that we knew the interior of the store, it was easy for us to move around safely. We had to go deeper into the store than we had ventured before, and it got darker the further we went. I held Gabby's hand and the flashlight, while Theo wielded weapons for protection.

Near the sporting goods and outdoor area, a smell came to me that made me freeze and pull Gabby to a stop. I flashed the light around. Theo turned in circles, also picking up on the scent of decay. Nothing moved near us, but something dead was in the store.

"I'll go. Stay still and scream if you see anything," Theo whispered.

I nodded and pulled Gabby to me so I could press her against my leg. I pulled my crowbar from where I stashed it between my back and Tina's pack. Tina fussed, but I shoved her pacifier back and she quieted down quickly. I listened to the sounds of the store. Theo's quiet footfalls moved into the distance. I could hear my heart pounding in my ears and Gabby's panicked breathing. But there was nothing out of place.

What felt like ages later, Theo appeared in my flashlight beam. His face was sad, but his weapons were still dry. He came close and brought his mouth near my ear.

"Dead body in the camping area. Looks like someone that came here to camp in a tent they had found. But I guess they decided they didn't want to live alone."

He didn't have to clarify beyond that. The smell told the story that the person had given up. I nodded. But then Theo held up his hand to show me a box. It had a picture of a pouch with a shower head attached. I had no idea how it worked, but it was one thing off of our list and I didn't want to go into the camping area again, knowing the dead body was there.

We moved toward kitchenware, finding three large stockpots. With those in hand, we couldn't carry much else. Gabby spied crayons and coloring books as we walked toward the door. Theo helped her fill her little backpack, but also tossed in the jelly beans that he saw on the end cap. We loaded her down, and she practically skipped. She was so happy with her haul.

He had just told her a joke and her giggle was bubbling out when we got to the open door. There was only a split second of warning before a zombie fell into Theo. Gabby's scream was ear piercing. Theo grunted under the weight of the zombie, as it was a large woman who was actually taller than him. It had Theo's shirt fisted in bloody fingers and he had a forearm up under its snapping jaws.

Before I could think of helping Theo, I pulled Gabby back and pressed her against my front. I spun in the open door, pulling her with me, ensuring nothing could grab her from me. Our movement brought us closer to the van, and I cursed when I saw another crowd of zombies coming toward us. I knew Gabby's scream was loud enough to call every zombie in a five-block area.

Looking back, I could see Theo was pushing the zombie off him, so he had the leverage to attack. I decided he could handle himself, so I rushed the last few steps to the van and slid open the side door closest to us. I shoved Gabby into the opening and sat down on the van floor. Unbuckling the backpack, I laid the whole contraption with Tina in it on the floor of the van and pulled the door shut on a screaming baby. I grabbed my crowbar from the front seat and turned toward the horror approaching.

The zombies approaching the van were too close for us to outrun, so I went around the vehicle to approach the nearest one. As I came into view, the zombie changed its direction and lunged for me. I swung my crowbar up and cracked the monster under its chin, causing its head to fly back. The momentum of the blow made it stumble several paces back, just enough that I could raise my bar again and slam it down on the side of its head.

With that zombie crumpled on the ground, I stepped around to attack the next. Just as I was pushing the reaching arms of the zombie away, Theo came running around the side of the van. He had his hunting knife out and he went for the next zombie in the group, trusting me to handle the one directly in front of me.

My swing of the crowbar this time glanced off the zombie's shoulder and I let out a grunt of frustration. The dead, with no ability to feel pain from the blow, came toward me with renewed vigor. It let out an animalistic growl and swiped at my face with clawed fingers. I jumped back, just missing being sliced open. The near miss just pissed me off, and I quickly retaliated with the bar, smashing across its face.

It flew back, off its feet, but not dead yet. I rushed forward and brought the crowbar down on the top of its skull. The sound of the skull giving way under the metal was loud, and I didn't need to check if it was dead for good now. I saw the zombie in front of Theo drop, and it ripped his knife from his hand. He cursed and rushed to grab it as another monster came for him.

I didn't take a second to think. I squared up with my crowbar like a bat and swung at the head of the zombie. Blood and black gore flew from the zombie and splashed across my torso and face. Dropping the bar, I started wiping my eyes frantically, afraid of getting any of the nastiness inside the vulnerable skin of my eyes, nose, or mouth.

Theo rushed over and grabbed my hands to stop the rubbing that had become violent. His eyes went over my face and he smiled.

"It's ok. It's only a little. And it's only on your cheek."

He used a clean corner of his shirt to wipe my cheek and we both evaluated the mess we had made. Four zombies in total and I had killed three of them on my own. It was a weird feeling to find my footing in killing something, but I was getting the hang of it. I looked down at my clothes and immediately wished I could learn to kill them cleanly.

"I'm dirty. Again." My voice was near a growl, and it caused Theo to laugh.

"We'll set up the shower, even temporarily, when we get back."

I looked over at the store and then around the parking lot. We had handled any threats, and I didn't think I could drive for an hour back to the airport with the nastiness that was coating my clothes.

"I'm going to find something else to wear," I said.

"I can go with you," Theo offered.

I shook my head. "The store is clear. I can do this. Keep the girls busy. I'll be just a few minutes."

Inside the store, I hurried toward the clothing section. We had so much from the suitcases on the plane we hadn't even bothered looking through what the store offered. But now, I was happy to find clothing that was actually my size. I had been living in sweats and leggings, but I really wanted something with pockets. When I found cargo pants, I grabbed all that were in my size and packed them in a bag.

There were graphic t-shirts, and I grabbed one with a cartoon character on it. Throwing my dirty shirt to the side, I pulled off the tags on the new one and slipped it over my head. Immediately, I could breathe a sigh of relief, to not feel dirty and infected. I saw the sign for kids' clothes and I rushed over, wanting to look quickly before I made Theo worry.

I picked items that would fit the girls and shoved them into another bag. I wanted them to have clean clothes, so after we could shower and really clean ourselves, they could go into clean pajamas. As I caught myself in overly domestic thought, I shuddered and promised myself a few bottles of booze when we got back to the plane. Worrying about clean pajamas for kids was something I never saw for my future.

As I walked back to the van, my mind whirled. We had nowhere else to go. No one else to find. No safe zone to speak of. I wasn't counting Rapid City as a safe zone, because I had a feeling things that happened there wouldn't be good for any of us. I stopped in the middle of the store and felt myself on the edge of hyperventilation. I wasn't equipped for any of this. The girls would be doomed if they were ever left with me alone.

Setting down my bags, I sat down heavily. I pulled my knees up and put my head down, trying to control my breathing. I thought about looking for a paper bag to breathe into. Then I quickly dismissed that idea, realizing I wouldn't know where to look for paper bags. I started rocking, trying to figure out why I couldn't control my heart rate.

That was how Theo found me. He came walking toward me and his shadow confused me at first. It looked like a body with a large circle taking up its head and shoulders. It was enough of a distraction to stop my labored breathing. When he came into view, I realized he was holding a big plastic kiddie pool over his head. Crouching in front of me, he shined a flashlight near my chest to see my face.

"What's wrong? Are you hurt?"

I shook my head and took a deep breath.

"Then what's happening? Taking a break? Wanna take a nap?" He asked.

"Freaking out, just a little," I whispered

Theo looked around, as if he thought the answer to his questions was hiding around a corner. When he saw nothing out of place, he looked back down at me, his face looking slightly baffled. It only made me feel more ridiculous for having a breakdown, when things weren't going all that badly for us at the moment. I realized, if I was going to be a group with Theo, if we were going to survive this all together, I was going to have to let him in somehow.

"Is this all that's left for us, Theo? Are we on our own? What business do I have, raising two children for the rest of my life? I'm going to die out here and then what happens to them? What if you leave us? We almost died the first time we were out on our own. That was a royal screw up on my part. What if one of them dies? Oh my god, I can't think about that, I'm going to be sick." My hyperventilation started up again, and I rocked faster.

Theo put down the pool and knelt in front of me. He put his warm palms on my shoulders to hold me still. When I didn't look at him, he grabbed my chin and tilted my face until I opened my eyes. It struck me again how stupidly handsome he was and how unfair the apocalypse could be. As if he could read my thoughts, he grinned his signature smile.

"Maybe this is all that's left. Maybe there's more. Maybe we meet more people, maybe Bet is all there is. Neither of us have business raising those kids, but we're all they have. You will not die, you just kicked butt out there. You're stuck with me and you won't make the same mistake twice. And the last thing we're going to do is lose either of those kids. Clear?"

All of his answers were so clear and made total sense. I tried to piece it together in my anxiety muddled brain, but all I really understood was, I wasn't alone in this. I nodded like a moron and let the death grip on my knees soften. Theo backed up and picked up the pool while I climbed to my feet and retrieved my bags. It was then that the question of the pool struck me.

"What's the deal with that?"

"Tina is going to need to take a bath. I figured it would make cleaning the girls way easier. Plus, you and I could stand in this while showering, instead of on the dirty asphalt."

He really was the smarter of the two of us, so I just grunted and started walking, feeling ridiculous that I hadn't thought of it myself. Outside, the girls were happily munching away on granola bars, and the parking lot was void of any more monsters. Together, Theo and I made the pool stay strapped to the roof with the gas cans.

With the van and gas cans full, we were ready to venture out to finish some of our shopping duties. We collected as many bricks as the van could hold, though as I watched the suspension take the pressure, I couldn't help but feel concerned. Then Theo scored by finding extra long matches, meant for barbecuing. That find led him to smaller grill sets, and he was excited when he found one that could fit inside the van with the bricks.

As we drove back to the airport, Theo chattered on about all his plans of building a fireplace with the bricks. And how we would boil water for the girls to have a bath in the pool. The word bath got cheers from the backseat and Theo grinned like a lunatic. It was good to see his positive side emerge again after his loss. I didn't want to remind him of his family or looking for them, but I knew we needed to go back to the house and leave the message if he had any chance of finding them again.

I watched as the buildings fell away and the open space appeared before we arrived at the airport. Finding anyone in this would be impossible.

CHAPTER 14

"KID, STOP SPLASHING ME AND RINSE!" I wiped water from my face as Gabby dissolved into giggles in the plastic pool that was our bathtub.

Domestic bliss in the apocalypse was a far cry from what we had found. But after a week of working on our little plane home, we had started to see some bright sides. It took a few days, but Theo finally figured out how to remove the plane seats. We now had three rows under the plane that we sometimes used to eat or just hang out when we didn't want to sit inside the plane.

Inside, we had scavenged two sets of utility shelving units. We put them up in the back flight attendant space and all our supplies were slowly getting organized there. Most of the food was stored above Tina's reaching height, because the kid liked to make a mess of anything she got her hands on. We had a good amount of food, but one thing I couldn't handle was waste. There was never any guarantee of what our next meal would be.

We had created a nest of beds for the four of us. We still slept in the same general area, but we had built a pen for Tina to ensure she couldn't wander off. Theo slept on one side of the pen with Gabby and me on the other. The mattress toppers were exactly what we had needed, and I found myself sleeping better than I had in weeks.

On the opposite side, we had created a play structure with colorful kiddie playpen panels. Gabby could almost climb over on her own, but she knew she wasn't supposed to. It completely trapped Tina, which made it easier for us to have the doors open for ventilation throughout the day. The toys seemed to accumulate overnight and each of the girls had plenty to keep them busy while Theo and I handled regular day-to-day things.

Our bathing situation was ever evolving. Currently, I had both girls in the pool, with water warmed over our fireplace. Theo had built one a few yards from the actual plane and we only used it during the day so the light couldn't give away our location. I was actually impressed with the ingenuity Theo showed with the design. He made sure just enough air got in to feed the fire with oxygen, but not so much that we were feeding it fuel the entire time.

Once we had time to search, we found a spigot with what we thought was potable water. We still boiled everything for over 20 minutes in the big stock pots we found. After it boiled, it cooled in the pot and was then transferred to one of the many water containers we had all over the place. Bath water was taken from already boiled water, warmed and then put into the plastic pool. The girls loved the treat every few days.

Showers for Theo and I were from the camp shower set up. The bag of water sat where the sun could heat it and then we'd hang it above our heads from the steps. It was normally a luke-warm, quick shower. But to feel clean was a benefit I hadn't realized I missed as much as I did.

With so much done the first week, we had slowed down and evaluated what else we needed to do to improve our home. I had finally started to think of the plane as home. We each had a crate for our clothes. We had dishes and silverware, a pantry to store our food, a system for water. It was more than I had working at my apartment before we had left.

Most of the time, I could find some happiness in the moments of the day. But I was also sneaking drinks whenever Theo wasn't watching. Gabby caught me once, but she didn't seem to realize what I was doing and hadn't said a word. And she was happy when I was in a joyous mood. And that's what the alcohol did, put me into a mood that didn't feel the despair of the situation. Or feel the anxiety of meeting people and not knowing who we could trust.

We had still only run into Bet and the woman loved to pop up whenever we were in town. She knew where we went to look for supplies, so it seemed like she just waited until we ran into each other. Once she showed up with Barbies for the girls, but I still didn't let her meet them. I knew we were going to have to have a conversation about trusting her completely, or finding a way to lose her.

The girls finished their bath, and I wrapped them in fluffy bath towels I had found at an expensive bed and bath kind of store. I hefted a wriggling Tina into my arms and Gabby slipped on her sandals to get up into the plane and put on clean clothes. I slowly followed her up the stairs, keeping a hand behind her, in case she missed a step.

Inside, I found Theo working to put together a small bookcase for the girls' books and coloring supplies. He had also built a plastic toy box to keep the toys when they weren't playing with them. Something about responsibility and teaching them to clean up after themselves. I personally didn't understand how we could teach them that, when the entire world was a wreck that couldn't be fixed.

"Laundry," I said when Theo looked up.

"What about it?" He went back to the bookcase.

"We need to find a way to do it. Maybe a second pool? Fill it with warm water and detergent? Shoot, maybe two pools, one for soapy water, one for clean." Tina tossed her towel off the moment I put her down, hitting me in the face, causing a portion of my words to be muffled.

"Huh?" Theo asked absently.

"Cleaning clothes. We need to do it. We can't just keep finding brand new stuff for each day." I slowed down my words, making sure he was hearing each syllable.

His piercing blue eyes shot over to me, finally focusing on what I was saying. I was busy wrestling Tina into a clean diaper and clothes, but I could feel his eyes on me.

"Right, yes. We need to work on that. The two pools make the most sense. Maybe set up laundry by the fireplace so it's easy to move the hot water?"

I nodded, glad he was finally hearing me and was adding the ideas to his mental to do list. I was horrible at planning, and I was happy to use Theo's desire for order to our benefit. He seemed content to run with things that we decided together and I couldn't think of a better setup.

With Tina tearing apart the cleaned play area like a tornado through a trailer park, I turned to Gabby. The little girl was fairly good at getting herself in order, but sometimes she had minor hiccups. Like putting her head through an armhole, which she had done again. She was confused and tangled, her little face getting red, the more frustrated she got. Without a delicate touch, I yanked the shirt up back over her head. I showed her again how to find the tag or the place the tagless area was printed. She nodded and soon she was dressed and playing with Tina.

Despite how nice things had been, I knew there was one thing that we hadn't done. With the organization Theo seemed to thrive in, I knew he hadn't forgotten. We hadn't gone to his family home again and fixed the mailbox and left a message. I wasn't sure if it was because he couldn't face the burned mess again, or if he didn't believe his family was out there. The desire to not upset him kept me from broaching the subject.

Dinner was canned tuna, mixed with mayo packets, until it was smooth enough for Tina to choke down. Gabby actually really liked tuna, so she never complained when we had it for meals. We added a can of corn to be shared between us and canned juices. The airport catering trucks had become an endless supply of small snacks and drinks. We appreciated the easy access, instead of having to drive all the way back into the city and search dark, dangerous stores.

Gabby picked a book for Theo to read at bedtime. She was aware I could read, but I didn't do the voices like Theo. When he read to them, the girls liked to giggle and climb all over him, until they finally calmed and were ready to sleep. As they read, I put away the dishes from dinner, piling the dirty things near the front door. We didn't go outside often when it was dark. There was no reason to take the risk if it wasn't warranted.

Next to the door was a case with a flare gun in it. It had been an odd gift from Bet at one of our meetings. She and Theo had finally started talking, and he charmed her like he did every other person he met. Though we had talked many times, we still hadn't shared where we were staying with her. She insisted that from where she normally camped, she could see most of the metro area and beyond. So, if we were to have a problem and need help, she wanted us to shoot off a flare. I ran my fingers over the case, wondering what problem she could fix for us.

Quiet had descended in the back of the plane and I snuck to my alcohol stash. I wasn't sure if I could even fall asleep anymore with the help of a small bottle or two, or even three. As I was downing the second bottle, Theo appeared, and I squeaked and began to choke. He just raised an eyebrow at me, but he didn't look surprised.

"You don't need to hide it."

"Hide...what?" I couldn't stop sputtering and coughing on the burning liquor that tried to go into my lungs.

"The drinking. Was it a problem before?" He asked.

The genuine concern on his face actually made me angry and feel defensive.

"Who said it's a problem at all?"

He slid open the drawer that held the bottles. Lifting one, he found it empty, nodded and repeated until he found the one that was still unopened. He counted and looked at me.

"You've been drinking these every night. They're almost gone. So, is this a problem, or you need relaxation or you can't handle what's happening in the world, or what?"

His tone only caused my spine to straighten further and a red blush to rise into my cheeks. I dropped the now empty bottle back into its space and tried to march by him. His hand shot out and grabbed my upper arm, stopping my progress. I froze, and a growl rose in my throat. But it did not deter him.

"You will not wake the girls with this discussion," he whispered.

I moved back into the small area between the cockpit and the bathroom. Theo blocked me and crossed his arms across his chest. The movement drew my attention to the way his muscles stretched the sleeves of his t-shirt, but I was too angry to really admire him.

"This is really none of your business," I said to fill the silence.

Theo turned his head and looked toward the girls and pointed.

"We are the only two adults protecting those kids. If you aren't up to the task, or will be impaired at some point, I need to know it."

"Their mother entrusted those kids to me. It's not your problem. You can walk away whenever you want." Even as I said the words, they felt like acid on my tongue. I didn't know what family felt like, but the four of us had grown close, so I thought it was something like that.

"You aren't going to shove me out the door, because you have some demons you can't face." His voice was even and placating, which did little to quell the anger I felt brewing.

"How about worrying about the demons you're avoiding, before you worry about mine." The way his eyes darkened, I knew my jab had hit the mark.

"You couldn't be talking about two more different things, Vicki. I get it. You didn't have a normal life. But you have to understand what it is to lose your family. I'm not trying to drink those sorrows away. Instead, I'm trying to help take care of our own small little family."

He was wrong in thinking I knew what it was like. How could I know what it was to lose something I had never had in the first place? My entire life had been about living at a bare minimum and having nothing that would be a loss. What I could understand was pain. And Theo was in pain. I could see it on his face, etched into every line and partial smile he gave throughout the day. And instead of being supportive, I was jabbing a knife into the wound and twisting.

I felt sufficiently chastised for saying what I did. But I couldn't articulate what the liquor was to me. It had been my coping mechanism since I had my first fake ID, which was much younger than I would admit to Theo. His entire vibe was good boy, doing good things, in a good life, with an excellent family. If he drank as a teenager, I was positive it was straight from a Boones Farm Strawberry Hill bottle.

"The drinking won't endanger the girls," I finally said.

Theo sighed, but he just nodded and walked away. It wasn't the entire answer he wanted, but it was all he was going to get.

Later, lying next to Gabby's sleeping form, I thought about how he called us a family. I tossed and turned, wondering if that was true. The nearest thing I could compare to was dysfunctional foster families that took on kids for the paycheck, while having their own biological kids that were treated like higher class citizens.

That night I barely slept. A nightmare crashed down on me, and it was a repeat of a previous one. I was smart enough to know that my nightmares were often my fears playing out. However, I was glad this time. I only woke myself up and didn't scream to wake up the entire group. I was drenched in a cold, sticky sweat. The plane was still fairly dark, though I could tell by the light starting to appear around the closed windows that dawn was breaking.

Carefully, I climbed from my bed and tiptoed to the front door. Swinging it open just enough that I could slip out into the cool morning, I took the stairs slowly to be as quiet as possible. Looking around, it still surprised me that our oasis hadn't been overrun with zombies, or other living trying to take what we had.

The thought had me looking toward the airport building. Sometimes in the early and late hours, when the sun wasn't a speck on the horizon, you could see movement in the windows. Those zombies would be more than we could ever handle. A shiver ran through me as the sweat dried on my skin, but also because the idea of the airport ever letting out its prisoners was unimaginable for me.

Since the sun was brightening the sky, I went to the fireplace and started the fire for the day. We had brought all the newspapers, magazines, puke bags and other paper products we had no use for, and stored them in a box near the fireplace. Theo had showed me how to take one and make it a tight twisting ball, so it could be a fire starter. Soon, I had a small glowing ember going that was catching the kindling I added, another thing he had taught me.

Building a fire had been far out of my life education. A lot of the survival things were. But Theo was patient and kind, teaching me whatever I needed to know to help him with building something out of the plane. A list in my head of things he taught me played, and I felt even more guilty for my outburst the night before. Attacking the nicest person I knew on the planet wasn't going to help anything in our survival situation.

Once the fire was going, I put a pot of water on to boil for cooking and drinking. The process took so long; we were basically boiling water the entire time we were home. Which was fine with me. Staying busy kept me from the despair that tried so hard to control my thoughts.

I also set up the solar charger, so it was ready to catch the morning rays. Even with no cell service, I had found a phone with downloaded music and movies within the luggage of the plane. I was sure if I charged up some additional devices, I would find even more entertainment options. The solar charger was Theo's idea, though he was thinking about rechargeable batteries, flashlights, and lanterns.

As the twenty-minute rolling boil finished, I carefully took the pot off the fireplace and put it to the side to cool before being transferred into the plastic holding containers. I started up a second pot and stoked the fire. Theo appeared next to me with two mugs and instant coffee. I wanted to fall to the ground and worship him with the coffee, but I remembered our tense night and busied myself with the camping kettle.

"Good morning," he said, his voice quiet and barely audible over the screech of the kettle.

"Morning." I didn't turn to look at him or confirm that he heard me.

"About last night—" he started to say.

"We don't need to talk about it," I interrupted.

"We really should. I wanted to apologize."

That made me turn and look at him. I hadn't expected an apology or for him to even bring it up. He smiled and continued.

"It's really not my place to confront you about anything. I just want to make sure you're safe. We're safe, the girls are safe. You've done nothing to risk anyone, so I shouldn't be interrogating you about it. I just want you to know that if it is a problem, or was a problem for you before the collapse of everything, we can work on it together. You aren't alone. And you're strong enough to not need it."

My mouth dropped open. The speech was excellent and shocking. You aren't alone. The words rattled around in my head like a pinball machine. I wasn't alone now, but I wasn't stupid enough to believe that couldn't change with one bite, one attack, one bullet or knife wound. We weren't a family that was only worried about freak accidents and beating the odds with illnesses like cancer. Every day was a threat to our lives and safety. There was nothing Theo could do to change that.

Theo's eyes searched mine, and I wondered what he really saw. I didn't have deep down secrets to hide or any fascinating life experiences for him to uncover. Feeling uncomfortable, I turned back to the kettle that was really screaming now. I poured boiling water into two mugs, and Theo added the instant grounds and stirred.

With a hot cup in my hands, I walked to sit on an airline seat and watch the sunrise. Theo followed, but was quiet the entire time. I could see his head turn toward me, but he never spoke. I knew I had to say something, and the truth found its way to my tongue.

"I've always drank. Not to the point of being an alcoholic. But the liquor has, at times, been a friend in the dark, if that's makes sense," I said.

Theo just nodded, which encouraged me to continue.

"I explained about my childhood. Once I was on my own, I was really alone. I wasn't good with people, not in the way people build bonds and trust. To most people, I was invisible, or just another random face in a crowd. So, when I started buying alcohol, they didn't even card me, even though I was much younger than twenty-one. Once I was legal, getting the job at the bar was the only place I really dealt with people. It was easy when I was short, to the point, and unfriendly. For some reason, patrons thought I wanted to hear their problems, but I just let them talk without responding. I had no experiences to garner advice from. It just worked."

I knew I was rambling about the randomness of my life and none of it really explained the alcohol, but Theo didn't respond or interrupt. It was probably the most words I had said to him at one time.

"The alcohol was like the one thing that I could rely on in life. It was there, it was strong, it always made me feel the same. So, when I wanted company, that's what I turned to. I guess maybe that is what alcoholics say." I finished with a shrug and kept my eyes glued on the sunrise.

There was a long silence, and I was just about to go back into the plane to check on the girls, or change the water out on the fireplace, but Theo cleared his throat.

"I appreciate your honesty. I can't understand what life looked like for you before, so I won't say I know where you're coming from. And maybe you aren't the best at building relationships, but you are not invisible, Vicki."

I wasn't sure why, but his words made me feel warm inside, but I wasn't sure what the appropriate response was, so I just kept my lips smashed shut. He downed the last of his coffee and stood and stretched.

"I guess we better get going, or those girls will rip apart the plane and all of our hard work," he joked.

"I'll be up in a minute."

He nodded and started for the stairs. The sun was halfway over the horizon, with beautiful blues, purples, and pinks staining the sky. I admired the colors for a long moment before moving to follow Theo. A weight was off my chest, now that Theo knew my secret. Now, I just had to decide what to do about the alcohol. Did I keep drinking, or was it time to let it all dry up?

CHAPTER 15

DOMESTIC LIFE WAS BORING. Which was exactly what we all needed. Boredom, without zombies trying to eat our faces, without running into demented living people who wanted to brand us and make us pets. Each day, we completed routines that were becoming second nature. It was coming to a point where I actually felt genuine hope for what we were building.

A few weeks after Theo and I talked about my drinking and my past, I ran out of little bottles of alcohol. At first, I felt nervous and panicked. It was a crutch I wasn't sure how to live without. Each night after I ran out, I'd lay in the dark plane, wishing for just a taste. Until one night, I was tired enough that I just fell into a dreamless sleep.

Each week, we had big tasks that we wanted to tackle. Theo and I talked about the best places to search for the supplies. He was more organized and took that role to heart, but he always let me be a part of the planning and executing plans. It made me feel useful, outside of being a caretaker for the girls each moment of the day.

Theo had taken my needs to heart, and we had created a place for laundry. We found metal buckets that were likely used for drinks at parties, that we lined up near the fireplace. One was for the warm water and detergent, one was for the first rinse and the last one was the final rinse. We had also scavenged a laundry drying rack from a house that still had towels hanging on it.

Doing the laundry was how Gabby found me one day, as I was agitating the clothes with a metal pole in the detergent tub. She watched for a long moment and then came to my side.

"Can I help?" She asked.

I paused, looking at the height of the metal pole and her height, and determined it probably wouldn't work.

"How about you help me when I rinse and hang things up?" I suggested.

She nodded enthusiastically. I had to wonder if it was the apocalypse, or if all little kids were excited to help with chores. The girls didn't seem to find our domestic life as boring as I did. Almost daily, Theo would take them walking around the runways of the airport, looking for little animals in the over-grown grasses, or running around under the other planes. Most nights, they were so worn out that bedtime wasn't a fight. I knew that parenting wasn't nearly that easy.

The clothes in my bin were done, and I started wringing out the soapy water to add them to the first rinse. Gabby used a small piece of wood and stirred the clothes, rinsing the soap from them. She smiled while she worked and I just shook my head at her enthusiasm for laundry. After the next rinse, we worked together to twist the materials to get as much water out as possible. Then Gabby took the job of hanging them over the drying rack.

When everything was hung up, she turned to look at me with triumph on her face.

"Thanks kid. Let me get more water boiling, so I can wash dishes next."

And that was how the day continued. Gabby shadowed most of my chores, handing me things or helping however she could. Theo found us drying dishes with Tina on his hip.

"We gotta get going, if we're going to meet Bet today," he said.

We had tried to keep a normal schedule of meeting up with Bet every other day, when we went into town. So far, it had worked for us all. The girls finally got to meet her on our last trip and they instantly enchanted her. The wistful look on her face made me want to ask about her family, but I didn't want to upset her already off balanced emotional state.

In town, we went to the same parking lot we always met in. We killed several zombies there, but each time we met Bet, the bodies were moved out of sight. I didn't ask Bet why she did it, but it always made the meeting more comfortable, without the overwhelming scent of decay around us.

We pulled in before Bet this time, which was odd, since she was always the first. I had told Theo that I thought she sat there all day just waiting for us to come because she was so lonely. She didn't tell me much about her history, other than the story of losing her husband. But she had made it clear that she was completely alone, living in the pop-up tent on the top of her Jeep.

Everything was quiet as Theo, and I climbed from our van. We needed fuel, and it never hurt to bring more food back home. But something didn't feel right as I looked around. Quiet was normal, but the silence felt different somehow. The hairs on the back of my neck stood up, and I looked around, trying to figure out what was out of place.

Theo had insisted I start carrying more than just my crow-bar. He had even started teaching me how to shoot, though my aim was still not great. I now had a hunting knife on one hip and a gun holstered on the other. We had tried several holsters until

I finally landed on one that felt comfortable and in the right position for me to pull the weapon should I need it. My hand laid on the butt of the gun now, as I tried to figure out what felt wrong.

It was then I picked up a noise that was hovering within the silence. Far enough that I hadn't noticed it right away, but my subconscious had known it was wrong. It was the echo of engines, more than one. We had only heard Bet around town before, so this wasn't normal. Theo's eyes met mine at the same moment as my brain was figuring out we had a problem.

Without speaking, we both jumped back into the van. Theo had it moving before I had even closed my door. Gabby had been in the process of removing her car seat straps, but she looked up in panic as we started driving again.

"Are we not seeing Bet?" She asked.

"Someone else is coming. Strap back in," I replied.

During quiet times in the days, Theo and I often talked about worst-case scenarios. We made plans for things we would do should anything happen. One of those was if we were to be taken unaware by other survivors. Theo's experiences had been so bad, I agreed we couldn't just trust any group that we might come upon. Bet had been one thing. She was one solitary old woman, that had a few screws loose, but was harmless beyond that. An unknown group was something entirely different.

Driving between the buildings, Theo went to the back alley. We had scouted around the entire area, since this was the major store we came to for supplies. There was a ladder that led to the roof of the store. Parking the van, we quickly strapped Tina to my back, after I convinced Theo I could climb with her and had done it before.

Theo carried Gabby quickly to the ladder, and she climbed up ahead of him. He stayed close to her, whispering encourage-ments as she grabbed for each rung and pushed up with her feet. Once they were halfway up, I started my climb with Tina, who was babbling behind me. She was talking about a princess and a tower, remembering a story Theo had read to her.

At the top, Gabby swung a leg over the edge and Theo followed. When I reached the top rung, Theo hung over and grabbed my hand and a strap on the backpack, to help haul us over onto the roof. We had only climbed up once to check the structure stability of the roof and knew there was nothing of note except air conditioning units and skylights. I pointed them out to Gabby and gave strict instructions to not walk near them or on them. She nodded her head solemnly. She knew we were trying to be safe.

As we approached the front of the store, we crouched and listened. The engines were loud now, almost on top of our little shopping center. My heart thundered in my chest, hoping the people would just move through without stopping. Theo took off his pack and pulled a pair of binoculars out. He searched the roads leading toward us and cursed quietly.

"Bad words," Gabby whispered.

"Sorry, little one," he replied.

"What is it?" I asked.

"I think I see Bet's Jeep. She weaving in and out of car wrecks, trying to move away from us."

"Her engine isn't that loud," I murmured.

"No, there's more. There's a van and someone on a dirt bike. They seem to be following her. But if Bet wanted to talk to them, I'm sure she would stop. She's trying to get away."

Suddenly, a gunshot rang out, and I had to cover Gabby's mouth as she screamed.

"No, she definitely doesn't want to talk to them. The one on the dirt bike is shooting at her," Theo reported from his perch.

Gabby pulled at my hand, and I looked down at her.

"Can you keep quiet?" I asked.

She nodded, and I released her. I moved with Tina still on my back, so I was next to Theo.

"Is there anything we can do?"

Theo just shook his head, still watching through the binoculars.

"She's definitely leading them away from us. That van...it can't be...," Theo trailed off, and more curses flowed from his mouth. This time, Gabby didn't call him out.

"What?" I demanded, when he didn't explain. I wanted to yank the binoculars from his hands to see everything for myself.

"It's The Children of Z. It's the same van, Vicki."

My blood went icy, and I almost stood up to see for myself. So many questions flew through my mind and I wasn't sure how to make sense of anything.

"How? Of all places, how did they end up in Denver?" I asked.

Theo didn't reply, and I grabbed his arm and squeezed until he looked down at me.

"How are they here, Theo?"

"The woman I told you about, the one that wanted to keep me as a pet? She tortured me for information. I admitted to her that my family was here. They could be looking for me." His voice was barely a whisper, laced with fear and shame.

I released his arm and let my hand slide down until I was gripping his hand.

"You don't know that," I whispered back.

His eyes took on a haunted look that made me wonder what else happened to him while he was with them. "If I'm right, that means Sister Ann, Father Allen...," he trailed off again.

"They didn't know you were on that bus, Theo. Those maniacs are just out killing anyone that won't follow their insane cult. It's not your fault."

"They KNEW I was coming here, Vicki. They're looking

for me. You and the girls aren't safe with me. You need to go. As soon as they are out of sight, take the girls and run. Go far away from here."

"Are you nuts? We are not leaving you. And we aren't leaving our home. They won't think to look at the airport. We just need to wait until they're gone and sneak back. We're safer together, Theo."

He just shook his head. His free hand ran through his unkept hair, causing it to look even messier than usual. He didn't pull his hand from mine though and I took that as a comfort, cradling it against both of mine. I knew the girls and I would have little chance of survival without him. Everything we had done was because of things he had taught me or had done for us. I wouldn't risk the girls' safety by leaving, but I also couldn't imagine abandoning him.

Theo lifted the binoculars again and searched the streets, but the engine noises had died and were far into the distance again. He slid down until he was sitting next to me. Our thighs pressed together, and I continued to hold his hand. He shifted so he could twine our fingers together. Gabby crawled over until Theo could put an arm around her shoulders and pull her to his side.

"I would never forgive myself if something happened to you all. It would be my fault," he said, his voice sad.

"You won't let anything happen to us. We'll take care of each other, just like we've been doing all these weeks. We built something good. I'm not just giving that up," I replied.

"Me neither," Gabby added.

That made Theo smile. He leaned toward her and kissed the top of her head.

"Ok, little one. Whatever you say."

We sat like that, shushing Tina as she became fussy, letting Gabby play carefully with the binoculars and snacking on things Theo thought to have in his pack. When an extra noise came to us, we all froze and waited. Gabby handed the binoculars back to Theo, and he released us to get back up and peer over the ledge.

"It's Bet's Jeep. She's driving really slow, but I don't see the van or dirt bike," he reported.

"We don't know for sure that it's her in the Jeep," I replied.

Theo nodded, but continued to watch. The engine's sound grew until I knew she was coming our way.

"It's coming around the back," Theo said.

He stood and rushed over to where the ladder was. He crouched and waited while I kept the girls on the far side of the roof. We had shared this plan with Bet only for this purpose. If something were to happen and we needed somewhere to hide, we didn't want her leading anyone to us. When he suddenly stood, I knew it was Bet in the Jeep and I moved across the roof as well. The old woman was climbing from the Jeep, but she leaned heavily against the front and slid around as she tried to make her way to the ladder.

"Bet?" I called.

Her head came up and when she saw us, she smiled her big smile and then her eyes rolled back in her head and she fell to the ground. Theo was on the ladder immediately, not even using the rungs. I watched in fascination as he slid down with his hands and booted feet on the sides of the ladder. He landed with bent knees at the bottom and ran to where Bet had collapsed. His hands moved her body until he found the problem.

Turning to look up at us, he held up a hand covered in blood. "She's been shot."

There was no rushing down the ladder for me, as I climbed down with Gabby slowly coming down above me. I had to keep myself aware of her movements, even as my patience was strung out. When I hit the ground, I reached up and grabbed the little girl to bring her to the ground.

Rushing over, I found Theo putting pressure on Bet's shoulder, on the front and back.

"There's an exit wound, that's good, no bullet stuck inside. But she's bleeding a ton. I can sew her up, if we get her back to the plane," he said.

"The plane? Are we ready for that?" I asked.

"We can't just let her lay here and bleed out," Theo replied.

"I know, I know. But I'm worried. I mean, I trust her, but bringing her home?"

"It was going to happen eventually, Vicki. We were moving toward that, with these visits and getting to know each other. Now, it's her life."

I couldn't disagree with that. We didn't want to leave her Jeep, knowing it was her entire life and home. After Theo packed her wounds, we laid Bet in the back of her Jeep and he got behind the wheel. I followed him in the van, with the girls in their car seats. I was acutely aware that there were other people in the city and they could come around any corner.

When the airport came into view, some of the tension knotted in my chest released. I checked the rearview mirror obsessively, and never saw the white van or dirt bike anywhere. Theo flung open the security bar and drove through, not waiting for us. I stopped to close it and caught up with him when he was parking the Jeep under our plane.

"Vicki, can you clear a spot, maybe in the front flight attendant area, where we could lay her?"

I nodded and jogged up the steps. We had moved a lot of the junk we had piled in the front; the disaster bothering us every day. Now the electronics that weren't helpful were piled inside an empty luggage cart. I used one of the clean bed sets we had and created a soft place to lay her while Theo worked on her. I also laid down extra towels to soak up the blood.

When I came back down, I found Bet on her feet and her eyes wide as she looked around, confused. She saw me and smiled and walked, but swayed in place. Theo grabbed her to keep her on her feet.

"Well, this is quite something you got here," she said on a groan when I approached.

"Let's just get you fixed up and then we can talk about a tour," I replied.

Theo helped her up the stairs and shockingly, even with a bullet wound, the old woman was spry and strong. She didn't lean on Theo much, only when it seemed like the blood loss was getting to her. Inside the plane, she let out a low whistle and chuckle.

"I should have known you were building something, with all the supplies you're always collecting."

"We wanted somewhere to call home for the girls," Theo replied.

Bet didn't respond, just nodded, her eyes understanding behind the pain. Theo helped her sit in the front seats of the plane. Now that she was awake, he didn't need to lay her down yet. He gave me quick instructions to boil some of the already cleaned water and bring it up, as well as a filled bottle for Bet to drink. I quickly went back down and started the fire and got water on.

The girls were still in the van, but Gabby, knowing something was going on, had let Tina out of her seat and they were playing quietly on the floor. When I opened the door, they both looked over at me, but neither seemed upset nor scared.

"You can come out. Let's just stay down here while Theo helps Bet."

The girls nodded and scrambled from the van. They ran to the circle of plane seats and sat on the ground to play with sidewalk chalk, another gift that Bet had brought them on one visit. They were fantastic about keeping themselves busy when Theo and I were busy. I went back to the water, which had just hit a rolling boil.

With the boiled water in a cooled pot and a metal water bottle filled with cooled water, I climbed back up into the plane. Bet was still sitting up, but her eyes were closed and Theo was fussing around with the first aid supplies we had scavenged. We had found an intact pharmacy during our first week and had taken anything that could be used for minor injuries. This wasn't a small injury, and I felt nervous about the results.

When I entered, I set the hot water near Bet and stood with nothing to do. Theo came to the row and his hands were full. He handed me a pair of surgical gloves and I just stared at him, confused. I knew nothing about first aid and wasn't going to be able to help Bet.

"I'll probably need you to hold her down. It's better to have everything clean. I have nothing for the pain, no more than pain meds. Those aren't anesthesia. She's gonna feel a lot of this," he explained.

I nodded and slid the gloves over my hands. Theo laid out the supplies he needed. I saw a needle and thread, rubbing alcohol, antiseptic wipes and an ointment for after he did the stitches. Bet's eyes cracked open when she heard him moving around.

"Let's get this over with," she muttered.

Together, Theo and I helped Bet out of her shirt. She cried out when we tried to work it off of the injured shoulder, so Theo just sliced it off with a pair of scissors. She wore a tank top under, covering a sports bra. I noted that all of her clothes seemed clean and wondered what type of setup she really had.

"Bet, this is going to hurt, bad. Vicki is here to help hold you still. I'm not the best seamstress out there, but we gotta get this closed up," Theo explained in his calm, kind manner.

The older woman looked at him with pure trust, just like every other person who met him. She nodded and squeezed her eyes shut. Theo started by pouring rubbing alcohol over both sides of the wound. Bet groaned, but she kept her teeth clamped together. I could see the sweat dotting her brow, as she did her best to not pull away. As Theo slid the needle into her skin for the first time, she jumped, and I had to put my hand on her uninjured shoulder to hold her still.

"Those...better...be straight, boy," Bet ground out.

"You'll have a great story to tell by these scars once you're healed up, Bet," I said.

She just grunted, her eyes still squeezed shut. As Theo continued, it was as if she was becoming numb to the experience. She stayed still, and I removed my hands, standing up to stretch my back. Theo finished the front with what he said was eight stitches. He gave Bet a break before turning to the back wound.

"I don't know what those crazies wanted," she said.

Theo shot me a look, and I just tried to convey to him that this was his story to tell. I wasn't saying a word.

"Did they say anything to you, Bet?" He asked.

"Well, at first, they were yelling at me about the zombies being god's children. What god could they believe in, to think those monsters are his children? So, I yelled back that they must have been referring to the devil himself. That didn't make them very happy. They called me a nonbeliever, and I realized I was dealing with something crazier than old Bet," she said, switching to talking about herself in their person.

I raised an eyebrow, wondering if we were losing her. But she just grunted and tapped her temple.

"I knew they weren't just in my head. Since I met you, I don't see people that ain't there no more."

"That's good to hear. We don't need any more friends," I replied.

That got a small smile out of Bet, that disappeared as Theo moved her body to angle for access to the exit wound.

"When did they shoot you?" He asked.

"When they called me a nonbeliever, I started to laugh, but then they started coming at me in that van and the man on the bike. So, I took off. But I knew you all would be at the store, waiting for me, so I made sure to go away from there, lead them away, ya know?"

"We appreciate your thoughtfulness, Bet," Theo murmured, as he studied the skin around the wound.

"The crazy guy on the dirt bike started shooting at me, and I guess one got through the window and hit me. But then I just kept driving until I could pull into a parking garage I know of. They didn't see me turn and eventually they disappeared."

"You didn't see where they went?" I asked.

Bet shook her head. "I was too busy hidin', honey."

"Ok, we need to get started. The one thing I don't have is blood to give you."

Bet nodded. She leaned forward slightly, giving Theo access to her shoulder. She gripped my forearm, so I crouched in front of her for support. I knew the moment Theo pierced her skin, Bet's nails dug into my skin and she grunted. This hole was slightly smaller and only took six stitches. She was almost silent through the entire process, though she left deep grooves in my forearm.

Theo liberally applied an antiseptic ointment and then taped on gauze to protect both sets of stitches. Bet sat back with a deep breath. She smiled shakily up at Theo as he cleaned up the supplies.

"Thanks. I sure am glad you're not in my head."

CHAPTER 16

IT WAS weird to have a guest in our little plane home. Theo worked to clear more chairs away, but these from the front of the fuselage, to put some space between us and anyone that might stay. Of course, the only person I could imagine being inside with us was Bet.

After a few days of recouping, the old woman got restless. She was thankful we brought her Jeep with us, so she didn't have to find something new or risk The Children of Z finding it. Theo had been honest with her about who had been chasing her. After she heard his entire story, she sat shaking her head. But then she grinned like a crazy woman and said, "Well, it's official, I'm not the craziest one out here."

In private, Theo and I had discussed our feelings about Bet staying with us. When I watched her with the girls, it was nothing short of a grandmotherly presence and the girls seemed to gravitate to her wild red hair and jokes that didn't make much sense. In my gut, I didn't feel like she was a threat, but I hadn't had many occasions to judge people and their motives. I felt better when Theo agreed, and we decided to let Bet know she could stay.

We told her over dinner one night and at first, I thought she was going to tell us no. She wistfully looked at Denver for a long moment.

"You don't have to stay, Bet. We trust you to not tell people where we are," I rushed to say.

She turned her face toward me and smiled.

"It's not that, girlie. Leaving Denver feels like leaving everyone behind. Even though everyone is gone. Starting somewhere new probably is the best plan for me."

Gabby stood up and cheered and started doing a silly dance in the middle of the circle. Tina giggled and tried to keep up with her sister. Bet clapped, some sort of pattern that could have been a tune, but nothing any of us knew. Theo and I joined and soon Gabby was collapsing breathless with smiles and a pink face.

We hadn't been into town in a week, while we nursed Bet back to health. But we were running low on a few things and now that we had another adult mouth to feed, we wanted to pack up the food storage even more. The van needed fuel and Bet came up with the idea to go into the airport parking garage to find gas.

With the girls in the van and Bet following in the Jeep, we slowly crept into the parking garage. I didn't know why, but the dim structure made me feel nervous and on edge. We found the first open spot and pulled in. Nothing seemed to move between cars, so Theo and I got out with our supplies. It didn't take long to fill the van and the gas cans again. We also helped Bet fill up the Jeep and the black gas cans that were strapped to the side of her vehicle.

A banging noise caught my attention, and I cautiously walked down the aisle of cars. A small white sedan seemed to shake in its spot. The interiors windows were covered with streaks of blood. Through the windshield, I could see two zombies that were fighting to get out to us. I just shook my head sadly and made my way back to the van. I wondered how people ended up like that, but chalked it up to bad luck.

We drove into town, following the path we normally liked to take. Everything seemed to be the same until we pulled into our shopping center. Theo slammed on the brakes as soon as the store came into view. Or what had been the store, where we had been getting all our supplies, where we had hid while Bet was being chased by The Children of Z. Now, it was a burned shell, nothing but smoldering lumber, melted shelving and freezers were left.

"Oh my god," I breathed.

To one side, on a nail salon, an immense piece of white fabric hung. Written in red letters, the word "Non-Believers" was painted with a crude skull in the corner. I had little doubt the dripping red was painted in blood. It would fit right in with the horror of the cult.

"The Children of Z," Theo said.

Bet had pulled the Jeep up next to us and her face had gone pale as she stared at the building.

"How did they know?" I asked, loud enough for Bet to hear me.

"They must have seen us, somehow," Theo responded.

"But how? We had been so careful. We never even came face to face with them," I replied.

I turned a circle, checking the shops that surrounded us. There were no faces peering out, no movement that shouldn't be there. But somehow, The Children knew we came here. What we couldn't be sure of was if they knew it was Theo coming to the store, or if they assumed it was Bet they were punishing for getting away from them.

I answered my question when I looked behind us at the building that sat next to the parking lot entrance. Another sign was there, and I cried out. In the same red lettering, the sign said, "Give over the one that has sinned with murder." There was no doubt they were talking about Theo. Bet stared at the sign I was looking at and she tilted her head questioningly.

"Bet, do you have somewhere else that has supplies? That's safe?" Theo asked, his teeth gritted.

The old woman nodded and motioned for us to follow her. She spun the Jeep in a wide circle, and Theo followed. We didn't speak as he drove. I wasn't sure what to say. This cult couldn't be so smart to hide so well that they had found our place of supplies without us knowing. But they had. And they had the chance to burn it down before we came back into town.

Thinking about everything still in that store made me simmer with anger. It was such a waste to destroy something just out of spite. But I guessed it wasn't just spite. They hoped to control and kill anyone that didn't follow their beliefs. They knew of at least Bet that was in town. I wondered if they knew Theo was here, and that they were this close to catching the one that had escaped.

Ten minutes later, Bet pulled into a similar-looking shopping center. A grocery store stood in the center, with a dollar store to one side and a clothing store to the other. Several other small businesses filled in the center, most of which didn't look useful to us. But nothing was burned down and there was no sign from a cult to warn us away.

Bet hopped from her Jeep, but winced a little when she used her injured shoulder a bit too much. Theo and I joined her in front of the vehicles.

"This is my local grocery store. My husband and I lived only a mile or so from here. We're still far enough on the outskirts to not run into the hordes that seem to dominate downtown Denver."

"Why aren't more of these places cleaned out, Bet? What happened to everyone?" Theo asked.

I knew why he was asking. It was a subject we still hadn't brought up. Though I knew one day, when Theo went into town by himself, he went back to the house and fixed the mailbox. Once it was done, he left his message for his family. He didn't give me details, just confirmed that he did it. And I left it alone.

"It was interesting what happened here. The smaller, outskirt towns emptied fast. People flew out or drove north. Canada was like this promised safe place, but as you learned, it wasn't to be. The government swooped in, making people think they would be safe. Instead, they set up blockades, keeping everyone in Denver inside. When they did that, they were trapping living people in too."

"They wouldn't let anyone leave? No one?" I asked.

Bet shook her head. "None. There were promises about testing people for the illness and letting healthy people out. But they did not set the testing spots up. The last few broadcasts I heard, were the empty promises. By the time people started to realize it was all lies, it was too late. There were too many zombies, too many military that were shooting anyone who tried to leave."

I just stared at her in shock. I thought of the government guys we had met and knew they wouldn't have a problem trapping living people anywhere. The living wasn't their problem, unless they had something they wanted. Like women and their bodies. I shuddered and looked over to see Theo's face just as shocked.

"Anyway," Bet continued, as she pulled a backpack from the Jeep, "Let's shop!"

I felt like I had whiplash. Bet had dropped a huge bomb on us, but it wasn't new information to her. It didn't seem to bother

her anymore. At one time, it could have been a contributor to her craziness, but now she brushed it off and led us into the completely intact grocery store.

The one problem with an intact store was all the fresh foods that had decayed and rotted. The smell was putrid inside. I coughed and gagged. Suddenly, a small container was shoved in my face, and it overcame me with a menthol smell. Looking down, I realized it was Bet who was holding a menthol rub under my nose.

"Put a little under your nostrils. It'll help with the smell. It's bad in here."

I nodded, and Theo took the same offer. With the menthol dominating my sense of smell, it was easier to be inside the building. Bet had obviously been here many times, as she led the way to the canned meats section. We filled our bags with canned chicken, tuna, spam, anchovies, and salmon. The last two were going to be for Bet, because there was no way I was touching them and I knew the girls wouldn't.

Our shopping didn't take nearly as long with Bet there to guide us in the store. It was darker than the store we had been in before, with no skylights to guide us. We used flashlights and a lantern Bet carried. Theo also filled a bag with batteries for other electronics we had gotten over the weeks.

I felt uneasy the entire time we were in town. We packed up more bottled water and canned juices. Bet chose things she preferred, which included things like cookies and candies. She claimed they were for her, but I had a sneaking suspicion they would be sneaking to the girls when Theo and I weren't looking.

As we drove back to the airport, Bet followed us this time. I watched her Jeep in the side mirror. At the security gate, Theo took the time to explain how we always kept the bar closed, just as a deterrent for any wandering person. It hadn't stopped us and we knew it was unlikely to stop anyone else, but it made us feel more secure. At the plane, Theo insisted Bet go upstairs and sit with the girls while he and I unloaded and put everything away. Her shoulder was still injured and by the pallor of her face, it was clear she had overdone it.

We were done by the time evening started to roll across the airport. We decided to not start a fire or the grill to cook anything for dinner. Instead, we used mayo packets to make up a chicken salad that could be eaten with crackers. The girls definitely ate more crackers than chicken, but they were both ready for sleep once their bellies were full.

Theo and I went along the plane to close the windows. Bet sat up near the front of the plane, where her bed was. When Theo and I circled toward her, she spoke into the darkness.

"Who sinned with murder?"

I froze. I had been waiting for her to ask, or had been waiting for Theo to offer his explanation. But neither had happened during the day. Now, we were all inside the fuselage of a plane, with two small children, and I wasn't sure how Bet was going to react to the information Theo was going to give her. After a long sigh, Theo collapsed into a seat across the aisle from Bet. I climbed over him to sit next to him, to be as supportive as I knew how.

"It's me," he said simply.

"Was it necessary?" Bet asked.

Theo seemed surprised by her question. He hesitated, so I covered his hand with mine, trying to encourage him to tell her the story. His hand turned and squeezed mine, but he didn't look at me as he dove into the story. When he talked about the woman trying to keep him as a pet and branding him, his hand tightened and I stroked the back of his fingers with my thumb.

When he finished the whispered story, the plane fell into silence again. I leaned forward to see if Bet had fallen asleep. She was so quiet. But her eyes were glued to Theo's in the limited light we had on. There was compassion there and understanding.

"It was necessary," she said with a nod of her head.

"Now, they must have tracked me to Denver, knowing my family lived here. I'm not sure what made them connect us with you, though. I feel bad about that. If you want to go back to your own place, if you feel safer not with us, we'd understand," Theo said.

He was speaking for both of us, but he knew I was with him no matter what. I already knew this story, had already seen The Children of Z in action. As far as I knew, they had killed the first friends I had made since the apocalypse. I knew how dangerous the group was. But I wasn't walking away from Theo or kicking him out of my group.

"Nope. Boy, none of that is your fault, and I hope you know that. You are the first trustworthy people I've met since losing my husband. Well, the first that weren't just in my head. So, I think I'd like to stick together. But what's the plan now that we know they're here, looking for you?"

Theo shrugged. "I wish I had a good idea. I had hoped we could stay here, create a world for the girls to live in, where they were safe and happy. But now, I'm not sure what the plan should be."

"We'll figure it out. Together," I whispered to him.

His hand squeezed mine again. I was finding reassurance in him, as much as I had planned on supporting him. I figured that was normal in adult relationships, friendship or beyond. A solid support structure, where you worked together. Sometimes I was sure our partnership was very imbalanced, with Theo being so strong and knowledgeable. But no matter my shortcomings, I followed his lead and learned what I could as fast as possible, so I could be useful.

Bet cackled quietly in her seat, and both Theo and I looked over at her.

"Told you he was your man," she said.

Theo looked over at me with his eyebrows raised. I just shook my head and made a motion with my finger around my temple, showing Bet was just slightly batty. I didn't believe Theo was my man. But he was my something. And I would support that and learn what it meant to be part of the group we were building together.

Later, as we were falling asleep in our beds, Theo chuckled quietly.

"Maybe you should say I'm yours, or Bet might take her chance."

I almost choked on my own startled laughter and slapped a hand over my mouth to keep from waking up Gabby, who was curled into my side. The girl had learned to be a fairly heavy sleeper with all the situations she'd had to sleep in. I fell asleep in a happy haze, on my side, with my body curled around Gabby.

I wasn't sure how long I had been asleep before someone shook me awake. My eyes snapped open, and I found Theo leaning over my head. He held a flashlight near his face. He tapped his ear, showing that I needed to listen. At first, I wasn't sure what I was supposed to hear, but then it came to me. A motorcycle. And it was moving fast.

Extracting myself from the cuddling five-year-old, I climbed to my feet. I shoved my legs into cargo pants, pulling them over my sleep shorts. I always slept in a sports bra and tank top, but I pulled a shirt on over, just in case. Quietly, we crept toward the front door that was slightly propped open for ventilation. We could hear the bike better here and knew it was coming our way, or at least in our direction.

A hand fell on my back and I jumped a foot before I realized it was Bet standing behind me.

"It has to be them," I whispered.

Theo nodded as he checked his gun. I hadn't thought of the weapon he had given me, so I hurried back to the shelves in the back, where we kept the guns on the top out of the reach of the girls. With my poor aim, I wasn't going to be any better at aiming from the plane. But if we ended up in a closer, hand to hand issue, I might be helpful. I also strapped on my hunting knife before joining them back at the door.

"It's definitely on the runway, but it changed directions suddenly and seems to be going back toward the airport building," Theo whispered.

I wracked my brain, trying to think of what they could be doing, what their plan was. We had only searched our side of the airport, finding what we needed nearby. So, if they went to the other side, there was no way of us knowing what they could find. There were probably unlimited supplies across the entire property, but The Children of Z didn't seem to only be after that.

As a realization came to me, I felt like a jolt of lightning had hit me on the top of the head. I grabbed Theo's arm, digging in my nails painfully. He stood from his crouching position, turning toward me. There was alarm in his eyes and I knew it matched my look.

"They're obsessed with the zombies, right?" I asked.

"Right," Theo confirmed.

"The airport, Theo. It's full of the dead. If they open the doors, let them out, we'll be trapped." My whisper cracked as the full understanding of my statement hit me.

Theo's eyes widened, and he looked back toward the door. He moved and dragged it open, keeping himself out of the opening, but making sure we could see what was happening. It was then that my fears were confirmed. The motorcycle was parked at the end of a jet bridge, its rider gone. The light from the moon was just enough for us to see the slight details, but the noise caught our attention the most.

A human voice echoed from the jet bridge, sounding like some sort of prayer or choir song. At first there was no answering noise, but as the person appeared at the end of the jet bridge and jumped back down the few feet to get to his bike, additional shambling bodies appeared.

"Theo, we have to get the girls out of here. If they let them all out, we'll never make it," I begged.

Theo looked around the plane. I saw his eyes go wistful over everything we had built and worked so hard on. I could feel the same pain in my chest over losing safety yet again. As we stared at our surroundings, Bet continued to watch The Children of Z member on the runway.

"He's not just letting them out, he's leading them," she said.

When I looked out again, I saw what she was saying. He was slowly driving toward our plane, but they were at least two hundred yards away for now. The zombies falling from the jet bridge took a moment to climb to their feet and get with the program, giving us just a small amount of a lead.

I rushed through the plane, grabbing our go bags. They were bags that Theo had insisted on. One for Tina and all her baby needs. One with toys for the girls, which Theo insisted were important. We had crates of food, ready to be carried down into the van. We had left bottled water packs near the bottom of the stairs, just in case.

Theo was on my heels, grabbing the portable bedding and the duffel of clothing we had always kept packed. Together, we ran down the stairs and straight to the back of the van. I always folded the third row of seats down, so we started shoving things in. Bet joined us, throwing her things into the Jeep, clearly deciding not to leave her vehicle behind.

Then the old woman did something I hadn't expected. She pulled forward the back seat of her Jeep and pulled out a long rifle. It was black, so I couldn't see all the details. But I watched her move with grace and confidence, to the back of the Jeep, where she could rest the gun and look down the barrel. She stood still, watching the rider as he approached.

"Murdering sinner! Come out and face your judgement!" The rider screamed across at us.

Headlights toward the security entrance we always used caught my attention and the roar of an additional engine added to the cacophony of noises in the night.

"There's more coming!" I cried out, no longer worried about being quiet.

Bet turned and nodded. I trusted her to know what was happening, so I ran back up the stairs for the girls. Gabby was already awake, sitting in the bed, fear painted across her features.

"What's happening, Vicki?" She cried.

Tina let out a loud scream from her bed, as she was scared from her slumber.

"Bad people here, kid. We gotta go. Don't worry about clothes, just come in your pajamas," I rushed to say.

I grabbed Tina from her bed and remembered to grab her favorite blanket and stuffy that she slept with. I also reached down and grabbed the same for Gabby, because I knew she'd forget them in her fear. With Gabby following me, I rushed back to the front door.

"Be fast, but be careful. Do not let go of the railing," I instructed.

Gabby's little feet pounded after mine. Just as we got to the bottom, a loud boom sounded from Bet's gun and Gabby screamed, her hands flying up to cover her ears.

"Got him," Bet called over her shoulder, before she adjusted to point her rifle toward the oncoming van.

Theo was suddenly at our side and picked up Gabby. The little girl wrapped her arms around his neck and her legs around his waist, her full trust in the man carrying her. When he put her into the van, she immediately climbed into her seat and strapped in. Another loud shot cracked and Gabby cried out in surprise, but not as much fear this time.

I ran to the other side of the van and quickly strapped Tina into her seat. The baby was still crying; her face red and covered in tears. My heart tugged, but there was nothing I could do for her now. I flung the door shut and ran back to the rear of the van, clocking the zombies that were now crossing the last strip of grass to get to us. Bet took aim and let loose another shot and the van's wheel squealed and the van slid to one side.

"Didn't hit anyone, but definitely hit the van," Bet called.

I was shoving all our bags, and the bottled water into the back of the van, while Theo brought more food down from our most recent run. Bet joined him. But as they came back, the first wave of zombies were reaching our vehicles. I pulled my hunting knife and had my crowbar in my other hand, and took a deep breath. I rushed to the other side of the van, ready to face the dead. We needed time to make sure we were prepared to leave in the middle of the night.

I flew at the first zombie that came close to the van, slamming its head with the crowbar. Before it could fall sideways, I kicked out, slamming my foot into its stomach, causing the pull of gravity to fling it backwards into the approaching dead. Another set of hands grasped for my arm and I pulled back, swinging with my crowbar again. I missed and hit it in the neck, not stopping it from diving at me. Slashing up with my knife, I slammed it through its chin, up into its brain. I pushed the body away from me, holding tight to my knife hilt.

Just as I was shifting my stance to face the next, I felt hands dig into my hair and yank me back. I let out a screech and heard my name being called from behind me. Twisting, I worked to keep my body away from the snapping teeth of the zombie pulling me in. The loud pop of a gunshot sounded and I was falling over the zombie that was still tangled in my hair.

"Let me go...let me go...let me go," I was yelling as I fell into a somersault with my hair still caught by the completely dead zombie.

Landing on my back, I reached up, trying to dislodge myself. I was vulnerable, and a zombie tripped toward me, seeing me struggling on the ground. Lifting my legs, I kicked out at its knees and heard a satisfying crunch as one knee crushed. The zombie tilted sideways and again I was working to free my hair. Suddenly, I felt fingers close around my ankle and I screamed.

I thrashed my body, just as my hair came free, and I was able to see the zombie on the ground that had grabbed me and was trying to bite into my leg. I had lost both my weapons when I went down and knew that was my biggest mistake. Scrambling backward, I kicked out with my free foot, kicking the arm that held me. A war cry came from behind me and suddenly a small body flew over me and a long weapon thunked into the top of the zombie's head.

Bet turned to look at me, a crazy grin on her face, as if this was just another evening for her. Arms came around me and yanked me to my feet, turning me back toward the van. I found myself looking into Theo's panicked face.

"We have to go, now."

I nodded, gripping his arms, looking around for my

weapons. I spotted my crowbar, and I rushed to grab it. Once I scooped it up, another zombie was coming toward me. I broke its jaw with a back armed swing as I ran by to the passenger door of the van. The engine was running the moment I got in and I caught sight of Bet running for her Jeep, zombies slowly following.

Theo threw the van into reverse and hit the gas. Tina was still crying and Gabby screamed as the van swung around until Theo could throw it into drive. I barely got my seatbelt clicked, before Theo was off roading and heading for the chain-link fence.

"Theo, we can't get through that!" I cried.

"No choice. The Children's van is near the exit. We can't risk going near them," Theo replied, his hands tight around the steering wheel.

As if she could read the plan, Bet sped the Jeep to pass us and moved to take the lead. Her vehicle was definitely more hardcore than the van and when she hit the weak spot in the chain-link fence, she easily opened a spot for us to fly through behind her. Her bright headlights illuminated the road and luckily none of the zombies had made it that far yet.

Looking across Theo, I squinted back toward our plane, and my stomach plummeted. I couldn't clearly see what was there, but movement was all over the runway, movement that could only be monsters filling the open space. The place we had created, worked so hard to make comfortable and safe for the girls, was overrun with the dead. To my surprise, tears pricked my eyes, and I felt warm wetness as they rolled down my face.

Theo's gaze moved over my face, and I could see his own devastation. He removed one hand from the steering wheel to grab my hand in comfort.

"We lost it all," I breathed.

"We saved what's most important," he said.

It was then I realized the girls had quieted finally. I looked back to find Tina asleep, her chest hitching with hiccups caused by her sobs. Gabby stared back at me, the whites of her eyes bright against the darkness. They were alive. We were all alive. We had saved what was most important.

CHAPTER 17

WE FOLLOWED BET BLINDLY, as we had no other ideas of where to go. When she finally pulled into a small gas station, the horizon was starting to brighten with dawn's promise. A new day could have felt hopeful and a new start. Instead, I leaned against the passenger window, lost in despair.

Theo shut off the engine of the van, and we all sat silently for a long moment. Then arms came around me and pulled me into an embrace. I was surprised and was on the verge of pulling away. But Theo was insistent as he crushed me to him.

"We're alive," he whispered into my hair. The hair that almost got me killed and was a more ratted mess than ever before.

"That won't do us a whole lot of good if we have nowhere to live," I mumbled.

Theo just shook his head and hugged me tighter. I finally gave in and wrapped an arm clumsily around his shoulders.

"I wasn't sure, for a long minute, if you were alive. When I saw you go down with that zombie, I thought you were dead." He pulled away and looked at me, then started inspecting my head.

I batted away his hands and leaned back into my seat. "I'm fine. My scalp hurts a little, but I didn't get bit."

I turned to look at the girls and found that both of them were still sound asleep. Gabby had taken the longest to calm down, but once she did, the movement of the van was enough to lull her back to sleep in her car seat. I studied them both, in their pajamas, surrounded by what had become their favorite blankets and stuffed animals. What did this world have to offer them?

Outside, Bet was hopping from the Jeep and making her way over to us. She looked no more frazzled than usual, with her red hair flying loosely around her head. Theo popped open his door when she approached, and she leaned into the van. When she saw the girls were asleep, she pressed a finger to her lips, as if we weren't both sitting silent, anyway. Then she motioned for us to get out and follow her.

I quietly opened my door and left it slightly open, so I could hear the girls if they woke up. They had enough nightmares for the night. I didn't want them to also think they had been abandoned. Theo and I met Bet near the Jeep. Now that I was closer to her in the waning light, I could see the fear in her eyes as well.

"How did they know where we were?" It was the obvious question, and I had to get it out immediately.

"They had to have followed us during a run. That's my only thought. But we were so careful," Theo replied.

"They could have seen our fire smoke, or the light from it. But they would have had to be all the way out by the airport to notice it," I added.

"Doesn't much matter now. We just gotta keep moving," Bet said.

Theo and I were quiet at that. Moving with the girls wasn't the easiest option. And it was also not what we wanted for them. We wanted stability. We wanted to build something where they could have a decent life, even if the world was crumbling around them. I knew we were on the same wavelength as Bet looked back and forth between our faces.

"We need somewhere safe for the girls. We can't make them live out of a van forever. There has to be somewhere," I said.

"I had so much hope for the plane. It was in the middle of nowhere. We had supplies nearby. I just feel like we'll figure nothing out," Theo said.

I reached out and his hand met mine. It wasn't normal for Theo to fall into the darkness like me. I knew one of us needed to have faith and belief that we could survive this. That person was normally not me.

"We'll sleep here, get organized. I don't think they'll recoup that fast and there's no way they followed us this time," Bet said.

Theo and I didn't have any suggestions otherwise. However, I was pretty sure I couldn't sleep a wink. He and I went to the back of the van to evaluate what we got away with. We quietly organized and counted the food, diapers, water and other items. We had a box of batteries now, with nothing that needed them. Neither of us had grabbed more than one flashlight and none of the lanterns that we had collected on the plane. We had well stocked our go bags with medications, fire starting supplies, extra sets of clothes, toilet paper, soap and more.

"We're probably ok for a week with this," Theo said, pitching his voice low so not to wake the girls.

"Probably doesn't feel great."

"I know. But it's all we have right now. We should look for a bigger vehicle if we aren't settling down soon," Theo said.

"Then we have to worry about gas."

"We'll have to worry about gas, no matter what. We'll be ok, Vicki. Losing the plane is a hard blow. But we'll figure it out," Theo said.

The positive Theo was back, and I was grateful. I wasn't

sure I could be the one to carry the happy train for our group. I didn't know how to be happy in normal situations. I definitely didn't know how to do that with the world giving nothing but death blows to us. Hearing Theo say we would figure it out made me actually believe we weren't at the end of our rope.

With so many supplies, we couldn't make a bed in the back like we used to. So Theo and I leaned back in the front seats as far as we could, without hitting the girls. They both still slept soundly, which had to be some sort of blessing only children had. As I lay in the front seat and the sky continued to lighten, I couldn't even think of closing my eyes. Nothing but the last few hours replayed over and over in my head.

I was pretty sure Theo didn't fall asleep either, but I didn't feel like a whispered conversation either. Bet had climbed up into the tent she had on the top of the Jeep and we hadn't seen a red hair from her since. When Tina started to fuss and try to get out of her seat, I carefully pulled her into my seat and got both of us out of the van.

At the back of the van, I had the supplies I needed to make her morning milk. I popped the sippy cup into her mouth to prevent her from crying and drawing any attention. She laid her head on my shoulder and made sucking and chewing sounds on the cup.

"Vick, go home?"

I had no idea how much an almost two-year-old should be able to say, but Tina was working on small sentences that we could almost always understand. She still didn't say my full name, but I didn't mind. Thinking about her question, I rubbed my cheek against her soft hair.

"No, kiddo. We're going driving for a while," I whispered.

She nestled deeper into my body, and I found myself rocking her back and forth without thinking.

"What am I going to do with you kids? Why didn't your

mom just stay with you? Take you somewhere safe? Why in the world did she think I was equipped for this?"

As I spoke, Tina's free hand came up to my cheek. Her warm palm slid down my face, over and over, as if to comfort me. The sippy cup popped from her lips and she smacked a kiss on my shoulder. I froze for a moment, not sure how to react.

Tina was pretty free with her affection, but it had always been hugs or her in the need of comforting so I would hold her in my arms. I hadn't known what appropriate affection was between adults and small children. Most foster parents I had throughout my life wanted little to do with me, as long as I was following the rules and staying out of the way.

I pulled myself out of the weird place I was trying to set up shop and rocked her again. I didn't return her kiss, but I let her nestle back into my neck and lowered my cheek to her head again. Holding the little girl wasn't a horrible sensation, it actually made a warmth spread through my chest sometimes. Well, except for the times she was fighting me with sleep or having her diaper changed and it was a battle to the death.

As she snuggled, she popped her milk back into her mouth and I could hear her breathing around swallowing. Suddenly, the feeling of something sliding down my chest made me jump. I pulled Tina away from me for a moment and noticed the milk that had dribbled from the side of her mouth and found its way down my shirt to soak my sports bra. And suddenly, the sweet baby moment was popped like an invisible soap bubble around us.

When I heard murmuring inside the van, I knew it was time to think about breakfast. Gabby climbed out, with Theo following from the driver's side door. We switched kids, and I took Gabby around the corner of the gas station and found a wall for her to lean against to do her thing. It impressed me she was getting better at balancing and relieving herself.

While she peed, I peeked through a side window into the store, noticing it looked lived in, with sleeping bags lined up against the back wall. As soon as Gabby finished, I rushed her back to the vehicles. Bet had appeared, her red, unruly hair, a frizzy cloud around her head. When she saw my face, she frowned and moved toward me. I quickly noted what I had seen through the window.

Theo could hear me as well, and he nodded, grabbing his gun and started toward the store.

"Theo, wait! We don't know who they are. It could just be other survivors trying to make it." I had to run after him to catch up with his long strides.

"And it could be The Children of Z camping here, in between their attacks on Bet and us. We have to make sure." His voice was colder and more menacing than I had ever heard. It freaked me out a bit. I grabbed his arm, yanking him to a stop.

"What is this? You want to go hunting them now? Why are you taking this risk?"

His eyes were full of fire as he stared at me. The jovial Theo was gone, hidden behind anger and revenge. The shock of the change only made me tighten my hold, without knowing what he would really do if he went into the store and found people inside.

"I have to protect us, Vicki. If I don't stop them, they could hurt you or the girls," Theo said.

"You don't have to do anything, especially not right now. And not alone. I'm pretty sure the building is empty. We should take whatever we could use and get on the road," I said.

"We'll do that too. But if it's The Children, I'm not letting them leave alive." He shrugged out of my hold and stalked toward the store.

With little thought, I ran back to the van, grabbed my crowbar, and motioned for Bet to stay with the girls. I ran to catch up with Theo, finding him peering through the side window, just as I had earlier. Looking inside, I confirmed nothing had moved or changed in the last five minutes.

"I think it's abandoned," I whispered.

Theo didn't respond, his hard eyes still staring, waiting for anything to move inside. I tired of waiting for him to move, so I circled around the corner of the store to approach the front door. The glass of the store was intact, so I tried to pull on the door. It easily swung toward me and the smell of musty air wafted out. I detected nothing dead, so I slowly entered. My hand was slick around my crowbar, but I felt prepared to swing at the first sign of trouble.

Behind me, the door creaked as Theo finally joined me. I was inspecting the sleeping bags lining the wall. There were small personal effects near each spot. I stooped and picked up a photo that had been left next to a pillow. A woman beamed from the image, a man's face hidden in her hair, as she flashed a large diamond ring. The sweetness of it made my teeth ache, but I felt like I was invading someone's privacy by looking at the captured moment. I carefully laid the picture back where it had been, a perfect square of clean floor surrounded by dust that had settled.

"No one has been in here in a while," I whispered as I stood and dragged the toe of my boot through the dust. "A long while."

Theo moved around the entire store, checking corners, checking the employee only area and bathroom. He moved efficiently; his plan clear in his mind. I started checking the shelves, trusting that Theo would let me know if there was a threat inside. When he came to my side, we both stared at the few things left. The survivors had cleared most of the edible items out.

"They lived here until they couldn't. I don't think this was The Children of Z," I said.

Theo grunted in response. He picked up one box of saltine crackers that was left and put it under his arm. The rest of the store was an empty shell. Without speaking, we went back through the door to leave behind what felt like a grave that didn't hold any bodies. I couldn't help but think about the items each bed had near it. The photos told me that the people had lost loved ones, and those photos were what they had left. The question that left me with was, why did they leave it all behind?

Back at the vehicles, Bet was giving the girls granola bars and dehydrated strawberries for breakfast. She was telling some sort of funny story, causing Gabby to throw her body back into the van and roll around with laughter. The sound was loud and echoed against the vehicles and building. As if on autopilot, I looked around to make sure nothing could hear her. I didn't miss the small smile that had appeared on Theo's face as he watched the little girl.

After everyone had eaten and the girls were running around, we pulled out the maps we had stored in the van. Theo, Bet and I were silent as we studied highways and side roads that could be an option. But with no specific destination in mind, our options were too endless.

Throughout my life, I had never had the tether of anyone pulling me to a place or keeping me settled. When I aged out of the foster care system, I just stayed where I was. I never felt a desire to go somewhere else, find a new start, or discover new places. I just stopped. Now that I faced this huge decision and a map with more roads on it than I knew existed, I had no idea how to proceed.

Bet disappeared into her Jeep for a moment and came back with a road atlas. She flipped through some pages and laid out a new map.

"I have an idea, since we don't have anything else," she said. She looked at us and I just nodded my head for her to continue. "Stick with me here. We're in Colorado. I had friends that lived in Utah back in the day. It's not a far drive from here. There was this place they took me once. They call it an island, though I don't actually think it is. When the water of Salt Lake is high, you can't get across. I think we'd be fine this time of year."

As she spoke, she pointed to the place she was describing. I squinted to read the label of Antelope Island. She ran her finger along a highway that would lead us to the city and then where we would have to exit and get to the island. I studied the number of miles we would have to travel with the girls and limited supplies. Math hadn't been my best subject, but I knew we wouldn't have enough to survive on an island.

Bet seemed to read my thoughts because she pointed to a major freeway that almost connected Denver and Salt Lake City.

"There are a lot of places to find supplies along the way. And once we get to Antelope Island, well, there's probably not much in way of supplies right there, but we can go back into town to scavenge and bring stuff back. What do you think?"

I looked over to Theo, and he was rubbing his stubble covered chin in thought. His eyes flicked over to me, his gaze locking with mine. I could see him asking me what I thought. The truth was, I had no other grand plans that would save us. I had no experience to speak of that would lend any advice to the situation. My only goals of the apocalypse had been to survive. Then it was to keep the girls and me alive. I had to add Theo and Bet to that, creating a group that I had never really asked for, but I was thankful.

"It sounds as good as anything else," I finally said, with a shrug of a shoulder.

"If Vicki is in, I'm in," Theo replied.

The darkness wasn't gone from his eyes, but he gave me a small smirk to let me know he was still in there. I nodded my agreement, and we bent over the map to discuss a plan. The drive seemed simple, but we needed multiple options if the freeway was blocked in any spots. From the road atlas, we could see there were plenty of off ramps and on ramps, especially near towns. Those were the areas Bet was most concerned about having congestion.

A cry from behind us made me spin with my hand groping for the crowbar I had leaned against the van tire. Theo was faster than me, as he took the few steps it took to get to Gabby, who was on the ground holding her leg to her chest. I dropped the crowbar, realizing there wasn't a zombie threat, and ran to meet them. Fat tears were dropping from her eyes and I looked around for a solution, as if something would just pop out of the ground and present itself.

Tina decided that her sister crying wasn't enough, and she plopped down next to Theo and started to wail as well. With some sort of practiced ease that I didn't understand, Theo scooped up Tina and let bury her scrunched-up face into his neck. He continued to talk softly to Gabby, who wouldn't look up at him and continued to sniffle.

"Hey kid, whatever it is, let us help. We aren't mind readers, ya know?" I said.

I tried to keep the edge from my voice. My patience was running thin with everything that had happened. Losing the plane, being run out of the place we thought was safe, The Children of Z stalking us, and trying to figure out a new plan. Theo's palm fell onto my shoulder and he squeezed softly. It was a reminder for my mind to breathe and calm down. All our problems were not caused by the five-year-old crying in front of us, and it wasn't right for me to take that out on her.

When Gabby still didn't speak, I decided leaving her on the

asphalt would not help anything. Carefully, I slid my arms under her body and lifted her up. I froze when she wound her arms around my neck and clenched. It was easier for me with Tina, because the baby didn't seem to expect much. Gabby was different. She had opinions and obvious needs she could, and always did, express. I wasn't always up to fulfilling those for her.

However, as she held onto me, I cradled her against my chest and murmured softly to her. Just random words of comfort that I wasn't sure actually worked. When I got her to the back of the van, she didn't want me to put her down, so I sat with her in my lap. I looked down at her and was finally able to see the rip in her leggings, on her knee, where she must have fallen while playing. There was red skin under, that was possibly bleeding.

"Hey Gabs," I said, the nickname popping out of my mouth, "let's take a look at your knee. I'll be careful."

She tearfully nodded, but barely loosened her hold on my neck. Carefully, I pulled the material of her leggings up until her knee was exposed. The scrape wasn't large, but it was bleeding. With Gabby still in my arms, I searched the back of the van for the bag we had the first aid kit in. She whimpered as I pulled out the supplies to clean up her knee.

As I dabbed softly at the blood, she jumped and cried harder. However, when I cleaned the scrape with alcohol, she started to wail. Her tear-filled eyes flashed up to mine, and she started to beg.

"You have to blow it! Mommy always blew it!" She screeched.

I froze. The last time someone told me to blow something, it was a drunk college preppy who had gotten lost and found his way into my bar. I refused to serve him and he yelled I should blow him. It was such a strange connection in my mind and I immediately started to laugh, to Gabby's abject horror. Theo suddenly appeared, his face a mask of worry. When he took in the scene, he immediately started to lightly blow on Gabby's knee, and I realized how ridiculous I was.

When she calmed down, Theo shot me a weird look, and I realized I was still chuckling quietly. I smothered it down and gave him a shrug.

"Weird memories at weird times. Sorry." Then looking down at the girl on my lap, I said, "Sorry, kid. I wasn't laughing at you."

Gabby sniffed indignantly and turned her face away from me.

"You're a little crazy, Vicki," she muttered.

She wasn't wrong. My mind wandered and sometimes tried to find solace in the meager life I had before zombies appeared. It wasn't much, but it was something I could rely on, each day giving me exactly what I expected. Now, everything was changing constantly, and I wasn't always sure how to keep up.

One thing I knew I needed to get better at was figuring out how to comfort the kids appropriately. Gabby still sat in my lap, but her face was turned away, her anger with my laughter stronger than the pain in her knee. I shifted, making her lay on my chest, as I opened a bandage to put on her knee. I was careful as I stuck the Band-aid to her skin. Theo watched over us and when the Band-aid was on, he bent and kissed it softly, smiling up at Gabby.

"See? All better," he said.

She graced him with a small smile, but she did snuggle back into me. I figured I was forgiven for my outburst, this one at least. With the drama of the skinned knee beyond us, we had to make an actual choice if we were going to continue going west. I held Gabby for as long as she wanted. But Theo sat next to us on the back of the van, both of us sitting and staring out into the parking lot around us.

"The Children of Z are more in the east, I think. Going west feels like the right choice," Theo said.

Thinking about The Children of Z only reminded me of everything we had lost. The plane, our safe haven, the place we were building as a home. I was tired of losing things, tired of not being safe and scrounging for every morsel we put into our mouths. Rationally, I knew that was just the way of the world now.

"Anywhere has to be better than waiting for them to find us here," I whispered.

CHAPTER 18

WE TOOK the day to organize and scavenge a nearby organic market. The market smelled rancid, with rotting food on every surface. It was one of the stores that had a full salad bar, complete with fresh deli meats and cheeses. Everything was rotting away, and the smell was thick in the building.

Bet stayed with the cars with the girls, while Theo and I worked our way through the store. I coughed and gagged, even with the bandana that was tied around my face. But in the end, it was worth the haul. We were able to find cans of beef and chicken broth and packs of rice. It was a lot of carbs, but the girls would love it. I also grabbed brown rice and quinoa. Neither things I usually stocked in my pantry of ramen and instant macaroni and cheese.

We got on the road relatively quickly. Bet guessed if we had mostly clear freeways, we would arrive in Salt Lake City in eight hours. I didn't have the same optimistic thoughts as she did, but I kept the negativity to myself. Theo was still on edge and I couldn't handle pushing him too far again. While he drove, I stole sideways glances. His body was more relaxed now, but his eyes darted between the mirrors often. I couldn't help staring at the side mirror myself, making sure no one was following.

Three hours later, a sudden popping sound and rattling caused the van to veer toward the freeway's shoulder.

"Oh crap," Theo mumbled.

He hit one short honk on the steering wheel, to notify Bet we had a problem. He fought with the steering wheel to get the van to the side of the road safety. Once we came to a stop, a string of curses came from Theo.

"Bad words," Gabby mumbled, by habit, clearly aware we weren't going to follow her rules.

"What is it?" I had zero experience with cars, just another way I was useless during the apocalypse. I was coming to the understanding that my skills of mixing drinks would not get me far in the world now.

"Something with the power steering, a belt or something broke," Theo said.

With an exhausted sigh, he climbed from the driver's door. After telling the girls to stay in their seats, I followed him. He popped the hood and stared at the engine. Bet appeared and scrunched up her nose.

"We aren't fixing that with duct tape," she said.

"No. We're not," Theo said, as he slammed the hood with more force than necessary.

The three of us stood and just stared at the van, as if we hoped it would miraculously start up again. Of course, magic didn't actually exist, something I was still pissed about.

"We need a new vehicle." I was superb at being captain obvious.

Unfortunately, the van we had been relying on for weeks decided to break down in the middle of nowhere. There wasn't a town in sight, or any abandoned cars we could try to hotwire.

It was clear the only option we had was to pile into Bet's Jeep. The car seats wouldn't fit, so I knew I would hear it from Gabby.

We turned to the job of sorting through supplies. Surprisingly, the Jeep had several storage spaces that Bet wasn't using. It took longer than we had wanted, but eventually we were able to cram food, diapers, and clothes into every open crevice of the vehicle. We even packed the footwells in front of the girls with supplies.

I stood at the back of the van, staring at all the things we had worked so hard to collect. Things we just had to walk away from. It wasn't nearly the same loss as the plane, but it just felt like it compounded that loss. Frustration rose in me, along with the familiar desire for a drink. Anything to make these big emotions manageable.

That's how Theo found me. He joined me, standing shoulder to shoulder in silence. I didn't have to ask. I knew he felt the same desire for things to just work out for once. His hand found mine and his fingers squeezed mine briefly, a sign of solidarity and understanding. He likely wouldn't understand how badly I wanted alcohol in a moment like this, but I appreciated him.

Without a word, we closed up the van. We didn't lock the doors. Maybe the supplies could help someone else. We strapped all the fuel cans to the Jeep, causing it to take on a Mad Max vibe with numerous items hanging all over. Theo sat in the front with Bet, while I sat with the girls. As expected, Gabby had words to say about leaving the car seats behind. Theo had the right things to say and calmed her before we had a full five-year-old meltdown on our hands.

Driving away from the van added more hurt to my already damaged heart. I could feel the sting of failure in the tears that tried to fall. Tina was squeezed into the seat between Gabby and me, sucking on her pacifier at warp speed. Tina and I had one large thing in common: we didn't appreciate upheaval.

"Ya know, that baby is getting old for that paci," Bet said from the driver's seat.

I just stared at the back of her head, having no clue what she was saying to me. Theo turned in his seat and smiled sweetly at Tina, who had her face pressed into my arm.

"It's the pacifier. Usually, babies are weaned from them around a year old."

The idea sent a shiver down my spine, the image of Tina screaming for her comfort object with no end in sight. I just shook my head at Theo, shooting daggers at him from my eyes. It didn't take him long to pick up on my subliminal message.

"Right. We definitely have more pressing things to worry about. Like Vicki and her looks that could murder me on the spot" "

With that jab, and Bet's chuckle, Theo turned back forward in his seat. Tina's body softened against my side, her breathing beginning to even. This was the magic of her pacifier, and no one would take that away from her or me. Not to mention how the noise the baby could make would just attract the dead for miles around.

As the sun dipped behind the horizon, Bet and Theo switched positions and Bet took over the navigation role. We agreed to get to our final destination first, before looking for a new vehicle to carry us and more supplies. The Jeep wasn't the most comfortable vehicle, but we were all eager to get some-where we could sleep safely.

My eyelids were heavy as the movement of the vehicle lulled me to sleep. But just as I was thinking about sleeping, Theo slammed on the brakes. My arm came up just in time to save my face from slamming into the seat in front of me. Gabby wasn't as lucky and her forehead slammed into the fabric of the driver's seat. She let out a shocked squeak before she started crying. Tina picked up her sister's song, and they both cried in tandem.

Looking through the windshield, it was easy to determine the problem. Bet held the map under a flashlight and she nodded to herself.

"We're getting close to the city. The freeways are probably like this everywhere," Bet said.

"Do we have an alternate route?" I yelled over the crying children.

Bet turned to study the map again. While she did that, I watched the girls out of the corner of my eye. I was wondering if I didn't acknowledge the crazy, would the crazy disappear? Theo shot me a look that clearly said I needed to do something. The sigh I let out was meant to communicate my suffering.

I removed Tina from her middle seatbelt and pulled her into my lap. This was all the permission Gabby needed to slide across to sit near me. The result was just two snot covered faces pressed against my body. I swallowed the gag that tried to rise at the idea of neon boogers sliding along my skin.

To try and distract myself, I stared forward, keeping my eyes open for any movement among the tangled wrecks and abandoned vehicles. Across the front of our side of the freeway, a semi truck had jackknifed, which caused the trailer to fall sideways. I could imagine the scene being like ours. The trucker coming over a rise and suddenly facing traffic for miles ahead.

The people in the cars ahead of the truck had no chance, and the collision likely caused the fire that burned part of the truck and the first few rows of stopped cars. In the dim light of dusk, I realized there was movement in some cars. I gripped Tina against my chest as I leaned forward, straining my eyes to determine what I was seeing.

"Are those...?" I trailed off, not sure I could vocalize what I was seeing.

"Zombies. Burned up zombies," Bet said, her voice a whisper.

I couldn't comprehend how that had happened, but I wasn't sure I wanted a genuine answer to that. While Bet studied the map and I stared forward, Theo was watching the rearview mirror. I caught his movement as he twisted in the driver's seat and looked back.

"We've got company and I don't think we want to know who." His words were like a grenade exploding in our vehicle.

I turned as far as I could with Tina clinging to me. Miles away, I could see headlights headed down the highway toward our position. We had been diligent in our movements, watching for anyone following the entire time.

"It can't possibly be The Children," I said.

"Doesn't matter. I don't trust anyone," Theo replied.

Without waiting for Bet to give direction, he threw the Jeep into reverse and went around the first section of wrecks, riding farther on the shoulder. It was only a hundred yards to the next exit, and he immediately took that, guiding the Jeep around the cars that were backed up on it. When we hit the road, Bet called out a direction and the Jeep's tires screeched as Theo took the turn too fast.

Gabby's body trembled next to me and I fumbled to get her back into her seatbelt. I trusted Theo's driving in normal instances, but he seemed like he was trying to outrun the devil as he wound around cars and debris littering the road. When he could, he pulled the Jeep into a residential area and immediately turned off the headlights and slowed until the vehicle was hidden from the main road.

We sat in silence, the only noise coming from Gabby as she sniffled. I wasn't sure how long we waited or what exactly we expected to happen. Bet continued to look over the map, mumbling that now she was even more lost than before. Theo stared into the increasing darkness around us, waiting for any signs of the vehicle following us.

The echo of a growl broke through the darkness and I swung my head around, trying to find the source. A moment later, a hand slapped the glass next to Bet, causing us all to jump. The bloody face of a zombie pressed against the window, broken teeth chomping, trying to get to the warm bodies within the Jeep. Theo started up the engine again and pulled away from the monster without a word.

He drove deeper into the neighborhood, quietly looking at each house. When he found one that looked mostly intact, he pulled into the driveway. Bet and Theo both climbed out, leaving me with the girls until the house was cleared. The Jeep doors were locked and the three of us sat quietly in the back seat. Sitting in what was becoming pitch black made goose-bumps pop up on my neck. Peering into the darkness, I couldn't shake the feeling of being watched.

Theo's face suddenly appeared next to me, and I clamped my hand over my mouth before I screamed out loud. Glaring at him, I unlocked the doors and handed Tina to him. He mouthed his apology with a small, sad smile. When it came to Gabby getting out of the car, she was still holding a hand to her fore-head, where it had struck the front seat. I let her climb into my arms and we followed Theo into the house.

Bet held a lantern, casting a small glow around what looked like a formal living room. Cream-colored couches created an L with a wall of bookcases along one wall. With the girls inside, Theo went back out to the Jeep and brought in supplies for dinner and sleep. He shouldered the makeshift baby bag we had been using with all of Tina's supplies, including several back up pacifiers.

Further into the house, we found a family room that was clearly for heavier use. A large flat screen TV was hung on a wall with a shelving unit that held several gaming consoles. I couldn't have named one of them, but it seemed like there was a lot of money on the shelves. I sat Gabby on one end of a couch, with Tina curled up next to her. There were blankets along the back of the couch, so I pulled one around them and motioned for them to stay.

In the front living room, I pulled the cushions from the couches and brought them to the family room. The house was a single story, but I had no desire to search the bedrooms. A big bed, where we could all be together, and hear if anything came for us, made me feel safest. With every cushion lined up, minus the one the girls were sitting on, the floor of the family room was covered.

The kitchen was just beyond the family room, and I could hear cabinets opening and closing. Bet and Theo murmured to each other as they searched. When I joined them in the kitchen, there was a small mound of canned foods on a small kitchen island. With my flashlight, I checked the labels, finding soups, vegetables and broths. Bet had carried in a small camping stove and got to warming up the hearty soups.

Back in the family room, I found the girls sleepy and on edge. I sat on the cushions on the ground and clumsily pulled them into my lap. Tina practically climbed up my body until she could press her face into my throat. Gabby curled up with her head on my thigh, looking up at me, questions swirling in her eyes.

"We're fine," I said, automatically trying to answer the big question I was sure she had.

"How do you know?" Her eyes searched my face in the limited light we had.

It was times like this, I knew I wasn't equipped to take care of kids. Under Gabby's scrutiny, I felt like I was at the front of an elementary class, naked, and everyone was staring at me.

"I just do," I answered lamely.

"But how?" Gabby insisted.

"I just do, ok? I know Theo will make sure we're all fine," I replied.

That was probably the most honest revelation I had given her. It wasn't me I trusted, because deep down I knew I had no clue what to do next. Theo was the one that seemed to know how to solve the big problems. And I knew he cared about the girls. I had faith in him, more than I had placed in any other human my entire life. That thought made me feel slightly queasy, but I pushed the feeling away and helped Gabby and Tina to sit alone while I helped get things situated for the night.

Once there was enough soup to feed the girls, Bet brought me a big bowl and a real spoon she had found in the kitchen. I sat with the girls and alternated giving them each a bite. Tina was full sooner, and I helped Gabby finish the soup, though she insisted on feeding herself at that point. I then gave each of them a pack of fruit snacks that were packed in Tina's baby duffel.

Later, the girls were curled up under a sleeping bag, fast asleep. Despite their nerves, as long as they were close to us, they seemed to have no problems falling asleep. Theo, Bet and I sat up around a lantern and the map Bet had of the area. It wasn't detailed in the neighborhood, but gave us some general ideas of major roadways that could get us to the island we were shooting for.

"We shouldn't stay here long. There's no way of knowing who was on the highway," Theo said.

"Maybe they found our van?" I added.

"Which would have only been evidence of which way we were headed. I don't like it," Theo replied.

"Let's not borrow tomorrow's problems. Right now, we're safe. The house is locked up tight. We'll take turns on watch. And when we're not on watch, we sleep," Bet said.

Theo's face was stormy, but he nodded. He immediately volunteered to take the first watch, and I didn't argue. I laid down next to Tina and put my arm over her and Gabby on the other side. Neither girl flinched, and I was glad they were so deeply asleep. From my place on the floor, I could just see the faint glow of the small lantern Theo had near the front window with him. It went dark, and I knew he was making sure no one could tell there were living people inside the abandoned house.

Before I had even realized I had fallen asleep, Theo was at my side, touching my shoulder. His eyes were no less turbulent, but he tried to give me a small smile as I yawned and stretched. We switched places, ensuring the girls were always within reach of someone. As I was about to walk away, Theo grabbed my ankle to stop me.

"There are a few instant coffee packets on the counter. I boiled water before I woke you up."

His kindness struck me speechless, but I gave him a small smile in thanks before heading toward the kitchen. I found a mug next to the camping stove and the steaming water. Mixing the coffee, I knew without sugar or powdered creamer; it was going to taste like sewage. But it was the fastest way to get the caffeine into my veins.

With the warm mug in my hands, I went to the front of the house. Theo had set up a chair with a pillow at the back for comfort. Sitting, I could easily see the side of the Jeep in the driveway and the street beyond. I sipped the hot liquid and forced myself to swallow as it assaulted my taste buds. There was no stopping the grimace on my face, but the only one to see it was me in the slight reflection in the glass in front of me.

I tried not to watch the clock and count the minutes until I could go back to sleep. An hour into my watch, movement on the street caused me to slowly stand. I moved, so I was completely in the shadows of the house and could watch what was coming down the street without being seen. I held my breath, wondering if anything could find us in the house we had chosen.

It was clear the figure was a zombie, as it walked on one good leg, dragging the other behind it slightly. As it got closer, the light of the moon illuminated the ripped nightgown it still wore. The pale skin was splashed with dried blood, crusted around bite marks along its leg that seemed partially useless. Even with the mutilated limb, the zombie continued on with the singular thought to find food.

The zombie's slack face swung from side to side as it stumbled along, reminding me of an animal on the hunt. There was no way to know if zombies could smell, but the way this one moved, it almost looked like it was sniffing at the air for clues. Once the zombie moved beyond our hiding place, I moved to the other side of the large bay window and watched it until it was out of sight.

The one zombie was the most excitement my watch had. A few hours before dawn, I boiled water and woke Bet with the same promise of crappy coffee. The old woman bounced out of her sleep much faster than I knew I did. She rushed to the kitchen, and I was only awake long enough to see her make her way into the front room.

When I opened my eyes again, the inside of the house was bright with sunlight and the girls were gone. An initial feeling of panic struck me and my heart thudded in my chest until I shot up and saw them both playing on the floor in the formal living room. Tina saw my movement, and she waved her chubby little hand. I threw up my hand in a response, before falling back into the cushions to give my heart the chance to calm.

Theo appeared above me with a packet of coffee and I couldn't contain the face I made. It only made him chuckle quietly before he headed into the kitchen. He knew no matter how nasty it was, I would still drink at least one in the morning. I missed all the supplies we had left behind on the plane. We had found boxes of sugar cubes and it made the instant coffee so much more drinkable.

In the kitchen, I found the makings for cereal and a small jug of powdered milk that had been mixed. I added the milk to the cereal before adding a large amount to the coffee Theo had set next to me.

"We have a bit of a complication out front, but we'll deal with it once we've all eaten," he whispered.

"Complication?" I spoke around the spoonful of sugary cereal I was shoveling into my mouth.

"Zombies that were attracted to the Jeep for some reason."

"Smell?" I asked.

Theo looked over at me with a raised eyebrow.

"Just wondering. I saw one zombie last night and I swear she was smelling the air. I've never studied them before, but it made me think."

"I guess no way of knowing. I was thinking maybe a squirrel or some other small animal ran by and they just got stuck bouncing around the driveway," Theo said.

"That makes more sense," I replied, spooning more cereal into my mouth.

Bet appeared in the kitchen, with the girls in tow. They settled on the kitchen floor with paper and pens that must have been in a junk drawer somewhere. Bet and Theo started packing up the items we brought with us. We then filled a few plastic bags with the remaining canned goods we could take from the house. The space of the Jeep was minimal, but I would rest my feet on cans if that meant we had food.

I looked down at the real bowl and spoon I was eating with. One thing I hadn't realized I would miss was real kitchenware. Eating from plastic silverware had been a regular occurrence for me, as I often ordered out for meals. But I always had real things in my kitchen should I want them. It felt weird to think about how we bounced around with nothing of our own.

Once I finished, I put everything in the sink, because that just felt like the right thing to do. I then went to the bay window and looked outside. I could see the zombies Theo referred to, five that I could see as I watched. They didn't know we were in the house, as they just bounced between the Jeep, the garage door and back. They seemed aimless in their movement. That would change the moment we opened the door and let them know warm bodies were just inside.

CHAPTER 19

"AND DO NOT LOOK out the windows, no matter what." My voice was stern as I hid the girls behind the couches in the front family room.

Gabby had her arms around Tina and nodded her head solemnly. Tina fussed and tried to pull away. I gave them a bowl of crackers and the baby immediately dove into the snack. I lifted my crowbar and tested the knife Bet had given me in my other hand. It felt lighter than the one Theo had given me before, but it was sharp, which was what I needed.

Theo, Bet and I stood behind the closed door, ready to rush out and meet the zombies between us and the Jeep in the driveway. We had all our supplies piled up and were ready to be loaded, but we needed the monsters away from our vehicle first. I nodded to Theo, and he flung open the door. He rushed out first, his knife held in a combat position. I followed quickly, giving us enough space to fight and Bet slammed the door behind herself.

Theo met the first zombie that he came to and pushed it into the yard and away from me and Bet. Spreading out the group was one of his strategies to make it easier for us to take them down, one by one. I figured he knew what he was talking about, so I agreed with the plan. There wasn't much time to think, because as the zombies noticed us, their movements became more focused.

A large female zombie came toward me, her mouth open in a growl with her hands out in front of her. I danced around it, toward the end of the driveway, making the zombie spin and lose balance for a moment. The confusion was long enough for a second, smaller monster to insert itself between the large zombie and me. As soon as it was within reach. I swung my crowbar with enough force that the vibrations from the impact almost caused me to drop the bar. I gritted my teeth and willed my fingers to hold on tighter.

The small zombie went down to the side, but the one blow hadn't killed it. The larger zombie, not having the chance to change direction, fell directly over the smaller one on the ground. I looked down and shrugged my shoulder, silently thanking them for making my job so much easier. I brought the bar down on the back of the larger zombie twice until it stopped moving and crushed the smaller one underneath. The smaller zombie continued to hiss and fight to get to me, but I didn't wait before slamming the sharp end of the crowbar through its forehead.

In the yard, Theo had taken down his first zombie, and a second was headed his way. Bet had a large cleaver she had found in the kitchen and was swinging it down on the top of a zombie's head. She had sworn the knife was quality, while I half expected the blade to break from the handle. But when she tore it from the zombie's head, brain matter sprayed in an arch and she still gripped the knife in her hand. She caught me watching and nodded with a big smile. I just shook my head.

In total, there were only six zombies in the group and we quickly handled it. As we moved the bodies away from the Jeep,

I didn't miss the little face that was peering at us through the front window. I swung my gaze toward Gabby and waited until she realized I had caught her. Her mouth dropped open, and I pointed back into the house. She disappeared quickly, but I knew we'd still have to have words.

Once the bodies were all out of sight of the car, we were all out of breath and I was feeling filthy. However, there was no stopping.

"We gotta go." I pointed down the road, toward the end of the street we had originally come down, where another group of zombies were gathering.

"Get the girls," Theo said as he ran for the door.

As we busted in, Gabby's head popped up from behind the couch.

"I'm sorry!" She exclaimed.

"Later," I growled, as I swung Tina up into my arms.

Gabby grabbed their bowl of crackers and ran after me as I went out the door for the Jeep again. Theo and Bet were behind us with bags. Gabby peered around the end of the Jeep and a small squeak came from her, indicating she had seen what was coming. Theo nudged her back toward me as he shoved supplies into the side compartment.

"Let's go, climb in," I said as I guided her to the Jeep door I had opened.

"They're coming," she said as she climbed into the backseat.

I was on her heels, so as soon as I sat down, Theo could slam down the seat and climb into it. Bet was behind the wheel and the Jeep roared to life seconds later. Without conversation, Bet threw the Jeep into reverse and turned toward the other end of the street. Theo barked out a few directions, since he now had the map open on his lap.

Gabby climbed to her knees and watched the zombies disappear into the distance. Once she seemed satisfied and we turned a corner, she sat down and put her seatbelt on. I had a sarcastic comment on my tongue about her need to follow the rules, but I bit it back and just let myself take a few deep breaths.

One of my arms had gore coating the skin, and I was pretty sure it was all over my pants. My crowbar was at my feet and I shoved the knife from Bet into a sheath in my back pocket. Since I couldn't exactly clean up, I just held the dirty arm away from the girls and watched the buildings go by as Bet drove. My eyes took in the general devastation of some areas. I felt surprised that other areas looked completely normal.

We wound through neighborhoods, from one end to another, avoiding big roads that were congested. When we found a large main street that had some room, Bet stepped on the gas and we sped by shopping centers, schools, gas stations and soda shops.

"What's with the soda shops? I swear I've seen like ten of them today," I said.

"Mormons. You'll see more soda shops than bars, I guarantee it," Bet replied.

That made me snort a laugh, but I smothered it when Gabby looked over like she was going to ask questions. I was not having the religion conversation with her. Tina started to get restless and without the harness of a car seat, it was easier for her to squirm. Theo glanced back and motioned for me to hand her forward.

"We can't sit up front. We're too small," Gabby piped up.

Theo shot her a soft smile and nodded. "You're right, little one. But we're going to break the rules just for now, so we can get to the next place we're going without her crying. How's that sound? I promise to keep her safe."

Gabby looked like she was actually having an internal debate, but she eventually nodded. I unbuckled Tina and handed the squirming baby up to Theo. He let her stand on his seat and hold the bar in front of him. She squealed and Bet laughed as she slowed down slightly. While Gabby was concerned with all the rules, Tina didn't care what she was supposed to be doing. Her little mind was just looking for entertainment and she got it from the fresh vantage point.

When I took my eyes from Tina, feeling sure she would not get hurt, I realized I had missed us leaving the city behind. We were on a road that seemed to cut directly through the salt flats of the great Salt Lake.

"This is the road to Antelope Island."

The mid day sun reflected off of the areas where there was water, but there was so much white beach as well. The further we drove, the further I got from the only place I had called home. I had never imagined seeing something so beautiful in person. The sunny day just looked different from this place.

I had to remind myself of the hell we were living, to push the smile back. But Theo had caught my gaze, and he turned to look at me. He smiled at my face and gestured around us.

"It's pretty, huh?"

"I've seen nothing like it," I replied.

"Wait till the sun goes down. That's when it's a real winner," Bet said.

I looked forward just in time to see the large concrete building we were headed for. But as we approached, an enormous animal blocked the road and Bet slowed the Jeep until we stopped.

"What is that!" I released my seatbelt and leaned between the two front seats. "It's a freaking buffalo!"

I had never seen any animal so large in real life. Foster families had never taken me to a zoo to see animals safely behind glass and bars. I had seen plenty on tv and learned in school to know what it was, but that it was standing in front of us sent my heart pounding.

"I think they're bison out here, but yeah, basically the same idea. They live on the island. I'm surprised the zombies haven't found them and had a feast, but the island seems fairly deserted," Bet said.

"They just live here? How is that a thing?" I asked.

Bet shrugged. "I don't know the complete story. I only visited with some friends and I never really read the stuff inside the visitor's center. I just know they have a lot of them and they're protected."

Shaking my head, I felt shocked that a place like this even existed. The bison watched us with his large dark eyes, but when we didn't move, he lost interest and slowly ambled off the road until he could find grass to chew on. I followed him with my eyes and squealed like a little girl when I took in the rest of the scene. I leaned over Bet and pointed.

"It's a baby!"

The large bison that had moved from our path had joined a few others who were grazing. A smaller animal, with orange brown hair, leaned against a full grown bison. I covered my mouth to stifle any more noises, but I couldn't get over how adorable it was. Gabby pressed against her window trying to see and I realized I needed to let the child get a better look.

I pulled back and indicated for her to lean forward like I had. She hesitated, so I popped her buckle and decided for her.

"Gotta see it while we can, kid," I said.

I didn't miss the way her eyes lit up when she could see the baby fully. A little gasp left her mouth, which was significantly better than my childish scream. The thought made me cough and cover my mouth with my fist, reminding myself I was a full-grown adult that shouldn't get so excited over baby animals.

Gabby took her time looking and then counting the number of bison she could see in the herd. When it looked like one wanted to walk our way, Bet softly told Gabby we had to go and started rolling the Jeep forward. That was all it took to make Gabby scramble back to the safety of her seatbelt.

"Don't worry, little one. We're here," Theo called back.

Bet pulled the Jeep up to a large building. There were walls of windows off to a side, but the majority of it looked to be composed of concrete. The engine cut off, and we all sat still, waiting for anything to surprise us. I looked back to make sure the bison didn't decide they were even more interested in us now. I remembered reading about how the animals could be very dangerous if you got too close and I wasn't in the mood to get trampled.

The building was labeled Antelope Island State Park Visitor Center. We slowly approached, the inside of the building was dark except for the places sunlight could stream in. Theo handed Tina to me so he could pull his knife and the gun he was carrying. At the door, Bet looked around and nodded.

"No one has been here in a while." She motioned toward the glass door and I immediately stepped back.

"Nope. I'm not walking through that," I said.

I had less trouble facing zombies than what was hanging in front of the door to the visitor's center. Spiders. I had an irrational fear of spiders. As I looked at them now, I shifted nervously, my skin crawling as if I could feel their eight legs scurrying across me. Gabby's hand found my elbow, and I jumped, causing her to let out a small shriek. She stumbled away from me, but Theo caught her before she fell into the webs that surrounded us.

"No human movement lately, so the spiders took over. I can handle it," Bet said, her voice completely too calm for my understanding.

I backed away until I was standing by the Jeep again. Theo followed with Gabby, his face split in a grin.

"I've watched you face down zombies more than once and spiders is what's going to stop you?"

"I don't want to talk about it."

Bet used her long weapon to swing through the spider webs. As spiders fell, she pushed them away from the building with the toe of her boot. I visibly shivered, wishing she would just stomp on them and snuff out their existence. Theo chuckled quietly next to me, but I ignored him. It only made me want to find out his fear and use it against him until he begged for my forgiveness. I filed that plan away for a later date.

"It's all clear of the eight-legged variety," Bet called.

I stepped forward, but I stopped when I saw her nudging something on the ground.

"Are you sure? Bet, seriously, I will make you think you're hearing voices again. Are you sure?" I called, my voice a higher pitch than it normally was.

She looked up at me, a weird look on her face for a moment, as she tried to process what I had said. Then she let loose a loud cackling laugh, smacking her thigh with her hand.

"You're a funny one, Vicki."

"I wasn't joking," I mumbled.

Even though I wanted to trust her, I held Tina close to my chest, and followed behind Theo, so he could catch any left over webs. When we made it to the doors without incident, I let out a whooshing breath.

"Vick, ow," Tina babbled.

Theo turned and tapped my arm. "You're holding on too hard, I think."

"Oh, crap. Sorry, kid." I loosened my hold and let her slide to my hip, where she stretched her arm out.

The sound of the jiggling door caught our attention, and Bet frowned.

"It's locked. Maybe they closed up in the beginning and never opened up again?"

"Or someone locked themselves inside," Theo said.

Bet handed her weapon to Theo and dug into her small day pack. She produced a small kit, and she bent in front of the lock. I watched in surprise as she picked the lock and soon the door was swinging out. Theo and I stood looking at her for a moment and she just shrugged a shoulder.

"Some skills are more useful than others these days."

Theo took the lead into the center. We all stepped through the door, but he used his knife and made a loud tapping noise against a metal sign hanging just inside the door. The sound echoed through the building and we all waited. When the door opened, I immediately noted the absence of the smell of the dead. But even with that, we had to make sure. A long moment stretched out as we were all quiet, except quiet babbling from Tina.

Once we were pretty sure we were alone, we moved further into the center. There was a welcome desk right in front of us and a gift shop on one side. I motioned for us to go into the shop when I saw clothing hanging from the wall. After handing Tina off to Theo, I stripped off my dirty shirt, wiping as much of the gore from my arm as I could. I threw it into a corner and grabbed the first souvenir shirt I found to pull over my head. When I turned toward Theo, he immediately burst into laughter.

"What?" I demanded.

Looking down, I read the shirt upside down and realized what the humor was. The shirt boasted something about a spider fest for the year.

"Freaking kidding me," I breathed to myself.

"It's perfect, Vick. Just wear it," Theo said, as he calmed himself down.

Tina had a huge smile on her face, not understanding why Theo was laughing, but his emotions were infectious. I couldn't stop myself from flashing a smile as well. I glanced around the gift shop and saw a small display of what looked like beef jerky, but the rest was normal knick knacks that would be more of toys for the girls than survival items.

Leaving the gift shop behind, we wandered through the displays that talked about the local wildlife, rocks and the great Salt Lake. Above some displays, stuffed heads looked down at us and I averted my gaze. I didn't like the feeling that they were staring at me. Theo didn't seem to have the same problem, as he studied each of them slowly.

I found myself in front of a wall of windows that opened the view over the lake. It was a beautiful vantage, but also gave us a good way to keep an eye around us. The building actually had several windows, giving us the chance to study the surrounding terrain.

"We'll need to cover some of these. We don't want light to show at night. I'm sure it would be like a beacon," Theo said.

"Can't cover these," I gestured to the wall.

He nodded thoughtfully, but continued looking around. Suddenly, Bet's voice came from across the room.

"Don't bring the girls over here!"

Theo and I exchanged a glance before I took Gabby's hand and he put Tina on my hip. Keeping the girls with me, Theo went to join Bet. Impatiently, I turned to show Gabby the rocks again, and she just rolled her eyes at me.

"They're rocks. The same as everywhere." Her voice was from a five-year-old, but the attitude felt so much older.

I just shrugged and looked at the display again, pointing out some of the different things because of the salt content of the area. Gabby wasn't interested. She turned and stared in the direction Theo had gone. She was too smart to be distracted by a museum display. I stopped trying and turned to lean against the display and wait for Theo and Bet.

They appeared a few minutes later and Theo stepped close to whisper in my ear.

"Looks like it was a ranger who might have worked here. Locked himself into the office and killed himself. Shot himself in the head. We're just keeping the office locked. There's nothing in there for us, except the gun, which I grabbed," he said.

I nodded, saddened by what the scene must have looked like. But I was glad Bet found it on her own and it wasn't something I would have to comfort Gabby through. After that discovery, we were careful opening a storage room, but were happy with only finding gift shop items and boxes of flyers and pamphlets for the museum. There was also a row of five gallon refill water bottles for a cooler that was behind the welcome desk.

"We can make this work," Theo said, when we made our way back to the front door.

"I feel really exposed here, yet we should be able to see anyone coming from far off," I replied.

Theo nodded at my comment and looked at Bet for her opinion.

"Honestly, I'm surprised no one else is in here. There might be people on the other side of the island, hiding, camping. But they aren't here. So I say we settle for a little bit."

"If anyone shows up, I think we move on," I suggested.

"Not everyone is a threat...," Bet said, but her voice trailed off as if she were remembering what had happened in Denver just a few days before.

With nowhere else to go, we agree to set up camp inside the visitor center for the time being. We brought in all the supplies, leaving the go bags in the Jeep. I was no longer willing to leave it to chance if we had to hit the road suddenly. Everything felt unsure, and I had to make sure I could take care of the girls, no matter what happened.

When we evaluated the small pile we had, we agreed that Theo and I would head into the edges of town to find something to make beds more comfortable on the hard ground and whatever food we could scavenge. Bet ripped the paper bags from the check-out counter in the gift shop to block the windows in that area. It was easy to decide to sleep on the thin carpet that was in the gift shop, instead of the hard concrete floor in the rest of the center. We would only use light at night in that area to minimize what could be seen from the windows.

I gave Gabby strict instructions to listen to everything Bet told her to do. We no longer had a playpen for Tina, so the baby was trying to run wild all over the visitor's center.

"It's really important you keep an eye on your sister, ok? No opening doors or messing with anything. And if you need to use the bathroom, ask Bet to take you outside. You do not go alone," I said.

Gabby looked up at me with a serious look on her face, but rolled her eyes at the last sentence. Her look told me she knew what the rules were, and she wasn't stupid, but she didn't say a word, which I counted as a win for the moment. Tina shrieked from somewhere and when I turned, Theo was holding her upside-down by her waist. The baby was laughing hard and her face was turning a shade of red, that made me worry. He flipped her the right way up and set her with Gabby, where she started to pout and hold her arms up for more.

"Later, little one," Theo said, bopping Tina on the nose.

The baby scrunched up her nose for a moment and I was waiting for a wailing to start. Instead, Bet appeared with a bag of mini chocolate chip cookies. I had no clue where she found them, but it sure quieted down the baby. Bet winked at us and made a motion for us to run while the coast was clear.

As the Jeep started up with Theo behind the wheel, I let out a loud sigh.

"This must be what parents feel like when they finally get a night out. Like, do they want to sprint out the door like I just did?" I joked.

Theo chuckled, but focused on pulling from the parking lot back onto the main road. I could see the bison in the distance again, but none were blocking the road this time. Rolling the window down, I allowed the clean air to wash through the Jeep. We both smelled a little ripe after running from the plane and fighting the dead. I wanted to feel the air on my face while it was safe to do so. There was no knowing when it would happen again.

CHAPTER 20

THE DRIVE away from the island to the edge of town didn't take long. At first it was only neighborhoods we rolled by, but Theo pulled into the first strip mall we saw. A burned-out shell of a gas station stood foreboding in a corner of the parking lot. I eyed the damage as we slowly entered, but nothing moved around it and I dismissed it as anything to search.

The shopping center wasn't burned, but there were signs of looting and damage along the fronts of the stores. Theo pulled into a parking spot a good distance from anything that could block our view. He pointed to one side, and I saw he was showing me the mattress store.

"Sometimes those places have sheets and blankets, ya know, to give away to buyers. Maybe we can find something in there."

I agreed with a nod of my head and picked up my crowbar as he turned off the Jeep engine. When we climbed from the car, I slammed my door, hoping to draw out anything that might look for a snack. A scuffing sound from the other side of the shopping center drew our attention to a lone zombie that was coming our way. The zombie woman had once been in a business suit and, amazingly, still had one high heel on.

"I got it," Theo said.

He jogged over and easily handled the dead. When he came back to me, he was wiping off his knife. He often kept a cloth in his back pocket for that exact purpose. I scrunched up my face when he shoved the cloth into his back pocket.

"I'll never get over feeling nasty every time we deal with those things," I mumbled.

"We definitely need a way to shower," Theo added.

I nodded as we made our way across the parking lot. The strip mall was home to the mattress store, a pet store, a gym, a small gift boutique and a taco shop. The taco place was the most destroyed, clearly people looking for food or money had gotten there early. We ignored it and continued toward the mattress store, focusing on what we needed most in the moment.

Trips into town would likely be daily until we collected enough supplies to create a stockpile inside the visitor center. Though it was on an island, I wasn't feeling as secure as I had with our plane. My chest ached when I thought about all the work we had put into it over the weeks we were there. And anger rose when I thought about how it wasn't the zombies that had ruined it for us. It had been other living people.

The mattress store had been slept in. That was the first thing I noticed. Some beds had abandoned sleeping bags on them, trash littered the show room and there was a smell of something rotting. We hesitated near the front, but there weren't many places for something to be hidden. Theo pointed, and we split to go to either side of the store.

My side had the register and desk for customers to complete orders. I walked around, looking through the drawers and cabinets, finding nothing but office supplies and forms. A pad of paper was on the ground, with crayon scribbles on it. I stared at the scribbles for a long moment, wondering what had happened to the child that had clearly stayed in the store at some point.

A loud crash and Theo's cry had me running to the other side of the store. The first thing I noticed was a row of mattresses that seemed to have fallen from the stand they had been in. The second thing I noticed was the growling zombie that was trying to crawl across to get to Theo, who had been buried by the mattresses and stand.

The zombie was a squat figure, a man if I had to guess, but there was a haphazard bun of hair on the top of its head. When I yelled to get its attention, it turned, and I noticed that part of its scalp was detached, waving with each movement, which caused the man bun to move. I gulped down the bile that tried to rise as it focused its dead eyes on me.

The zombie was partially stuck, not able to get to me, but I couldn't reach it without climbing into the mess. I could barely see Theo as he fought to get from under the mattresses and the zombie who had crawled on top. The zombie seemed confused, as he knew there was something close, but he couldn't get to it. But he could see me. So, he continued to try to get across the mattress to me.

Taking a deep breath, I stepped and put one leg between two mattresses and swung the crowbar down on the zombie's head. The swing threw my balance off and my body fell to the side, causing me to land on the metal stand. A searing pain radiated through my leg as I fell, and I couldn't stop the scream that erupted from my throat. My leg felt stuck, despite trying to pull it free. Each movement only made the pain radiate further up my leg.

"Vicki!" Theo was finally sliding from under the pile.

Luckily, my one blow to the zombie had killed it and it now rotted alone in the middle of a twin sized mattress. Theo started pulling mattresses away, that were between us, before he could get to me. He tried to pull me to my feet, and I cried out in agony.

"My leg...something's wrong." A million thoughts were flying through my head. Was it a bite? Is it broken?

He bent to look at my leg and the curse he let loose told me what he saw wasn't good. I couldn't see him where he crouched near my leg, but I felt the sudden tug of my pant leg as he ripped it away from whatever was hurting me.

"So, we have a problem..." he started, but his voice trailed off as I felt his fingers move over the bare skin of my lower leg.

"Spit it out, Theo. I know there's a problem. One that hurts badly." My teeth were gritted tightly as I tried to speak.

Another mattress moved and Theo shoved the zombie body away from us. I was grateful, because I kept sucking in its rotting smell as I was trying to calm myself.

"There's a metal piece of the rack that has dug into the side of your lower leg, Vicki. It's bleeding pretty heavily. We need to get the metal out and slow the bleeding, or the problem is going to be bigger," he finally explained.

"Metal stuck into me? How are we going to get it out? Am I going to bleed to death...OH MY GOD!" My rambling ended in a scream as Theo yanked out whatever was embedded into my leg.

As soon as the metal was out, I felt a relief, but I could feel the warmth of my blood as it flowed. Theo ran to the nearest bed and ripped off a decorative sheet. With his knife, he cut several long strips.

"I'm going to wrap this up before we move you. I'm afraid that any movement is just going to open the wound more. You need stitches. I have nothing with us to do that."

Tears were streaming down my face at this point. I punched a mattress, cursing the God that forced me to no longer drink. Then I muttered prayers under my breath, begging for alcohol to appear and help the pain go away. Stars danced in my vision and I started to have an actual concern about how much blood I was losing.

"Theo...I'm not feeling so good...," I muttered.

"Vicki, keep talking. Hold on. I'm going to tie this tight. It's going to hurt like crazy," he said, his voice becoming loud and commanding.

The blinding pain of the wrap being tied off made me scream again, even as I tried to grit my teeth against it. I couldn't stop the sound, knowing I could draw more zombies to us. In my mind, I tried to compartmentalize the pain, push it to a corner and make it stay. But I had never felt anything so extreme in my life.

"Why do they say women are good with pain? I can't handle this," I tried to say, but my words came out muffled and confused.

When Theo cursed again, it sounded alarmed, and I tried to turn my head to look at him, but everything was swimming in front of my face. I let my head fall to a mattress, before I lost my stomach contents all over the place.

"Vicki, put your arm around my neck. Can you do that?" Theo was saying near my ear.

I could feel his arm under my knees, but I could barely help him pick me up. I could feel my strength draining from me, like the pool of blood I had left under the mattress pile. As he stood, my head lulled over to his shoulder and his short beard tickled my face. I didn't have the strength to pull away or itch my face, so I just let my muddled thoughts go.

"You need to stay awake, Vicki. You're suffering from blood loss. We gotta get fluids in you. We gotta get back to Bet. The supplies for stitches are there." Theo was talking faster than I could understand.

What I did know was when we left the mattress store, zombies were descending on us. My screams had called them all as if I were ringing a dinner bell in the middle of the strip mall. Theo rushed to the back door of the Jeep, his breathing coming out roughly as he tried to run with me in his arms. In my mind, I wanted to hold myself up, hook my arm around his neck, make it easier on him. But my limbs felt heavy, and I was confused.

At the door, Theo had to shift to open the door and my leg hit the Jeep, causing me to cry out. I didn't miss the sounds of growling nearby, but there was nothing I could do if I was going to be a meal for them. The door swung open and Theo unceremoniously shoved me across the seat, causing another scream to rip from me. It was the last thing I experienced before everything went black.

The next thing I knew Theo was shaking me, one hand on my shoulder and the other on the steering wheel. When he looked back at me, I could see blood and gore splashed across his handsome face.

"You're dirty, again," I mumbled.

"Oh, thank the lord. Vicki, honey, I need you to stay awake," he said.

Theo put both hands back on the Jeep and we bumped violently as he drove. Though I cursed, he just pressed his foot harder against the gas pedal. I looked around and tried to take stock of what was happening. Theo's backpack was under my wounded leg and I could see where the sheets were soaked through with blood, the dark red liquid seeping up my leg.

"It's bad, isn't it?" I asked.

My mouth felt like a bag of cotton balls had been shoved in and then down my throat, but the words were loud enough for Theo to hear.

"It's not great, but we're going to fix this. I just need you to stay with me."

"You'll take care of the girls, right? If I can't...if it's too bad...don't leave them. Please," I begged.

"You are going to recover and take care of them yourself. And I'll never leave them, no matter what," he replied with a hard, determined voice.

"What happened in the parking lot?" I asked.

I didn't see how many zombies there were, but I knew I had heard more than a few. And Theo had been alone, trying to protect me in the Jeep.

"Nothing. Everything is going to be fine," he said.

But his shoulders were stiff and his eyes stayed glued ahead. As I stared at his profile, from where I laid, a new feeling combined with the pain in my leg. Fear. I tried to pull myself up toward Theo, to see with my own eyes that everything would be fine. But my fatigue pulled me down and I could only watch him as my vision faded to black again.

I was lost in a sea of pain, crying, screams, and deep fear. My dreams were a mixture of reality and pieces that my brain tried to fill in when I passed out. I saw Bet and her face scrunched up as she studied my leg. I felt the pain as they poured saline solution over the wound to clear it of debris. I screamed as the needle entered my skin, before my mind spared me and I passed out again. The last vision I remembered was Gabby's pale, tear-streaked face and her hands reaching for me.

Light was streaming into the visitor's center when I tried to open my eyes again. I didn't move, allowing my mind to catch up with the sensations in my body. A moan couldn't be stopped as the pain from my leg reached my brain. One of my hands was being gripped by a smaller hand, which I was pretty sure was attached to the warm body pressing against my side.

Theo suddenly blocked the light in my face as he leaned over to look into my eyes.

"Vicki? Can you hear me?"

The cotton balls were still living in my mouth and I made a motion for a drink. Theo rushed away and came back with a canteen. Sliding his hand under my neck, he helped prop my head up so I could sip water and try to rinse away the dryness. My tongue felt as if it was glued to the top of my mouth, but the water started to loosen things up.

"I hurt my leg, which is far away from my ears," I mumbled.

"Sarcasm, intact. Check," Theo replied, his face lighting up with a smile.

"Vicki?"

Gabby's voice was tentative and just above a whisper. It took a lot for me to turn my head in her direction. When I did, she let out a little sob and buried her face into my chest. The impact caused a groan to pop out of my mouth, but I didn't stop her. Carefully, I tested my arm and found I had enough strength to put it around her.

"I'm fine, kid," I mumbled.

"I thought you were dead." My shirt muffled her voice, but she didn't pull away to speak more clearly.

Her words caused moments in my broken memories to come together. I turned my head to look at Theo. His eyes were clear. He looked warm and alive. He didn't seem to sweat or look sick. When he realized I was studying him, he turned and pulled the neck of his shirt away. My mouth dropped open when I saw the perfect circle of a bruise on his shoulder.

"The teeth didn't break through my jacket, but there was a moment there...," he trailed off, looking at Gabby and back into my eyes. He was clearly telling me we'd talk about it later.

The relief I felt almost took away the pain in my leg, but that was an almost. I cringed as I tried to shift on the ground.

"Don't move. Bet sewed you up, but we haven't been able to give you any pain meds since you were sleeping. You could probably use some ibuprofen at least, now."

Footsteps announced the arrival of Bet. When I glanced her

direction, I realized someone had found a play pen, because Tina was standing in it, watching events unfold in front of her.

"How long have I been asleep?"

"A day and a half," Bet said.

She crouched with Theo and opened her hand to show three small reddish pills. I opened my mouth obediently, and she fed them to me, followed by Theo lifting my head for water again.

"Are these going to cut it?" I asked.

I found myself wondering again if there was any booze in the visitor center. Maybe one employee had a drinking problem and hid a flask or a small bottle of something in a drawer. I was pretty sure the small pills Bet gave me weren't going to take the pain away. The most I hoped for was taking the edge off as I laid on the ground with Gabby splayed across my chest and my foot elevated to keep pressure off of my wound.

"Your blood loss was more than we'd like, but with the wound closed up, you should be on the road to recovery," Bet said.

She moved toward my leg, beyond my field of vision. Gabby stayed where she was, so I looked over at Theo.

"I knew something was wrong when I woke up in the Jeep the first time. I didn't wanna fall asleep again. I was so scared," I whispered, just loud enough for Theo to hear.

He bent low so he could speak directly into my ear and hopefully limit what small ears could pick up.

"After I got you into the Jeep, they converged really quickly. I lost my jacket to the one that got a hold of my shoulder. Somewhere along the way, I had cut myself, so when I saw my own blood, I freaked out a little. But Bet has reassured me she didn't find any bites when she looked me over."

"Looked you over, huh?" I glanced down at his fit frame. "Are you sure she wasn't too distracted checking you out?"

Theo pulled back to look at me with a small smile.

"Can't decide if that was a compliment or a smart ass remark."

"Bit of both, I guess," I replied, my voice losing its strength.

"Well, it's been over a day and I'm not sick, so I'm most likely in the clear," he replied.

He leaned back and put his hand on my head. I wanted to push up into his palm, because it felt cool against my skin. But when he frowned, I had a feeling something was wrong. I forced my eyes to stay open and watched his face as his hand slid from my forehead to my cheek. Bet leaned close, and they exchanged a few words I couldn't hear. The old woman disappeared again toward my leg. I couldn't hold back the wince as she moved my leg, prodding the injured skin.

Bet walked away and came back with a large white pill between her fingers. Theo nodded and helped my head up again.

"What is it?" I asked.

"Maybe a slight infection. Can't tell yet, since it's only been just over a day. But you are a little warm. We should just give you the antibiotics in case," Bet said.

"Do we have enough? If something happens to you two, or the girls, is there enough medication?" I asked.

"We'll be fine on supplies. I can find a pharmacy too, to restock if we need to." Bet's voice was soothing, but I wasn't sure I liked the idea of wasting the medication on me.

They did not give me a choice in the matter, as Bet slid the pill between my slightly open lips and Theo poured water into my mouth. I couldn't stop myself from swallowing the cool liquid, because it felt like heaven in my mouth and down my throat. Once the pill was gone, Theo carefully laid me back. He wet a small cloth and laid it over my forehead.

"You can sleep, Vicki. We've got everything covered," Theo said.

I nodded, but it was hard to feel comfortable in the position I was stuck in. Gabby finally moved from my chest at the insistence of Theo. But her little hand slid into mine and she laid down again, not leaving my side. I felt guilty for scaring her so badly. Though I often tried to deny it, the connection between her and me was growing and I didn't want to let her down. I squeezed her hand as I felt my eyelids growing heavier.

The meds did little to ease the pain radiating from my leg. But the blood loss made my thinking foggy and everything, including talking, made me exhausted. I fell into a deep, dreamless sleep for the rest of the day. I only realized time changing when I noticed the sun had set and everyone was sleeping around me.

Gabby hadn't left my side and her breathing tickled my bare arm, where she clasped it against her body. My fingers were numb from lack of circulation, but I didn't want to wake her and have her worry, so I left my arm where it was. I turned my head to find Theo sleeping an arm's length away. Tina was curled up in the safety of his arms, one of her little arms around his neck. A low lantern gave off enough light that I could study their sweet picture for a long moment.

Movement near the lantern had me looking over to find Bet still awake, moving toward me with the canteen. Soundlessly, she slipped more pain killers into my mouth and helped me sip water to swallow. She pushed my hair from my face and I didn't miss the frown when she held the back of her hand to my forehead. Wiping her face off any reaction, she helped me get comfortable, with a soft smile toward Gabby, before walking back to the lantern. I got one more look at Theo and Tina before the light went out.

Morning was much of the same, except I was starting to feel

worse. When I mentioned I was cold to Theo, his face took on a look of concern as he bundled me in a sleeping bag. Bet fed me more ibuprofen and another antibiotic pill that was hard to swallow. I fell in and out of sleep for a lot of the morning. But when I woke up fully, I found Theo packing a pack and Bet playing with Tina.

"What's going on?" I croaked.

Gabby was near my head, drawing in a book. She dropped her crayon, to lean over me. Her upside-down face swam and went in and out of focus. I tried to rub my eyes, but my arms were stuck inside the sleeping bag Theo had wrapped me in.

"I'm going to find a pharmacy. You need stronger meds. We think your leg is infected. We've cleaned it and you've had a couple doses of antibiotics now. But it seems to be getting worse. Paired with the blood loss, your body is having a hard time," Theo explained softly.

"Bet is going with you?" I asked.

Theo shook his head and slid a knife into a sheath on his hip.

"You can't go alone." I tried to struggle free of the sleeping bag, but my body felt heavy and my teeth chattered with the chill that went through me.

He came to my side and tucked the sleeping bag in again, making sure I was completely covered. He then pushed my hair out of my face and the same look of worry was in his eyes. I was getting used to that look on his face and I shook my head, not wanting him to do something risky because he wanted to help me.

"It'll be fine. Don't worry. I'll be back before you can wake up again. And hopefully I have a stronger antibiotic to fight whatever is going on with you. Behave yourself and listen to Bet."

I raised an eyebrow weakly and shook my head again.

"She'll behave. She's in no condition to cause me trouble anyway," Bet called from across the room where she was putting Tina in her playpen.

"Don't be so sure, old woman," I muttered.

Theo caught my words, and he gave me a sideways grin before climbing to his feet. Gabby came to him and hugged him around the legs. He hugged her back tightly and whispered something to her. She let out a little giggle and looked over at me. I plotted my revenge on everyone once I was feeling strong enough.

Gabby turned from Theo and plopped down next to me. She turned and just stared at me, and I stared back.

"What did he tell you to do, kid?"

"Watch you."

"I'm not exactly going anywhere," I huffed.

"Not on my watch," she replied, crossing her arms across her chest with a serious look on her face.

She sounded more like Theo every day, and she took his instructions very seriously. Both girls were attached to him. And that thought made me try to call out to him. He couldn't risk himself, not when the girls needed him. I felt like hell, but I refused to believe I couldn't get over it on my own. What I wouldn't survive, was the girls' heartbreak if they were to lose one more person they cared about.

My voice was only a cracked noise that didn't rise loud enough to reach Theo. He moved with purpose to the door and threw a smile over his shoulder before disappearing through the gift shop entrance. I heard when the door opened and closed again behind him. Moments later, the Jeep came to life, and it only took a few moments for the engine to fade away.

Bet busied herself with warming a plain vegetable broth for me to drink. With my fever and shivers, she was afraid actual food would upset my stomach. I hadn't thought about food, but when she spooned the first bit of warm broth into my mouth, I groaned out loud. The warmth moved through my chest and settled in my stomach, heating me from the inside. However, by the third spoon, I was chattering so badly, Bet couldn't give me anymore.

"Your body is really fighting, sweetie. You're going to be ok," Bet said in a low soothing voice.

Gabby still sat next to me, watching my every movement. When Bet lowered my head back to the camping pillow, I couldn't stop my eyelids from fluttering closed. My leg hurt, but the aches in my body were trying to fight an internal competition to see where I could feel worse. Even with the shaking and the pain, I passed out, completely mummified with Gabby, staring at my face.

CHAPTER 21

GABBY'S SCREAM echoed throughout the gift shop, yanking me from the multicolored dreamscape I had been trapped in. My first few moments of blinking only revealed blurry figures moving around the gift shop. I was still wrapped in the sleeping bag, unable to move, but I quickly realized that was a good thing.

I could finally focus on a small blurry figure that proved to be Gabby. She was on the ground near the playpen, crying next to a wailing Tina. Confusion clouded my mind as I tried to understand why both girls were so upset. Where in the hell was Bet? A person walked in front of my vision and immediately my body went cold. I didn't recognize the man that was pacing between me and the girls.

"You're going to give us everything. And then we're going to take the kids. They belong with The Children of Z, people who can save them," the man was saying.

He was clad in all black. The largest knife I had ever seen was strapped to his leg, and he held a handgun in one of his hands. He waved the weapon in a direction away from the girls, and I let my eyes follow. Bet was crouched on the ground, her face twisted in fury as she watched the man pace. Next to her was the crumpled form of something, but my mind was slow in processing.

The longish brown hair that stuck out at every angle from the head on the ground made a scream echo in my brain. It was Theo on the ground. I was coming awake faster, the synapses of my brain finally starting to fire and try to connect the dots of what I was seeing. The man that was pacing did not know I was awake, so I continued to stay still to take in the information.

"This guy thought he could run from us. But he was marked. We don't lose the ones we mark," the stranger was saying.

There was no way to know or understand how The Children of Z had tracked us across so many states. Or how they had taken out Theo without a fight that would have woken me. I hadn't heard a gunshot, but there was no way to know what I could have slept through in my state. I stared at his body, trying to tell if his chest was rising and falling, but even when I squinted, I couldn't tell.

Slowly, I let my head fall to the side and focused on the girls. Gabby immediately saw my movements, and she fidgeted. I shook my head in the smallest movement possible and the little girl froze in her spot. I was thankful that she listened without thinking; her fear a big motivator to listen to the adults she trusted in the room.

In the smallest movements possible, I adjusted, trying to work my arms from the sleeping bag around me. If the man continued to think I was sleeping or dying, I could have the chance to distract him for Bet to take him out. I moved my eyes toward her and I could tell she was trying to not look in my direction, to be sure to not draw attention to me.

The man continued to rant about The Children of Z and how they were going to save the world. As he yelled, he drowned out the sounds of the rustling sleeping bag. I was partially blocked by a rack of clothing near my head, but if he really looked, he would have noticed one of my arms free. Once the second one popped out, I pushed the sleeping bag down my body.

"We save the babies that are left. Do you want to come with us kids? We'll keep you safe, protect you from people that would hurt you," the man was speaking directly to Gabby now.

I winced as I watched her lift her chin and lock a hateful gaze on the man.

"We are with people that don't hurt us now. You're the only one hurting people. You should leave!" She yelled.

When the man stopped in front of her, I froze, afraid I was going to see the man harm the little girl. I could see Bet starting to rise to her feet, but the man caught her movements too, and he pointed his gun at her.

"Sit down, grandma. There's nothing you can do. And you," he said as he swung back toward Gabby. The little girl winced, but her chin stayed raised. "Someone needs to teach you manners."

"My mommy told me to be nice to people that were nice to me. And people that weren't, I didn't need to like. I don't like you."

Somehow the insult from the little girl sounded like a cutting string of words and I wanted to high five her. I focused on the man as I tried to continue to move the sleeping bag. He was large, with a belly that should have started to disappear with the lack of fast food available. His height was towering, but he didn't seem to move fast. His hair was to his shoulders, falling in greasy strings around his ears and face.

My leg screamed in pain, but adrenaline seemed to have stopped the uncontrollable shaking from my fever. I used my good leg to push the sleeping bag all the way off my injured leg.

I was barefoot and the leg of my pants was gone from where Theo had cut it so Bet could treat my wound. Carefully, I pushed backward with my good foot, gritting my teeth hard as my injury stretched and moved against the stitches.

When I got behind the clothes rack, I took a moment to breathe. My head swam, and I felt as if I could pass out at any time. The Children of Z member was still going on and on about Theo's transgressions. He talked about the murder Theo committed, which I knew was only to save Theo's own life. For a moment, I wished he had taken out a whole lot more of the cult members when he escaped.

I propped myself up on my uninjured leg and slowly rose on the one foot, holding onto the rack so I didn't tumble over. When I set my other foot on the ground, I gasped in pain, but the man didn't even notice. He was so obsessed with looking the girls over that he didn't know I had moved. Not that I was much of a danger at the moment, but I would do whatever I could to get him away from my girls.

He moved toward Bet again and in that moment, Bet looked at me and she shifted her chin slightly, indicating the gift shop entrance. Instinct told me she was telling me to run, though I wasn't sure how good I would be at that. In my mind, I pictured the office across the museum. I tried to remember if Theo had locked the door or left it open. Either way, I knew it was my only chance to hide the girls and maybe save them.

"Hey, jack off. You aren't just walking out of here with those girls. I won't allow it," Bet said, getting the guy to focus on her.

As soon as his back was turned to the girls, I limped toward them. White fiery agony was shooting through my injured leg, but I bit down on my pain and continued moving. Gabby was on her feet waiting for me, and I leaned down and grabbed Tina as I moved. I waved for Gabby to follow and we headed for the museum as Bet's yelling followed us out.

"You are nothing but a cult of murders and sadists! You aren't saving anyone. Theo told us about you feeding the living to the zombies. How is that saving anyone?"

The walk out of the gift shop was the longest few feet of my life. I could barely hop on my good leg and had to use my injured one to move. At the entrance of the gift shop, I had to stop and breathe. Sweat was soaking my shirt and dripping down my face. Gabby grabbed my hand that wasn't holding Tina to me. She pulled me forward softly, and I knew I had to keep going.

"What the hell?"

The bellowed yell told me we had been found out, which I figured would happen. I leaned down and put Tina on her feet and pushed her toward Gabby.

"Run!" I said.

Gabby's face was white, but she grabbed Tina's hand and pulled her sister into the museum. Just as they were rounding the corner of the welcome desk, I was tackled from behind, sending me sprawling into the museum entrance. A scream tore from my throat, as my injured leg slammed into the wall and I came to a rest. Black spots threatened my vision, but I shook my head and looked up to find Bet swinging a knife at the cult member. Theo was nowhere to be found, and I had to push it from my mind. I would face the news later if one of my only friends in the world was dead.

Digging deep down, I found what strength I had left and pushed myself up against the wall. While Bet had the man distracted, I limped toward the welcome desk, looking for the girls as I went. I leaned heavily against the desk and slid along its surface. Around the side, I almost stepped on Gabby, where she was crouched, holding Tina around the waist. Both of their faces were streaked with tears.

There were only two options from where we were. The

door, into the wilderness of Antelope Island, or hiding some-where in the museum. The sun was low in the sky, but it was still light enough outside to see and hopefully maneuver to somewhere I could hide with the girls. I had no weapons on me, but if the Jeep was outside, I knew that Bet kept extras in one of the storage bins. Hope bloomed, as I imagined those items still being there.

That hope was squashed as I heard Bet scream and then a loud crash. I glanced back just as I saw the man stalking toward the woman, who was climbing to her feet. She was shaky, but her knife was still clutched in her fist. She braced herself as the cult member moved toward her. I knew it was now or never if I was going to protect the girls.

Swinging Tina back onto my hip, I grabbed Gabby by the arm and shoved her toward the door. She got the message quickly and scrambled toward the exit. I limped after her and she stopped at the door, waiting for me to guide her. Popping the door open slowly, I looked outside. The Jeep was parked in the first parking spot where we had always parked it. But now, there was a bright red pickup blocking it from behind.

We slid through the open door and I watched the truck as we moved along the wall toward the Jeep. Suddenly, movement inside the cab of the truck caught my attention, and I fell to my knees, pulling Gabby to the ground with me. The impact on my leg shot spikes of pain through my injury, but I ground my teeth together to keep any noise from coming out of my mouth.

I set Tina next to Gabby, and the girls held each other tightly. I looked into Gabby's overflowing eyes and forced my voice to be calm.

"There's someone in that truck. I need to get to the Jeep and find a weapon. You stay here until I come back to get you. If anyone else comes before I do, you run and hide. Run and hide, you got it?" I said.

Gabby's head bobbed as I spoke, and I worried her panic was going to prevent her from listening. I crawled along the wall and motioned for her to follow. When I got to the wheelchair ramp that had concrete walls, I pointed toward a corner that would hide them from the truck, as well as the door of the museum, if the guy was to come out before I could get a weapon.

Crawling the wheelchair ramp felt the safest thing to do, but it also caused me white hot pain. Halfway down, I wondered if I would pass out from the pain. But my mind fought through it, digging into my anger and determination to protect the girls. My body had little choice but to keep going as I got to the end of the ramp and peered around the side.

From the side of the Jeep, I didn't think the truck occupant could see me. Staying low, I continued to crawl until I reached our vehicle. The storage locker on the side of the Jeep I was on was the exact goal I had. Slowly, I stood, until I was stooping to remain hidden against the body of the vehicle. I couldn't see into the truck from my vantage, which I hoped meant they also couldn't see me.

I popped open the top of the locker and slid my hand in without looking. My hand closed around the first thing it touched and I knew it was a gun. Theo had said multiple times that I needed to learn to shoot, but we never got to the actual teaching. Now, the weapon was probably the only way I could protect the girls against the cult members that wanted to take them.

I looked at the gun in my hand and remembered what Theo had pointed out about the safety. I clicked it off immediately, not wanting to be confused if the sudden need for it arose. It didn't feel as heavy as I had expected and fit into my palm with little thought. I curled my fingers around it and let my pointer finger find the trigger, while pointing the weapon away from me. I would do this if it was the last thing I could do.

The opening of the museum door caught my attention, and I went to my knees again. I crawled as fast as my body would let me back to the wheelchair ramp. I heard heavy footsteps pound down the front steps, telling me it wasn't Bet coming to look for us.

"Little girls! Where did you run off to? We just want to help you!"

The stranger yelled, his voice bouncing off of the museum's concrete walls. To the girls' credit, they were silent, and I continued to crawl until they came into sight. Gabby's face was turned toward the sound and she was pale. Her hand was over Tina's mouth and I could see the baby clawing at her sister, wanting to scream, wanting to be free, wanting anything but to be silent.

When I came into view, Gabby trembled, her fear pumping too much adrenaline into her. I took Tina, letting the baby burrow into my neck. I shushed her, hoping that our small noises didn't carry. But just as I thought it, the man started yelling for the girls again, this time further away. I guessed he was near his truck now, looking out into the parking lot and beyond.

Gabby clung to my arm, but it was the only arm I had for the gun. Setting down the weapon for a moment, I brushed my palm over her head. A sudden thought had me leaning down and pressing a kiss to her forehead. With my mouth near her head, I whispered.

"I need you to listen to everything I tell you to do and do it immediately, ok? We're going to hide until Bet or Theo can come help us."

Gabby nodded, her sweet, sweaty scent invading my senses.

"We're going to crawl back up to the top. Instead of going

toward the door, go to the left and keep going until we get to the end of the building."

With that, I pushed Gabby on her back, and she crawled. I put Tina down and she mimicked her sister, though she moved faster than either or us. I had to grab her ankle twice to keep her from passing Gabby completely and giving us away. When we got to the end of the ramp, the man's yelling had moved further into the parking lot. I didn't know how long our luck was going to hold out.

Just as I was about to pray to God and beg him to keep the man away, the sound of a vehicle door opening and slamming came. And I knew God wasn't listening to me at the moment.

"Joel! They didn't go that way! I would've seen em'!" A woman's twang filled voice rang out.

Cursing under my breath, I tried to crawl faster along the building toward the back. All I wanted was to get the girls around the back so we could run and put some space between us and the cult members. As we neared the side of the building, I heard mumbled talking, once the man named Joel met back up with the woman at the truck. I pictured the area behind us and knew he only had to walk a few more feet before he would have a clear view of us.

The sweat was dripping off of me in rivulets, but I didn't stop. Gabby was the first to the edge of the building and I waved for her to go around. She disappeared just a moment before Tina and I caught up. But it was in that split moment that I heard Gabby scream, before something cut it off, muffling her voice. I clambered to my feet and lurched around the side of the museum wall, keeping myself between whatever I was facing and Tina, who was still on the ground.

A third person I hadn't known existed was holding Gabby with an arm around her waist and a hand over her mouth. When she saw me, tears erupted and flowed down her red cheeks as she tried to fight. I held up my free hand and made a calming motion toward her, but she couldn't stop. Her fear was the only thing raging in her mind.

"Well, looky here. You're the one they said was dyin'. But you're on your feet now. You ain't one of the blessed though, are ya," the man said, staring hard into my face.

"I have no idea what you're talking about, man. But you need to put her down right now. She's with me."

Behind my hurt leg, I hid the gun, the grip digging into my palm. I kept my trigger finger along the slide, as Theo had told me to do once. Don't shoot yourself, was his specific instruction. I had no intention of hurting anyone except the man that had my girl clutched in his arm. The pain in my body seemed to fade away, and I focused hard on Gabby, trying to get her to meet my eye.

Her blue eyes were crystal pools, full of tears that didn't seem to have an end. I felt hands on my leg and I knew Tina had appeared because the man holding Gabby was momentarily distracted. It was in that distraction that I finally got Gabby to look in to my face and I mimicked biting down. I did the motion a few times before Gabby seemed to understand what I was telling her to do. But once she got it, a look of determination crossed her face and she stilled.

Bringing up her free hand, Gabby pressed the man's hand against her mouth harder and her eyes squeezed shut a second before the man bellowed. The little girl didn't let go, and he released her waist, using both hands to pry his flesh from her teeth. The moment he let her go, Gabby released him and fell to the concrete. It was the opening I needed, and I raised the gun.

Aim for the largest part of the body. Another of Theo's pieces of advice. I didn't question the idea as I aimed directly at the man's chest and pulled the trigger. The impact of the bullet threw him back off his feet, and he screamed in pain. I didn't wait, didn't hesitate and watch him lay on the ground as blood began to pool below him. I grabbed Tina by an arm and awkwardly swung her into my arms. Gabby was next to me and we began to run into the desert, hoping for anything to give us cover.

I knew the noise of the gun would draw the other two cult members, but I wasn't sure how long we had. I didn't look back, even when I heard the scream of the woman when she found the man I had shot. Her sobs followed us across the barren landscape and I turned away from the building, to put the museum between us if I could. I knew the moment Joel saw us. His bellow echoed off the walls of the museum and out into the open.

"Vicki..." Gabby said, her voice breathless.

"I know, kid. We just gotta keep going."

I could barely speak, pushing the words through gritted teeth and thin lips. But I couldn't stop. I still gripped the gun, though I did not know how many bullets there were. The sound of commotion vaguely registered behind me, but I didn't even think to look back. I heard the pounding of feet and I knew there was no way for me to out run whoever was coming.

"Take your sister," I cried, putting Tina on her feet and pushing her toward Gabby.

The little girl only hesitated for a moment before she pulled a tottering Tina along with her, away from me. I spun and found Joel baring down on me. His face was blotchy and angry. As he got closer, I could see a vein popping from his temple. I started talking to God again, letting him know that an aneurysm could be quick and painless for Joel at that moment. But that made me wonder if God would listen to me calling for the death of another.

When Joel got within arm's reach, his arms came up, one of

his fists was balled. I braced myself for the impact, but the man slowed and studied me instead.

"You killed my buddy back there," he said.

"I sure did. He wouldn't let go of my girl." My chin came up in defiance, and I stared back at him.

"There's some fire in there, even if you were dyin'. Why doncha come with us? The girls, me and my other friend. You could join us. Help us spread the blessin' and word of the Z."

My mouth dropped open at his words, and then I snickered. The blotchy red of his face spread as he realized I was laughing at him.

"You have more than one screw loose. Zombies don't talk, they don't have a word to spread. You all are just psychos using a made up cult to murder people. I won't be joining you. And neither will my girls."

With surprising speed, Joel closed the distance between us and wrapped a hand around my throat. On instinct, I tried to raise the gun between us, but Joel was faster. He knocked it across the dirt and then wrapped his other hand around my neck, squeezing.

"Well then, you aren't necessary. I'll get the girls next and they'll be raised right. To respect the dead and know we don't own this planet no mo."

I scratched and swung at his face, but he just pushed my body back, using his long arms to keep me from hurting him. I pulled at his fingers, scratched his arms, but his hold didn't loosen. My lungs screamed for air, my mind begged me to fight and get the oxygen flowing back through my body. Forgetting my injured leg, I tried to kick out at Joel, but all I did was collapse in his hold.

Just as black began to seep into the sides of my vision and my eyelids slid closed, Joel's grip suddenly released and I sucked in a lungful of the cool air of evening. I was crumpled on the ground, but I raised my head, trying to figure out what had happened and why Joel had released me.

Standing, like an avenging angel, was Theo. His long hunting knife protruded from the side of Joel's neck. He viciously pulled it free, causing blood to spray across him and across me. As Joel tried to press his hands against his wound, Theo kicked his legs out from under him, making him fall in the dirt a few feet away from me. I just stared dumbly as I struggled to suck in as much air as my body truly wanted.

When Theo came to me, his arms went under my arms and helped me to my feet. The adrenaline in my bloodstream was still doing its job, and the pain hadn't caught up with me. With a hold on my chin, he moved my neck around. Running his fingers across the skin, he pressed in a few places, but nothing felt broken.

"Are you ok?" I asked, noticing the hair matted with blood and dirt on the side of his head.

"You're asking me that?"

His hand was still on my chin, and I was suddenly aware of how close we were. Before I could think anything of it, I threw myself into his arms, burying my face in his neck. That was when the tears started. I wasn't sure what I was crying over. The pain. The people we had killed. The fear of losing the girls. But as I cried, Theo held me tightly, one of his hands sweeping circles on my back.

Pulling back, I suddenly realized I was crying, but I had no idea where the girls were. I turned and looked, only to find them a foot away. Tina was sitting in the dirt, playing with rocks, but Gabby was staring at the dead body of Joel. I limped over to her and stood between her and the man.

"You know, he was an evil man. We had to do what needed to be done," I said, trying to figure out how to rationalize murder to a five-year-old that followed all the rules.

"I know. Just wish it had hurt for longer."

My eyes widened, and her determined gaze turned to me. Her eyes were now dry, and she was angry. I couldn't think of what I should say to her. But before I could botch the job, Theo appeared next to us. He crouched, so he was at Gabby's level, and he drew her into his arms.

"I know it feels like that right now, little one. But killing anything is hard. A zombie, an animal, even bad people. We should never enjoy it. We should only do what we have to, to survive and protect our family. Ok?"

Gabby didn't answer, but she nodded her head against his shoulder. He stood, picking her up with him. Bet came running toward us from the museum. Her wild hair looked as if she had just come from an electrocution.

"The woman is gone. She took off in the truck," Bet said when she reached us.

From where we stood, we could see the distant lights of the truck as it sped down the road that went back to town. Letting her go was the right thing to do, the moral thing to do. But something in the back of my mind knew it wasn't what would protect us in the long run. I had a sick feeling in my stomach that we would see that woman again.

CHAPTER 22

ONCE THEO CALLED US A FAMILY, Gabby seemed to look at us differently. She didn't want to leave our sides, made sure we ate meals together, and asked for a book to be read to her at night. I hadn't really picked up on the changes at first, but Theo spelled it out for me and I was slightly dumbfounded. We had a family unit? What did I know about that?

The first evening after the attempted kidnapping, Theo and Bet loaded up the two dead bodies in the Jeep and drove them to the middle of the salt flat. When they got close to the water, they dropped them both and left them to rot, or be eaten by whatever was surviving the harsh landscape. I stayed in the gift shop with the girls, as they played and got ready for bed around me.

I had torn my stitches and Bet was pissed about having to clean up the wound and close me up again. The pain was raging and my fever hadn't disappeared. I could admit, looking at my leg, that it didn't look good. Bet didn't hold back as she cleaned it out, making sure she had rinsed all the puss away before stitching it up again. Theo finally convinced Bet to tap into the harder pain meds for me. That night, I floated away in a pain med fueled stupor and it was the best sleep I had experienced since the beginning of the apocalypse.

The next day, I finally got the full story of how the cult members had come upon us. Theo had gone into town to find a pharmacy, that much I remembered. He told us how he went around to three different pharmacies before finding one that had something left that he could sort through. The only thing he had to deal with was zombies. He never came across anyone alive. When he drove back, he saw no one following him. He brought the meds in, but the limited view from inside the museum had given the cult members the opening they needed.

"They must have been following me from a distance the whole time. But I never noticed. Everything was so quiet, it didn't even occur to me there could be a threat. That's on me," Theo said.

"There's nothing normal about what we're living through, son. You can't take the blame for everything. We're all doing the best we can," Bet said.

I just nodded from where I was laying, because I still didn't have the strength to sit up on my own. The weakness in me now made me marvel at what I had been able to do when we were under attack.

"Either way, they got all the way into the parking lot and jumped me when I went outside to bring in the other supplies I had collected. That's all I remember until waking up in here," Theo said, motioning to the gift shop slash home area that we were all in.

"I can pick up from there. I heard the commotion outside and rushed to see what was happening. The big one, the one you killed with the knife, was dragging you by your arm, up the stairs. When he saw me, he came straight for the door. I didn't have the chance to find a way to lock the door, only run back in here and try to hide the girls. He saw them before I could."

"You didn't wake up," Gabby whispered, from her place next to me.

She was laying with me again, whenever she wasn't coloring right next to me, or sleeping. I was wrapped in a sleeping bag again, to ward off the chills I was getting with the fever. But it was the third day on the stronger antibiotics and I was pretty sure I was improving.

"Sorry, little one," Theo murmured.

I tried and failed at imagining how scared Gabby must have been. Tina was still young enough that she seemed to bounce back from anything that scared her at the moment. Gabby, though, could absorb and hold on to those emotions, and I could see them replay across her eyes. I hated that for her. I hated the world she was going to have to grow up in. I hated that I couldn't seem to provide stability and safety for any long period.

"Theo was out cold, unfortunately, from the blow to the head. Before you came to, Vicki, the big guy was going on and on about the Children of Z and how they would take the girls and raise them right. The guy also knew who Theo was and said he was going to take him back as an offering to their mistress. I figured that meant they wanted to kill him, but they didn't want to do it here. They wanted to let this woman see it happen," Bet explained.

"That's what they called the woman that wanted to keep me, their mistress." Theo visibly shuddered, and his eyes got a faraway look.

"Well, I wasn't going to let that happen, of course, but I had to think of the girls, too. Vicki woke up then, and I just kept the guy distracted as long as I could. What happened when you got out of the building, Vicki?"

I cleared my throat, or tried to. It started a coughing fit, in which Theo had to lift my head and pour water slowly into my mouth. I felt ridiculous being tended to. But my strength was slow to come back, so I kept my thoughts to myself and enjoyed the liquid coating my sore throat. Once I could speak, I recounted what the girls and I had gone through before Theo found us trying to get away from the man named Joel.

"Vicki was brave. She told me to bite the man who was holding me and then she shot him!" Gabby exclaimed, chomping her teeth down to illustrate exactly what she had done to help.

"You were brave, kid. And you actually followed directions, which was helpful. We wouldn't have got away if you hadn't bitten him as hard as you did," I said.

Theo ruffled Gabby's hair, smiling fondly down at her. Her smile was bright as Bet also gave her compliments on her fighting spirit. I hoped she'd never have to fight like that again, but there was no way of knowing what we would face each day as we tried to survive. I finished the story of running into the wild, with the girls running and me lagging because of my leg.

"And then Theo came and saved me...again." I mumbled the last word, because I felt like I had played damsel in distress more times than I wanted to count.

Theo swiped his thumb along my cheek briefly before pulling his hand back and clearing his throat awkwardly. I saw Bet's eyes following his movements and her smile increased its wattage until it was practically blinding.

"That's what you do for family. Help each other," Theo finally said.

"Some more than others," I groaned.

"You took care of the girls. That's your number one job. And you've always done it the right way. That's all I need." His eyes were locked on mine and I wasn't sure how to respond, so I just nodded my head.

With the stories out of the way, Theo and Bet settled the girls across the room so they could play and snack. Gabby didn't like being taken from my side, but I pointed out that she could still see me, so she could look over and make sure I was ok as often as she wanted. Theo helped prop me into a sitting position against the wall. It felt good to let the sleeping bag slip to my waist and feel fresh air across my skin. Bet checked my fever and nodded as she fed me another pill that was large enough for a horse.

"We need to make a new plan," Theo said, as they settled around me.

"That woman knows where we are. I have no doubt she'll come back if she can get reinforcements," Bet said.

I nodded, though again, we faced a blank slate of ideas.

"Do we just keep going west?" I asked.

The question hung heavy, with us all thinking our own thoughts and worries.

"What about the installation in Rapid City?" Theo asked.

I gaped at him. "You've got to be kidding. I'm not going anywhere near a place that has soldiers that clearly are looking for women to do their bidding. Even when you told them we were together, they still tried to get me to go with them."

When Bet looked confused, Theo explained the story the soldiers told us and the impression they gave. She shook her head when he was finished.

"We're not going anywhere near there," she said.

"I've always wanted to go to Oregon," Theo said, after we had sat in silence for a while.

"I don't have any maps that go that far, but if we head north-west, we'll go in that general direction. Pick up maps along the way," Bet said.

"We need a better way of traveling, no offense." I nodded my head toward the Jeep parked outside.

"A van is better with the kids. But if we could find something bigger than a mom's soccer van. More room for supplies and sleeping," Theo said.

With a shell of a plan happening, we settled in for a fitful sleep. My pain meds helped me, but everyone else was restless with the fear preventing true sleep. I had Gabby on one side of me and Theo on the other, since he was worried I would roll over onto Tina in my drugged up state. That's how I knew keeping him around for the girls was the right thing to do. He always had worries for them I hadn't thought of yet.

As he fell asleep, he had found my hand and twined our fingers together. I didn't know what it meant, but I didn't feel the sudden need to yank my hand away. Theo was solid and dependable. He was more things than anyone I had ever known in my life. And though he felt like the last sane man on Earth, that wasn't the only thing that drew me to him. My drug muddled mind threw thoughts around like it was creating a Jackson Pollock painting. I couldn't grasp any of it, so I just let myself fall into sleep without a worry. I knew Theo would watch over us.

Morning came, and though the pain was still present, I felt much better than I had. Bet confirmed I had no fever, but I still had to finish a regimen of antibiotics. None of us were doctors, so she was taking a running guess of two weeks, since that was how much medication we had left. I could get up and use some of the bottled water to clean up, while Theo and Bet packed up our supplies. I limped out to the Jeep when it was time to go.

Struggling at the door, I had to figure out how to put up my good foot and climb in, so Theo just lifted me and sat me in the passenger seat without a word. Bet drove us away from Antelope Island, back into town. We were all on high alert, looking for the truck with the remaining cult member. But when nothing seemed to move or follow us, I felt like I let out a long sigh of relief. I glanced back and saw that Theo was more relaxed, sitting between the girls, both of them leaning against his sides.

Suddenly, Bet jerked the wheel, and I was thrown against the passenger side door. Theo cursed loudly and Gabby squealed as he smashed her in surprise.

"What is it?" Theo demanded.

"That's what we need," she said, pointing at a large van parked in front of a house.

"Jesus, Bet," I mumbled, rubbing my shoulder.

Despite our reactions, Bet's excitement couldn't be abated. There, parked along the curb, was a large, older model van. It was bigger than a commercial van, tall and bulky, with some sort of electrical unit on the top. Bet pulled the Jeep behind it and turned off the engine. We waited in the silence, to see if anything was going to come out and greet us. Nothing moved in the street, or behind the windows of the houses around.

"It's creepy how quiet it is," I said, keeping my voice low so only Bet heard me.

"Most people thought evacuation was their only option."

Up and down the street, there was evidence of people panicking and rushing out of their homes. Garages left open, trash littering the road, a suitcase that had burst open, spilling clothing across a yard. And there were stories of zombies as well, blood and bodies, that I tried to not focus too strongly on. As long as they weren't moving, I didn't want to study them.

Bet climbed from the Jeep and Theo joined her on the street. They slowly approached the van and peered into the windows. Bet did a little jig, her excitement overflowing. Theo said something to her and started toward the house. Bet came back to the Jeep and explained that before we broke into the van and tried to hot wire it, Theo wanted to check the house for keys. I tried to climb from the vehicle to help, but she waved me off.

"Nothing you can do limping after him. If there's trouble, he'll be more worried about you. He's got it handled."

I tapped my fingers along the dash, waiting for him to reappear. It never felt right when we split up, for whatever reason. But just as I was really going to worry, he rushed out with his fist above his head, telling us he found the keys. He went to the driver's door and disappeared into the van. A second later, the van's engine growled to life and I could hear a quiet cheer from Theo. Then the engine was cut, and he climbed back out.

With Theo helping me, we opened all the doors to check the interior. The front had two captain's seats with a large console between them. Each nook and cranny of the console was full of receipts, books, and maps. Behind the passenger seat was one additional captain seat and a couch across from it. Gabby immediately climbed up and went to the couch. She sat on it and bounced a few times, as if testing it out for purchase.

Bet climbed in as well and moved toward the back of the van. I waited with Tina in my arms.

"There's an electric stove back here! And a sink, which means it probably has a water tank and a gray water tank. And a small fridge! Not that we can find anything that's perishable now, but if we mix milk or something, we can keep it cold," Bet said from inside.

"Do I want to ask what a gray water tank is?" I asked.

"Motorhomes and trailers have gray and black waste water tanks. Gray for sink and shower, black for sewage," Bet explained.

Theo had moved to the back of the vehicle and had popped open the two doors there.

"It must have a black water tank too," he called.

"There's an actual toilet?" Bet cried, jumping from the van and rushing to join Theo.

While Bet gushed over a toilet, I looked around the inside. It wasn't big enough for all of us to have beds, but I imagined the couch folded down and would be large enough, at least for the girls. I pictured them being able to nap as we drove and cooking actual meals on the stove. It was the picture of domestic life that we had tried to create in Denver that was too quickly snatched away from us.

I had no way of knowing how long the drive to Oregon would take. But this vehicle would clearly be more comfortable than the Jeep. For the first time since we left Denver, something seemed to click, and I could smile. I put Tina on the floor of the van and she immediately went to join her sister on the couch. Theo joined me, and we watched the girls giggle and play.

"This feels good," Theo said.

"We can do this," I replied.

With everything I had been through since the apocalypse started and then with the girls thrown into my life. From being saved more times than I could count to losing people that did nothing but protect us. I was finding a determination that I had never possessed in my life. I was truly beginning to believe that I could be the babysitter of the apocalypse and more.

————

The story doesn't end here! Vicki's story of survival continues in Babysitter of the Apocalypse, Book 2: We Don't Talk to Strangers. Find it by clicking here!

LOOKING FOR MORE?

If you'd like a preview of book one of my highly rated zombie series, The Sundown Series, you can get that by clicking here!

ACKNOWLEDGMENTS

Thank you so much for taking a chance and joining Vicki on her insane survival journey! Writing about Vicki has been a whole new experience. Normally, I like survivors that know what they're doing, but Vicki isn't that. But she's trying! To keep up with more of their stories, be sure to follow along on my website courtneykonstantin.com. I also post updates on my Facebook page at https://www.facebook.com/AuthorCKonstantin.

I have to give a shout out to my best friend and chosen sister, P. I appreciate all of the support she has given me through the writing process (even when some of it was yelling at me to hurry up).

Thank goodness for a fantastic editor that keeps my comma mess to a minimum! Angry Eagle Publishing keeps me on track with those evil little things, making sure I am able to concentrate on the bigger picture. Not to mention the cheerleading!I appreciate you!

Thank you to JS Designs Cover Art for my amazing cover! https://jsdesignscoverart.com/ I really appreciate the feeling of ruin that was captured in the creation of the cover.

Finally, this interior wouldn't be so amazing without the assistance of Emcat Designs. https://www.facebook.com/EmCatDesigns I love being able to open a book and have a little surprise with each chapter!

Stay tuned for more from Vicki and the girls in book 2 of the series. Coming soon!

ALSO BY COURTNEY KONSTANTIN

The Sundown Series

Prepared

Alone

Survive

Alive

Torment

Vengeance

Ruination

The Babysitter of the Apocalypse

Babysitter of the Apocalypse: Prequel (Freebie!)

Babysitter of the Apocalypse, Book 1

Babysitter of the Apocalypse, Book 2: We Don't Talk to Strangers

Echoes of the Flare

Whispers in the Dark

www.ingramcontent.com/pod-product-compliance
Lightning Source LLC
Chambersburg PA
CBHW020910200626
46814CB00001BA/265